...aries

D0278510

SHANKILL LIBRARY

Inv/07 : L285   Price E19.13
Title: Barking
Class: f

BARKING

TOM HOLT

BARKING

BAINTE DEN STOC

WITHDRAWN FROM DÚN LAOGHAIRE

orbit

www.orbitbooks.co.uk
www.tom-holt.com

ORBIT

First published in Great Britain by Orbit 2007

Copyright © The One Reluctant Lemming Co. Ltd 2007

The moral right of the author has been asserted.

*All characters and events in this publication, other than those clearly
in the public domain, are fictitious and any resemblance to real
persons, living or dead, is purely coincidental.*

All rights reserved.
No part of this publication may be reproduced,
stored in a retrieval system, or transmitted, in any form
or by any means, without the prior permission in writing of the
publisher, nor be otherwise circulated in any form of binding
or cover other than that in which it is published and
without a similar condition including this condition
being imposed on the subsequent purchaser.

A CIP catalogue record for this book
is available from the British Library.

ISBN 978-1-84149-285-8

Typeset in Plantin by M Rules
Printed and bound in Great Britain by
Clays Ltd, St Ives plc

Orbit
An imprint of
Little, Brown Book Group
Brettenham House
Lancaster Place
London WC2E 7EN

A Member of the Hachette Livre Group of Companies

www.orbitbooks.co.uk

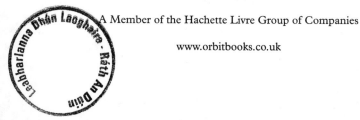

For Mike Hughes,
Without Prejudice

CHAPTER ONE

Wee small hours of a cold, moonlit night; last call of the shift, nothing more urgent than a drunk with a broken leg, so no need to floor the pedal or burn rubber on the way back to the hospital. In the front passenger seat, the driver's mate glances at the wing mirror.

'There's a dog following us,' he observes.

'Mphm.'

'Yeah.'

There's a slight edge to his voice, which makes the driver check his own mirror. 'They do that,' the driver says, frowning as he speaks. 'More in the country than in town, but—'

'Big dog.'

The driver nods. 'Alsatian, right?'

'Yeah. Or one of them – what're they called? You know, they pull sleighs.'

The driver's frown deepens. 'Reindeer?'

Behind them, the big dog runs, red tongue lolling. The driver checks his speed – just legal – and feels his right foot nudge the pedal just a little harder, for some reason. Then the mirror again. Big dog still there. Big dog apparently not bothered.

'There's another one – look.'

The driver can't look just now, since he needs to keep his eyes on the road as they round a corner. When he has attention to spare again, he sees not two big dogs, but three.

'What speed are you doing?' the driver's mate asks.

Not enough. The driver's right foot urges the pedal down, and he reaches forward to flip on the siren. Two or three seconds pass before he looks again. Still there. Three big dogs. Four.

Five.

'Shit,' says the driver's mate, with feeling.

Just as well there's no traffic on the roads, in the suburbs at four in the morning. *Silly,* the driver can't help thinking as he nudges the needle up to forty-five, *it's just dogs. They like to chase cars. Man's best friend, and all that.*

How fast can dogs run, anyway?

Forty-five, no problem: by amber light and moonlight he can see their backs flexing with the pace, powerful easy movements, muscles rippling with fierce joy under the thick grey-white coats. At fifty, though, the stride gets laboured and more determined. In the back of the driver's mind an ancient memory stirs; because once upon a time long ago, dogs weren't dogs. They were something quite other.

'Put your foot down,' the driver's mate urges, unnecessarily. 'Jesus, they're gaining on us.'

Fifty-five, and the dogs' backs are bent like drawn bows as they force the pace. Sixty beats them, and gradually they dwindle, from dogs into dots into specks. The driver begins to slow down.

'Shut that bloody siren off,' he mutters.

A steady, law-abiding twenty-nine, as if to demonstrate that nothing really happened back there; no yellow eyes and swaying tongues in the rear-view mirror, no pursuit, or fear—

'You get that a lot in the country,' the driver's mate says, his voice rather higher than usual. 'Dogs chasing cars. Not so much in town, because of getting run over. My cousin Norman—'

For some reason, however, the narrative urge fails him. He

sits quiet for the rest of the ride, and keeps checking the wing mirror. When the white glare of the hospital lights blots out the darkness, he says, 'Huskies.'

'What?'

'Dogs that pull sleighs; at the North Pole and stuff. Saw a programme about them once. Fast as shit, and they can run seventy-two hours without stopping.' They pull up, and reach for the door handles. 'Didn't know you get them in this country, but there you go. I blame the Internet.'

The driver doesn't answer as he steps down onto the tarmac, his feet not quite steady. Just one of those things, he tells himself; but even so he can't help wondering whether, somewhere on the B2043 between the multiplex and the slip-road for the Ash Grove garden centre, five big yellow-eyed dogs were still grimly, determinedly running.

In every working day there is a still moment, a point of balance; a fulcrum, if you like, around which the scales pivot. The slightest nudge at this point decides whether it's going to be a good day or a bummer. It can come at any stage in the proceedings; it can be a massive boot on your instep in the crowded rush-hour Tube, or a call from a rabid client at 5.29, just as you're pulling your raincoat sleeve up your arm. It can be a fleeting wisp of a smile from the new girl in Accounts, the dismissal of a loathed superior, an unexpected and undeserved pay rise or a bluebottle floating in your mid-morning coffee. But it will come, every day, and leave its little scar.

On the twenty-sixth of January it came at three minutes past nine. It hummed along the phone wire from Reception and shrieked to be picked up, like a fractious baby, before Duncan Hughes had even had a chance to sit down.

Duncan knew it for what it was before the receiver brushed his ear. 'Hello, Mr Martinez,' he said. 'How can I—?'

Help you. But nobody could help Mr Martinez. Not in a jurisdiction that outlaws euthanasia (or, in his case, justifiable pesticide).

'That's terrible, Mr Martinez,' Duncan said after a while. 'I'm really sorry to hear—'

But not nearly as sorry as he would be. 'And that's not all,' Mr Martinez went on. 'They came back.'

'Did they?'

'They fucking did. And you know what they did *then*?'

You couldn't help feeling sorry for him, up to a point (the point, usually, on which the balance of your day teetered, as noted above). Anybody into whom the Revenue has got its needle-pointed teeth to that extent has to be pitied on some level, even if it was seventy-five per cent his own fault. But, as raids followed investigations and hearings before the Special Commissioners were appealed to the Chancery Division, there came a moment when pity ran out, and the hiatus flooded with a vast, horrified weariness; a longing for the wretched man to bugger off and take the pity and the terror with him.

'And on top of that,' Mr Martinez said, 'now they're asking for the deposit-account statements right back to 1987.'

What really puzzled Duncan about the Martinez case was the poor fool's ferocious tenacity. Anybody with the brains of a carrot would have given up long since: changed his name, emigrated, his quietus made with a bare bodkin, whatever. Not Ricky Martinez; which meant—

'I think the best thing,' Duncan sighed, 'would be for you to come in and see me, and we'll talk it through. Today, if—'

'I can make five-fifteen.'

Whimper, Duncan thought. 'You couldn't possibly get here a bit earlier?'

'No.'

'Fine. Quarter past five, then, and –' Duncan took a deep breath '– please be sure to bring all the papers with you.'

'All the papers?'

'All of them,' Duncan said bitterly.

'*All* of—'

'Yes. See you then.'

'All right,' said Mr Martinez. 'Cheers.'

Click-buzz, said the phone. Duncan held it at arm's length and scowled at it for a moment before putting it back. In many ways it reminded him of the former Mrs Hughes: every day he held it close to him, and every day it whispered in his ear horrible things that ruined his life. He reached for his diary and pencilled in the appointment. Then the phone rang again.

So, people tended to say when meeting Duncan for the first time, *what do you do, then?* And, when he told them he was a lawyer, and they'd deliberately restrained their lips from curling and asked what sort of lawyer, he'd reply, 'Oh, death and taxes, mainly'; and then, inevitably, would come one of the Sixteen Jokes – there are only sixteen, and he'd heard them all, so very many times – and after that, the question, 'But don't you find all that stuff pretty depressing?' And he'd answer, 'Yes.' Then, of course, they'd change the subject. It wasn't that he minded being universally regarded as somewhere between a vulture, a hangman and the jolly gravedigger in *Hamlet*; that was a fair cop, after all. It was partly the fact that everybody assumed he really wouldn't want to talk about his job; partly the fact that they were right—

'Mr Woodcock for you,' said Reception. To her credit, she didn't snigger.

– And partly the fact that, every time he met up with someone he hadn't seen for ages, their first question would be, 'So what are you doing *now*?', as though it was inconceivable that anybody could still be doing his rotten, shitty job, a whole six months later—

'Mr Wood—'

'We've decided,' said Mr Woodcock. 'She's having the shoes, and I'm keeping the costume jewellery. Thought you ought to know, so everything's above board.'

Wait for it, Duncan told himself.

'But it's still not right.' The words gushed out of Mr Woodcock like poison from an abscess. 'She distinctly told me, the last time at the nursing home, I was to have everything in the big suitcase; and what I'm saying is, why would she think I'd want a load of old shoes and plastic bloody beads? It could only be because she didn't want Dolly to have any of it, so—'

'Mr Wood—'

'And I've only agreed because the worry is killing my wife, she's lost four pounds in weight and the physio says her wrist is all just nerves, so I just can't go on living like that, and if Dolly's set her heart on hounding an innocent woman to her grave over a few pairs of old shoes that're only fit for the skip anyhow, well, what can you do with someone like that? So anyway, I thought I'd better just check with you, make sure it's all legal and proper.'

'Absolutely, Mr Woodcock. The will just says—'

'Oh.' Disappointment. 'So there's nothing in the will says Dolly can't have the shoes.'

One good thing about the phone: the man at the other end can't see the faces you pull. 'Really it's a matter of being practical, Mr Woodcock. I suppose you could argue, strictly speaking—'

'Yes?'

Duncan had completely forgotten what he'd been going to say. Probably just as well. 'That's fine, Mr Woodcock,' he snapped politely. 'Glad to hear that's all sorted out. Now we can crack on with selling the house and the stocks portfolio and the investment properties in Surrey, and it should all be wrapped up by June. The way the market's shaping, it should be a good—'

'Yes, right. But about the shoes—'

That, Duncan thought as he put the phone down some time later, was the really weird, scary thing about the death biz. Greed – naked, vicious, more than happy to tear out its own sister's throat rather than cede her a few clapped-out old shoes with the heels trodden down; but the money, the seriously big money, didn't seem to interest him. So he stood to cop for over a million and a half quid. So what? Dolly was getting the shoes. The fact that, with the money he'd flushed down the bog through whining to his hourly-paid lawyer about the injustice of it all, Mr Woodcock could've bought enough shoes to satisfy the wildest dreams of Imelda Marcos was apparently neither here nor there.

People, Duncan thought.

Work helped calm his jangled sensibilities: standard letters to banks, building societies, stockbrokers, National Savings, estate agents, the Probate Registry, the Revenue. As he droned them into the dictating machine, he spared a thought of deep pity for his secretary, who had to put up with his voice reverberating through her headphones all day long. *Kindly forward us a note of the closing balance at your earliest convenience, together with the sum total of deposit interest accrued at date of death.* What a thing to whisper in the ear of a sensitive young girl, or even Tricia (sensitive as a shock absorber, delicate as the Atlas Mountains, quick as a glacier, his girl Friday). Did his numbing bleat echo through her nightmares, a voice in her head that only she could hear, like God and Joan of Arc? The possibility twisted in his conscience like an arrowhead.

Duncan tended to think of his progress through the working day in terms of Frodo's journey through Mordor; in which case, his eleven-thirty meeting with Jenny Sidmouth was Shelob's lair. Not that Ms Sidmouth looked particularly like a giant spider. She was long and thin, like a skewer: sharpest around the eyes, which could pierce any armour as effectively as the English arrows at Agincourt. Her dark hair was precisely straight (she must have it engineered, rather than cut) and her slender, bony fingers tapered eventually down to close-bitten nails.

As always, she let him stand in the doorway for seven seconds before acknowledging his presence; then she laid down her sheaf of computer printouts, and smiled right through him.

'Not so bad this month,' she said. 'Up seven-point-six-three on this time last year.' But her eyes were narrowing, like the diaphragm of a laser lens. 'That said, we did decide on a target increase of ten-point-seven, which leaves you three-point-o-seven per cent short. Perhaps you'd like to explain that.'

Duncan shrugged. 'I'm sorry,' he said. 'People just aren't dying fast enough, I guess.'

You could get away with saying something like that to Jenny Sidmouth, if only because she regarded anything you said to her with equal contempt. Humour, irony or rank insubordination – she swept over them all like flood water. 'Let's see,' she went on. 'Billable hours are up, that's encouraging, but charges rendered are down, and there are a number of discrepancies I'd just like to run though with you.' Instinctively, Duncan groped for the arms of the chair – something to hold on to as the wave crashed down on him – but of course there weren't any. 'For example, the Hohenstaufen file. On a time-plus-value basis, you should have charged twenty-seven thousand, but you only billed nineteen. Why was that?'

Because—

(Because the money-grubbing bastards would've screamed the place down if I'd charged them that much; which was why I did most of the work at home, on my own time, so I wouldn't have to bill them for it. But of course I daren't tell you that—)

'Goodwill,' he said. 'Sort of a loss-leader. Like Captain Scott,' he added, mostly because he still could.

'Strictly speaking,' (did she know any other way?) 'you should have cleared that with me first. And then there's the Martinez file. You haven't rendered an interim bill for three months. Standard procedure for long-running cases is a bill every six weeks. Can you perhaps—?'

'Well, yes,' Duncan said, and for some reason he thought of the Polish cavalry in World War Two charging the German tanks with lances. 'I sort of used my discretion there a bit. It's sort of an unusual case, really.'

Jenny Sidmouth nodded. 'Very unusual. It's the only case in my department where an interim bill hasn't been sent out for three months, which makes it actually unique. Perhaps you'd like to do something about it. By Friday.'

No need to say *yes* or *of course* or *I'll see to it immediately;* just as there's no need for the grass to acknowledge the edge of the scythe. Ms Sidmouth rolled on over him, her voice sandpaper, her eyes drills: Parsons, Barlotti, Singh, Bowden Allshapes, the

Atkinson Will Trust – all the sleepers, cupboard-skeletons and too-difficults that lurked in the places in his filing cabinet where he was too scared or too ashamed to go. It was, Duncan decided, a bit like the Last Judgement would be, if Margaret Thatcher was filling in for God. With an effort he tuned out the voice and did a few quick calculations. A three-point-whatever shortfall wasn't bad enough for the sack, so the only possible way for the ordeal to end was The Speech. And, sure enough—

'Duncan,' she said, tightening the apertures of her eyes down to pinpricks, 'let's make no bones about this.'

Thought so. And, of course, he'd heard The Speech before. Parts of it he could recite along with her. Somehow, though, knowing exactly what was coming didn't make it any easier to handle. If anything, the reverse. Like injections: you know it doesn't really hurt, far less actual pain than a paper-cut or stubbing your toe. But as you sit there in the waiting room, your knees can't help shaking and the knot in your stomach slowly gets tighter than a schoolboy's tie; and then when the buzzer goes and it's your turn—

'Actually—'

He'd said it before he'd realised he was speaking. Pure reflex: he didn't have anything to say. A bit like raising your arm to shield your face when a fifteen-storey building's about to fall on top of you.

'Yes?'

'No, sorry. You first.'

The look on Ms Sidmouth's face quickly reduced Duncan from three dimensions to two. 'As I was saying,' she said, 'in the final analysis, it all comes down to attitude. In this business, Duncan, we're all predators.' Her nostrils twitched slightly, as if scenting the prey. 'There's no room for herbivores in the legal profession. You can't just mumble along, chewing the cud. If you want to eat, you've got to hunt and kill. We're not just a team, you know, Duncan, we're a *pack*; and a pack runs at the pace of the fastest dog. So it's no good waiting for work to come to you. You've got to go out there into the long grass and flush it out; and when you've got hold of its neck, you've got to *bite*. Letting clients off the hook just because you're sorry for them isn't predator thinking, Duncan. That's your dinner you're letting get away from you. If it moves, you go after it; that's the rule you've got to learn to live by. Remember: we're here to get paid, so if you've done the work, you've got to charge, and charge, and keep on charging—'

'Like the Light Brigade.'

As already noted, using humour against Jenny Sidmouth was pointless, like trying to stab a dragon with a rose. '*Exactly* like the Light Brigade, Duncan, yes. No matter what the enemy throws at you, no matter how tough it gets along the way, you've got to keep going until you get there. It's survival of the fittest, it's natural selection, it's the thrill of the chase and the law of the jungle . . .'

'Ah,' Duncan said sagely. 'Only I didn't do jungle law at college. Timetabling screw-up: you could do either jungle law or tax and probate, and I thought—'

'Attitude.' She stared through him, as though he was one of those transparent tropical fish and she was a cormorant. 'That's what it comes down to. In this business, you're either a wolf or a sheep; and I want to you ask yourself, really deep down: which one are you?'

Baa, Duncan thought. 'I see,' he said. 'Now you've explained it to me, I think I understand.'

'Excellent.' A smile you could've shattered into chunks and stuck in gin and tonic. 'I'm so glad.' Jenny Sidmouth looked past him, towards the door. 'I'll be keeping an eye on your printouts from now on, Duncan. I'm sure you won't let me down. Thanks so much for your time.'

The law of the jungle, he thought as he wandered slowly back to his office; yes, well. It was all very well telling himself it was high time he got away from this bunch of Neanderthals and found himself a proper job, but it wasn't as easy as that. He'd been trying for – what, six months? During that time, the agency had set him up with half a dozen blind dates. He'd built his hopes up, trotted along to the interviews, sat down in the chair with his confident, capable look smeared all over his face; and guess what? Each time, the eyes that had stared back at him across the interview desk were exactly the same as the eyes he was trying to get away from: the same greedy, vicious glow – predators, Jenny Sidmouth had said, and for once he reckoned she was spot on. He hadn't needed to listen to the words they said. The eyes told him everything he needed to know. It didn't matter what sort of face they were lurking in – round and chubby, thin and pointy, smooth or hairy. They were always the same eyes, identical to the ones that glowered at him here, and they gave him the creeps.

But (Duncan reminded himself as he sat down and reached for the drift of yellow Post-It notes that had settled round his phone while he'd been away from his desk) it's all very well fantasising about chucking in the legal profession for good: going straight, retraining, carving out a new and meaningful life for himself as a restaurant critic or a gentleman thatcher. The simple fact was, he was a competent lawyer and no bloody good at anything else. True, he had a crummy job, but not so crummy that shelf-stacking or burger-flipping would be better. Besides, he had a mortgage and a credit card to think of.

Even so. Predators. Well.

One good thing about being a tax lawyer. When you're sunk in a bottomless slough of depression and self-loathing, you can always phone the Revenue and reassure yourself that you're not the greenest, slimiest breed of algae floating on the surface of the gene pool – not by a long way. He returned a call from Our Ref X/187334/PB/7 at the Capital Taxes Office, and it made him feel a lot better.

Even so . . . It wouldn't be all that much to show for a life (Duncan mused, as he pencilled in figures in a draft Form IHT200) if all they could find to inscribe on your tombstone was *At least he wasn't a taxman*. No, there had to be something better than this, somewhere over the rainbow; not a daydream or a TV lifestyle make-over, but a better, less painful way of being a moderately competent lawyer for eight hours a day. Fix that, and the other stuff – the dustbin bag full of old broken junk he was pleased to call his personal life – would sort itself out without any conscious effort on his part. Or if it didn't, he wasn't all that bothered, just so long as he could find a way of making work just a tiny bit less shitty. Possible, surely. Hardly rocket science, but think of how it'd improve his quality of life. One little change was all it'd take. One small step for a lemming; a giant leap for lemmingkind.

At his elbow the phone burbled. One good thing about being a lawyer: the phone rings so often, you never have a chance to concentrate long enough to get really depressed.

He didn't recognise the name of the firm that apparently wanted to talk to him: Ferris and something. 'Yes, all right,' he grunted, and there was a click.

'Dunc?'

Duncan Hughes was six foot two in his socks and no beanpole; there had only ever been one person big and fast enough to call him Dunc twice. But he blinked three times and stared at the receiver as if it had just kissed his ear; because he hadn't heard from that one person for fifteen years—

'Luke?'

He could hear the smile; and two uninsulated wires in the back of his mind brushed together, and he thought, Ferris and something. Luke *Ferris*—

A big smile, full of teeth and good humour; he could picture it now. He could picture himself, all spots and elbows, trying to punch it through the back of its proprietor's neck, and always missing. 'I thought it must be you,' the voice said, and fifteen years crumpled up like the front end of a Volvo. 'I saw your name on this sheet of letterhead – down at the bottom of the cast list, I couldn't help noticing, in with the lighting assistants and the location caterers – and I thought, could that possibly be my old mate Duncan Hughes, who fell off the edge of the world fifteen years ago and was never heard of again? So,' the voice added, 'how are you?'

Duncan thought long and hard before answering. 'Oh, fine,' he said. 'And you?'

'A bit like the *Mary Rose*,' the voice replied. 'In remarkably good shape, all things considered. Look, is it true what it says on your firm's notepaper?'

Duncan frowned. 'Depends,' he said.

'You're at 32 Fortescue Place, EC2?'

No harm in admitting that. 'Basically, yes.'

'Upper storey? Facing the street?'

'If I could see through walls.'

'Ah. Well, if you were to climb up on the roof and look sort of east, you'd see a big black glass thing a couple of blocks over, sort of like a minimalist Borg cube. 97 Mortmain Street. That's us.'

Us, Duncan repeated to himself; Ferris and somebody, note the word order. 'Small world,' he heard himself say.

'Fucking tiny,' the voice replied. 'And talking of geography, doesn't it strike you as significant that the Bunch of Grapes in Voulge Street is exactly halfway between your place and mine?'

'Well, not—'

'See you there, then. One-fifteen?'

'No,' Duncan started to say, but the disconnected-line buzz drowned him out. Which proved, if there was any residual doubt about it, that he'd just been talking to the authentic Luke Ferris, who never took no for an answer, or gave a shit about anybody else's—

Hang on, he thought.

To test out a theory, he asked himself a question: define Luke Ferris in no more than five words. Easy: *my best friend at school.* The fact that he'd never been able to stand him for more than ten minutes without wanting to hit him had, somehow, never been incompatible with that definition. A more precise and informative version would've been *not an easy person to get on with*, but that was eight words, not five. All right, then; how about *a complete pain in the—* Nope, six.

So he glanced at his diary: one-fifteen. Of course, he had

mountains of work to be getting on with, and although slipping out of the office for a bit at lunchtime wasn't exactly forbidden, it was more frowned-on than the foot of Mount Rushmore. On the other hand: my best friend at school. What harm could it possibly do?

You go through life thinking of yourself as a tall person – brushing snow out of your hair in summer and ducking in the late afternoon to avoid nutting yourself on the setting sun – and then you come across someone who makes you realise you're merely a slightly elongated hobbit.

'You've grown,' Duncan said.

Luke raised an eyebrow. 'You sound just like my aunt,' he said. 'What're you having?'

'You *have* grown.' Duncan wasn't quite sure why he needed an admission at this point, but he knew somehow that it was important. 'I mean, at school you were a tall bastard and a hazard to aviation, but –' He shrugged. Luke was looking through him; the way Jenny Sidmouth had done, like *management*. 'Coke, please,' he said.

A slight frown; then Luke turned to the barman (who'd materialised out of nowhere like a Romulan battlecruiser) and said, 'Two pints of Guinness.' No *please*; just the peremptory order. The barman nodded quickly and flipped the tap. 'And yes, I have,' he said. 'I put on a late spurt while I was at college. I put it down to beer, healthy exercise and clean living.'

'Right,' Duncan said doubtfully. 'Clean living.'

'Mphm.'

Duncan wasn't quite sure about that. True, Luke looked almost grotesquely fit in an Arnie's-big-brother sort of a way; he also looked *terrible*. As far as Duncan could remember, Luke was older than him by no more than a month or so, but his hair (augmented by a shaggy beard and bushy, three-dimensional moustache) was nearly all grey, with only a few untidy-looking splodges of its original black, like paint splashes on a dust sheet; and what little was visible of his face under all that fur was lined and worn, almost as if it had been sandpapered, with craters under his eyes like meteorite strikes. His suit was expensive and immaculate, but his hands were scarred and the nails bitten and torn. He looked like all sorts of things – a Viking, a sixty-year-old rock star, Dorian Gray's passport photo, a tramp in a millionaire's suit.

'Table free over there,' Luke said, nodding at a far corner. The two pint glasses stood on the upturned palm of his hand, as steady as though they were on a tray. 'So,' he went on, 'how are you keeping?'

They sat down; Luke arranged his enormous legs under the table like someone stacking luggage in the corridor of a train. 'Oh, not so bad,' Duncan replied. 'Bit of a coincidence, isn't it, both of us ending up in the lawyering racket. I thought you were going into the family business.'

A faint, sad look. 'I did,' Luke replied, 'for about six months, until it went bust. We got run out of town by the Spanish. Cheap imports,' he explained. 'It broke dad's heart, but I didn't mind so much. I never quite managed to regard the glove trade with the same crusading zeal as he did. The law biz is much more my style.'

'It must be,' Duncan said, trying not to let the sourness leak through. 'Your name on the stationery, and an office in Mortmain Street. I get the impression you're doing well.'

'It keeps the wolf from the door,' Luke said, and for a moment his face split around an enormous, humourless grin. 'Don't ask me for the secret of my success, because there isn't one. I mean, we must be doing something right, because people keep bringing us work to do, like a cat brings you dead mice. Beats me what it is, though. The best explanation I've been able to come up with is, we don't *try*. I mean, we don't chase after people saying how wonderful we are, we just get on and do our best, and when we haven't got a fucking clue, we say so. I think people respect that. It's either that or there's another firm called Ferris and Loop, and people come to us thinking we're them.' He lifted his glass and swallowed its contents in five enormous gulps. 'Either way I'm not bothered. How about you? Getting on all right?'

Duncan opened his mouth, then shut it again. Given his vocation he could lie, just as Michelangelo could paint a bit. For some reason, however, he felt a powerful urge to tell Luke the truth.

'No,' he said. 'I'm stuck in a boring job with a rotten firm, bugger-all chance of promotion and a boss who models her management style on Lord Voldemort. Apart from that, it's all peaches and cream.'

'Good heavens.' Luke was staring thoughtfully at him, as though he was Fermat's last theorem. 'You surprise me. I'd have thought you'd have done all right for yourself. You were always the clever bastard.'

'Was I?' Duncan raised his eyebrows. 'You sure?'

'I always thought so. Well, not as far as maths was concerned, I grant you. Not in the fifteen-A-stars-at-GCSE sense so much: more a happy blend of intellectual muscle and low cunning. What went wrong?'

Duncan shrugged. 'No idea,' he said. 'After I left school I did law at uni, got a decent degree, applied for what looked like a good job, made the fatal mistake of getting it. And here I still am, like Robinson Crusoe.'

Luke smiled. 'Ah,' he said, 'I see. Brains but no drive.'

Duncan suddenly wished he was somewhere else. 'Absolutely,' he said. 'That's what my boss thinks, too. According to her, I lack thrust, hunger and the killer instinct.'

'I'm sure she's right,' Luke said mildly. 'It'd explain why you aren't in prison. All right, if it's such a dump, why don't you leave?'

'I'm trying. Have been for the last six months.'

Luke looked puzzled. 'Picky? Spoilt for choice?'

'No.'

'Oh.' Luke considered him for a moment, as though he was a crossword clue with a misprint in it; then he glanced down at Duncan's unmolested beer glass. 'Same again?'

'Actually, I don't drink at—'

Luke had gone; and a path opened up before him across the crowded bar. It was like watching slowed-down film of the shock wave that precedes a high-velocity bullet. The barman was waiting for him, practically at attention. Duncan – one of those people who have trouble getting served in pubs without the aid of a time machine – couldn't help feeling slightly jealous.

'So,' he said, as Luke did the leg-stacking thing again, 'are you in touch with any of the old crowd? I haven't seen Micky Halloran since—'

'Actually, he's my partner. One of them,' Luke added. 'Micky and Kevin and Clive all came in with me when I set up the firm; Pete joined up about six months after that. More or less the whole of the gang,' he added, 'apart from you.'

'Oh,' Duncan said. 'So they all became lawyers, then?'

'I suppose you could call us that, at a pinch.'

For a second or two, Duncan couldn't think of anything to say. Envy, of course; but mostly a curious and quite unexpected feeling of resentment at being left out. Irrational: he'd been the one who'd decided he wanted to break with the old crowd, the one who'd changed his address and phone number without telling anybody, made no effort to keep in touch. Even so; all of them except him. It surprised him to realise that the prickle at the back of his mind was anger, but he couldn't deny it.

'I thought Pete was going off to be a teacher.'

Very quick grin. 'So did he. For a little while.'

Duncan waited for Luke to expand on that, but he didn't. 'Well,' he said. 'Like you said, all of us except me. Must be like old—'

'Yes.'

That bewildering, walking-into-a-plate-glass-door feeling, when you know you've said something wrong, but you don't know what it was. 'Times,' he said quietly. 'Who's Loop?'

'What?' Luke must've been thinking about something else for a moment. 'Oh, right. Wesley Loop. Came in with us to start with, left after eight months. Should've changed the name when he buggered off, only we'd just ordered a big lot of letterhead and it seemed silly to let it go to waste. And by the time we'd used it all up, people had sort of got used to the name. Corporate identity and all that garbage. Can't be bothered to change it now.'

One of those silences, the sort unique to the reunion of old friends who suddenly realise that they no longer have anything to talk about. He's lost interest in me, Duncan thought; any moment now he'll make an effort and ask—

'So,' Luke said. 'Work aside, how's things?'

Sometimes it's a pain when you're proved right. 'Oh, I just sort of wander along,' Duncan said. 'Nothing to say, really. I mean, if this was *Mastermind*, I wouldn't choose my personal life as my specialist subject.' He paused, took a breath, not too deep. 'Got married; we met at law school, got hitched as soon as we both qualified, didn't last five minutes. No big deal. In fact, in my list of Bloody Stupid Things I've Done Over The Years, it's somewhere down around number seven hundred and fifty. Since then—' He shrugged. 'I could never see the point, really.'

'Mphm.' Luke nodded. 'You lost the only woman you ever loved, and since then life's been an emotional black hole seething with despair and existential doubt. It's a right cow when that happens.'

'No, it wasn't like that at all,' Duncan said, only realising as he said it that he wasn't really telling the truth. Occupational hazard. 'Blessing in disguise, really. The way I see it, work's bad enough without relationships as well. Mostly I sit at home in the evenings watching the box and hoping that one day I'll evolve into plankton. Too tired and emotionally buggered to do anything else, really.'

Luke was frowning. 'That doesn't sound much fun,' he said.

'No. I think fun's a bit like Father Christmas. You believe in it passionately when you're young, but eventually you figure out it never really existed. What about you, then?' he said, seconds before embarrassment made them both die of hypothermia. 'Married? Kids?'

A smile; superiority and compassion, mostly. 'Not in any meaningful sense,' he said. 'But you don't want to hear about that. What happened? You can't just say *didn't last five minutes* and leave it at that.'

None of your damn business, Duncan thought. 'I don't really know what happened,' he said. 'We got married straight out of law school, like I told you. She got a job with Crosswoods – you know, the family law specialists?'

Luke nodded. 'Impressive,' he said.

'Oh, she was the clever one, not me. Anyhow, as soon as she started there, she seemed to change. Funny little things, to start with. Like, she always used to love eating out at swanky French restaurants; then suddenly, if I ever suggested it she'd get all up-tight and bite my head off. Which is odd, when you come to think about it. I mean, when we were students we couldn't afford to go to places like that, but we did; then, when she's working at Crosswoods and money's not a problem—' He sighed. 'Stuff like that, anyway. Cut a long story short, I came home one evening and found a letter on the mantelpiece. Both of us being in the trade, we got the divorce practically at cost.'

Luke was looking at him , as if trying to diagnose where the fault lay. Time, Duncan decided, for a diversionary counter-attack. 'I'm surprised at you, though. Weren't you and Hannah Schlager—?'

'Yes.' A gentle scowl, such as you'd imagine on God's face as He contemplated a blatant case of TV licence evasion. 'But it was a bit like the Roman Empire. Came to an end eventually, and that was that. Since then – well, I've had other things on my mind.'

In other words, a big Keep Out sign, backed up with razor wire and searchlights. Duncan could take a hint; besides, he realised, he wasn't all that interested. Whoever this person was, he wasn't the Luke Ferris he'd gone to school with. It was like driving past the house you used to live in twenty years ago; and in this case, he really didn't like what the new people had done to the old place.

After that, things went downhill like a bobsled. All Luke seemed to want to talk about were the circumstances of the failure of Duncan's marriage, and as far as Duncan was concerned, even if there had been anything more to say on that subject (and there wasn't) he really wasn't inclined to say it. The usual conversational gambits suitable for failed reunions were a wash-out. Luke seemed preoccupied; he sat with his stanchion-like elbows parked on the table, gnawing vigorously at the end of a pencil grasped in both enormous hands. If Duncan started to say 'Do you remember the time when you and me and Steve—' Luke simply said 'Yes,' closing the conversation like someone squashing a spider between the pages of a heavy book. There didn't seem to be much point continuing; so, when Luke stood up to buy yet more beer, Duncan did the looking-at-watch-and-tutting thing and said he had to be getting back to the office.

'Oh.' Luke frowned. 'That's a nuisance. Give me your home number – I'll ring you.'

Why? Duncan thought; but it was an order, not a request. He noticed, however, that Luke didn't offer his own number, and he felt no urge to ask for it. He stood up to go; Luke was already on the move, reprising his Moses impression through the Red Sea of lunchtime drinkers. Along the way he nudged against a table, dislodging some female's powder compact; it fell on the floor, landing on its rim, and began to roll, but before it had travelled ten inches Luke pounced on it, a blurred, smooth motion of almost deadly grace, and put it back without a word. As they walked out into the street Luke glanced at Duncan quickly, nodded and strode away through the crowd, the tallest tree in Birnam Wood.

As a hatter, Duncan thought. But, as he headed back up the street, he decided that was oversimplifying. Whatever it was that was strange about newly rediscovered Luke Ferris, comparisons with hatters, brushes, jay birds and fruit cakes proved unhelpful in isolating it. Quite possibly it would have bothered him, if he'd had any desire whatsoever to see Luke again.

One good thing about the legal profession is the extraordinary range, depth and variety of counter-irritants. No matter how grim or niggling a problem may be, in a matter of minutes you can be sure that something else even more exasperating will come along and flush it out through your ear. Five minutes into a call from the accountants in the da Soto probate, the eccentricities of his old school chum were the last thing on Duncan's mind.

'But can't you *see*?' the voice quacked in his ear. 'If we do a Section 56 election, that'll mean we trigger an event under Section 8(b) of FA77, which'll have a knock-on effect on our Schedule D, quite apart from the CGT implications, which in themselves—'

(Yet another joy that goes with the trade. You don't have to poke about in the backs of dusty old wardrobes to find a way through into a strange, unreal world populated by freaks and monsters. We deliver to your desk.)

Maybe the worst part, Duncan thought, is that if I was actually listening, I'd probably be able to understand what he's talking about. 'Point taken,' he said. 'So what do *you* think we ought to do?'

That always shut them up. A silence. 'Hello?' Duncan asked, out of wickedness. 'Are you still there?'

'On the other hand,' the voice said, 'there's a very real risk from the anti-avoidance provisions in section 106 FA98, which means we'd be treading a very fine line—'

'I agree,' Duncan said. 'So what do you think we should do?'

Very long pause. Amoebae that had been crawling across the bottoms of lightless oceans when it started had evolved into sharks, crayfish and dentists by the time the voice spoke again. 'I think,' it said, then hesitated. 'Let me run through the figures one more time, and I'll get back to you,' it mumbled; then there was a click and a buzz.

Duncan grinned. Just occasionally he was able to control his environment one teeny-tiny bit, and when it happened, it never failed to please him. He reached for the summit of the mountain of green wallet files on his desk and tried to remember what he was supposed to be doing with it.

Just more death, that was all. Back in the unfairly stigmatised Dark Ages, they knew a thing or two. When you died, they buried all your stuff with you: your spear and your shield, your favourite cup, your string of shiny beads that the Roman trader had promised you were genuine amber. In a way, it was a kind of golden age of mankind. No need for jumble sales, dejunk-your-life TV make-over shows, or probate lawyers: you simply took it with you, on the assumption that, when you reached Valhalla, Odin had infinite cupboard space. Simpler times, simple faith. Of course, it helped that only Iron Age Gettys and Gateses had more than one pair of shoes.

Yawn, stretch. The soldier's definition of war is an infinity of boredom punctuated by moments of unspeakable horror. The working day ground on, one begrudged tick at a time. As he read, cross-referenced and dictated, Duncan allowed his mind to wander a little. He considered, among other things, the curious return of Luke Ferris. It had been an odd, faintly surreal business, rather like a dream, and he found it hard to shift the mental image of the huge white-haired man who'd once been his best mate at school gnawing the end of a pencil, looking for all the world as if he was about to crack it with his teeth and suck out the graphite. Memory and the passage of time don't just revise the past, of course. They cover it up, like a government burying bad news. The fact was, he'd never liked Ferris much; the confusing thing was, he hadn't actually realised it at the time. What had confused the issue (he could see it clearly now) was that Ferris had apparently liked him; and, being a commanding sort of personality and a born leader, it hadn't ever occurred to him that anybody he liked wouldn't automatically like him back. Now he came to think of it, there'd always been that undertone in their relationship: *like me or I'll break your arm.* Teenage boys are, of course, the crudest form of pack animal, their obedience to the alpha instant and unthinking, at least until the alpha is deposed and replaced. Duncan smiled at that. Just as well he'd made the decision on the day he left school to forget all about his old friends. By the look of it, the rest of them – Micky, Clive,

Kevin, even Pete – hadn't moved on at all. The Ferris Gang still defined them, as it had all those years ago. There but for the grace of God, Duncan thought—

(Except that the Ferris Gang had an office in Mortmain Street and were presumably swimming in money; and if they were still being ordered around by their boyhood Il Duce, how could that be worse than having to listen to inspirational speeches from Jenny Sidmouth? Fine. It'd be easier to count himself well out of it if he hadn't contrived to get himself bogged down in something worse. Which raised the question, of course—)

The door opened and Tricia came in, with the wire basket of freshly printed letters for him to sign. At one time he'd rather enjoyed this particular ritual. There was something rather medieval and grand about having your chamberlain waiting on you while you affixed your royal seal to a consignment of writs and charters – *le roy li volt*, and all that. And signing his name, over and over again, like a film star conceding autographs on his way to an awards ceremony; it's not for me, you understand, it's for the Maidenhead branch of the Midshires Building Society. He'd taken a perverse pleasure in gradually eroding his signature into a wild, Dadaesque squiggle, something to be executed with panache and plenty of wrist. But the sad reality is that even kings and earls and margraves reach the point when they groan and say, 'Not more bloody charters', and Duncan's signature had long since degraded into a squirly mess. He groped around his desk for a pen.

'Under your elbow,' Tricia said.

'What?'

'Pen. You're leaning on it.'

Of course, he had two different squiggles: Duncan Hughes for the yours-sincerelys, Craven, Ettin and Trowell for the yours-faithfullys. Over the last few months they'd gradually begun to merge into one another. Occasionally he still tried to make believe he was the Booker Prize-winner signing copies at the front of a queue that was paralysing traffic as far back as

Holborn, but each time he tried it the illusion frayed a little bit more. 'That the lot?' he asked.

A nod, and Tricia was gone. Once the door had shut behind her, Duncan realised that she'd changed her hair yet again; now it was black, straight, vaguely Goth. Was there a reason for it, a little bit of human interest, or had she just woken up that morning with the fanciful notion that it'd make her look nicer? He shrugged, and picked up another green folder. The trouble is, in order to do human interest, you have to be interested in humans.

Mail call meant it must be around half-past four; in which case, in just under an hour he'd have Mr Martinez to deal with, complete with his self-propelled miasma of doom and invisible albatross necklace. Did they do post this way over in Mortmain Street? Hard to imagine the Ferris Gang having proper grown-up office routines. All right, so presumably they'd found a way to suppress the urge to roam the corridors writing rude words on the walls and beating up the typists; even so, it was a set-up he found practically impossible to visualise – because, in his mind's eye, Pete's tie knot would still be buried under the wing of his open collar, and his shirt-tails defiantly free-range; if Kevin was still at his desk at five forty-five, it could only be because he was in detention yet again, not because he was finishing up a few things he needed for an important meeting next day. Suddenly, and without serious provocation, Duncan felt *old*. And what in God's name had happened to Luke's hair? Now he realised what was so badly wrong with the picture that haunted his mind's eye. Somehow, his best mate at school had mutated into the headmaster.

Mr Martinez, he ordered himself sharply.

Four big fat green files, not to mention two stocky pink files, for the court case. In a way, they were as eloquent a testimony to human suffering as any war memorial. He looked at them and did some quick and dirty calculations. A sheet of paper: let's assume an average thickness of one five-hundredth of an inch. The correspondence clip of the first file was easily two and a quarter inches thick: call that twelve hundred and fifty sheets of paper; each sheet was either a letter in, at a fiver each, or a letter out, twelve quid. Average that: eight-fifty. Twelve hundred and fifty times eight-point-five—

Mr Martinez came, unloaded his sorrows like a contractor tipping topsoil, stayed for an hour and went away again, leaving Duncan with a headache and a powerful thirst. He thought of home (the frozen pizza, the microwave, the TV and early to bed) and, as he dragged the sleeve of his coat over the sleeve of his jacket, a vision flooded his mind of a crowded bar, deafening noise, stale air and, the not-so-still centre of the hurricane, Luke Ferris and the Ferris Gang letting off steam after a long but boisterous day in the office. It was inevitable, surely: the pack that plays together stays together, and there they apparently still were, as inseparable now as they'd been in the corridors and behind the bike sheds at Lycus Grove.

Duncan expected to feel a great reassuring surge of superiority welling up inside him, purging him of his earlier self-pity like a pressure washer; the righteous contempt of the cat that walks by himself for mere dogs. He waited, but it didn't come. Instead, he caught himself thinking that it'd be rather nice to have friends again; not his sort of friends, the kind you see every now and again, who never just pop in uninvited, who'd probably frown and say 'Oh dear' when they heard you'd died. Proper friends, the sort who shared their lives with you, the sort who were actually pleased to see you—

He buttoned his coat. He'd turned his back on the Ferris Gang because they had swamped him; told him what he could do and what he couldn't; unsettled him, belittled him, cramped his growth, tried to turn him into someone he didn't really want to be. In the event, he'd managed to do most of those things quite well on his own without any help from them. It hadn't taken much; he'd mumbled 'I do' in a registry office, and the rest had been so much downhill freewheeling.

He thought, as he left his office and turned out the light: I've reached a point in my life where I can try to do something about all the crappy stuff, or else I can go home, defrost a pizza and watch *Celebrity Love Island*. As he headed through the maze of corridors and landings toward the main stairwell, he caught a glimpse, in his mind's eye, of the great crossroads in Life's dark and shadowy forest, where the arms of signposts point away from each other at right angles: this way Work, that way Fun. Never mind, he thought, it may still be there tomorrow. He stumbled down the stairs into reception, barged through the fire doors and let himself out into the street.

Sardined in a Tube train, Duncan tried to think about something else; anything. Good heavens, he thought, any day now I should be due for an electricity bill. There's another crucial moment in a man's life: should I stay with my present supplier, or should I compare tariffs and look for a more competitive source of supply? And then there's the larger issue: in my use of electricity, am I doing everything I can to reduce my reliance on fossil fuels, curb emissions and stave off the next Ice Age and the twilight of the human race?

Somehow, he couldn't quite bring himself to focus on the issues with the laser-like concentration that they required. Instead, through the perished gaskets of his mind seeped the thought of company, the tantalising notion that if you can be with other people, you no longer have to be yourself.

No man is an island; define island. There are some pretty big islands, after all. Being an island is no big deal if you can be Australia. Things only get depressing if the most you can aspire to being is Rockall.

No messages on his answering machine. Duncan poured himself a nice tall glass of water, and shoved his pizza into the microwave.

CHAPTER TWO

He was dreaming that he'd died; and Uncle Norman and Aunt Freda, being his closest living relatives, had come in to the office to see him, to sort out the paperwork. Can we start with the full name of the deceased, he asked: Duncan Maurice Hughes, Uncle Norman replied. Did he make a will? No, he never got round to it – silly, really, him being in the trade; cobbler's children, as they say. He nodded, and made a mental note to sell Uncle Norman and Aunt Freda a will before he left the building. So, he said, what does the estate consist of? Uncle Norman smiled; couldn't really call it an estate, he said, just a few bits of old junk, an overdraft, mortgage, credit cards . . . He frowned, and got ready to do the speech about What Happens When The Loved One Dies Insolvent . . .

And the box, of course, Uncle Norman said.

Box?

Nod. He had this box.

From a Morrisons bag, Uncle Norman produced a box. It was small and black, clearly quite heavy for its size: cast iron, or something like that. There was a tiny keyhole in the lid. It's locked, of course, Uncle Norman said, we've looked all over for the key, but he always was a messy devil.

I see. Do you happen to know what's inside it?

No, Uncle Norman replied, just that it's very valuable.

Fine, Duncan replied, and reached for the sledgehammer leaning against his desk. You don't mind if I—?

You go ahead, said Uncle Norman. So he hefted the sledgehammer in both hands, took a big, slow swing and brought the hammer head down on the box lid with all his strength. The box exploded in a glittering shower of burning sparks, and he woke up.

Duncan Hughes adhered to the school of thought that maintains that you shouldn't buy newspapers, because it only encourages them. Nevertheless, he had a guilty feeling that he really ought to keep up with current affairs, as a sort of miserable civic duty. The best compromise he could handle was a radio alarm clock.

Straight from the dream, then, to the collapse of the EU budget negotiations, the latest suicide bombings Over There somewhere, factories closing, oil prices rising, some political scandal he'd stopped trying to understand weeks ago, a disturbing rise in cases of dognapping in the Home Counties, and finally time is running out for Cuddles the giant hammerhead shark stranded in the mouth of the Severn Estuary—

Yawn; shut the bloody thing off, cold feet groping for slippers, cold lino tiles in the kitchen as he waited for the kettle to boil. Tiny fragments of dream-shrapnel still dug into the lining of his brain (hammer head, hammerhead; he was lashing out at Uncle Norman's little black box with a seventy-foot shark) as he thumbed the lever of the broken toaster a couple of times before remembering. At least, he told himself, I was sensible last night and didn't go out drinking. Just think how much worse all this would be if I was hung over.

Train full of people, their feet on his feet, their elbows in his ribs; do they still have manned lighthouses any more, or is it all automated? A thousand mirror-lemmings sharing one escalator. The front office; two minutes late.

'That Mr Martinez rang. I told him you weren't in yet. Could you call him back soon as possible?'

Nod. (Marvellous. Now Mr Martinez would picture him dallying over hot buttered toast in front of a roaring fire, probably wearing a silk dressing gown, instead of making the effort to be at his post at nine sharp. Not fair, really.) Up the stairs, through the maze. Big tray of post. Another day.

'Hello, Mr Martinez? Sorry I missed you, what can I—?'

More stuff like that; also standard letters, probate valuations, the Capital Taxes Office, capital gains tax implications, Nottingham and Swansea. At eleven-fifty, the phone rang.

'Mr Ferris for you,' said Reception. 'Ferris and Loop.'

'What?'

'Ferris,' Reception explained.

But – 'Oh, right, yes.'

Click; and he was about to say *I wasn't expecting to hear from you so soon* when Luke's voice thundered in his ear:

'Did she really just up and leave you, out of the blue?'

'What? Oh, yes.'

'That's terrible. Bloody cow. Anyway, see you at the Bunch of Grapes at one o'clock.'

'No, I can't, that's—'

Click.

Duncan felt a surge of anger, like stomach acid refluxing through a hiatus hernia. Bloody Ferris, ordering him about— He was still holding the phone; tightly, as if he was about to strangle it. He frowned (don't strangle the phone, Duncan, it's not its fault) and put it carefully back.

I'm buggered if I'll go, he thought.

He picked up a letter and stared at it, but it could've been written in classical Sanskrit for all the sense it made. What's going on? he asked himself. Fifteen years since he'd last run with the Ferris Gang, and now they wouldn't leave him alone.

Possibly, he thought, just possibly, Luke Ferris wants to see me again because he likes me.

He held the letter in front of him and picked the words out one by one. *Dear sir, we thank you for your letter of the 21st and note what you say. However, we cannot agree that the property referred to in the third schedule to the conveyance dated 17th January 1946—*

There is a moment, a watershed in one's development as a human being, which must be passed before one has any claim to enlightenment and understanding. It's the moment when you come to realise that, just because somebody likes you, you're under no legal or moral obligation to like them back.

Even so—

Duncan shook himself like a wet dog. Third schedule to the 1946 conveyance: there was a photocopy of that in the file somewhere. He scrabbled for a bit until he found it. *All that freehold property more particularly described in a conveyance dated the 4th March 1926—*

In which case, he told himself, he didn't really have a choice. He'd go to the stupid pub and tell stupid Ferris to quit bothering him: straight from the shoulder, no messing, polite and civilised but firm. He could hear himself: *To be quite frank, Luke, I think it's been too long for us to be able to pick up the threads just like that. And besides, I never really liked you anyway.*

Ring. He opened his fingers, letting the sheet of paper flutter unhindered to the desktop, and picked up the phone.

'Crosswoods for you.'

'What?'

Of course, he didn't even know if she was still with Crosswoods; it had been a long time, and ambitious go-getters like Sally don't hang around out of sentiment or loyalty. 'Crosswoods,' Reception repeated impatiently. 'You want to take it or not?'

'Put them through,' he replied, with a shrug that nobody was there to see.

Click; and then a voice that, thankfully, *wasn't* hers.

'Imogen Bick, Crosswoods,' the phone said chirpily. 'Barker, deceased. You act for the plaintiffs.'

Do we? 'That's right,' he said. 'What can I—?'

'I've got your letter of the twenty-sixth of November here in front of me,' said the voice; and thereafter it was just legal stuff, and he disconnected his brain from his tongue and let it drift. Coincidence, he told himself. Big firm like Crosswoods, very highly regarded in the death-and-taxes game. Absolutely no call for him to assume it was personal. However, when the legal stuff had finished and the woman was about to ring off, he said, 'Excuse me, but can I ask you something?'

Slight pause. 'Go on.'

'It's just a personal thing. Have you got someone called Sally Hughes working for your lot? Sally Moscowicz, I mean. Of course, she'll have gone back to her—'

'Well, yes,' the voice replied, rather as if he'd asked her if the big yellow bright thing in the sky was really the sun. 'My boss.'

'Oh.' He frowned. 'She's a partner now, is she?'

'Head of the probate department. Why?'

But not the *whole* truth. 'Oh, we were at law school together,' he said. 'Thanks. Bye.'

This time Duncan ground the phone into its cradle like someone stubbing out a cigarette. Not that he was jealous, or resentful. Good heavens, no. No skin off his nose, even though she'd never have scraped her pass in Probate and Trusts if he hadn't lent her his notes a week before the exam and spent hours and hours of his own precious revision time drilling the rudiments of discretionary settlements and the perpetuity rules into her short-plank-thick skull. Bloody good luck to her, even if but for him she wouldn't have known the rule in *Saunders v Vautier* if it had bitten her on the bum. Obviously, she must have hidden depths, like the Atlantic (dark, murky, inhabited by pale creepy things with huge eyes and rows of needle-sharp teeth). For some reason he could hear Luke Ferris – *Did she really just up and leave you, out of the blue? That's terrible. Bloody cow.* There, he suspected, had spoken a true misogynist; whereas he, Duncan, liked women, admired and respected them, enjoyed their company, even forgave them for fucking up his life and leaving him an emotional and spiritual wreck. *My boss,* the Bick woman had said. Well, that he could believe. If Sally was good at anything, it was ordering people about. He yawned. The past was apparently coming back to haunt him like London buses, all huddled together in a flock. But as far as he was concerned, the past was a horrible place, only marginally preferable to the present and the future.

He checked his watch; 12.15 already. To walk to the Bunch of Grapes, seven minutes. Except that he wasn't going. Wild horses—

'There you are,' Luke said. 'You're late.'

'I'm—' Duncan resisted the urge to defend himself. He wasn't late, he knew that, and even if he was, so what? 'Look,' he said, 'I can only stay for a minute, I've got to prepare for a meeting with—'

'Sit down.' He saw that there were two pints of Guinness, huge and black as the gaps between galaxies, already waiting on the table. He sat, feeling uncomfortably like a well-trained dog.

'Well, cheers,' Luke said, and his share of the black beer vanished down his face in eight enormous, throat-convulsing gulps. In a way it was a sight to admire, but only if your taste also ran to volcanoes and the like. 'Glad you could make it. Look,' he went on, before Duncan could draw breath, 'I've been thinking about what you were saying yesterday, and I sort of got the impression – put me straight if I've got this wrong – that you're not exactly thrilled with your job. Right?'

'Well, it's all right,' Duncan replied without thinking. 'I guess.'

'You like it there, then.'

Lying to Luke was a bit like supporting the weight of the Albert Hall on your shoulders. You could do it, for perhaps as long as a millionth of a second, before you got squashed flat. 'Actually, no,' Duncan said. 'It's rotten, it sucks. But it's the only job I've got, and the only one I'm likely to get, so—'

'Really?' Luke put his head on one side as he looked at him. What great big eyes you've got, Grandma. 'Why's that?'

Shrug. 'Well, I guess I'm not the greatest solicitor who ever lived.'

'You reckon? Why do you say that?'

'Because I'm useless.' Again, the insupportable weight of his own dishonesty; he knew he wasn't as bad as all that. In fact, he'd be all right at it, if only— 'Not good enough, at any rate. It being such a competitive business and all.'

Luke seemed to find that amusing. 'Who says?'

'My boss. All the partners. Everybody else in the office. Everybody I ever met in the business. My Aunt Freda. My Aunt Freda's friend Sharon—'

'I see. And you believe them.'

'Well, yes.'

'Oh.' Luke's lip curled a little, a sort of handy combination smile and sneer. 'You surprise me. Personally, I've never seen it that way.'

Too stunned to react. 'You haven't.'

'No, not really.' Luke stared absent-mindedly into space for a few seconds. 'Competitive means everybody fighting each other all the time, right? Well, that's not how we run our business. God, no. I suppose it helps that we've all been friends as long as any of us can remember. But it's just common sense, really. How can you concentrate on doing a good job if you're at each others' throats all day long? Stupid.'

'Yes, but—' Yes, but that seems to be the way the whole world's run, not just the law business; and if it wasn't a good thing, all those clever people who run things wouldn't do it. Would they? 'All right, it sounds fine in principle. It's just not the way they do things at our place.' He frowned without knowing it. 'We work more on the gladiatorial system, I guess. We all fight each other to the death, and the ones who're left alive at the end get thrown to the lions. Standard British management philosophy, I'd always assumed.'

Luke shrugged. 'It may be, for all I know. It just doesn't make much sense, that's all.'

The discussion was leading somewhere, Duncan could tell; he could almost see the tour guide's raised umbrella. 'So you don't—'

Luke smiled. 'Thought so,' he said. 'I told Kevin and Pete and the lads, after I'd seen you yesterday, he doesn't like it there much. Not his style, my guess was. And then we had this sort of collective brainwave, lightning flash of inspiration, all of us simultaneously. Sort of like a multiple pile-up on the road to Damascus. Why don't you chuck in your job with the arseholes and come and join us?'

Mostly, Duncan wanted to scream. It was intolerable; sheer torture. The choice: stay where he was, for ever, and wake up every single morning cringing, or rejoin the Ferris Gang, with the subtle distinction of being the lowest form of life. 'Come and work for you, you mean?'

'Not *for*,' Luke said irritably. 'With. Join us.'

Penny dropping, burning up in the atmosphere, splattering the ground below with droplets of molten copper. 'What, you mean, as a *partner*?'

'Mphm.'

'But—' Well, at least he had a reason to refuse, and so end the torment. 'No, I couldn't. I can't afford to buy into an outfit with an office in Mortmain Street.'

Luke's tongue clicked like a bullwhip. 'You don't need to worry about all that rubbish,' he said. 'All we do is, we get a whole load of new stationery printed with your name in the list of partners – roughly in the middle, because we do it in alphabetical order. Simple as that. After all—'

Duncan knew what was coming. It was like the end of the world; the trumpet had sounded, and the Messiah was swooping down to earth in His winged chariot, and *scrunch* – guess who just happens to be standing underneath its wheels as it touches down. *After all, you're our friend, one of us.*

Trouble was, he wasn't. That had been his choice, and he could still remember why he'd made it. No use worrying about that now; he'd left the band before they became famous, and he couldn't go back to them now, on these terms. Could he?

'After all,' Luke said, 'it's not like you're a stranger. We've all known you since you were the little fat kid with the really bad acne, who got crispbread and lettuce for his packed lunch instead of proper sandwiches.'

A shrewd point to raise. The only reason he hadn't starved to death before he reached sixteen was because the others had shared their lunches with him; because (he couldn't help remembering) Luke had *made* them share their lunches with him. But that recollection started a whole new rail network of thought, and he didn't want to go there.

'It's very kind of you, really—'

'But.' Luke pulled a sad face. 'You're about to say *but*, aren't you?'

Nod.

'Why?'

Duncan remembered a playground: early autumn, dry leaves drifting in on the wind from the plane trees that grew just outside the school gates. Hughes the new boy, just moved into the neighbourhood, uncrinkles the silver foil in which lurks his first packed lunch at Lycus Grove. He's nervous about anybody seeing; understandably, since inside the foil are three slices of Ryvita spread with couscous, two cherry tomatoes and a short stick of celery.

He knows why it has to be that way, of course. His mother and father had explained to him, kindly and patiently, why he was a vegetarian and why we don't eat processed bread and chocolate and biscuits and all that rubbish. It had made sense at the time; it always did, except that shortly afterwards the sense would always evaporate, like the ramparts of Elfland, and that could only be because he was too dim-witted to have understood properly. And, if he couldn't remember the sense himself, he knew for certain that he'd have no chance of explaining it to his contemporaries and so excusing himself of the mortal charge of being different.

One last furtive glance over his shoulder; then he pinches the edges of the first crispbread between forefinger and thumb—

'What've you got there, then?'

Terror and despair; because he recognises the voice, though

he hasn't yet spoken to its owner. That Luke Ferris, the dark lord of the Ferris Gang; the sort of kid his parents have warned him about. Rough, uncouth, no respect for rules, almost certainly a vandal and a bully. The last person on earth who'd be prepared to overlook Ryvita spread with couscous, cherry tomatoes and a stick of celery.

He knows he's done for; but a tiny spurt of courage burns inside him, like a rat at bay turning on the terriers. 'Mind your own business,' he says.

'What've you got there?'

'Piss off.'

That Luke Ferris doesn't say a word; but two of his trolls materialise on either side of Duncan, taking firm but ineluctable hold of his elbows. Ferris advances slowly and takes the foil parcel from his hand like someone picking a ripe apple off a tree.

He looks at it. 'You like this stuff?'

Duncan looks up, meets his dark, terrible eyes. As he does so, an urge rises inside him to tell the truth; a truth he'd never quite admitted to himself before.

''Salright.'

'Looks like shit to me.'

'Yeah.'

Ferris's head dips ever so slightly, and the Stilson-like grip on Duncan's elbows relaxes. Ferris is still staring into the foil, as if he's looking at something bizarre and inexplicable. Then, with a move as graceful as it's swift, he lobs the package underarm into the nearest of the four tall plastic trash-cans parked twenty-five yards away, by the alley that leads to the kitchens.

'You can share ours,' Ferris says.

Duncan is still recovering from the amazing spectacle of Ferris's throw – could've been a fluke, sure, but he really doesn't think so. 'What?'

'Our sandwiches. What d'you want, ham or chicken?'

As soon as he says it, the attendant trolls unzip their school bags and produce flat wedges wrapped in plastic. *Sandwiches*:

slices of toxic plastic bread with scraps of butchered flesh entombed between them like the dead at Pompeii. *No, thanks, I don't eat meat*, he doesn't say. Instead: 'Dunno.'

'Make your mind up. It's not astro-bloody-physics.'

'I don't know,' Duncan repeats. 'Never had either of them.'

– Which should, according to his mother and father, have unleashed on him the full fury of their unenlightened wrath (because nasty people who eat animals always make fun of nice people who don't; but you mustn't tell lies and pretend, because you must always stand up for what you truly believe in . . . There were times when Duncan wondered if his parents had ever been to school; and, if they had, how they hell they'd survived.). Instead, that Luke Ferris stares at him. Not mockery or bigotry, but compassion.

'You what?'

'I never had either of them.' *I'm a vegetarian.* 'My mum and dad are vegetarians.'

'Oh.'

Ferris shrugs. Duncan watches him. Even he can see that a great deal depends on what happens next.

'You poor bastard,' says Ferris. 'Try the ham.'

He doesn't signal, but a troll steps forward with a plastic packet, which he unwraps.

'That's ham, is it?'

'Think so. Pete?'

The troll nods. 'Ham,' he says.

Duncan hesitates. 'That's murdered pig, isn't it?'

'Mphm.'

And now he has no choice. He takes the object in his hand, tries not to look at it, bites until his top and bottom teeth meet through the unfamiliar textures; chews before swallowing.

'Hey,' he says, with his mouth full. 'Cool.'

Ferris nods slightly, acknowledging a truth too obvious to need expression. 'Now try the chicken. That's murdered hen,' he adds.

Yummy murdered hen. Duncan pauses for a moment, trying

to catch words that come somewhere near the turmoil of lights and explosions inside his mind. 'I like the ham best,' he says, 'but the chicken rocks too.'

A troll grins; but not unkindly. 'There's murdered cow and murdered sheep too,' he says. 'My mum does me murdered cow on Thursdays – you can try some.'

'And murdered turkey,' adds another troll. 'And *corned* murdered cow. You want to try some of that, it's amazing.'

The trolls had closed in round him, but not in any threatening way. For some reason, Duncan almost expects them to start sniffing him. 'My mum's going to be so pissed off,' he mutters.

Ferris grins; a very slight movement, nonetheless showing the teeth. 'Only if you tell her,' he says.

Which Duncan never gets round to doing; which is why, every lunchtime until the day comes when he dumps his tie in the bin on his way out through the school gates for the last time, he ritually discards an unopened tinfoil packet before seeing what his mates have brought him to eat. Over the years, he wavers in his loyalty. Sometimes his favourite is roast murdered cow, sometimes it's murdered salami. (Nobody would tell him what sort of animal a salami was; at first he assumed it was short for salamander, until he saw a whole one hanging up in a delicatessen shop. For a while he felt guilty about eating cold sliced dachshund, but he came to terms with it in the end.) His greater loyalty, however – to Luke and the gang – never falters even for a split second, in spite of the detentions and suspensions and awkward times down at the police station; not for an instant, until the very end—

'Why?' Luke repeated.

'Because—' Duncan hesitated for a split second, then exploded, 'Bloody hell, Luke, you can't just spring something like that on someone and expect an instant yes-or-no answer. I've got to think about it.'

His explosion had been more like a damp Catherine wheel: two or three unconvincing twirls and a few farted sparks. Luke was grinning, his teeth still as straight and white as ever. 'Why not? I mean, what's there to think about? You hate this shit-hole you're at now, your whole life's a complete mess. You need looking after.'

This time, the flare of anger was hot enough to light the blue touchpaper of self-expression. 'Absolutely,' he snarled. 'My whole life's a complete mess—'

'Well,' Luke interrupted reasonably, 'it is.'

'I *know*.' Not quite loud enough to silence the bar and turn heads, but almost. 'You don't actually need to remind me, thank you so very fucking much. And it's been a complete mess ever since—'

'Since she dumped you.'

In the Middle Ages, they hunted the wild boar with a spear. You dug the butt end in the ground, shoved the pointy end at the approaching boar, and let the stupid creature kebab himself on it. 'Well, yes,' Duncan mumbled; but what he'd been about to say, because until Luke spoke it had been what he'd believed to be the truth, was *ever since I left your stupid gang*. And he'd been about to add that his decision to turn his back on the Ferris gestalt had clearly been proved to be disastrous, and he wasn't fit to run his own life and obviously needed Luke to run it for him; but, regardless and in spite of all that, fuck off and die.

He didn't say any of that. He felt like a physicist who's spend twenty years working on a theory, spending millions in hard-won research grants and devoting his life to the cause, and who finally achieves final and irrefutable proof that his basic hypothesis is a load of old socks.

'The bitch,' Luke said sympathetically. 'But what the hell, it's still no reason why you should carry on having a horrid time when you could be having a slightly less horrid one. Well?'

But he couldn't just roll over on his back and admit it. 'Like I said,' he muttered, 'I need time to think about—'

'Chicken.' Very slight pause. 'That's murdered hen, to you.'

You can't really be offended and want to laugh at the same time, not unless you're Duncan Hughes. He opened his face to say something, but closed it again, as it occurred to him to consider the significance of the fact that his ex-wife had also been a vegetarian.

Then Luke said, 'So, what was she like?'

There's a drug that supposed to make you tell the truth, whether you want to or not: the CIA buy it by the tankerload, presumably. Luke could've spiked Duncan's beer with it, except Duncan hadn't drunk any.

'Tallish,' he said. 'A bit on the chunky side, though she lost a lot of weight. Straight dark hair; she was a lot into the Goth sort of look when I first met her, black clothes and spiky silver jewellery. A bit on the quiet side to begin with. She changed a lot after we left law school and started work.'

'It happens.' Luke nodded. 'I gather it's called growing up,' he said. 'I don't reckon it much, and neither did Peter Pan.'

'It wasn't just that.' Duncan frowned. For some reason, things long obscure were beginning to clarify in his mind. 'She was always – well, quiet.'

Luke nodded. 'Quiet,' he said. 'Didn't say a lot.'

'That's right.'

'You sure she was female?'

Girls had always liked Luke, of course, and Duncan had assumed that his air of arrogant disdain for them was just catnip; it certainly seemed to have that effect. But now there was an edge to his voice. Not bitterness, an echo of Duncan's own attitude. More the unconcerned dismissal of the man who's never been to a particular place and never wanted to. He bookmarked the insight for later.

'Serious,' he said. 'I don't mean no sense of humour, just – well, quiet.'

'Boring.'

'No, not boring. Just—'

Luke shrugged. 'Quiet, right. Nice-looking?'

Duncan pulled a face. 'Yes.'

'I see. Nice-looking and didn't talk all the time. You wouldn't happen to have her phone number?'

Duncan sighed; Luke frowned. 'Go on,' Luke said.

'That's about it, really. We met, we fell in love – well, I know I did, and she said she did too.'

'Quietly?'

'And when we both finished law school and qualified,' Duncan continued sourly, 'we got married. She'd got this job at Crosswoods lined up, I'd already got a place at Craven Ettins. We bought a flat in Battersea – it was just before it got too expensive – and everything seemed more or less OK. And then, one day out of the blue—' He snapped his fingers. 'And that's all there is to it,' he added sadly. 'My life down the toilet, basically.'

'Ah well.' Luke shrugged again. 'Spilled milk, plenty more fish, all that crap. I don't really see, though, what any of that's got to do with you quitting your job and coming in with us.'

'You raised the subject,' Duncan snapped back.

'Yes,' Luke said. 'And obviously it's relevant. It's left you with a raw, bleeding hole where your self-esteem used to be, and that explains why you can't be bothered to try doing something about your wretched, pointless existence. Fair enough; I can see exactly where you're coming from. What I'm having trouble with is your reluctance to leave the barren desert island and let yourself get rescued by the passing ship. Can't see the problem myself. Perhaps you'd care to explain.'

It had never been what Luke Ferris said; always the way he said it. How else could anyone explain why instructions like *you take this bowl of cold custard and balance it on top of the Head's office door while I nip back and set off the fire alarm* had, at the time, seemed not only wise and sensible but the only possible course of action in the circumstances? Later on, in the still calm of triple detention, it was possible to unpick the strands of his logic and trace the fatal flaws. But when Luke was giving you your orders, it was as though the Oxford University Press had recalled all the earlier editions of the Dictionary and replaced them with one containing only the single word *Yes*.

'I need time to think about it,' Duncan repeated.

And Luke shrugged again. 'Sure,' he said. 'You'd be an idiot to take a big decision like this without weighing up all the pros and cons, considering the implications, really thinking hard about what you want to do with your life.' He smiled. 'You can have as long as it takes me to get in another round. Then you can toddle back to Craven Ettins and clear your desk.'

In spite of his mental turmoil, Duncan couldn't let that pass. 'Does alcohol have any effect on you at all?' he asked.

Luke smiled. 'Long story. Be back soon.'

There was, Duncan decided, only one thing he could sensibly do. He waited until Luke reached the bar and turned his back on him; then he jumped up and scuttled out of the pub as fast as he could go.

Reception glared at him as he loped through the front office, looking nervously over his shoulder. 'There you are,' she said. 'You've had ever so many calls in the last ten minutes. Ferris and Loop—'

He leaned on the desk, both hands planted, fingers spread, so that Reception leaned back nervously. 'If Mr Ferris rings,' he said loudly and clearly, 'tell him I died. Got run over by a bus at the corner of Barditch Alley. Private funeral, no flowers. You got that?'

'Yes, but—'

'Bus. Brakes squealing. Squelch. Flat as a pool table. Come on, picture it in your mind, it'll help you sound convincing.'

Duncan couldn't stop himself sprinting up the stairs, hardly stopping to draw breath until he was back in his office with the door shut. He was tempted to drag the filing cabinet over to block the doorway with, but he guessed the partners might not approve. To hell with Luke Ferris and his rotten gang, he said to himself. I've been there once, I'm not going back. Ever.

All that afternoon he felt as though his chair was stuffed with six-inch nails, and every time the phone rang he cringed. But apparently he'd shaken them off, at least for now. As four o'clock dragged by (it was one of those days when the Chariot of the Sun gets a flat tyre, and its fiery Charioteer has to get out and push it all the way to the portals of the sunset) he felt brave enough to suggest to himself that maybe, over the last fifteen years, Luke Ferris had learned how to take a hint. Curiously, in spite of the painfully slow movement of the clock hands, it turned out to be a reasonably good afternoon. No accountants rang in to point out his mistakes; no clients turned up unexpectedly to see him; no partners sent for him. He sat with his feet propped up on the opened bottom drawer of his desk, slowly enunciating a draft Deed of Trust into his dictating machine. Today, for a change, he was Richard Burton, with occasional intervals of Alec Guinness when the context called for it; and when he'd finished that he did Ian McKellen for the first sixteen clauses of a nil rate band discretionary will trust. Of course, when he hit the rewind and played any of it back, it sounded just like a duck quacking in an echo chamber.

Quarter past five, and it occurred to him that maybe Luke and the gang might be waiting for him outside the building, ready to pounce as soon as he set shoe-sole to pavement. He fretted over that one for five minutes or so until the answer came to him: work late. After all, he had nothing special lined up for the evening (nothing special? Nothing at all: frozen pizza, TV, bed) and in the top drawer of his filing cabinet lurked the Allshapes estate accounts, which he'd been putting off revisiting for weeks. Two birds, one stone; he'd get that particular albatross off his neck, and by the time he'd finished, Ferris and the lads would've long since given up and gone away.

Fine, he thought. Win/win scenario.

The Allshapes file. Duncan took it out and looked at it for three minutes before opening it. All solicitors know that certain files have curses on them: it's a simple fact, something they teach you on day two at law school. Sometimes the curse is relatively trivial: you buy the wrong house or, halfway through the case, you suddenly realise you're supposed to be acting for the defendant, not the plaintiff. Other files bear the weight of darker spells: inconvenient misprints (remarkable, the effect of leaving out a little word like 'not' in a contract or a lease); title deeds that only show up once every hundred years, like the enchanted village in *Brigadoon*; as often as not, the real curse is the client himself. In the case of Bowden Allshapes, deceased, the curse seemed trivial at first sight but, after nine months of trying to deal with the bugger, it had grown so huge that it blotted out the light.

Quite simply, there was something squiffy with the maths. Every now and again, when he felt brave or reckless or so demoralised he didn't care, he'd get an up-to-date printout of the client account ledger, stick a new battery in his calculator and try and get the bastard thing to balance. Take a sheet of A3, draw a freehand line down the middle. On the left hand side, list all money paid into the account. On the right, payments made and cash in hand. The proverbial piece of cake; except that, each time he spread the printout in front of him on the desk, it was—

And that's where the Allshapes file got a bit spooky; because it was demonstrably the same as the previous edition: you could put them side by side, tick off the new entries and match the remainder with the earlier version. Except that it was also, in some way he simply couldn't put his finger on, different. Something happened to all the numbers while Duncan's back was turned; maybe they sneakily converted themselves from base ten to base eight (though he'd tried compensating for that and it made no difference). The visible symptom of this silent alchemy was that, no matter how many times you added up the numbers – the same fucking numbers, every time – they always came to a different total. One day the difference could be thousands; another, it'd only be out by 46p (but then you added it up again, and the discrepancy would swell to twice his yearly salary). Not that he'd have cared a damn if only he could have got the two sides of his A3 sheet to balance. But they wouldn't; not ever.

Perhaps the weirdest thing about the Allshapes file was that the deceased's heirs (two nieces and a nephew in South Africa) didn't really seem to care that their uncle's estate had taken six years to wind up and wasn't settled yet. The revolting thing was worth two and a half million, give or take a few thousand, and they'd never had so much as a penny piece or a paper clip out of it. Instead, Duncan sent them interim bills, which they blithely approved by return of post; and Sarah, the younger niece, had taken to sending him cards at Christmas and, for some reason as yet obscure, the Chinese New Year. It was the saintly, unclient-like behaviour of people who should by rights have been his principal natural predators that made the file rather more than he could cope with.

He opened the file and checked the date on the latest print-out; recent enough that nothing on it should have changed, apart from the deposit interest. With a newly sharpened pencil he went down the page, drawing a little sun next to all the receipts and a tiny crescent moon beside each payment out. The famil-iar crawling feeling at the nape of his neck; but he washed it out of his mind with the image of Ferris and the gang standing out in the street shivering in the cold. This time, he said to himself (and his lips curved in an unconscious smile), let's do this as slowly as possible.

Outside in the world, he knew, it was cold and dark by now; and say what you like about Messrs Craven Ettin, they weren't cheapskates when it came to light and heat. He had a radiator of his very own, and above his head the fluorescent tube burned brightly. His fingers on the calculator keys were as light and swift as a concert pianist's, and he was nearly at the bottom of the first column of figures when the door opened and his con-centration shattered like a glass dropped on a stone floor.

'Oh,' said Jenny Sidmouth, staring at him round the door frame.

He was so pleased that it wasn't Luke Ferris that he almost smiled to see her. 'Hi,' he said.

'You're still here.'

'Yes.'

'It's a quarter to six. You usually go at half-five.'

This time he did smile. Her accusation was well founded. Duncan never stayed late if he could possibly avoid it, and Jenny Sidmouth, in common with her partners, held the view that people who downed tools and walked out at five-thirty on the dot ought really to be rounded up and burned alive in wicker cages, as an example.

'Thought I'd polish off these accounts tonight, while it's quiet,' Duncan replied cheerfully. 'You know what it's like trying to concentrate with the phones ringing all the time.' He took a surreptitious breath, then added, 'I always reckon the real working day doesn't start till five-thirty.'

She stared at him as though he'd just sprouted wings. 'But you're always the first one out of the door—'

He nodded. 'I take work home with me,' he said. 'I find it's easier to pace yourself in a less formal environment.'

She narrowed her small, vicious eyes. 'You take work home?'

'Yes.'

'What in? You haven't got a briefcase.'

If it hadn't been for the thought of Luke and the boys shivering in the frosty darkness below, that would probably have beaten him. Instead he shrugged. 'Big pockets,' he said, and although it was obviously blatant drivel, the words came so freely and easily to him that they must have carried conviction, because Ms Sidmouth frowned and said, 'Oh.'

'That's all right, isn't it?' Duncan went on. 'Of course, I never take important documents or stuff like that out of the office, just photocopies.' Just the right modulation of self-doubt, as if it was something that had been preying on his over-conscientious mind. He could see from her expression that he was doing well.

'I suppose,' she said. 'I mean, obviously we prefer it if you do your work here in the building, otherwise there's not much point having an office, is there? But,' she went on, 'if you feel there're some things you can do more productively at home, on your own time—' Baffled, Duncan decided, like a terrier that can't quite reach the rat. 'It's entirely up to you,' she said after a pause. 'Just so long as the work gets done and the staff's happy, we don't mind in the least.'

That's the thing with lawyers and lies, Duncan thought. They lie so often and so fluently, it can only be because on some level they can make themselves believe what they're saying; as if they had the power to reshape the world with a few words. Ms Sidmouth was a very good lawyer, and when she said the words there was a tiny part of Duncan that couldn't help believing them, just for a fraction of a second; in which time, perhaps, a small, sealed universe in which they were true came suddenly into being, glowed for an instant intolerably bright, and then went out, like a shooting star.

'Great,' Duncan said. 'Oh, while I think of it, that Sudowski file you were asking about the other day. Should have it wrapped up this week, and then if it's OK I'd like to have a word with you about the bill. I was thinking, we can probably justify charging the full five per cent value element, but I'd be glad of your thoughts on that.'

For a moment, Jenny Sidmouth almost glowed at him. Then she left; and he thought, there must be some truth in it after all. Because, for a split second there, I really believed that there's an ice lolly's chance in hell of getting Sudowski sorted out this week; and when I said it, for another split second she believed me, even though she knows it's a complete fuck-up that'd have all the king's horses and all the king's men quitting the service and moving to the private sector. Between us, we made a little bit of magic that actually existed for a while. Like antimatter. Of course, it wouldn't get the mess sorted or bring him any closer to the point where he could ram in a gigantic bill and close the file: that was where the magic failed, he presumed, and why the whole world wasn't run on it.

Any hopes he might have had that the enchantment might have extended itself to the Allshapes estate accounts withered quickly. He added up the figures four times and got four differ-ent results. Since he had a bit of time on his hands, he decided to experiment a little. He worked out the discrepancies between the four different totals and averaged them, eventually arriving at a figure of 4,337.97. He wrote it in big numbers in the middle of a blank sheet of A4, and stared at it for a while. Then he added up the columns four more times, resulting in four more completely different totals. He was about to start averaging them too when the door opened again.

'Oh.'

This time, though, it was only a cleaner, who muttered something under her breath and withdrew almost immediately. Duncan scowled at the closed door for a moment or so, then sighed. It was, he realised, half past six, and he was still in the office. No magic could make that into a good state of affairs. Did the Ferris mob have the endurance to hang about in the dark and the cold for a whole hour? Chances were, no. He packed away the Allshapes accounts – that was another five minutes – tidied his desk, sharpened a few pencils; put down an hour and a half on his timesheet (nobody would ever know, after all, that he hadn't stuck it out for the extra thirty minutes), put on his coat and went down to the front office. Nobody around to see him leave, which was a pity; it'd have been nice if all the partners had chosen that moment to come out of a meeting and see him, but no such luck—

Which told him, he realised as he let himself out into the street, what he needed to know. His decision had been made; because if he still cared about sucking up to the bosses, it meant he'd decided to stay at Craven Ettins, instead of obeying the call of the Ferris Gang. Until then, he hadn't really been sure.

Nervously he peered up and down the street, scanning for shadowy forms in doorways. It felt like a silly thing to do, and it occurred to him that a busy, successful lawyer (which was, apparently, what Luke Ferris had morphed into, at some point when Duncan's back was turned) probably had better things to do after all than stand around in the street waiting to offer a job to a loser who ran away from him while he was buying him a drink – Duncan shook his head and started to walk to the Tube. His head always seemed to be full of shit these days. Some of it came from the job, sure enough, but not all of it.

Because it was that much later, of course, the Tube wasn't quite so hellishly jam-packed: another advantage of working late, he realised, and he began to wonder if maybe, just possibly, there was a greater lesson in there somewhere. Maybe (just possibly) his life was wretched because he fought it so much. Think: he made a point of leaving at five-thirty sharp because he had an inalienable human right to his spare time, but he spent those precious hours of freedom watching TV game shows and sleeping, so what was the point? As a result of his obsessive reverse punctuality, his bosses had reached the quite reasonable conclusion that he wasn't partnership material, and despised him accordingly. As a result, his time at work was nothing but trouble and sorrow. Now: if, instead of sitting bored and lonely in his grotty flat, he could bring himself to sit bored and lonely in his grotty office till, say, quarter past six every weekday, he'd soon come to be regarded as a dutiful predator and made of the right stuff; they'd start giving him the decent jobs instead of the garbage, he'd begin making them some decent money and they'd promote him—

More of the same magic, he realised, a lie that'd slowly make itself true. But that didn't really matter. In the country of the lawyers, the selectively sighted man is senior partner; and if you can work the magic and make yourself believe, quite soon what you're seen as turns into what you are. It was rather like what he'd told Reception when he'd come back from lunch: *picture it in your mind, it'll help you sound convincing.* Once you saw it in your mind, seeing was believing. And, on top of that, he'd get to arrive home in three dimensions rather than two, not having been squashed flat by ninety million people all trying to occupy one Underground carriage at the same time.

Win/win scenario.

Usually, as he walked from the Tube to his flat, he tended to huddle, as if braced against a mighty wind. Tonight he practically strolled. It clarifies things tremendously once you've finally figured out who your worst enemy is, particularly if it turns out to have been yourself all along. And Sally, he realised, didn't really enter into it at all. True, she'd ruined his life and left him feeling about as valuable as a bounced cheque, but that wasn't the reason he was a miserable failure in the office. All his own work, that was.

So: tomorrow, he'd throw himself into it, make believe that all the daily garbage – the accountants and the clients and making sure the bills went out on time and getting the accounts to balance – actually *mattered*, and that the stuff he did all day was worth doing and a valid use of his lifespan. Only believe; only in faith lies salvation.

He unlocked his door and moved his hand up the wall towards the light switch. Then he realised that the lights were already on. Bloody fool, must've forgotten to turn them off before he left that morning; except that he distinctly remembered having done so. But here the lights were, distinctly on, so his memory must be—

There was someone sitting in his chair: feet propped on his battered coffee table, shoulder-length white-black-grey hair just visible above the back of his chair. Before he could react, the intruder stood up, turned and faced him.

Luke bloody Ferris.

CHAPTER THREE

'You're late,' Luke said. 'Never mind. Come on in, sit down. Have a crisp.'

On the coffee table, a packet of crisps, savagely torn open. 'What the hell do you think you're . . .'

'Just the one chair,' Luke said, tightening the corners of his mouth in a small grin of scornful compassion. 'I take it you don't entertain much.'

'How did you find out where I live?'

Apparently Luke hadn't heard him. 'I was expecting bachelor squalor,' he said. 'Obviously she got you well trained before she left. Not a sock or a styrofoam tray full of cold chips anywhere to be seen.'

'That's none of—'

'A little palace, you might say,' Luke went on, looking through Duncan at something clearly far more interesting – the wall, say, or the windowsill. 'A little palace that's been burgled by professionals and stripped of all its contents, but a little palace all the same.' He drew a long forefinger across the top of the coffee-table. 'You don't *dust*, do you?' he said, and there was a hint of genuine awe in his voice, mixed with the barely repressed amusement. 'Bloody hell, mate, my *mother* used to dust.'

The instinct is to fight, but giving in is often easier. 'All right,' Duncan said. 'Sit down if you want to.'

'Thanks.' Luke smiled, turned back to the chair, turned round three times and sat down. Duncan noticed that the top pocket of his suit jacket was lined with pencils, all heavily chewed. 'You're a bastard, you know, sneaking off like that. I had to drink your beer for you.'

'My heart bleeds.'

'So it should. Oh, don't stand there like a butler, sit down. It's hurting my neck peering up at you.'

Duncan scowled at him, then got down and sat on the floor. His master's voice, he couldn't help thinking.

'The answer's no,' he said.

'Sorry?' Luke replied, 'Don't quite follow. Answer to what?'

'The job offer. I've thought about it, and it's really kind of you, but I think I'll stay where I am.' No sudden violent interruption; Luke was looking over the top of his head. 'No offence,' he went on, 'but I've come to the conclusion that— Look, would you mind bloody well not doing that?'

For a moment, Luke seemed puzzled. Then he seemed to notice that he'd picked the TV remote up off the coffee table and started chewing it. He lowered it, but didn't put it back. 'That's daft,' he said. 'You don't want to stay there. You told me yourself, the whole gig sucks like a Dyson.'

'I exaggerated.'

'Balls.' Luke stood up, and Duncan saw that he'd left a few white hairs on the chair-back. 'I've heard all about Craven Ettins,' he went on. 'Typical London law firm. They treat you like dirt, pay you peanuts, the only reason they don't sell their grandmothers to the glue factory is that you don't make glue out of grandmothers—'

'Yes,' Duncan said. 'But—'

'Well?'

And Duncan smiled as he said, 'But at least they're not you.'

Luke's body slammed into the back of the chair as if he'd

been shoved, and his bushy eyebrows shot up like house prices. 'What did you say?'

'They're not you,' Duncan repeated, amazed at how calm he felt. There now, he was saying to himself, that wasn't so bad, was it?

For the first time – yes, dammit, for the first time since he'd known him, Luke seemed genuinely bewildered, as if he didn't know what to do. 'I don't understand,' he said.

'Really?'

'Yes, really. Bloody hell, Dunc, you make it sound like you don't like me.'

And Duncan smiled. 'Don't call me Dunc,' he said pleasantly.

'What? Oh. You don't like—'

'No.'

Pause. Luke was watching him, like a cat at a mousehole. 'I didn't know that. You never said.'

'I did, actually. You never took any notice.'

'Didn't I?'

Duncan shook his head. 'You never do. That's your trouble, you hear things but you don't *listen*.'

'Oh.' Luke had his head slightly on one side. 'Right, fine, I won't do it again if it bothers you.' He paused, frowning. 'Is that it, then?'

'What?'

'Whatever it was that was bugging you,' Luke said. 'The name thing. Was that why you said you don't want to—?'

'Don't be stupid.' He saw Luke's eyes grow very big and wide, and if he didn't know better he'd have thought he heard a very low, faint growling noise. 'It's not just that. The name thing was just the tip of the iceberg. It's—'

'It's what?'

Luke, he realised, genuinely didn't know; which made it next to impossible to explain. It was like trying to tell a five-year-old about the causes of the Seven Years War in three sentences. 'It's everything,' he said; and then he added, 'Oh screw it, you wouldn't understand.'

Luke frowned. 'It's not just dusting, is it?' he said. 'You even talk like a girl these days. She must have—'

'Oh, for crying out loud.' Then Duncan realised that he was sitting on the floor, in his own flat. It struck him as a really stupid thing to be doing, when he had a perfectly good chair, the only problem with which was that it was currently full of Luke Ferris. He stood up. 'How did you get in here?' he snapped.

Luke shrugged. 'Climbed,' he replied.

That made no sense. 'Are you kidding? It's the fifth floor.'

Luke grinned. 'Piece of cake,' he said. 'I went round the back and saw you'd left your kitchen window open; so I shinned up next door's drainpipe to that little balcony thing, and jumped across onto your windowsill. Really, you should be more careful with your windows, there's—'

'You jumped?' In spite of everything else that was going on in his mind, Duncan was doing mental triangulation. From the third-floor balcony of the building next door to his kitchen windowsill: easily thirty feet. 'Bullshit,' he said. 'That's not possible.'

'I'm good at jumping.' Luke was nibbling at the TV remote again. 'Don't you remember at school—?'

'Look.' Duncan pulled himself together. 'Forget how you got in. All I'm interested in is how you're getting out again. How quickly, actually.'

'Hm?'

'Leave.'

Immediately, Luke put the TV remote back on the coffee table, but stayed in the chair. There was something about that; a point that Duncan felt he was missing, but was too annoyed to clarify. 'Steady on,' Luke said. 'There's no need to go working yourself up into a state. Calm down, get a grip, stop looming over me and tell me what's bothering you. I mean,' he added, sounding a bit like God forgiving the ninety-seven-billionth sin of Mankind since breakfast, 'how am I supposed to know what the matter is if you won't tell me?'

A sort of reckless fury filled Duncan's mind, sweeping away a lifetime of careful training and programming in the ways of peace and non-violent persuasion. He leaned over the table, grabbed a handful of Luke's jacket lapel, and tugged. But Luke didn't move, and cloth, even the really expensive stuff that Luke could apparently afford these days, isn't that strong. Something tore, and Duncan staggered back. There was something in his hand.

He looked down at it. Out of context, it was practically unidentifiable: a triangular piece of cloth, neatly seamed on two sides, frayed and ragged on the third. If it had been dripping with blood, Duncan could hardly have felt more guilty. He opened his mouth but nothing came out of it, and all he could think of was, *I'm going to be in so much trouble—*

'Duncan?' he heard a voice saying. 'Are you all right?'

Duncan, he noted: both syllables. 'What?'

'Are you OK? You look like you're about to have a fit or something.'

'I'm fine,' he mumbled. How much did a suit like that cost? Not a hope of getting it mended so the damage wouldn't show. He tried to remember how much he had in his bank account. 'Luke, I'm really sorry, I'll pay—'

'Your phone's ringing.'

'What?'

'Telephone.'

For a moment, he couldn't remember what a telephone was. 'Oh, right. Sorry. Would you excuse me a minute?'

'Sure.'

Duncan stumbled into the bedroom, still holding the scrap of cloth. It looked very much like an ear. Hadn't there been a long and bloody war fought once over someone's severed ear? Or was he thinking of Van Gogh? He groped for the phone and picked it up.

'Duncan?'

A female voice. 'Who's this?'

Pause. He'd said the wrong thing; in which case, it could only be—

'Sal?'

'Please don't call me that.' Yup, it was her all right. He wondered how he could possibly have failed to recognise her voice; the only possible explanation was that when she said his name, she was sounding reasonably civil. 'Look,' she went on, 'were you talking to someone from our place this morning?'

Our place. As in our movie, our song; no, probably not. 'Crosswoods?'

'Yes. Well, were you?'

He remembered. 'That's right, yes. Some female—'

'My assistant, Imogen Bick.'

'That's her, yes.'

'You asked after me.'

'Yes.'

'Well, don't.'

'Sorry? I don't—'

'Don't ask after me,' Sally said, cold and precise as an ice scalpel. 'Do you understand?'

'I was just—'

'Don't. Come on, it's simple enough.'

'Well, all right.' He hesitated. 'I was only—'

Click. He stared at the receiver for a moment, as though it was something he'd found in an apple he'd just bitten a chunk out of, then put it back on its cradle, carefully, as if afraid of waking it up again.

'Let me guess.' Luke's voice, behind him. 'One of those telesales people, right?'

Certainly the most striking example of cold calling he'd come across in a long time. 'Yes,' he said.

'Not your ex, then.'

Duncan closed his eyes; his hands clenched, and he felt his fingernails digging into the torn-off lapel. He turned round slowly.

'Look,' he said, 'I'm really sorry about ruining your jacket and I'll buy you—'

Luke did a really rather fine dismissive gesture. 'Forget it,' he said.

'I'll buy you another one,' he repeated. *If it's the last thing I do*, he didn't need to add. 'But the answer's still no; I'm not packing in my job and coming to work for you lot. I've made my mind up, and nothing you can say will—' He broke off. Luke had jumped up, crossed to the window and twitched aside the curtain.

'What's the time?' he asked.

Duncan checked his watch. 'Quarter to eight,' he replied. 'Why?'

'Sod.' Luke seemed agitated about something. 'It is the twenty-first today, isn't it?'

'Yes. What's that got to do with—?'

Luke was walking towards him; he felt an urge to get out of the way. 'Well,' Luke said, 'sorry to hear you're not interested, but it's your life.' He was rummaging in his side pocket. 'I'll see myself out. There isn't a back door to this building, is there? No? Oh well. See you around, I hope.'As he opened the front door, he slid a pair of sunglasses onto his nose. 'Take care, all right?'

'Luke,' Duncan said to the closed door.

He stood quite still for the best part of a minute, trying to clear his head. Then he crossed to the window, pulled back the curtain and looked down into the street. In the moonlight he saw Luke crossing the road, his maimed lapels drawn up round his face as though it was raining. He wasn't actually running, but he moved quickly. He stopped beside the driver's door of a new and illegally parked Ferrari. Apparently he'd left it unlocked. He drove off like a drag racer.

Duncan let the curtain fall back. 'Don't understand,' he muttered to himself. But then, he'd never really got a handle on what made Luke Ferris tick, not even at school. There didn't seem to be any point, somehow. You don't need a degree in mechanical engineering to know not to play about with an unexploded bomb that suddenly stops ticking. No; the strange and alarming behaviour wasn't what was bothering him. It was the fact that Luke Ferris had apparently accepted defeat. That, he realised, was definitely a new one on him; and, although it meant

he'd apparently won, he couldn't help feeling decidedly appre-
hensive about it.

Next morning he arrived at the office twenty minutes early.

It was the first time he'd ever done such a thing, but he knew
what he'd find when he got there: a small knot of his colleagues,
standing about aimlessly, waiting for a partner to arrive and let
them in. The point of the exercise was to be noticed, and
recorded in the corporate mind as keen and dedicated. Actually,
Duncan suspected as he looked at their faces, it was probably
subtler and darker than that. Once the custom had become
established, it was more a case of not daring not to be there on
the doorstep bright and early, for fear of being classified as not
keen and non-dedicated, like that Duncan Hughes. At any rate,
they stared at him when he joined them, and nobody spoke to
him.

Tony Utgarth-Loki, the senior litigation partner, arrived to let
them in at a quarter to. He carried a briefcase the size of a small
trunk in each hand, and three pink wallet folders wedged under
each armpit, and he gave the impression that he hadn't seen
any of them.

Never mind. Obviously, it'd take Duncan time and perseverance to build his new persona, and one had to start somewhere.
He dashed up the stairs two at a time instead of trudging – there
was nobody to see him to do it, but it helped him establish the
all-important mindset: the Stanislavsky approach, as he was
coming to think of it. He sat down at his desk and, instead of sitting motionless and struggling to cope, which was what he
usually did for the first quarter-hour of the working day, he
grabbed the nearest file, opened it and tried to remember the
plot so far.

The crazy thing was, the Stanislavsky approach did seem to
have a grain of merit in it. Simply by pretending very hard that
the work was worthwhile, interesting and urgent, he found it
easier to bear. The Chapman tax-planning file, for example. It
had pottered along at the speed of tectonic shift for the last two

years and finally come to monolithic rest, simply because he didn't want to take responsibility for doing the calculations, and neither did the accountant. Since Mr Chapman appeared to have forgotten all about it, there was nobody to make a fuss and get things moving again, and the file nestled peacefully in his cabinet, as safe from disturbance as a Martin Amis novel in a library. But (protested the character Duncan was method-acting) that wouldn't do at all. There were hours of unbilled chargeable time on the file; thousands of pounds ready and waiting to be invoiced for, just as soon as the finger was extracted and applied to the keys of a calculator.

So he did the sums, which turned out to be not nearly as scary as he and the accountant had thought; then he incorporated them in a letter to the client, copy to the accountant, and added *Finally, please find enclosed a note of my firm's charges for work done to date.* He should then have gone through the file costing it, letter by letter, phone call by phone call, but by now he was feeling far too dynamic and motivated for that sort of nonsense; so he looked up the client's telephone number, doubled it, added seventeen hundred pounds for luck, and dictated an invoice.

Piece of cake, he thought. I could get the hang of this.

Encouraged, he took a similar approach to the Thorketil, Morrison, Ganga Ram and Danby Trust files (the Danby file was so ancient, he half expected to find ammonites pressed neatly between its pages like dried flowers in an Edwardian lady's diary), bunging down any old thing to gloss over the original insoluble problem, and enclosing with each letter a suitably awe-inspiring bill, its initial integers trailed by a string of noughts as long as a comet's tail. This, he began to understand, was how partnerships were come by. As for the money: that, he realised, was the key to the whole alchemical miracle. It's a fundamental law of economics that a thing is worth what someone's prepared to pay for it. If his client paid five figures for his advice, it inevitably followed that his advice was very valuable; by the same token, the more he charged the more precious it became. The fact that in many cases his advice wasn't capable of being put to any useful purpose was neither here nor there. A Ming vase is, after all, just a very old flowerpot if looked at in strictly utilitarian terms, and a genuine Titian is just a bit of canvas covered in paint, no good for anything except hiding a damp patch on a wall. They're only worth anything because people pay money for them; and the same was true of his legal services. So: all strictly fair and above board.

He'd just cleared up the Ibbotson file (wouldn't Mrs Ibbotson be delighted to find out that for years she'd been the owner of legal advice worth a small fortune without even knowing it; like finding a Leonardo sketch in the attic) when the door opened and Jenny Sidmouth came in.

'Got a moment?' she said.

Duncan put down the file (very busy man, but never so busy he couldn't find time for her) and smiled, keenly and with dedication. 'Sure,' he said.

She sat down. 'I've got something to tell you.'

Duncan suppressed the urge to raise an eyebrow. A partnership, already? He'd only been doing the Stanislavsky thing for – well, less than twenty-four hours, but evidently the partners could spot potential in the bud. 'Fire away,' he said.

Jenny Sidmouth sort of grinned, then straightened her face. 'Funny you should say that,' she said.

'Excuse me?'

'You're sacked.'

Once upon a time, many years ago when he was a small, vicious child, he'd gone to use the lavatory and found a large spider crawling up the inside of the toilet bowl. He'd immediately pulled the chain, and to this day he could picture the spider swirling round in the vortex of foaming blue water, its repulsive legs vainly pumping up and down. Now he knew how it must've felt. 'Sorry, what did you—?'

'There's a cardboard box behind the desk at Reception,' Ms Sidmouth went on. 'You can use that for clearing out your things. You needn't bother about bringing it back,' she added magnanimously. 'We'll send on the paperwork.'

'You're sacking me?'

'Yes.'

'Why?'

Duncan thought he could see the tiniest glint in her eyes, like the final twinkle of a star sucked deep into the heart of a black hole. 'Breach of duty of care and confidentiality,' she replied. 'Which reminds me. You can have a reference if you insist, but if I were you I wouldn't. I don't think it'd help you get another job, if you follow me.'

'But that's—' He shook his head. 'What did I do?'

She looked gravely at him. 'You've been taking confidential material out of the office,' she replied. 'Files, clients' documents, that sort of thing. If you look at your contract of employment, page 476, paragraph 98 (c), you'll find that it's expressly forbidden.'

Incy-wincy spider, its eight eyes blinded by Harpic. 'But—'

She sighed, like St Peter bouncing a sinner at the Pearly Gates. 'Imagine if you took a sensitive file home,' she said, 'and you got burgled, and the thief stole the file. Or what if your house burned down? I'm sorry, but we can't make exceptions. We've got our professional-liability insurance to think of.'

'Just a minute,' Duncan objected feebly. 'Mr Utgarth-Loki takes work home with him, doesn't he?'

'Of course not. Like I said, it's strictly—'

'Really? So what's in those two sodding great big briefcases he lugged in this morning?'

She looked straight at him. 'Sandwiches,' she said. 'He has a thyroid condition.'

In popular folk tales, of course, the spider is proverbial for its dogged perseverance. The difference was that, if Jenny Sidmouth had been Robert the Bruce, she'd have smeared the spider all over the cave wall. 'Fine,' Duncan snapped. 'I'll clear my desk.'

'Good.' She stood up. 'Oh, while I think of it: did you manage to get the Sudowski file wrapped up, like you promised last night?'

'No.'

'Oh.' Disappointment filled her big round eyes, so that she looked like a pedigree Jersey deprived of its daily silage. 'Well, never mind. Goodbye.'

After Jenny Sidmouth had closed the door behind her, Duncan sat staring at it for at least four minutes. Then, as the implications started soaking into his brain like acid, he squirmed in his seat. Sacked; no reference; thirty-four years old, with a law degree, a mortgage and some extremely valuable credit-card bills. While he was striving not to accentuate the negative, the word *screwed* did seem to cover the situation like a bespoke shroud.

Options, he thought. I must have some, somewhere. This has got to be one of those moments you look back on in later life, while you're watching the Caribbean sun go down over the rim of your banana daiquiri, and you say to yourself, *getting the sack from Craven Ettins turned out to be the best thing that ever happened to me.* No doubt; unfortunately, this particular blessing appeared to be a master of disguise, like Inspector Clouseau.

He went downstairs to the front office. 'I need a middling-size cardboard box,' he said to Reception, as casually as he could. 'You wouldn't happen—'

She'd produced it before he finished speaking. 'Will that be big enough?' she asked. 'I mean, you haven't got a lot of stuff, have you?'

The box turned out to be slightly too small, but Duncan couldn't face the thought of making two journeys, so he balanced a few books and the spare pair of shoes he always kept at the office on top, and staggered back down the stairs. He stopped at the desk, still half expecting to find all his colleagues gathered there, with cakes and champagne, to reassure him that it had all been a merry prank, and really he was being promoted—

'Jenny said you're to hand over your keys before you leave,' Reception said cheerfully. Why was it, he couldn't help wondering, that she always called the partners by their first names and got away with it? He dumped the box awkwardly on the desk, tried in vain to catch a fugitive shoe as it slid past, and pulled out his keyring. Needless to say, the office keys were stuck, and he broke two fingernails trying to prise them out.

'I think that's everything,' he said briskly, when Reception had taken the keys away from him and locked them in a drawer. 'Well,' he added, 'it's been—'

''Scuse me.' Reception darted past him to pick up the phone. 'Craven Ettin solicitors, how can I help you? No, sorry, Mr Hughes isn't with us any more. Ms Sidmouth is handling his cases for the time being – shall I put you through?'

He waited till she'd transferred the call, then asked: 'Who was that?'

'Oh, just a client.' She was looking through him, as if he wasn't there.

'Well, bye, then.'

'Bye.'

The phone rang again; she swooped down on it. Duncan juggled with his box for a bit, then stuffed the leftover books in his coat pockets, binned the shoes and walked out.

Out in the world, it was drizzling. The box was heavy, and he knew that everybody who passed him on the pavement couldn't help but realise what it signified; if a passing artist had happened to be looking for inspiration for an updated Business Tarot pack, he'd have needed to look no further for the perfect image of the Sacked Man. Needless to say, nobody looked at him. It's a well-known fact among office workers that unemployment is contagious, and is passed on by eye contact.

I'm an eccentric senior partner, he muttered under his breath all the way to the Tube. *I carry all my stuff with me wherever I go because I don't trust the cleaners.* But it appeared that the Stanislavsky effect didn't always work, because no matter how passionately he struggled to believe the lie, it still wasn't true by the time he got off the train at the other end. The weight of the box was making his shoulders and elbows ache. It felt bizarre and unnatural to be walking home in the middle of the day. The

streets were much emptier than they were during the morning
and evening lemming-runs, and he was reminded of all those sci-
fi films where the Last Man In The World wanders through the
deserted city.

When Duncan finally got home, he dumped the box on the
kitchen table and left it there. It contained, he realised, nothing
he actually wanted: pencils, a calculator, his desktop electric fan,
the strange and vaguely disturbing paperweight he'd been given
by his aunt for his last birthday but one. He wondered why he'd
bothered bringing it all home, when it'd have made much more
sense to have dumped it in the first rubbish-bin he'd come to.

He flopped into his chair and shut his eyes, asking himself,
What the hell just happened to me? It made no more sense here
than it had back at the office. Why had they fired him? Well,
because he wasn't exactly an asset to the firm: clash of mindsets,
difference of attitudes, square pegs and round holes. Fine; but
why now, so suddenly? Sacking the unwanted staff wasn't the
Craven Ettin way; instead, they made life so miserable for them
that they quit of their own accord. He'd seen it happen half a
dozen times, he knew the drill, and that wasn't what had happened to him. It must have been something he'd said or done,
something so intolerable that they'd reacted with the swift,
sudden, bloody stroke rather than the gradual easing-out. He
had no idea what the something could have been; but anyway, it
didn't matter now.

Quick ransack of his memory, followed by a flurry of mental
arithmetic. Add the interest on his credit-card debts to the mortgage, the bills and even the bare minimum for subsistence, and
you came up with a depressingly substantial sum of money,
which he now had no way of earning: because nobody would
give him a job without some kind of reference.

Nobody. No normal employer—

He groaned out loud. *No*, he thought, *I'd rather stack shelves or
clean toilets*. No doubt; but neither of those vocations paid well
enough to keep him solvent. Working for Luke Ferris, on the
other hand – assuming the offer was still open, after he'd

insulted, abused and practically assaulted his well-meaning old friend, who'd only been trying to be nice.

It was, he decided, his Japanese game show moment; a point in his life where he had no choice but to embrace the humiliation, plunge right into it as if immersing himself in a hot bath. As he called directory enquiries for the number of Messrs Ferris & Loop, Mortmain Street, he tried out various opening gambits in his mind—

'Hello, could I speak to Mr Ferris, please? Duncan Hughes.'

The being-put-on-hold music buzzed in his ear like an electric hornet, disrupting his attempts at structuring a well-turned phrase. Count to five, he told himself. If they don't put me through by then, put the phone down and think of something else.

Three, four – 'Duncan?'

'Hi, Luke.' Just enough of a pause to swallow some breath, then: 'I've been sacked.'

'Sorry, what did you—?'

'They fired me. Craven Ettin. This morning.'

'Bloody hell. Why? What'd you done?'

Duncan laughed, for some reason. 'No idea.'

'Any warning?'

'Clear blue sky.'

'What an absolute bugger. So, what can we do to help? You want us to sue them for unfair dismissal?'

Duncan closed his eyes. One small step for a lemming. 'Actually, Luke,' he heard himself say, and he sounded very far off and strange, 'I was wondering if—'

'Did they give you the proper written warnings; you know, the section one stuff? Because if they didn't—'

'No. Look—'

'What about dispute-resolution procedures? Are there any in your employment contract? The tribunals come down like a ton of bricks—'

'Actually,' Duncan repeated, 'I was wondering if I could have that job.'

Silence. You could have skated on it, or smashed it up to go in whisky. Floating chunks of it could've sunk liners.

'I thought you'd decided you didn't want to come in with us,' Luke said.

'Yes. Sort of.' A mammoth trapped in the pause that followed would keep fresh for a million years. 'But I've been thinking about that, and—'

'Yes?'

He gave in. 'The bastards say they won't give me a reference,' Duncan said.

'That's nasty,' Luke replied. 'You sure you don't know what it was you did? You must've got up their noses so far you were practically coming out of their ears.'

Duncan counted to three. 'Well,' he said, 'is the offer still open, or what?'

'The partnership, you mean? Joining us?'

'Yes.'

'Oh, sure.' Completely offhand, as though Duncan had just asked him for a light. 'No problem there. Only, I got the impression you'd rather starve in the gutter and be eaten by rats.'

'No, not really.'

'Well, then.' Luke sounded *happy*, for crying out loud. 'Sorted. Tell you what. Drop in some time tomorrow morning, give us a chance to clear all the crap out of the upstairs front office. Do you prefer tea or coffee mid-morning?'

'What? Oh, tea.'

'Fine. No rush. I generally drift in around ten-ish, unless I've got to be in court. Give me half an hour to get the morning clutter out of the way, any time after that that suits you.'

'Um,' Duncan said.

'That's really good news,' Luke said. 'The others'll be chuffed to buggery when I tell them.'

How could he be so sure of that? 'Listen, are you absolutely sure—?'

'See you tomorrow. Bye.'

'Bye,' Duncan replied into the dialling tone. He put the phone back, then wandered into the kitchen and opened the fridge. One can of beer, a packet of plastic ham slices and a carrot. He ripped open the beer and drank it, but it bloated rather than anaesthetised him. He went back to his chair, sat down and closed his eyes.

Whether it was nervous exhaustion or the beer, he fell into a doze, which in turn slipped gradually into a dream. He was still in his chair, but in front of it was an office desk: a big, impressive thing made of shiny golden oak, with a green leather top. There was another desk next to his, and another in front of him; in fact, the room was full of the things, like a classroom. He looked up, and found that he was being glowered at by the teacher.

'Duncan,' the teacher said. 'Perhaps you'd like to share the joke with the rest of the class.'

'What, sir?' he heard himself say.

There was something in his hand. He clenched his fist around it, but too late; the teacher had seen it, and advanced on him like a siege-tower. He knew that if he opened his hand and let the teacher see it, whatever it was, he'd be in all sorts of trouble.

'All right,' the teacher said. 'Let's see what you've got.'

He knew what it was: the ripped-off lapel of a jacket. To be precise, the lapel from the teacher's suit. 'I haven't got anything, sir, honest,' he said. 'You can trust me, sir, I'm a lawyer.'

He raised his hand, opened it and showed that it was empty. The teacher nodded, then vanished in a shower of green sparks, as the rest of the class cheered.

The architecture of the office in Mortmain Street was early Mordor with strong Dalek influence: a gleaming rectangular tower of black glass, with fountains and palm trees in the entrance lobby, and doormen who looked as though they'd turn to stone in an instant if they happened to be exposed to direct sunlight. Ferris and Loop were on the twenty-first floor. The lift moved so fast, Duncan had an unsettling feeling that he arrived before he'd left.

The twenty-first floor, seen through the lift doors as they opened, wasn't what he'd been expecting at all. There was a great deal of oak panelling, dark and glowing as though beeswaxed by generations of housemaids. The carpet on the floor was deep and expensive but softened with long use; old and very well cared for. The front desk was apparently genuine antique, beautifully figured and carved walnut but with heavily scratched legs. On the walls hung ancient, slightly faded tapestries, in what Duncan guessed was supposed to be Elizabethan style: hunting scenes and so forth. In one corner stood something that looked like a sawn-off church font: a large granite bowl on a marble plinth.

Reception was a small, elderly bald man with a pointed nose and very large ears. 'Ah yes,' he said, when Duncan told him his name. 'Mr Ferris is expecting you,' he added, making it sound as if Duncan was either the Messiah or Quetzalcoatl the Feathered Serpent. 'If you'd care to take a seat.'

Duncan looked round. One thing there wasn't, in all this genteel splendour, was a chair. The old man was muttering into a phone, like an elderly clergyman intoning responses at evensong. On his desk, a VDU the size of the screens they show football on in pubs flickered and dissolved into a screen saver of prancing antelopes.

'Do please sit down,' the elderly man said. 'Mr Ferris will be with you directly.'

Duncan glanced round again, but saw no chair. He turned away and pretended to be fascinated by the nearest tapestry – a bunch of big, nasty-looking dogs bothering an anatomically improbable unicorn, wearing what looked like a gold Christmascracker party hat.

'Duncan. You're here at last. Come on through.'

There was Luke. He wasn't wearing a jacket, and his shirttails hung out over his trousers, as they had all those years ago. There was an enormous grin on his face as he lunged forward. For a moment Duncan thought he was about to offer to shake hands; instead, he walloped Duncan between the shoulder-blades like a cyclops performing the Heimlich manoeuvre, then grabbed him by the arm and dragged him towards a panelled oak fire door.

'Guided tour,' Luke thundered in his ear, as the door swung shut behind them. 'The others'll be down to see you in a tick, but I thought you might like to see the old dump first.'

Dump, oddly enough, wasn't too inappropriate a term. A great deal of money had been spent at some point on decorating and furnishing; there was enough solid hardwood around the place to account for decades' worth of despoiled rainforest. But every single desk, chair, table and door he saw as Luke whisked him along was chipped, scratched or gnawed up to a height of about four feet off the ground. The filing cabinets were more than usually battered, and the flex spaghetti that hung out of the back of the technology like disembowelled entrails was heavily patched with black insulating tape. The fabric of all the chair seats was frayed, and covered in grey and white hairs. All in all, it was a bewildering mix of industrial extravagance and lived-in scruff. There was also a curious smell, which Duncan couldn't quite place.

'Library,' Luke said, as they swept through a huge room, floor-to-ceiling with the usual black, blue and fawn-spined volumes – law reports, forms and precedents, the loose-leaf planning encyclopedias, Kemp and Kemp on mutilations, a whole wall full of tax statutes. On the floor, next to a battered grey waste-bin, something had apparently savaged an elderly and obsolete edition of Megarry and Wade's *Law of Real Property*; it lay open on its broken spine, and several pages had been torn out, screwed up and shredded. In the opposite corner, a bank of computer screens showed the same running-antelope screen saver he'd seen in the front office.

Duncan frowned. 'Does someone around here have a dog?' he asked.

'What? No,' Luke snapped. 'Why? You're not allergic to dogs, or anything like that?'

'No, I don't think so. I'm not exactly what you'd call a dog person, but they don't make me come out in spots or anything like that.'

'Cashier,' Luke said, pushing open a door like the DEA pulling a dawn raid. A little white-haired man with enormous glasses looked up at him from behind a huge desk, then went on with his work. None of those cloying how-utterly-wonderful-to-get-to-know-you introductions in this office. Back out into the corridor again; another swift forced march.

'This is where we've parked you for the time being,' Luke said, opening another door. 'If you absolutely hate it, we'll have to sort something out, but I hope it'll do for now.'

Duncan's office at Craven Ettins had, once upon a time, been a boiler room. It was small, windowless, cold in winter and murderously hot in summer; three people turned it into a Bakerloo Line carriage in the rush hour, and the door didn't close properly. This office wasn't like it at all. You could've staged the Olympics in it and still had room for a modest international airport.

'You don't like it,' Luke said.

'No, I mean yes.' Duncan scrabbled frantically for words. 'It's *big*.'

'What? Oh, I see. Well, it's all right, I suppose. A bit cluttered for my taste, but you can chuck out anything you don't want, obviously.'

Define clutter. There was a desk you could've landed Sea Kings on (but the legs were grooved with scratches) and the sort of chair that emperors used to sit on; a huge leather-covered sofa out in the western prairies; the wall opposite the door was one huge window, with a view of all the kingdoms of the earth; against the north wall, enough raw computing power to send a manned probe to Andromeda. If you lived in a room like this, sooner or later you'd be overwhelmed by the urge to be discovered sitting in your chair stroking a big fluffy Persian cat and drawling, 'We meet at last, Mr Bond.'

Duncan found he was clinging on to the door frame. 'It's nice,' he said.

Luke shrugged. 'It's an office,' he said. 'And at least you can sneeze without the walls getting wet. Seen enough?'

'Luke.' Duncan took a deep breath. 'I think I ought to tell you something.'

'What?'

'All this—' He made a vague gesture. 'Must cost a fortune.'

Luke frowned. 'Well?'

'Which means you must be pretty bloody good at the job in order to pay for it.'

'We manage.'

'The thing is,' Duncan said, slowly, in a very small voice, 'I'm not a particularly wonderful lawyer. Like, on a really good day, I'm sort of middling to average. What I mean is, if I had a place like this, I wouldn't hire me to wash down the bogs and frank the letters.'

Luke grinned at him. 'Oh, come on,' he said. 'You were always fairly bright at school. Except maths, of course.'

'Yes, but—' Sort of a surreal feeling about this. 'School's different, isn't it? Just because you can do French irregular verbs—'

'You can do French irregular verbs?'

'Well, yes. At least, I used to be able to. I've probably forgotten, of course.'

'I'm impressed,' Luke said. 'I sort of tuned out at *nous sommes, vous êtes.*'

'But that's not important, is it? What I'm trying to say—'

'The only maths I can do is adding up and a bit of subtracting,' Luke said. 'And I learned that from playing darts in pubs. No,' he went on, shaking his head, 'you don't want to worry about not being bright enough, God knows. Lawyering isn't exactly rocket science, after all. If I can do it, so can any bloody fool. The important thing is getting on well with your mates and having a reasonably good time while you're at it. At least,' he added, 'that's how we do things, and it seems to work all right for us.'

'Oh.' Definitely surreal; a job interview conducted by René Magritte and Salvador Dali, wearing silly hats. 'Well, I suppose that's all right, then.'

'Excellent.' Luke sounded like he'd just fixed up peace in the Middle East. 'Well, you've seen pretty much everything. Come and meet the lads. They're dying to see you again.'

The moment, in fact, that Duncan had been dreading. Luke on his own, he mused as he followed his soon-to-be partner down a long corridor, was one thing. Meeting the whole Ferris Gang again, on the other hand, was going to be—

Luke shoved open a door and called out, 'He's here'. He took a step back. Duncan couldn't see past Luke's substantial bulk, but on the other side of it a chorus of voices was baying his name. Then Luke grabbed his shoulder and bundled him into the room.

They crowded round him, their faces bobbing up and down in front of him, their hands hammering his back and pounding his shoulders, until all he wanted to do was sink to the floor and curl up into a ball. He heard himself mumbling names – hi, Micky; hi, Kevin; hi, Clive; hi, Pete – as though reciting the names of Santa's reindeer or the Seven Dwarves. As for the faces, they were both strange and familiar. They'd aged, all of them. They all seemed to share the same greying hair, worn unflatteringly long. They also looked *battered*, like boxers who'd retired a couple of fights too late. Kevin's nose had been broken at some point, and Pete had a long white scar on his left cheek, only partly overgrown by a bushy white-and-ginger beard. Most surprising of all, however, was the almost inhuman pleasure they seemed to get from seeing him again. He was looking great, really fit, he'd grown, they'd never seen him looking better; and as they laughed and barked and chuckled round him, they kept on pummelling and slapping at him until he felt like a slice of flash-fry steak. But when Luke cleared his throat, they all stopped their onslaught and stood still and quiet.

'Guys,' Luke said, 'the man from Del Monte says yes.'

Kevin hugged him. Pete let out a rebel yell. Clive hammered him between the shoulder blades, while Micky punched him savagely in the solar plexus. For a moment, everything went black and wobbly; then he could just about make out Luke saying, 'I've got the paperwork here on the desk, let's all sign up before he changes his mind. Sod it, witness – Pete, get Bruce in here, he'll do.'

Pete bounded away, as though chasing a rubber ball; the other three frogmarched Duncan over to a desk, on top of which were six shallow stacks of typed-on A4. 'We're all supposed to be lawyers,' Luke was saying, 'so I suppose you'd better read the thing first.' Duncan found some papers in his hand, and looked down at them. *This Deed of Partnership made the   Day of   Between* and then a lot of names; legal mumbo-jumbo, wodges of it.

'Finished?' Luke said.

Duncan nodded. 'Seems all right to me,' he said. (But he was thinking: everything ready and waiting for me as soon as I arrive; a bit premature, surely.) 'Bruce, over here,' Luke was shouting, and the bald, pointy-nosed man from Reception squeezed through the slim gap between Clive's and Kevin's shoulders. Then Duncan felt a pen in his hand, and saw Luke's fence-post-sized finger pointing to a dotted line.

He signed: six copies. The others were signing too, using each others' backs to rest on, while the little bald man from reception sat behind the desk and witnessed each signature. He looked tiny in the shadow of the Ferris Gang – not one of them, Duncan noticed, under six foot – and he seemed to be curled in on himself, a hedgehog without the prickles. He'd barely finished writing when Pete barked, 'Right, fetch the champagne,' and the little man jumped up and scuttled away, head bowed, legs pumping. He was, Duncan thought, either terrified or very well trained.

'Everybody signed everything? Hang on, what's today's date?' Luke was sitting on the edge of the desk, riffling stacks of paper like a Vegas blackjack dealer. 'Pete, you missed one; here, look. Right, that's it, we're legal.'

A cheer that made the floor shake. This is very strange, Duncan thought, as the little bald man scampered back carrying the biggest champagne bottle he'd ever seen in his life.

'Great stuff,' Luke said; and the others stepped away, like veteran soldiers not volunteering. Duncan realised they were all standing behind him, as Luke slid his leg off the desk and came towards him. 'Just one last thing,' Luke went on, 'and then we're done. Duncan Hughes,' he continued, as his hands reached out and pinned Duncan's arms to his sides, 'welcome to the partnership.'

And everybody cheered again as Luke leaned forward, bared his teeth and bit deep into the side of Duncan's neck.

CHAPTER FOUR

The world had changed.

It was like fiddling with a TV's tracking or vertical hold: one moment everything's blurred and fuzzy, and then quite suddenly the picture's crystal clear, the sound's loud, distinct and in perfect synch, the colour's right and you know that everything's how it should be.

Little short of miraculous; because, a second or so ago, Duncan would have sworn blind that the fuzzy, blurry, foggy, mumbling reality he'd lived in for the last thirty-three years was about as good as it was likely to get, in terms of clarity and definition. All completely wrong, of course. For the first time in his life he could actually see, and hear. And smell. God almighty, he could smell. He had no idea how he'd contrived not to notice them before, but the world was crammed with an unbelievable wealth of scents, smells, odours and stenches; seven different flavours of incredibly rich and complex sweat, for one thing, not to mention the almost stifling perfume of the furniture wax, the dry, mellow background of dust, the bewildering medley of shoe polish and toothpaste and peppermints and stale beer and blood and bath salts; far more vividly perceptible than mere sight could ever be, and phase-shifted backwards through time, so that he felt he was taking in a whole week's worth of perceptions simultaneously in a fraction of a second.

'Fuck it, Luke,' he heard himself squealing, 'you *bit* me.'

Laughter all around him; loud enough to float the top off his head, but not loud enough to drown out a million other distinct and fascinating sounds – a phone ringing on the floor below, the beating of six hearts, someone talking out in the street.

(In the street; and I'm on the twenty-first floor, and all the windows are sealed and double-glazed.)

'That's right,' Luke said. 'How do you feel?'

Three days ago, Luke had eaten curry; to be precise, roghan ghosh with tarka dal, pilau rice and sag aloo. Since then—

'Weird,' Duncan said, clapping his hand to the side of his neck. Cocaine? LSD? Could Luke's teeth have been carrying enough drug residue to get him instantaneously stoned out of his brain? Instinctively, however, he knew it wasn't anything like that. It was more like coming down out of a really bad trip back into blissful reality. Even the air was as delicious as chocolate. It smelled completely new and different. It smelled of *air*.

Then Pete said, 'You did tell him, didn't you?'

Pause. Then Luke growled.

What Luke growled was, *No. Want to make something of it?* There were no words, just as you don't get English subtitles on English-language films. Pete lowered his head and his shoulders slumped.

'Tell me what?' Duncan said.

Another pause. Then Luke said, 'You might want to sit down for a minute.'

Duncan's legs were wobbly as he walked over to the chair behind the desk. He pulled it out, turned round three times and sat down. Then he raised his head and said, 'Why did I just do that?'

'Ah.' Luke grinned. 'Let's say it's something you're going to have to get used to.' Apparently absent-mindedly, he'd snatched a biro out of Micky's top pocket, and was chewing it. 'Pete, you tell him.'

The world might have changed, but not the hierarchy of the Ferris Gang. Pete Thomas had always been Luke's duly accredited herald. 'It's quite simple,' Pete said. 'Smart bloke like you, I'd have thought you'd have figured it out for yourself. We're werewolves.'

At some point over the last ten days, someone had eaten peppermints in this room. Duncan sniffed again to make sure; then he realised what Pete had just said.

'Bollocks,' he protested. 'There's no such thing as—'

Something whizzed through his field of vision; something small. Without thinking, he sprang out of his chair and caught it. A small rubber ball; and, to his deep embarrassment, he appeared to have caught it in his mouth.

'Actually, there is,' Luke said, retrieving the ball from between Duncan's teeth (Duncan felt a strange but strong urge not to let go) and dropping it back in his pocket. 'Are. Whatever. The lightning reflexes are a definite plus; the short attention span's a bummer, but you learn to work round it, if you see what I mean. The biggest problem, of course,' he went on, 'is lamp-posts.'

The others were nodding sagely, as if to say that they too had been sorely tried in the furnace of temptation.

'The heightened sense of smell and hearing should already have kicked in by now, so you don't need me to brief you on them,' Pete said, scratching behind his ear. 'You're going to love the extra strength and stamina; also, you can eat and drink anything you like, as much as you like, and no worries about putting on weight or anything like that. You may find it a bit awkward keeping your temper around humans for a day or so, because patience isn't really one of our top virtues, but it's like everything else, you find your own ways of adapting. Really, it's just the little things, like not jumping up at people when they come into the room, or begging at tables in restaurants.'

There had been a key word in there, Duncan realised. 'Humans,' he repeated.

'Ah.' Luke gave him a thin-lipped smile. 'It's probably best you don't dwell on that side of it for a while, at least till you're more settled,' he said. 'But sooner or later, you're going to have to square up to it. Everybody else out there is only human. We, on the other hand—' He shrugged. 'Welcome to a small, under-represented but basically extremely fun minority.'

Duncan thought for a moment, very hard indeed. 'I'm a werewolf,' he said; and to his surprise, it wasn't a question, it was a statement. 'Hang on,' he said, as panic flooded his mind, 'does that mean—?'

'Once a month, yes; and then things get, well, let's say they can get a bit hairy, if you follow me. No bother at all if you follow a few simple precautions and then just go with the flow.'

'Once a month,' Duncan said, raising his voice a little, 'I turn into a wolf. Right?'

'It's not as bad as it sounds, really.' Clive talking; he had thickets of hair in his nostrils and his ears, and two of his front teeth were missing. 'You don't actually feel a lot while it's happening, especially if you're completely rat-arsed at the time. I find that helps a lot.'

'You carry on being you, if that's what you're concerned about,' Micky put in. 'In your case, a mixed blessing—'

'The walking-on-all-fours thing's no bother,' Clive went on, 'though it helps if you practise a bit first; really, just to get used to seeing what the world looks like when you're two feet closer to the floor. It's also a good idea to have a really good blow-out half an hour beforehand.'

'Plenty of red meat,' Pete added. 'Mixed grill's my favourite: the steak not too well done, and loads of black pudding. Let's say it helps you keep a sense of perspective, if you start off with a full stomach.'

'And of course we'll be there, to see you through it all.' Luke was looking at him, head slightly on one side. 'After all, that's what it's all about.'

Duncan blinked. 'Is it? What?'

Luke grinned. 'Loyalty, my old mate, loyalty. That's the whole essence of the thing. It's something humans can never hope to understand, not the way we do.' He laughed, drawing his lips well away from his teeth. 'That's the secret of our success in the legal profession. We're not just a partnership, we're a *pack*.'

Duncan studied him for a moment, then said: 'Fine. What's the antidote?'

'There isn't one.' Pete sniffed; an unmistakable and unique sound, something between a pistol shot and tearing calico. The sound of Pete's sniff was an abiding memory, part of the fabric of Duncan's youth. Hearing it again now brought the past thundering back, six years of concentrated memories all coming at once, like buses. 'That's why I was a bit puzzled when Luke said he hadn't explained to you first; I mean, before—' Pete caught Luke's eye and stood back a little. 'Anyhow,' he said, 'it's permanent, there's no cure. You might say a wolf is for life, not just for Christmas.'

'Talking of which,' Clive put in, 'a considerably prolonged lifespan is definitely part of the package. Double, possibly even triple.'

'Right,' Micky said. 'We don't just chew old bones, we make them. And we're obnoxiously healthy, and very hard to damage; unless you stop a silver one, of course, but that's hardly a problem these days. After all,' he added with a grin, 'nobody believes we exist. Culling mythical beasts isn't really a priority, not even for DEFRA.'

'So there you have it,' Luke said, with extreme mock gravity. 'You're practically immortal. You can stop a bus just by standing in front of it, and the worst you'll get is torn trousers. You can appreciate the world around you the way no human could ever do. You can run fast enough to interest the speed cameras without even getting out of breath. And once every thirty days or so, you get to party like you wouldn't believe. All that, and you're also a member of a very small, select community that'll look out for you, do anything for you, till the day you eventually die. All in all, looking at it in the round and not letting yourself get sidetracked by conventional, trapped-inside-the-box-hammering-on-the-lid thinking, wouldn't you say it's a pretty good deal? Also,' he added, with a twitch of his nose, 'it's done now and you're stuck like it, so accentuating the negative's not going to do you any good. All right.' He clapped his hands together, and all of them (Duncan included) were suddenly still, silent and alert. 'I think it'd be nice to round off a pretty good day by doing some lawyering.'

A moment later, Duncan and Luke were alone. 'Now then,' Luke said. 'Wills, probate and tax planning.'

It was like hearing someone talking your own language after you've been stranded on a desert island for twenty years. 'What did you say?'

'Administration of estates. Trust management. I sort of got the idea it's what you do for a living.'

'Oh, you mean *work*.'

Luke smiled pleasantly. 'That's right,' he said. 'We do dabble in it occasionally. We find it's a nice, easy way of making money, among other things.' He took hold of Duncan's arm and led him out of the room, back into the corridor. 'We don't actually have a death-and-taxes bloke at the moment,' he said. 'Clive's been doing it up till now, but he's really conveyancing, commercial leaseholds, that sort of thing. I got him to dump all his death files in your cabinet; you might like to browse through them, see what sort of an unmitigated bog he's been making of them. Death's an area we're really keen to get into, but none of us has got the divine spark, if you know what I mean.'

How Luke could be prattling on about work at a moment like this was beyond Duncan. He wanted to shake free of Luke's grip, charge down the stairs out into the street and chase taxis. Instead, he asked if he could meet his new secretary.

'There aren't any,' Luke replied cheerfully. 'We do our own typing – piece of cake with computers and voice-recognition software – and all our own filing and copying and all that sort of thing. Even make our own coffee. Oh, I forgot, you're a tea addict, aren't you? Sorry, but you'll have to make do with coffee till I get a chance to go out and do some shopping.' He yawned. 'Apart from the six of us, and Bruce on reception and Arthur the cashier, that's it as far as personnel's concerned.'

'The cashier and the receptionist; are they—?'

Luke shook his head. 'If they were, they wouldn't be doing boring rotten jobs like answering phones and counting the petty cash. But they're all right, they know what's going on, and they do their jobs well, which is all that matters, isn't it? Oh, stationery. The cupboard's down the corridor, second left then right and right again, just past the photocopier room. Help yourself to pencils and stuff.' He was chewing on one again, pausing to crunch the end between his back teeth. Was he going to suck out the graphite and eat it? Duncan wondered. The thought made him feel hungry. 'Just remember,' Luke went on, spitting out a few splinters. 'The rule here is, anything goes, so long as you do the job, get money and don't do anything to let down the pack. Other than that; if you want to chew through the phone cables or wee on the carpets, that's fine. This place is as much yours as mine or anybody else's.' He stood up and grinned. 'Enjoy,' he said. 'It's actually a bloody good life once you stop worrying about it.'

He closed the door behind him, and Duncan crossed to the huge, valuable-looking desk, sat down in the amazingly comfortable chair, and began to shake all over.

Obviously, he thought, it isn't *actually* true; because werewolves don't exist. They're like vampires and zombies and all those other high-camp horror clichés. When Newton and Einstein and Hawking created the universe, they didn't allow it any scope for men who turned into wolves at the full moon. But, undeniably (he paused for a moment to eavesdrop on a girl in the street talking into her mobile phone; she was wearing expensive scent, but her breath stank of coffee and peppermints) *something* had happened to him, and whatever it was, he didn't feel inclined to complain about it.

That reminded him. He put his hand to the side of his neck, expecting to feel wet blood, or at the very least a big clotted scab, but there was nothing there. Maybe he'd imagined the bite after all. He looked round the office for a mirror but there wasn't one. He frowned, but then he heard the sound of a cistern flushing, not terribly far away.

Duncan had gone through life hampered by a pathetic sense of direction; but he could have found the bathroom with his eyes shut, and all from hearing that one sound. Out of his office, up the corridor, left then right and there it was. He went in, bolted the door and looked in the mirror.

It didn't work. At least, the middle of it didn't. The edges were working just fine; he could see the wall behind him, the door he'd just come through, all that. But the centre of the mirror, the place where his face ought to be, was on the fritz, because all he could see in it was the wall, the door &c.

Oh, he thought.

Among other things, he said to himself as he walked slowly back to his room, it's going to make shaving difficult. Probably why the others all have those great big bushy beards. Also, there's this business of not being human any more—

Bollocks, he thought. Of course he was human – how could he not be? It wasn't like renouncing your citizenship when you emigrate. Of course he was still a human being; just one that could hear voices in the street twenty floors below, and who didn't show up in mirrors. A bit different, but basically the same.

He sat down at the desk again. Inhuman; no, superhuman, like Superman. That was more like it. What had Luke said? Greatly increased strength. Well, he could do with some of that. He reached under the desk with his left hand, pressed his palm against the underside and tried to lift it. No bother; it was like balancing a tray. He let it down gently and grinned. What else? Practically immortal, couldn't be injured. That would account for there not being a scab where Luke had bitten him. Very much like Superman, in all sorts of ways. A smile slowly spread across his face, like a slick of oil under a British motorbike. A person could have all kinds of fun if he had superpowers, and couldn't be killed or hurt.

Furthermore – Duncan stood up, crossed to the filing cabinet, and chose a file at random from the half-filled top drawer. Furthermore, he told himself, if Luke was right and there was no cure or antidote; if he was stuck like this for ever and ever and nobody could do anything about it, not even Luke and Pete and Clive and the gang; what was to stop him walking out of here, quitting the legal profession for good and getting a job as James Bond or a superhero or something? Much more fun than boring old wills and probate.

He turned that possibility over in his mind as he quickly skimmed through the file on his desk. They might not like it if he walked out on them, but so what? Nothing they could do to stop him. Presumably they'd taken it for granted that he wanted to belong to their gang again, so it hadn't occurred to them that he might just up sticks and push off. But why not? The world was full of grand and glorious things, particularly for someone who could smell the roses in the posh florist's three blocks away, or the exhaust fumes of a 747 just leaving Gatwick. There was absolutely no reason—

He frowned. Without realising it, he'd just read the whole file from cover to cover. What was more, he'd understood it; he could have recited most of it by heart if he'd wanted to. How long had it taken him? Remarkable. He'd just done four hours' work in as many minutes. Absently, he picked up a biro as he reflected on that. No effort; his mind certainly hadn't been on it. He picked out a blank IHT200 form, remembering how much he loathed filling out the wretched things: all the complicated sums and having to keep looking up dates and figures as he went along. He remembered; but it was like thinking back to when you were a kid, and you needed to stand on the footstool and use both hands to turn the sitting-room doorknob. Just for the heck of it, he started jotting things down on the form – he didn't have to look anything up in the file, because he could remember it all, and he could do all the sums in his head. Not only that; he could write so much more quickly than he used to. He could even write *legibly*.

The form took him just under a minute, and there was about fifty seconds' worth of other stuff to do on the file to bring it right up to date; half a dozen letters – he did the first three on the keyboard (couldn't he type fast now), then remembered that

Luke had said something about voice-recognition software. He'd never used it before, but it only took him a moment or so to figure out how it worked. A heartbeat or so later, the letters came spooling out of the printer; he folded them, tucked them into their envelopes and tossed them into his post tray. All done.

It had been like doing things in a dream; the sort where you're an airline pilot or a brain surgeon, and you can do all the incredibly difficult and dangerous stuff, even though in the back of your mind you know you wouldn't have a clue where to start if you were awake. It was, of course, impossible for anyone to do the best part of a thousand quids' worth of legal work in less than seven minutes. By the same token, it was impossible to be a werewolf.

He stared at the desk: the wire tray full of letters to be posted, the completed IHT form. A man who could work at that sort of speed could make himself a fortune in the law business, where work is charged for on a time basis: a hundred and fifty, two hundred quid an hour. You could earn a million in a day; or, if you preferred, you could earn a hundred thousand before elevenses and spend the rest of the day just slobbing about—

His eyes widened (what great big eyes you have, Mr Hughes). The hell with being a ninja special agent or a supermercenary. Too much like hard work. To test the theory he got another file from the cabinet and attacked it. Apportionments, drafting assents, drawing up estate accounts for approval and signature. Six hours of slog for a mere human, but Duncan got it done in about the time it took his clunky old kettle to boil. Then he leaned back in his chair, threw his arms wide, kicked up his legs and yelled 'Woo-hoo!' at the top of his voice.

Bugger Superman, he told himself. Faster than a speeding bullet; well, fine. Leaps tall buildings at a single bound; yawn. Duncan Hughes, on the other hand, can earn sixty thousand quid in an hour, of which he gets a one-sixth share, less tax and overhead; say four grand. He followed the entrancing trail of figures through weekly and monthly into yearly net earnings, assuming a five-hour working day and generous holidays – Fuck me, he thought. Not, of course, as much as Julia Roberts or David Beckham or Robbie Williams, but he found he wasn't really bothered about that. He was, after all, basically a simple, modest person at heart. Doing a short but honest day's work, doing it well and earning a revoltingly large amount of money would suit him very nicely.

Just to make sure it really worked and hadn't merely been a fluke, he hauled all the remaining files out of the cabinet, dumped them on the desk and set to work. Far from wearing off, the superpowers seemed to grow with use, as he got used to them and figured out the minutiae of how they worked. For example: he found that he could read to the end of one line, left to right, and then read the one underneath it right to left, as though it was Arabic. He could turn pages quickly and accurately just by blowing on them, which left his hands free for typing. (Multi-tasking? No problem.) Mental arithmetic soon became practically instantaneous, while his newly acquired photographic memory was clicking away faster than a pack of paparazzi. But the strangest, and also quite possibly the most helpful thing was that, the more of it he did, the less tiresome and dull the work became. It was, he realised, the old rule of human nature: we enjoy doing stuff we do well. The faster he went, the more absurdly pleased he was with himself, which in turn boosted his productivity. Not so much a piece of cake as a slice of Black Forest gateau with whipped cream and cherries.

Then, abruptly, he reached the end. He'd finished it all, every last scrap of the work he'd been given to do. The stack of neatly addressed envelopes in his post tray rose like a bonsai mountain, and the finished-with files lay discarded on the side of the desk, like the washing-up after a feast. *I can't have done it properly*, he accused himself; but he thought about it and yes, he'd been thorough, accurate, conscientious and in places more or less inspired. The faster he went, it appeared, the better the quality.

He'd also lost track of time. He glanced up at the clock on the wall opposite; then, because what it told him seemed so absurdly improbable, he looked down at his watch. No mistake: it was ten to one. Just in time for his lunch break; and when he came back from that, he'd have no work at all left to do. He could skive off, go home early—

The thought of home – his grubby, cramped little flat – made him feel ill. What possible reason could he have for wanting to spend a minute longer in it than he absolutely had to? Home: sit around on the sofa until it was time to microwave his evening pizza, then telly, indigestion and bed. No way could you describe that as a life, not even if you were using a dictionary compiled by Alistair Campbell. This office, on the other hand – well, it was everything his miserable hovel of a flat wasn't. Big, for one thing. Roomy, tidy, beautifully furnished, smart but comfortable at the same time. And, of course, the major difference. Where he lived, the building, the street, the borough, he had no friends. Here—

Duncan frowned, and checked the clock again. Lunchtime; he could trek over to the dreary little sandwich bar he usually went to. Or he could stay here, in his personal pocket Versailles. He realised he wasn't a bit hungry (possibly because, while he'd been working, he'd chewed up a dozen pencils) and lunchtime drinking just made his head hurt. Wouldn't it be much more fun to go and find his friends and spend the rest of the day with them?

His friends. His fr. His fruth. No; try as he might, he couldn't quite get the idea to fit into his mind. His oldest and dearest friends, the lads, the gang. They'd always been there, hadn't they, ever since that first dramatic encounter in the playground. Every memory of his youth that he'd seen fit to keep had them in it; they were the monosodium glutamate of his life, the universal preservative of his past, colouring and flavouring everything that had made him who he was.

He leaned back in the chair, scowling. Question: how had it happened? Logically, it would have to have started with Luke; he must have been bitten first, and of course he'd immediately shared the gift with the others. He remembered what Luke had said about Pete; he'd wanted to be a teacher, but they'd changed his mind. He wondered: had it happened before they all went to law school? He could picture Luke making the decision, choosing the most appropriate career for a werewolf from some handbook. For a nutter, he'd always had the knack of being very calm, deliberate and sensible; that, in fact, was what made him so dangerous. An ordinary nutter decides to do a bloody stupid thing, like fusing all the lights in the street or stealing a police car, and charges at it wildly, cluelessly; he's caught and stopped straight away, or he winds up in hospital, and no real harm done. It's Ferris-grade nutters who plan and consider and bring the full force of their intelligence to bear on the slice of mayhem they have in mind who do all the damage.

His friend. My friend the superhuman nutter. Presumably, Luke's world-view had widened as he'd got older and put away childish things. But it seemed too perfect, somehow; that someone so innately suited to the werewolf life should just happen to get the opportunity to live it. Duncan couldn't help but suspect, however irrational it might be, that somehow or other Luke had been planning this all along. At the age when other kids want to be footballers or starship captains when they grow up, Luke had already decided, and started to frame his long, patient design – choosing, building and training his future pack, searching for an existing werewolf who could pass on the gift. (Gift? Infection? Whatever.) In which case, his plan must at last be complete, now that he'd retrieved the one little lost cub that had gone astray—

He considered the implications of all that. Then, gathering together every last scrap of honesty he could muster, Duncan asked himself the question. If this is all part of some demonic scheme of Luke Ferris's and I'm just a component in his machine, does that spoil it?

The faintest trace of the scent of blood and roast chicken, dragged in off the street by the air-conditioning system, caught his nose and he sniffed at it as though smelling the rarest of orchids. Nah. Did it hell as like.

All right; assume for now that Luke had planned the whole thing back in Year Seven, and that Duncan Hughes's life had been callously steered and manipulated to bring him to this point. So what? It was a *nice* point. He felt sure he was going to like it. Money, luxury, superpowers, not having to work himself into the ground; guaranteed health and strength throughout an unnaturally long life. If it was true that he'd spent his childhood being hunted and trapped, it was a bit like being stalked by Father Christmas. Drawbacks few and nebulous, advantages manifold and bloody obvious—

(So that's why they'd all been wearing pure wool suits, he suddenly realised, the way you do. Sheep's clothing.)

Suddenly Duncan felt an irresistible urge to bite something. He looked round the room and decided on a fine old-fashioned free-standing coat-rack. He knelt down and clamped his jaws on it. The squashy crunch of the wood fibres under his teeth was simply delicious, like the very best fillet steak. He steadied the base of the stand with his hands, arched his back and tore away a chunk of splintered wood.

'Duncan?'

Pete was standing in the doorway looking at him; deliberately not laughing. Duncan spat out the wood and scrambled to his feet. 'I was just—' he started to say, but even a master of instant-excuse fabrication like himself couldn't do anything with that. He smiled instead.

'You'll find it's like that for a day or so,' Pete said. 'After that, you'll be able to control it.'

Duncan frowned. 'Why would I want to?' he asked. 'It's fun.'

Apparently he'd said something slightly wrong; tasteless, perhaps. 'Well, fine,' Pete said. 'After all, it's your furniture. Anyhow, we're all off down the pub. Coming?'

Immediately he was ready to go, like a dog wanting to be walked. Pete led the way, walking briskly, not looking round to see if Duncan was following (had a voice in Pete's head just said *Heel*? If so, Duncan fancied he might have heard it too) and he had to trot for a few paces to keep up. 'Pete,' he said.

'Mm?'

'When's the next full moon?'

But Pete didn't seem to have heard him, so Duncan quickened his pace a little and followed him to the front office, where the rest of them were waiting. Luke led them across the landing to the lift; nobody spoke on the way down, or as they headed off along the street. Twice Luke stopped to sniff the air. Somehow it was very controlled and disciplined, like a school outing.

The pub was, of course, stuffed to the doors when they got there; but Luke seemed to have no trouble getting to the bar. He didn't push or shove, because there wasn't any need. People got out of his way, as though he was an ambulance in a traffic jam, and the rest of the pack followed in his wake like the body of a wedge. A barman was standing ready to take his order: six pints of Guinness. Apparently, that was what werewolves drank.

(In werewolf bars, do they have bowls of bones on the bar instead of peanuts?)

No chance of getting a table; but Luke led them to one. Its existing tenants all got up at once as he approached, like ducks off a pond. They weren't even looking at him, but they went away in the opposite direction, even though it wasn't the way out. Duncan watched them; they kept going until they reached the back wall and then stopped, looking rather confused. He wondered if Luke could herd sheep as well.

Luke chose the seat facing the door and the outside world. Nobody said anything, but Duncan somehow knew he was going to sit down last, in the chair that nobody else wanted. He didn't mind; he hadn't given it any conscious thought, but he knew it was the right thing to do. Same with drinking; first Luke gulped down his beer – seven convulsive movements of his neck and all gone – and then the others. To his surprise, Duncan found that he was very thirsty. The beer tasted like water and there didn't appear to be any alcohol in it. Two seconds of dead silence; then Duncan was on his feet, collecting glasses.

'Same again?' he asked. Nobody answered; polite silence, ignoring the social gaffe. He headed off to the bar. People got out of his way, and when he got there, a barman was ready and waiting to serve him.

'Six pints of—' he began to say, but the barman was already busy. 'They come in here often, then,' he said, trying to sound normal.

The barman looked at him. 'What?'

'The crowd I'm with. Only, you seem to know what they—'

It struck him that the barman didn't know what he was talking about. 'It was Guinness you wanted?' he asked.

Duncan nodded. 'That's right, yes.'

He'd never tried that thing where you sort of squash all the glasses together and lift them up all at once; apparently, though, it worked. He set them down on the table and then remembered. He'd forgotten to—

'It's all right,' Luke said. 'We don't.'

'Sorry?'

'Pay for drinks, in pubs. At least, nobody ever asks us for money.' He smiled. 'The subject never seems to come up, funnily enough.'

'Oh.' Duncan sat down, as suit-sleeved arms all around him secured the beer glasses like the tentacles of an octopus. 'Is it the same in shops and restaurants as well, or just pubs?'

'Depends,' Luke replied, after he'd finished drinking. 'Some places they do, others they don't. It also seems to depend on whether we're all together in a group; also, whether it's a man or a woman serving. To be honest, I haven't figured it out yet, but there's bound to be a pattern to it. So,' he continued, as Micky got up to go to the bar, 'how's it going?'

'I finished all the work,' Duncan said. No reaction. 'Didn't take me long.' Pete shifted a little in his seat; the others appeared not to have heard him. Another faux pas, obviously. 'It's a great office, by the way,' he said, mostly because he couldn't think of anything else to say.

Luke looked at him steadily for what seemed like a very long time. 'How do you like being—' He paused, and twitched his nose. 'One of us again. Settling in?'

Duncan nodded, relieved to have been pardoned for whatever it was he'd done. 'Loving it,' he said. 'It's so – well,' he added, trying to marshal his thoughts. 'It's completely different, of course, and yet at the same time it feels sort of—' He'd been about to say *natural*. 'Meant,' he compromised. 'Like this is what I was always supposed to be, if you see what I mean. It's as though I've had to be someone else all my life.'

'Splendid.' Oh good, Duncan thought, just for once I've said the right thing. 'Told you, didn't I?' Luke went on. 'You belong with us. The old gang.'

Wasn't quite what he'd meant, actually, but he didn't want to upset anybody by correcting the slight misunderstanding. Micky came back with more beer. This time Duncan drank his almost as quickly as the others did. Three pints; but he didn't feel the slightest bit drunk. Rather, he felt relaxed and alert at the same time. If someone were to throw a rubber ball for him right now, he was pretty sure he'd be able to jump right out of the chair and catch it in flight, in his mouth. Only . . . why would anybody throw a rubber ball for a probate lawyer?

'Plans for this afternoon, anybody?' Luke said. No reply, and Luke didn't seem to have been expecting one. He went on, 'I thought we might have half an hour up on the roof, then do the bill reminders. I've got clients coming in at three-fifteen.'

General nodding, putting Duncan in mind of the little furry toy that used to hang from the rear-view mirror of his Uncle Norman's Cortina. 'I'm in court at four,' Clive said, 'so that suits me. It's only an interlocutory, so I'll be back in plenty of time for the run tonight.'

Run, Duncan thought; compulsory corporate keep-fit? But that was fine. After all, running is one of life's greatest pleasures, isn't it? He considered that, and it occurred to him that he hadn't run more than ten yards since 1989. God, what he'd been missing.

'You'd better be,' Luke was saying; both mock-stern and serious at the same time. 'We can't hang around waiting for you. Pete, when's lighting-up time?'

'Ten to five,' Pete answered promptly. 'I checked on the Met Office website. It should be properly dark by five-thirty.'

Luke nodded. 'Let's say quarter to six, then. Kevin, beer.'

Six more pints, drunk swiftly and in silence and followed by six more. Since nobody was talking to him, Duncan let his mind drift. Why the deathly hush? That wasn't hard to guess. Twenty-odd years of living in each others' pockets meant there was nothing much left to say that hadn't been said already. A bit like a marriage, really, except that they didn't bicker. And why the massive alcohol intake, when the stuff clearly had no effect whatsoever? Might as well be drinking tea, or water. Also, nobody had said anything about getting something to eat. On the other hand, he didn't feel particularly hungry, so maybe werewolves simply didn't do lunch. The important conclusion, though, was that none of it mattered terribly much. The strange, quirky little details were mildly interesting, but they weren't taking the edge off his pleasure in what he'd just become. On the contrary: for the first time since childhood, there were all sorts of new and interesting things for him to find out about himself. Just one example: swilling down a pint of Guinness in one go isn't nearly as hard as it looks. You've just got to open your mouth wide, relax your throat and sort of breathe it down, as though you're a fish.

'Well.' Luke had been lolling back in his chair. Now, quite abruptly, his back was straight and his head slightly lifted. He twitched his nose a couple of times, then said, 'I'm going back to the office.'

Four chairs scraped simultaneously and for about half a second, Duncan was the only one still sitting down. It was half a second of excruciating embarrassment, a bit like farting just as you're about to make your Oscar-acceptance speech. He jumped out of the chair, forgetting for a moment that he was now in the tall buildings/single bound category. Very briefly he hung in mid-air; then he landed half on and half off the table they'd just been sitting at. He could see an empty beer glass apparently rushing to meet him; he saw it break as his forehead slammed into it.

He'd been told that if it doesn't hurt under such circumstances, it's probably very bad indeed. It should've hurt, he knew. Quite apart from the broken glass, he'd hit his kneecap on the edge of the table, rolled onto the back of a chair, smashed it and dropped three feet to the floor. If he couldn't feel any of it, the only logical conclusion was that he was dead.

He stood up. Everybody in the pub had turned to look, but instead of staring at him they were looking puzzled, as if they couldn't see where the noise of breaking wood and smashing glass had come from. Luke, on his way to the door, hadn't even turned round. Pete gave Duncan a very small wry grin, a don't-you-hate-it-when-that-happens sort of look. Apparently he wasn't the tiniest bit dead.

All *right*, he thought, as he quickened his step to keep up with the others. Until then he hadn't really believed in the invulnerability thing: too perfect, his inner sceptic had sneered, too Marvel Comics. But he'd seen the glass break with his own eyes. In fact— He paused, tweaked the bridge of his nose between forefinger and thumb, and from the corner of his eye he retrieved a splinter of glass shrapnel about the size of a small shirt button.

There are those moments when you realise how very close you came to doing yourself a really horrible injury; your stomach muscles crimp, and everything you ever learned about toilet training threatens to slip away like mist through a sieve. He stared at the bit of glass, balanced on the tip of his forefinger, then quickly flicked it away.

Of course, he tried to explain to himself as he followed the others back to the office, I wouldn't have fallen on the table and bust the glass if it hadn't been for the amazingly enhanced strength, so really I wasn't in any danger . . . But even a lawyer, even the incredible superlawyer he'd now become, couldn't kid the jury into going along with that. On the other hand (the realisation seemed to burst up into his mind, like a rose forcing its way between two paving stones) Luke hadn't been exaggerating about the invulnerability business. It worked.

Duncan tried to think about that, but it proved to be too big for his head; and besides, they were back at the office. In the lift, nobody spoke; but Micky leaned across him and picked another glass shard out of his hair. When the doors opened, the pack dispersed, leaving him standing by the front desk.

The little old man, he noticed, was looking at him furtively. He gave him a friendly smile. 'Hi,' he said. 'I'm Duncan Hughes. I've just joined the partnership.'

The little old man's eyes opened wide, and he shivered a little, as if he'd just been caught by a chilly draught. Maybe he said something, but all Duncan heard, even with his amazing new hearing, was a vague little squeak.

Even so. 'Luke Ferris told me your name,' he went on, 'but I'm ashamed to say I've forgotten it.'

No reply. The little old man was completely motionless, like a rabbit caught in the glare of headlights. Duncan wasn't quite sure what to make of that, but it seemed fairly obvious that the little old man wanted him to go away, so he smiled vaguely and headed for his office. Halfway down the first long corridor he realised that he couldn't remember how to get there, but he found it quite easily by listening out for the distinctive tick of his wall clock.

While he'd been out, someone had collected his post tray. There were also two yellow while-you-were-out notes, stuck to the receiver of his phone.

Please call Imogen Bick, Crosswoods, urgent; followed by the number.

He frowned. He'd been warned off having anything to do with Crosswoods, hadn't he? Even werewolf concentration couldn't clarify that one, so he looked at the other note.

Felicity Allshapes, re Bowden Allshapes deceased.

Odder still. The Allshapes file was part of his ridiculous, pre-transformation past. Mostly it was a set of estate accounts that refused to balance, along with a gang of beneficiaries who didn't seem to care a damn that years had gone by and they hadn't had a penny of their money. Felicity Allshapes, he remembered, was one of these. He'd never met her or spoken to her on the phone; he'd sent her interim bills, which she'd dutifully approved by return of post, but that was all he knew about her. He reached out and tapped in her number.

'Thanks for calling back.' She had a nice voice, anyway. 'I gather you've left Craven Ettins.'

'Yes.' He felt an urge to confess that he'd been fired, and only just resisted it.

'A bit sudden, wasn't it?'

'A rather good opportunity came along,' he said.

'Oh, splendid. Congratulations. Anyhow,' Ms Allshapes went on, 'I've been talking to the other beneficiaries, and we all think it'd make much more sense if you carried on looking after Uncle's estate for us, since you've done all the work on it so far. I mean,' she went on, 'where's the sense in someone new having to read all the letters and stuff, when you know it all already? Besides, you said in your last letter that it was all very nearly sorted out, so—' She paused, apparently expecting enthusiastic agreement. 'What do you think?'

'Well, yes,' Duncan replied. 'If that's what you want, then yes, fine' Being a werewolf didn't seem to have improved his people skills. Pity. 'Of course, you'll have to get Craven Ettins to send us the file, and I imagine there'll be a final bill to settle.'

'Oh, that's no problem. Can you write us a letter we can all sign to ask them to give you the paperwork? I'll just give you my address.'

Should be flattered, he thought; for some reason, they like me, or at least they think I'm competent. (But now, of course, he really was competent. Quite possibly, his werewolf superpowers would make him able to balance the bloody accounts.) Even so, there was something about it that disturbed him, and he felt hackles rise on the back of his neck; a bit like an ache in the tooth you had out last year.

Which left the other message. He read it again. *Crosswoods. Urgent.* Oh well, he thought; if I can't be bruised by tables or blinded by smashed glass, I don't suppose there's an awful lot Crosswoods can do to me.

He dialled the number, and they let him listen to music for a while, which was nice of them, before putting him through to Ms Bick.

'You left Cravens, then.'

He sighed. 'Actually, they fired me,' he replied. 'But I got lucky. An old school friend, actually. Gave me a partnership in this outfit. Seems all right, though it's only my first day, of course. What can I do for you?'

A silence at the other end of the line gave him a clear impression of what Ms Bick thought about divine justice. 'Fell on your feet, didn't you?' she said, but there was a sort of cautious awe in her voice. 'Well, that's neither here nor there. It's not about work, actually. I wanted to know when you last heard from Sally.'

Sally. Sally? Oh, yes, right. 'Actually,' he said, 'she rang me. Night before last, I think.' He grinned. 'It's been a busy few days, so I'm a bit vague about details.'

'The night before last,' she said. 'Damn.'

'Is something the—?'

'Well, I thought I'd try you just in case, you being the ex. But—' Sigh. 'Sorry to have bothered you, then.'

'What's happened?' he said, just a bit louder and more forcefully. Practically a growl, in fact.

Ms Bick sighed impatiently. 'If you must know,' she said, 'she's disappeared.'

CHAPTER FIVE

It was a last-step-of-the-escalator moment. 'What do you mean, disappeared?' Duncan said.

'Gone. Not there.' At the other end of the wire, Ms Bick clicked her tongue, and Duncan instinctively sat up straight in his chair. 'I don't mean vanished in a puff of smoke or put on the Ring or anything like that. She left the office at a quarter past ten yesterday morning, telling Reception she was just nipping out to buy a pound of liver, and that's the last anybody's seen of her. She's not at her flat, her mobile's switched off and she's not answering texts or e-mails, and her car's sitting in the underground car park in Bat Street with a big yellow ornament on its front offside wheel. *That* sort of disappeared.' Pause, while Ms Bick refrosted. 'We thought she might have been to see you,' she said quietly.

'Me?'

'She's been talking about you,' Ms Bick said. 'Quite a bit, lately. More than usual.'

You can do it in several different ways. You can stick a sheet of six-inch-thick glass across the fast lane of a motorway, or you can breed pterodactyl-sized pigeons and train them to precision-crap on people's heads from a thousand feet; or three little words can have the same effect.

'More than usual?'

'Yes. So we thought, well, maybe you two had sort of got back together . . .'

(If only they'd stop messing about with nuclear physics and putting men on Mars, and knuckle down to the job of perfecting the video phone; then Duncan could have seen the look of embarrassed revulsion he knew Ms Bick was wearing when she said that.)

'Well, no,' Duncan replied. 'Sorry.'

'Oh.' Long pause. 'In that case, sorry to have bothered you.'

'No problem.' He hesitated. 'Quarter past ten yesterday, you said.'

'That's right.'

'Does she do that sort of thing? Go off suddenly, I mean.'

'No.' She made it sound as if he'd implied something disgusting. 'And she's got a diary as long as your arm, and she's really conscientious about appointments. That's what's so—'

'I see.' Duncan unleashed the full power of his werewolf brain. 'You don't think she's been in an accident, do you? Have you—?'

'Tried the hospitals, yes. And the police, and the airports and the ferry terminals.'

That gave him pause for thought. 'Ah. What about—?'

'And the leading health spas, rehab clinics, monastic retreats, all that. And the Air Force.'

Duncan blinked. 'Air Force?'

'For reports of unidentified flying objects, in case she's been abducted by aliens.'

'Oh,' Duncan said. If he'd been a cartoon character, a little halo of singing birds would have circled his head at that point. 'Right. No joy there, either?'

'No. Anyway, you've been a great help, good—'

'Hang on.' Not quite sure why, but: 'When she turns up, could you let me know?'

Two-second Ice Age. 'Why?'

'Well, I'm concerned, naturally.'

'Oh.' Three seconds. 'All right, then. But don't call us, all right? Wait till we call you.'

Bzzzz. Duncan put the phone down. He'd said it, he realised, almost as if he'd meant it. *I'm concerned*, he'd said, *naturally*. But he wasn't, of course. He hated the bloody woman. After all, she'd screwed up his life (his other, his pre-bite life; had that really been him, that passive and unsatisfactory creature, now mercifully extinct?) before walking out of it for ever, making it plainly, viciously clear that she never wanted to see or hear from him ever again, not until the skies fell and the seas ran dry and the dead were raised incorruptible. Nothing natural, therefore, about being concerned about her, except in a vague, woolly, no-man-is-an-island sort of a way, the concern a normal person feels for whales stranded in the Thames estuary. The right to worry about her had been taken away from him years ago, after all.

He leaned back in his impossibly comfortable chair and closed his eyes. Without quite realising he was doing it, he was listening; as though his extraordinary hearing might be able to pick up her voice, faint and distant, moaning 'Help!' somewhere. Not that he cared, of course. Quite the reverse. If something bad had happened to her, he'd want to know about it, of course, so he could gloat, possibly revise his hitherto negative opinion of cosmic justice. Other than that, couldn't care less. Honest.

And then the penny, burning up in the Earth's atmosphere, streaked across his plane of vision like a shooting star. She'd gone out at a quarter past ten yesterday, that foul woman had said, to buy a pound of liver. Strange behaviour, all things considered, on the part of the most adamant and proselytising vegetarian he'd ever met in his life.

Sometimes, conclusions are like bits of driftwood floating past a sinking ship; we leap to them for our very survival. Think about it. She wasn't likely to be buying liver for herself. Therefore, inevitably, she was buying it for someone else. Further: if she was prepared to defile herself with the flesh of murdered animals, it could only be because there was someone whose heart she was anxious to short-cut to via his stomach. Apparently, Ms Bick's guess hadn't been so wide of the mark. He quickly pieced together a storyline: unexpected phone call (on her mobile, so it didn't go through Reception). *Darling, I'll be stopping off in London on my way to LA, but I've only got thirty-six hours*; drop everything, quick dash to the butcher for the makings of his favourite liver, bacon and onions, then a fast taxi to his penthouse flat – You didn't have to be Sherlock Holmes or a werewolf to figure that one out.

Duncan frowned. Not that he cared any more. He was tempted to phone up Ms Bick and share his insight with her, but he decided against it, if only because he didn't relish the prospect of getting frostbite in his ear. She was a smart girl, she'd figure it out for herself sooner or later. Besides, if his hypothesis was right, Sally would be back at work in a day or so, smiling a lot and walking awkwardly. Problem solved. The whole issue flushed from his mind.

His mouth, he discovered, was full of little crumbs of wood, all that remained of a perfectly good pencil. He spat them out. It'd have been nice to have some work to do right now, to take his mind off the whole tiresome business; some nice, difficult work, something he could really chew on. Right now, in fact, he could even tackle the Allshapes estate accounts—

Which reminded him.

One of those little things, like bits of grit in the corner of your eye. How had Felicity Allshapes found out so quickly that he'd left Craven Ettins? Furthermore, how had she known that he'd joined Ferris and Loop?

Particularly the latter; because he knew for a fact that he hadn't called up his old employers to share the happy news with them, and he doubted very much whether Luke would have done so, unless it was some fine detail of professional etiquette, the sort of thing senior partners do when they're not nibbling canapes and swigging Bollinger. But presumably he had; or else how come Ms Bick had known where to find him?

Another insoluble mystery solved, ahead of schedule and

within budget. Duncan relaxed. Away in the distance, up against the opposite wall of his office, he noticed for the first time a large padded thing, a cross between a paddling pool and a coracle but made out of foam rubber covered in soft, warm fabric, inside which someone had thoughtfully placed a delightful-looking old blanket. It seemed to call to him, promising warmth, comfort and safety; so much nicer than this horrible, limb-cramping chair. He stood up and walked across the room.

(This is silly, he thought. Whoever heard of a grown man curling up in a doggy-bed at three o'clock in the afternoon? But it looked so soft and cuddly, and the blanket so gorgeously fuzzy and frayed—)

Without knowing that he was doing it, he got down on his hands and knees and approached the padded thing warily. When his nose was about six inches from it, he stopped and sniffed.

He felt his ears twitch. There was something about the smell; that who's-been-sleeping-in-my-bed blend of apprehension and annoyance. He was new to all this stuff, of course; but he knew enough to recognise the scent of his own kind. The last occupant of the bed had, beyond question, been One of Us. That, however, didn't make a whole lot of sense.

He hadn't been conscious of uploading the information, but he knew the scents of the rest of the Ferris Gang. The whole building was filled with them; so much so that he could have drawn a diagram showing which rooms each of them had been in over the last week, with detailed itineraries and timings. The smell from the bed, however, most definitely wasn't Luke (a sort of fiery dark red with cinnamon and a hint of tenor saxophone) or any of the others. He could hear a low growling noise, which he quickly traced back to himself.

Silly. So somebody else had slept in it at some stage: so what? Did this mean he'd never be able to stay at a hotel ever again without barking himself hoarse? He sniffed a little more, but the lure of the bed had evaporated and he went back to his chair and picked up the phone.

'Hello,' he said, and dried. Luke had told him Reception's name, but it had slithered out of his mind like a wise fish in a net. 'You there?'

Someone at the other end of the line squeaked.

'Great.' He was finding the conversation a bit trying, but he soldiered on. 'I was wondering if you could do something for me.' Squeak; oh, for crying out loud. 'Come in here,' he said firmly, 'and, um, get rid of something.'

That made him sound like a little boy scared of spiders. He put the phone down, and a few seconds later the little bald man from the front office knocked at his office door.

'That bed thing,' Duncan said, pointing. 'Chuck it out, would you?'

The little man stared at him as if he'd just been ordered to woodchip over the ceiling of the Sistine Chapel. 'Squeak?' he said.

'I don't like it,' Duncan said. 'If you'd just get rid of it. Throw it out, or,' he added, as the little man's eyes widened like sunflowers, 'stick it in a cupboard somewhere out of my way. Thanks.'

The man stood there. He was quivering slightly.

Duncan sighed. 'Here,' he said. He stood up, went across and picked the padded thing up. 'Take it,' he said. The little man stared at him sadly, so he shoved it into his arms. 'Thanks,' he said; then, as the little man seemed rooted to the spot, 'Go away,' he added. That worked, at any rate; the little man walked backwards to the doorway, then turned and scuttled away, leaving the door wide open.

Strange. But strangeness was the livery around here. Other firms had monogrammed carpets or colour-coordinated open plan, Ferris & Loop had weird. He yawned. He really did fancy a little nap, after the day's exertions. Pity about the padded thing, really. He could see how comfortable one of those could be, for a busy man in need of a quarter of an hour's down time.

He looked up. The little bald man was back again. Only the shiny top of his head was visible. The rest of him was obscured by a colossal quantity of pink, blue and green wallet files.

'Hello,' Duncan said, trying a bit too hard to sound breezy and relaxed. 'What've you got there?'

No reply. The little man dumped the stack of files down on a table that Duncan hadn't got around to noticing yet, stared at him for a moment, then fled. At least this time he remembered to shut the door.

Ah well, Duncan thought, then frowned. One pink, green or blue file looks pretty much the same as any other, but there was something familiar about these specimens. He advanced quietly and carefully, as though stalking wary prey, until he could read—

– His own handwriting on the cover of the file on top of the heap: *Bowden Allshapes dec'd*. There was a single sheet of A4 folded under the flap.

Dear Mr Hughes,
Further to our phone conversation, I have asked Craven, Ettin &
Trowell to forward the files to you ASAP. My fellow beneficiaries
and I look forward to hearing from you in due course, although
naturally there's no rush.
Cordially yours,
Felicity Allshapes

Ask, apparently, and it shall be delivered unto you by Federal Express. It'd have been fun, he thought, to have been a werefly on the wall when the Sidmouth woman found out that one of her department's files was being snatched away from under her nose. She hated it when that happened. He smiled.

Dear old Bowden Allshapes deceased, may he rest in peace. Duncan pulled out the third file from the bottom, the one containing his twenty-seven attempts at drawing up estate accounts. A fine coup, he decided, on his first day as a partner, to clear up this trifling spot of unfinished business and whack in an eye-watering final bill for the first scrap of meat he'd personally brought to the communal feast. He flicked open the file and took out a computer printout. Today's date; efficient. The most recent entry was a debit for £4,337.97. He checked the correspondence. Sure enough, the top sheet was a bill: Messrs Craven Ettin & Trowell, final account to date of transfer of file: £4,337.97. He grinned. Credit where it was due; when it came to gouging the punters, Jenny Sidmouth sometimes displayed a reckless arrogance that was beautiful to watch.

The accounts. He took a sheet of A4 and a biro, drew his centre line, his sun and his moon, and set to work. Amazing, the difference; rather like the contrast between a fish in water and a man wading through waist-high slurry. He dived, gambolled and spun in the flow of the figures, and the mistakes fled before him, their cover blown, their pathetic attempts at deception laughable. When he'd made the last entries and drawn his bottom lines, he began to add – first the left side, then the right.

For a breathless second, he thought it was going to balance. Almost; very nearly. The discrepancy was a trivial 43p. You couldn't buy a second of a solicitor's time for that. He grinned so widely that his face nearly came unzipped. Just once more, to check; he did the sums.

Discrepancy £7,973.34.

Oh.

Panic grabbed him. Had it worn off? Was he going to have to go back to being a stone-deaf, puny, fragile, unable-to-smell human again? That would be more than he could bear. He had to find out. He held his breath and listened; and down in the street, someone sneezed. Joy.

Encouraged to hope, he stood up, crossed to the far wall and took down a framed print of some miserable-looking dead judge or other, the sort that seem to grow on lawyers' office walls like honey-fungus on rotten trees. He smashed the glass against the edge of the desk, picked out a jagged shard and ran it across the palm of his hand. It tickled a bit. No blood.

Relief surged over him like car-wash suds. He was still a werewolf. He went back to his desk and added the figures up for the third time. The discrepancy had shrunk to £677.31.

He sat at his computer and wrote a letter:

Dear Ms Allshapes,
I acknowledge receipt of the files in this matter, which will receive
my full attention at the earliest possible opportunity.
Yours sincerely –

Some things, apparently, don't change just because you stop being human. Duncan shrugged. Maybe it was just as well. His life would be that little bit emptier, he decided, without Bowden Allshapes deceased. There has to be a challenge, an impossible dream, or we stop trying.

Just for fun and something to do, he added the figures a fourth, fifth and sixth time; then he screwed up the sheet of paper, ate it and started again from scratch.

He was running, bright eyed and bushy-tailed, through a misty forest of tall grey pines. His nose was full of the intoxicating scent of the prey: delicious, unfamiliar, so rich and strange that it made every nerve in his body hum and tingle with the desire to catch, kill, eat. The scent was like a filament of burning gold; it was silk and chocolate and Beethoven, and no more than a minute old. He was running impossibly fast (he could feel his lungs bursting) but not fast enough. He needed more strength. He found it.

A great leap over a trackway in a ride, flooded with stagnant water. The shock of landing squeezed air out of him like water from a sponge. He forced his back and hind legs to kick back against the mat of rotting pine-needles. Faster now. Fast enough?

The scent was almost strong enough to choke him as he flew over the trunk of a fallen tree, landed, recovered his stride. He could feel the weight of his lolling tongue.

He saw movement. Up ahead, a flash of white between the trees, moving. He arched his back and lengthened his stride. He knew he was running well, fast even for one of his kind; he also knew that he wouldn't be able to keep it up for more than a minute, ninety seconds at most. He was burning too much energy, putting too much strain on his joints and tendons. No stamina; he'd have to do something about that. Meanwhile, the prey—

He saw it. Only for a quarter of a second, the time it took to cross a ride. It was about the size of a small horse, slender and fine-boned, with a coat improbably white for a natural creature, and in the centre of its forehead stood a single slim golden horn.

Ah, he thought, as his mind filled with love and hunger. *We meet at last, Bowden Allshapes.*

Then it was gone, but the scent was still there. Incredibly, he found a little more speed from somewhere and drove himself on; he knew he was damaging himself, that a professional predator can't afford to carry an injury, no matter how slight, but this wasn't about feeding any more. It was love at first sight, the obsessive love of the hunter for his prey, an overwhelming desire to reduce the fugitive thing into possession. Closing his mind to the pain and the warnings, he forced himself to maintain the pace. Run yourself to death rather than give up; that's what love's all about, isn't it?

A blinding sparkle up ahead, so bright it blinded him (which is also love; blind in perpetual light instead of darkness). For a moment he almost believed it was the glow of the prey's white coat. Instead, it was the sun reflected on the face of a broad river.

His strength left him, like a bird escaping from a cage, and he tumbled to a halt on the very edge of the river. No sign of the quarry. The scent ended at his feet, and the rushing of the river water over its stony bed drowned out all other sound. He lifted his head and, with the last dregs of his strength, prepared to howl, as a spasm rocked him—

'I said wake up, for crying out loud.'

Luke was shaking him by the shoulder. 'Woof?' Duncan asked; then, realising the question was rather vaguely phrased, added, 'What time is it?'

'Five to six. Come on.'

Pressed between his elbows and the desk was a sheet of A3 paper, densely covered in scribbles. He remembered: his sixteenth (or was it seventeenth?) attempt at balancing the Allshapes estate accounts. There had come a point when he'd had to close his eyes just for a second or two, to rest them. That had been two hours ago.

'Fell asleep,' he explained. 'It's these accounts. Can't quite figure out where the problem is.'

Luke didn't seem interested. 'Come on, if you're coming,' he said. 'Otherwise, we're going without you.'

The thought of being left behind (from what? Something had been scheduled for six o'clock, but he couldn't remember what it was) panicked him, like vertigo. 'I'm coming,' he yelped, stumbling to his feet. Werewolves get pins and needles just as badly as humans do. Possibly worse.

Luke led the way down the corridor, going left down a turning that Duncan hadn't noticed before. It led to what Duncan deduced must be the service lift; a battered old grey steel door with a panel of plastic buttons on the wall beside it. The others were gathered there. When they saw Luke, they stopped talking immediately, as though someone had hit the mute control.

'We all fit?' Luke called out.

The door slid open. No brushed chrome or mirrors in this lift. It opened onto an underground car park, in which there were no cars.

'Fifty laps to warm up,' Luke said. 'Ready? Go.'

Fifty laps? Duncan opened his mouth to protest, but the others were already running. He didn't seem to have any choice. He ran after them.

– *Game of soldiers*, he gasped to himself as they passed the lift door for the fifth time. He felt shattered; his chest was heaving and his throat burned. '– The fuck are we running for, anyway?' he mumbled. But Pete, directly in front of him, gave no indication that he'd heard.

Then he remembered. Silly mistake to have made, actually. Of course; he wasn't human Duncan Hughes any more, the pathetic sedentary blob who couldn't have run ten yards if all the bulls in Pamplona were after him. He explained it to his lungs; they understood perfectly and stopped hurting.

I could get to like this, he thought.

Indeed. The hearing had been pretty good, likewise the sense of smell. Being able to do a day's work in a matter of minutes had a lot going for it, and he wasn't exactly turning his nose up at invulnerability, either. But if he had to choose just one of the strange and wonderful transformations he'd experienced today, it'd probably have to be this. For more years than he could remember, Duncan (shallow and unregenerate creature that he was) had dearly wanted to own a Ferrari. Nuts to that, he realised. Why settle for owning one when you can *be* one?

And oh, the difference. It was nothing at all like running as a human. As he indulged his legs in bliss, a small, objective part of his mind paused to analyse. Not rocket science; simply a matter of evolution and instinct. Humans run to get away from danger. We *chase*.

Which made him realise what was missing, the one ingredient that kept this experience from being quite perfect. He was chasing Pete, he supposed, in the sense that he was following him, but that wasn't the same thing at all; like going to the pictures with your sister instead of your girlfriend. Once he'd figured that out, of course, it spoiled the whole thing. What the hell was the point of running round and round a car park, with nothing to run after?

'OK.' Luke was slowing down. 'That's fifty.' He wasn't even breathing hard. 'Now then, where do we fancy going tonight? Don't know about you lot, but I'm getting a bit sick of St James's Park.'

There blossomed in Duncan's mind the image of six men in business suits and shiny black shoes yomping grimly through the dark greensward, terrorising the sleepy ducks. Someone was sure to notice; and anyway, didn't they shut the gates? It was bound to be against the law. Most things were, these days. On the other hand, he had a feeling that the Ferris Gang probably wouldn't be too fussed about breaking laws. Werewolves *and* lawyers: all the bases covered, when you thought about it.

'How about Richmond?' Clive asked hopefully. 'It's been

ages, and you said we'd probably be all right to go back there once things settled down again.'

Luke shook his head. 'They're still running extra patrols,' he said. 'I checked. Apparently the RSPCA gave them a hard time, so we'd better stay clear of there for now.'

'Hampstead,' Micky said. 'We'd have to take out the CCTV cameras on the way in, but that's a piece of cake – you just bite through the cable.'

A popular suggestion, but Luke shook his head again. 'I thought we'd save that for later in the month.'

'There's always Wimbledon,' Kevin said. 'There's usually masses about round there. And my aunt Carol says they've got these new recycling bins with lids that don't shut properly. Bringing 'em in from miles around, apparently. And rats.'

A look of disdain from Luke. 'Well, that's fine if being a terrier's the limit of your ambition. Personally, I like to think we can aspire to better things.'

'They move fast, though,' Kevin said wistfully, 'specially if you get them cornered in among the bins or something. Besides, where there's rats, there's always—'

'No.' His master's voice, Duncan couldn't help thinking. That little extra touch of firmness, and Kevin subsided immediately, as if the gas under him had just been turned down. 'No more cats, not after Putney. Call me a shrinking violet, but I don't particularly enjoy reading about myself in the papers. No,' he went on, 'I was thinking of Chiswick.'

Silence. Then Pete said, 'That's a thought.'

'Quite.' Luke grinned smugly. 'One of the best preserves north of the river. All those yuppies, chucking out their past-its-use-by-date Ardennes pâté; and if we're lucky and find them in the right place, there's that cracking run along the river. The only problem's if they go to ground up by the Fullers brewery, but—'

Some of the terminology was beginning to ring bells, but Duncan wanted to be sure. 'Excuse me,' he said. 'Are you talking about, well, *hunting*?'

Luke's eyebrows raised. 'Yes.'

'Hunting what?'

Luke frowned, but the others laughed. 'Foxes, what d'you think?' Pete said. 'They're an absolute godsend, urban foxes. Don't know what we'd do without them.'

'But that's illegal,' Duncan pointed out.

The laughter was mostly kind. 'Only if you use hounds,' Luke replied. 'And why on earth would we want to do that? It'd be like barking yourself and having a dog, if you see what I mean.'

'Oh,' Duncan said, and he thought: Richmond Park, deer, no wonder they can't go back there again in a hurry. And no more cats. No *more* cats—

'Don't tell me,' Micky said, 'you've got ethical issues. In which case—'

'No, of course not,' Duncan heard himself say; and, just for once, he agreed with himself. The unicorn dream was still there, deleted from his conscious mind but still present in his mental Recycle Bin. Even now he could just about catch a faint flavour of that scent, and the desperate need to run. A great longing came over him to recapture that feeling for real, not just in a dream. Maybe that was what was really meant by the pursuit of happiness. Happiness that stands still and lets you take it probably isn't worth having. If it's going to mean anything, you've got to chase it first. 'I just thought, if we got caught, we'd be in all sorts of trouble—'

Laughter, not kind. 'It's all right,' he heard Luke saying. 'It's his first day. He'll be settled in fine by the weekend.'

Stamina was clearly going to be a problem. According to Luke, Victoria Embankment to Chiswick along the banks of the Thames was a nice brisk little jog, just right for warming up before the fun started. By the time they eventually got there and stopped, however, Duncan was unmistakably out of breath. But there were worse things than puffing a little, and the run had been wonderful; as though he'd been cooped up in a confined space for thirty-odd years, and this had been his first opportunity to stretch his legs a little.

'Right,' Luke was saying. 'We've got Chiswick House behind us over there, so watch out they don't double back; and it'd be better if we stay clear of Kew tonight – we don't want the Osterley mob getting uptight with us for poaching. Otherwise—'

'Just a second,' Duncan interrupted. 'What Osterley mob?'

Broad grin. 'Oh come on, Duncan,' Luke said. 'You don't imagine we're the only pack in Greater London, do you? No, we've got our territory, we respect other people's boundaries and they respect ours. Besides, the Osterley boys are all right, for dentists.' He shook himself and clapped his hands. 'Too bloody cold for standing about,' he said, 'so I suggest we wind up the debating society and get down to business.'

Instantaneously and simultaneously, like well-drilled soldiers on parade standing to attention, all five of the Ferris Gang lifted their heads and sniffed. Pathetically inadequate word for what they were doing. Nostrils flared, eyes half-closed, they sampled the air like wine-tasters, turning their heads slowly like searchlights, drawing the delicately flavoured air smoothly and evenly down into their lungs. Duncan tried his best to follow suit. There was obviously a knack to it that didn't come entirely by light of nature. In spite of his inexperience, however, he was stunned by the tidal wave of information that broke over him as he inhaled. Why the hell, he wondered, do people muck around smoking grass or hash, when you can get so unbelievably high on just plain ordinary air? In a split second he became aware of every living creature that had passed that way during the last forty-eight hours: species, gender, size, age, weight, and all superimposed, like seeing an entire movie in one frozen image.

One of the scents was unfamiliar but extremely strong; not only that, it was *scrummy*. It was Stilton cheese, the Stones, the feel of sandpaper on the skin and a sort of garish rusty purple. He wanted it, very badly.

'I think he can smell it too,' Micky said.

The others were looking at him, smirking, and Duncan felt like a toddler observed doing something unbearably quaint. 'That smell,' he said. 'Is it—?'

'Dog fox,' Luke said. 'About six hundred yards south-east, elderly with a touch of mange, twenty minutes ago. Not in the peak of condition, so it should be a nice, easy run. Ideal for a beginner, in fact. Mr Hughes,' he added, with a slight bow. 'Would you care to do the honours?'

No second invitation required. Duncan found himself breaking into a trot, which quickly flowered into a fast, almost desperate run. From time to time stuff got in his way – walls, gates, fences – but he hurdled them without thinking. Every last scrap of his attention was fixed on the golden filament of scent and he had to follow it, almost as though it was a thin but strong wire looped round his neck.

Over a low wall, through a bit of a shrubbery; each step he took made the scent stronger. He was dimly aware that the others were just behind him. He could sense them holding back, to allow him to go first. He wasn't sure whether he should resent that or feel grateful, but it didn't matter in any case. The scent drew him on, whether he wanted to follow it or not. *Three years of law school*, he thought, *two years articles, and here I am, being cruel to animals with the Ferris Gang*. But the thought was synthetic. This was *right*.

He vaulted a garden wall and landed in a cold frame. Glass shattered around his ankles, but he knew it couldn't cut him. A dog barked somewhere – bloody hell, he said to himself, I can understand what it's saying. The wonder was diluted a little when he realised that all it was saying was 'Intruder alert! Intruder alert!' like the ship's computer in a sci-fi movie. Nevertheless.

The scent tugged impatiently as he scrambled over a flimsy featherboard fence and waded through a tangle of knee-high flowers. They erupted scent as his shoe soles bruised them, but he couldn't stop to savour the explosion. Another dog had started barking; a bitch this time, and as far as he could gather it was making improper suggestions. He shoulder-charged a rickety trellis, cleared yet another fence, and found himself in the open. The moon gleamed silver on the sinuous curve of steel rails. They reminded him of the river in his dream.

Railway lines: he tried to remember the geography of Chiswick from the fleeting glance he'd had at Luke's *A-Z* during the run from the City. He knew that the line ran from the river in the north-west to Mortlake in the south-east; interesting, but not exactly relevant. Knowing where he was didn't really matter; what he wanted to know was where the prey had got to. He sniffed, but the scent was too faint, overlaid by oil, dust, exhaust fumes, rats, cats, dogs and God only knew what else. He'd failed.

He wanted to kneel down and weep. His first hunt; the others had trusted him, and he'd let them all down. The others; of course. They were much better at this sort of thing – they'd be able to pick up the scent and carry on in spite of his gross inadequacy. He looked round for them, but they weren't there. Marvellous, he thought, I'm useless *and* lost.

Human thinking. All he had to do was use his senses; listen out, sniff. Now that he'd evolved, he need never be lost again. He flared his nostrils and jerked air into his lungs.

Luke was about two hundred yards away, with Pete close behind him. The others were a bit further off, and he could hear Clive muttering something, though he couldn't quite make out the words. In other news, the bitch was still trying to open negotiations, and someone was yelling (in human) at the intruder-alert dog. The fox was well away; it had doubled back at the railway track, following its own scent backwards (crafty bugger). Duncan unilaterally declared the hunt at an end, and was plotting a course to rejoin Luke when he caught a taste of a new scent.

It was, beyond all doubt, the most wonderful, tantalising thing he'd ever encountered; so intense that all he could do was close his eyes and shake his head, to try and keep from being overwhelmed by it. Beauty, beyond all hope of description or analysis; but mostly it made him feel desperately hungry, in every literal and figurative sense of the word. He forced his head to clear and opened his eyes.

A horse, no bigger than a child's pony, slender and white as paper, stood perfectly still on the railway track about thirty yards away from him. Although Duncan found it hard to concentrate or think at all, he couldn't help noticing two things. One was the golden horn, fluted, slender and perilously sharp, in the middle of its forehead. The other was the fact that it was standing on the live rail.

Its ears were back and it was staring at him wide-eyed, its tail swishing just a little. Moonlight made it glow like a filament, and its breath was cloudy white in the chilly air. Duncan knew for a certainty that if he moved, or breathed, it would take fright and run; and if it ran, he would chase after it. He knew that he could never catch it, but that he'd never stop trying, not until his heart seized up or a blood vessel burst in his brain. He could feel the danger as if it was something physical, a net or a spider's web brushing softly against his raw skin. The urge, the longing to make the movement that would start the hunt that could only end in his ruin and death was almost unbearable; the pain of keeping still was worse than hanging by one hand from the edge of a cliff. He also knew that sooner or later the horse would move away, even if he didn't spook it. There would be some other noise, a barking dog or a rat scuttling, the vibration of a distant approaching train felt through the rail it stood on. Despairingly, he tried to convince himself that he was asleep and dreaming the dream again, but that was too big a lie, even for an experienced lawyer. It was real, more real than anything he'd ever seen, and it had him pinned down, poised for the kill, and there was absolutely nothing he could do to save himself.

He could hear it breathing: short, snatched gasps in and out, implying apprehension. Could it see him? One thing he'd noticed about his new and improved senses: there was a kind of built-in filter, which made it possible for him to tune out the vast swell of background information and concentrate only on those things that interested him. Just as well, or his head would've exploded hours ago. He narrowed the focus of his attention down to a fine point, until there was nothing in the world except the—

Unicorn. It was a massive word to have to accept; like swallowing a mountain. But there was no doubt about it. The thing he was watching wasn't a small white pony with a brass spike sticking out of its head. It was a unicorn, a mythical beast, a medieval allegory of something or other, innocence or purity or some such. It was also real: a real unicorn, being observed by a real werewolf. And if anybody had told him, fifteen hours ago, that by ten o'clock that night he'd have no problem with either of those concepts, there would have been a brief, embarrassed silence and then he'd have changed the subject. Talk about a rich, full day.

The unicorn's left ear twitched and went forward; the right ear stayed back. Quickly, Duncan realigned his hearing to pick up whatever it was that had startled it.

That bloody dog: a quarter of a mile away at least, but it must've picked up the unicorn's scent, because instead of *intruder alert* it was now barking *strange horse smell, does not compute.* Which said a lot, Duncan reckoned, about canine intelligence, and maybe explained why so few dogs win scholarships to Cambridge University.

The unicorn's ears were back now, and it was snuffling the air. Fortunately, Duncan was downwind of it, but he wasn't sure about the dog. The unicorn was alert, unquestionably, but it didn't seem unduly concerned. After what seemed like a very long time, it lowered its head a little and sniffed at an empty hamburger box lying on the ground a foot or so away from its front legs.

A thought began to quiver in Duncan's mind, like an egg on the point of hatching. How far away was it? His first estimate had been thirty-odd yards, but on further reflection he was inclined to cut that down to twenty-five. In which case, it'd be a straightforward case of drag racing: which of them could do nought to sixty in the shortest time. If he could accelerate from a standstill significantly quicker than the unicorn could, he stood some sort of chance of catching it. If he managed to catch it, he might still have a chance of getting out of this in one piece. If he missed and scared the unicorn away – well. Try and make sure that doesn't happen.

A whistle; some bloody inconsiderate fool was blowing a whistle. The unicorn must've heard it just before Duncan did. Its legs and back tensed up and it jumped forward; not going away, but sauntering straight at him. Twenty yards; *I can do this*, he told himself. *One good spring—*

'Duncan!' Luke's voice, bellowing. Immediately the unicorn spun round and leaped, all four hooves off the ground, into the first stride of a gallop. Duncan hurled himself at it, as if his body was a stone he was throwing. Not a hope. Three paces and the unicorn was out of sight, and Duncan was following the scent blind—

Something grabbed him; he twisted, desperate with anger and fear, and tried to grapple, but the constraining force was much too strong for him. It lifted him off the ground and held him in the air, his legs pumping like the cat in a Tom and Jerry cartoon when it runs off a cliff.

'Duncan,' Luke said, his voice infuriatingly calm. 'Slow down, it's OK.'

Luke Ferris. For a full second, every part of Duncan's body and soul concentrated on hating Luke Ferris. He stopped moving, and Luke put him down.

'Arsehole,' he said. '*Arsehole*.'

Luke punched him in the solar plexus. For a moment he blacked out; when he came round he was gasping like a fish dangling on a line. Even so, he knew somehow that the punch had been kindly meant. 'It's all right,' Luke was saying. 'Pull yourself together, it'll be fine.' Duncan managed to get about an eggcupful of air back in his lungs. 'Ar—' he mumbled, and collapsed in a heap.

Some time later, he sat up. The Ferris Gang was clustered around him, exuding a mixture of concern and contempt. 'Talk about jammy,' Micky was saying. 'First time out and he scents the unicorn.'

Duncan could feel it draining out of his mind, just as the dream had faded when he woke up. 'It's real, then,' he said. 'I didn't just imagine it.'

'Oh, it's real, all right,' Pete said, with just a sprinkle of bitterness. 'Luke, you'd better clue him in, before he does himself a mischief.'

Instinctively, Duncan turned his head and looked at Luke. 'I think you've probably figured out the gist of it for yourself,' Luke said gravely. 'Yes, it's a unicorn. As far as we can tell, there's only one. I've tried making discreet enquiries of the other packs, but when I start talking about unicorns they act like I'm taking the piss. Anyway, that's not important. What matters is, when you smell it, for crying out loud *don't chase it.*'

Murmured agreement from the rest of the pack. Still, he had to ask. 'Why not?'

'Because you'll never catch it, that's why,' Micky said sourly. 'She's fast. Even when it's that time of the month and we're, well, *normal*, we can't get anywhere near her. When we're like this, human, we don't stand a chance.'

'Pete chased her once, didn't you, Pete?' Clive put in. 'Luckily we realised what was going on and there was a short cut; we managed to catch up with him and pull him off before it was too late. Even so, he was flat on his back for six weeks, couldn't eat anything except single cream and Heinz vegetable soup.'

'That's right,' Pete said. 'If the lads hadn't rescued me, I'd have been a goner. Once you start, see, you just can't stop, even when your eyes blur over and you're spitting up blood. Of course, I'd actually caught a glimpse of her, which made it so much worse—'

'I saw her,' Duncan said.

Dead silence.

'I did, really,' Duncan said. 'Smaller than a proper horse,

white, with a golden horn. She was standing there, about twenty-five yards away.'

For a long time, none of the Ferris Gang breathed, let alone spoke. Then Micky whispered, 'Fuck me,' in the voice of a man who's just seen a miracle.

'That's more than I have,' Luke said, and his voice was very slightly shaky. 'Look, Duncan, no buillshitting: did you actually *see*—?'

'Yes, I just told you.' Duncan made an effort and calmed down. 'I was following the scent of the fox and I came out on the railway line. I realised it'd given me the slip, and then I saw her. She was just standing there looking at me. I kept still so as not to spook her; then Luke came along, she ran off, I started to follow—'

'Shit,' Luke said, with deep and sincere emotion. 'Look, standing around next to the railway lines isn't the cleverest thing in the history of the galaxy. Let's get out of this and go somewhere we can talk.'

By a delightful stroke of synchronicity, the pub they ended up in was called the White Hart. For the first time, Duncan had no trouble swilling down his pint of Guinness as quickly as the others.

'We know bugger-all about her,' Luke was saying, 'where she comes from, what she's in aid of, what she *means*. Obviously we've done the research. Unfortunately, the only proven and unassailable fact we've been able to find out about unicorns is that they don't exist. That and a load of thinly veiled soft porn about horns and virgins is all there is to it. Which is interesting, actually, now I come to think of it.' Luke paused for a moment, frowning. 'The thing is,' he went on, 'Pete's the only one of us who's ever actually set eyes on her; and we thought, bearing in mind the medieval legends and all, that was because he's the only one of us who's still—'

'Shut your face, Luke,' Pete growled. He'd gone a sort of beetroot colour.

'But obviously not,' Luke went on. 'I mean, since you were married, I'm assuming – yes, fine. Another theory blown out of the water. Not that it matters a damn, at that.' Luke put down his empty glass and took its replacement off the table. 'There's only one thing you need to know about the unicorn, Duncan. Leave it alone. Ignore it, don't chase it; because if you do—' He scowled, as if remembering something very bad and stupid he'd done once, a long time ago. 'She's already cost me one very dear friend,' he said quietly, 'and I'm buggered if it's going to happen again. All right?'

He swallowed his beer and wiped his moustache on his sleeve; and then the grin was back on his face. 'We call her Millie, by the way,' he added.

'Millie?'

'Mphm. No reason, I just happen to like the name. Knew a girl once called Millie. Never managed to catch her, either. One more, I think, and then we'll call it a night. Duncan.'

Automatically, Duncan stood up and went to the bar. As the Guinness surged lava-like up the glasses, he tried to purge the memory from his mind; a glare of pure white, burned on his mind's eye like the residue of a welding flash. Millie, he thought. Well, quite.

They ran back to the City in silence; outside the office building in Mortmain Street they split up without goodnights or see-you-in-the-mornings; each went his separate way into the darkness, until Duncan was standing alone. He shrugged; it was the only gesture that seemed to help.

He walked to the Tube, but didn't go down the stairs. Screw riding in trains, he thought. Instead, he ran home, rejoicing in each long, effortless stride. There were still a few people in the streets but nobody stared, or even seemed to notice him (a man in a business suit, tie flapping in the slipstream, tearing down Kingsway faster than Seb Coe, at a quarter to one in the morning). He arrived home pleasantly warm, not at all breathless; trotted up the stairs, let himself in, switched on the light.

His Aunt Christine had said once that he was so untidy that if ever he was burgled, he wouldn't notice for a fortnight. It was good to be able to lay that old slander to rest. He noticed as soon as he walked through the doorway. Not, however, because of the mess. It was the smell.

Intruder alert; so much for *x* million years of evolution. He stood rooted to the spot, and the hair on the back of his neck was bristling. He sniffed, and growled; and then he noticed the yanked-out drawers, overturned furniture, scattered books, DVD-player-sized void, et cetera.

Bastards, he thought; then he was grinning, and he had a good idea why. He sniffed again; then he knelt down next to one of the discarded drawers, put his nose to the handle and breathed in.

Fine: that told him everything he needed to know. His only regret as he slammed the door behind him and set off down the stairs, snuffling as he went, was that he didn't have a tail. If he'd had one, it'd have been wagging so hard he'd have sprained a buttock.

Their scent disappeared at the kerb, but Duncan picked up a strong smell of diesel and sump oil, so he followed that instead. He lost the diesel after a few hundred yards, blended hopelessly into the general traffic stench, but the oil smell was clear and distinctive. He didn't have to trail it very far, no more than four or five miles. It took him to a lock-up workshop under a railway arch. He knocked and waited for six seconds before kicking down the door; after all, just because he was a werewolf, there was no call to go acting like a wild animal.

'Here, what d'you think—' said the man in the grey parka, just before Duncan sprang. He went down on his back with a thump, with Duncan's hands round his neck, too startled and terrified to move. Duncan knew the drill. One hard bite into the throat, then shake vigorously until the prey stops moving. He could smell the prey's fear, and it made him feel painfully hungry. He bared his teeth—

And then he thought, *No, this is wrong. No – I'm a human being. Well, a lawyer. Tearing people's throats out, for a straightforward domestic burglary? Even David Blunkett never went that far.*

He lifted his head. Out of the corner of his eye he could see two more men. They were frozen, staring, making no effort whatever to intervene. He looked up at them and growled.

Sometimes, you hear your own voice and somehow, for a split second it isn't you. On this occasion, he was glad it was him. He wouldn't have wanted to be in a confined space with whatever had made that noise otherwise. Instinct or deep-seated genetic memory was keeping the three men from moving, and that was probably just as well. Anything remotely resembling a threat or hostile action would have given his own instincts the shred of pretext they needed. He growled again. The man whose throat he was gripping had gone ever such a funny colour, and you didn't need a werewolf's nose to tell you that he was in urgent need of a change of undergarments.

He relaxed his grip, and the man gasped, gulping down air like Luke with a glass of beer. 'All right,' Duncan heard himself say. 'But I want my stuff back. And God help you if you've buggered up my PC. Have you any idea how long it takes to install broadband?'

They hadn't unloaded his things from the van yet, so he took the keys and quickly checked everything was there. Fine. He climbed into the driver's seat while they opened what was left of the doors. The man he'd jumped on, he noticed, was wiping drool off his chin. Yuk, he thought.

'I'll leave the van outside, with the keys in,' he said. 'You can pick it up in the morning. Oh, and you've got an oil leak somewhere.'

It didn't take him long to put everything back and get the place straightened up; another werewolf superpower, he supposed, because usually tidying and housework took him for ever. When he'd finished, he looked the place over and decided he wasn't going to be staying there long. A dump, by any meaningful criteria. Most definitely not suitable for his new, evolved self; an aristocrat of the animal kingdom, one of supernature's gentlemen. The hell with grotty little flats. Something large and detached was what he deserved, with a nice big garden you could run in; down by the river, maybe. Chiswick, somewhere like that.

Even the bed felt small and cramped, and he found it hard to get to sleep. By rights he should've been exhausted after the day he'd had, but instead he was bursting with energy. After an hour of fidgeting and listening to next door's clock he jumped up, burrowed around in the coal seam of papers and junk in the kitchen drawer, and found the calendar he'd been given last Christmas and never got around to putting up. It was one of those information-packed calendars, detailing among other trivia the phases of the moon.

Only two weeks to go. He couldn't wait.

CHAPTER SIX

'To begin with, it was cats,' Pete said, idly nibbling a plastic ruler. 'Everything else I could pretty much take or leave alone, but just the faintest whiff of a moggy and I was completely out of control.'

A week since Duncan had joined Messrs Ferris & Loop, solicitors. Quarter to twelve; all the day's work long since done and profitably dusted, and the lunchtime drinking ceremony only fifteen minutes away. Duncan had come to look forward to it, even though the procedure was invariably the same. Quick march to the pub, drink twelve pints of Guinness, leave, and no more than a dozen sentences spoken from start to finish. But, as Pete had pointed out, when you've known each other as long as we have, you don't need to be forever chatting away.

Pete was by far the most talkative of the gang. Duncan wondered whether this was because he'd briefly escaped to teacher training college before the long arm of Luke Ferris reeled him back in again, or whether he'd made his abortive break for freedom because he wasn't quite like the others. Probably the latter; which in turn might account for his habit of dropping by for a chat around half-eleven, which had become something of a daily ritual. None of the others had come by for a chinwag; indeed, their chins generally only tended to wag when they were drinking beer or baying at the moon.

'I quit, though,' Pete went on. 'I just told myself one night: from now on, no more cats. And it worked. Haven't had a cat now for – what, three years this April. Sheer will-power, too. No support from the rest of 'em, and bugger-all from anywhere else, either. You can't just stroll into Boots and buy yourself a cat-impregnated patch or a box of cat-flavoured chewing gum.'

'I see,' Duncan said. 'So it was simply guts, determination and strength of character.'

'Exactly,' Pete replied, yawning. 'That and Luke telling me he'd rip my throat out if I ever so much as sniffed another cat as long as I lived.' Pete frowned. 'Luke can be a bit of an old worry-wart at times,' he said. 'Apparently we were getting in all the local papers – well, you know how people are about their pets. And I'd be the first one to admit, I was laying into the suburban moggy population a bit, people were bound to notice sooner or later. That's the thing about Luke: like it or not, he's always right.'

There was something about the way he'd said it; almost the way you'd imagine Lucifer talking about God, when he was plotting the rebellion of the fallen angels. Maybe, Duncan told himself, there's more to this than just cats. Maybe.

'So,' Duncan said, mostly just to keep the conversation going, 'you're cured as far as cats are concerned.'

'Yup.' Pete spat out a few shards of scrunched plastic. 'And besides,' he went on, glancing at Duncan out of the corner of his eye, then looking away, 'once you've seen Millie, it's hard to work up much enthusiasm for small game. I mean, I can show a little polite interest in a fox or a dog – a proper dog, I'm talking about now, a Labrador or a Staffordshire, not the small fuzzy rubbish – but let's face it, it's not the same. Luke says I should try and get over it, but it's not as easy as that.' He sighed. 'Ah, but Man's reach must exceed Man's grasp, or what's a Heaven for?'

A quotation, presumably. Pete went in for quotations; probably a legacy of his time in teacher training. He never talked about his brief sojourn in the Real World, but he carried a sort of aura of difference around with him that was hard to overlook. Obviously Luke was prepared to tolerate it, though presumably there were clearly established limits. He tried to remember what Pete had been like at school; but when he cast his mind back, all he tended to get was a series of group photos. Remembering the gang, the gestalt, was easy enough. Trying to prise the individuals out of the group was as tricky as catching eels while wearing boxing gloves.

'Anyhow,' Pete went on, adjusting his perch on the edge of the desk. 'The billion-dollar question: how are you settling in? On balance a good career move, or would you rather still be at Craven Ettins?'

'On balance?'

Pete nodded. 'On balance.'

'Fucking wonderful,' Duncan replied with a huge grin. 'I mean, the superpowers—'

Pete nodded gravely. 'They are rather nice, aren't they? After a bit, you start to forget what it was like, back before you could do all the cool stuff; when you couldn't smell worth shit, or hear. Really, I don't know how the humans survive, with only fifty per cent sight and about ten per cent of the other senses. You're so vulnerable, for one thing. Like, how the hell can anybody get run over by a car? You think, surely they must've heard it coming from miles away. And then you remember, sort of. No, that's a lie,' Pete said abruptly. 'The nearest you ever get is sort of like history, or archaeology even. You know more or less what happened in the past, but you can't begin to imagine what it must actually have been like.'

Poetry, almost. Duncan raised his eyebrows. This took slightly more effort than it used to do; his eyebrows, like his hair, were growing at a remarkable rate, and shaving was getting to be such hard work every morning that he was seriously considering growing a beard.

'I've got that to look forward to, then,' he said. 'I take it you've got no regrets.'

He'd said the wrong thing, yet again. On the other hand, it wasn't so scary saying the wrong thing to Pete, without the others there. Transgressions committed in front of the whole pack were met with about half a second of total, frozen silence, and then the subject was changed and it was as though it had never happened; Micky might laugh, if it wasn't too dreadful an error, but otherwise the protocol was unvarying. Pete on his own might look shocked or disgusted, but there wasn't the same desperate   falling-overboard-in-the-North-Atlantic-in-winter drop in temperature that'd probably kill you if it lasted for more than a second and a half.

'Regrets?' Pete said, without much expression. 'I've had a few, but then again, too few to mention. Why? You wishing you hadn't joined?'

'Me? God, no.' Duncan meant it, too. But that wasn't the same thing as having no regrets. 'I can honestly say I've never been happier in all my life. I mean, it's perfect, isn't it? Not just the superpowers,' he added, 'the— Oh, I don't know. It's sort of the Three Musketeers thing, all for one and that stuff. Being part of the group again. Knowing you belong.'

(Knowing your place? Well, if you put it like that.)

'Quite,' Pete said. 'It's very important, belonging. Though a certain amount depends on who you belong to.' He lifted his head and sniffed. 'They're coming,' he said. 'Pub time. You realise I haven't had a single cold since I got bitten? Marvellous. Not a single snuffle. Worth it just for that, if you ask me.'

Apart from the Allshapes estate accounts, the work part of Duncan's working day was generally short and sweet. The Ferris Gang didn't tend to talk about work much. Their attitude seemed to be that it was a bit like ironing: it had to be done and you were better for it, but it did so cut into your free time. Nevertheless, Luke had taken the trouble to reassure him that he was performing up to expectations; *doing all right* were the words he used, but from Luke that was high praise, practically gibbering with enthusiasm.

Two new estates to start off when he got back from the pub. He tore into them, got the initial letters written, drew up the schedules of assets, all that. The clock said two-thirty. He sighed happily and looked out of the window.

Nothing to do.

There was always Bowden Allshapes. Duncan frowned. He didn't like to admit it to himself, but his repeated failures with those bloody accounts were starting to prey on his mind. He'd even mentioned it to Luke, who looked at him oddly and asked if the punters were getting difficult. No, he'd replied; well, then, Luke said, and that had been the end of the discussion. Even so; he'd had the feeling that Luke had been a bit taken aback, as though Duncan had used a word he hadn't understood. *There's no such word as can't*; which of his annoying female relatives used to say that? He couldn't remember offhand, because his family belonged to the unsatisfactory part of his life, which was now over. He couldn't quite see Luke Ferris as an aunt, even if he sounded like one sometimes.

Nothing to do.

When they had nothing to do, the rest of the Ferris Gang slept. They had little beds, like the one in Duncan's office. They curled up in them (not forgetting to turn round three times first) and went to sleep until it was time for their next meeting. It was, Duncan had to admit, supremely logical, like all the things animals do: conservation of energy, which to animals is as valuable as money is to humans. Unnecessary exertion to a werewolf would be like setting fire to a wad of banknotes. He'd tried nodding off like they did himself. Sometimes it worked, though he slept in his chair, slumped forward over his desk with his head pillowed on his forearms. It wasn't something he could do at will, however; he couldn't use sleep as a way of fast-forwarding through the boring bits of the day, as they could. He hadn't got the knack of switching off his brain. He could close his eyes and practise deep, even breathing, but his thoughts carried on spinning round, like the tumblers of a fruit machine. Simple, really. They could sleep because they had no cares or troubles. He—

Sod it, he thought, this is silly. Outside, it was a bright, crisp day, and the streets were humming with remarkable sounds and smells. He got up and headed for the front office.

In the corridor he bumped into Clive.

'Going somewhere?' Clive said.

Duncan nodded cheerfully. 'It's a nice day and I've got nothing much on. Thought I'd go for a walk.'

'Oh.' Clive looked at him. 'I see.'

'I might stroll down to the river, maybe.'

'Fine.' Clive frowned. 'Well, why not? Yes, I'm sure that'll be all right. Excuse me, I've got to get this lot copied before the punters arrive.'

Something about Clive's manner suggested that he didn't want to be caught associating with dissidents. Duncan hesitated, but for the life of him he couldn't see that he was doing anything wrong. He carried on, and met Micky coming out of the lavatory.

'Where are you off to?' Micky said.

'Just going for a walk,' Duncan replied. 'It's a nice day, and—'

'Outside?'

'Yes.'

'On your own?'

Something prickled against Duncan's collar. 'Well, yes,' he said. 'I'll be careful crossing the road, if that's what you mean.'

'Why?'

'Well, I don't want to get run over.'

'Why are you going outside on your own?'

Suddenly, Duncan understood something that had been puzzling him on and off for eighteen years. The reason, he discovered, why he'd always felt uncomfortable around Micky Halloran was that they didn't like each other very much. One of his oldest and closest friends, yes, but not a friend he *liked*.

'Because it's a nice day and I'm bored stuck in here with bugger-all to do,' he said pleasantly. 'That's all right, isn't it?'

Micky gave him a look. 'We usually do things together,' he said. 'Or hadn't you noticed?'

Duncan shrugged. The truth had set him free, just like it's supposed to do, and he didn't feel uncomfortable any more. 'Sure,' he said. 'But the rest of you are busy, so I thought—'

'I'm not busy.'

'Clive is,' Duncan replied, quick on the draw, like a gunslinger. 'He's got a client coming in, he just told me.'

Micky nodded. 'Well, then,' he said, 'you can wait till he's free, and then we can all go out. Go and ask Luke, I expect he'll be up for it.'

'I don't want to bother anybody,' Duncan said sweetly. 'Luke's probably having a nap, if he hasn't got a meeting or anything. Why go disturbing him, just because I fancy a breath of air?'

Duncan could have sworn that Micky's ears twitched, as if they wanted to go back but were restrained by the stupid inflexibility of human anatomy. 'You don't want to go wandering about outside on your own,' Micky said. 'Where's the point? You go out, you walk around for a bit, you come back in. What exactly does that achieve?'

The difference was, Duncan realised, that eighteen years ago he'd never have dared to stand up to Micky Halloran like this. It was an issue they'd never resolved by combat or any other formal means, but Micky had always been above him in the hierarchy, for some reason never explained or analysed. Perhaps it was just because he was slightly taller, or had a deeper growl; maybe subconsciously, Duncan had always known that Micky could beat him in a fight. Unimpeachable logic for fourteen-year-olds in a playground gang; didn't cut it as between two adult officers of the supreme court of judicature.

'Oh well,' Duncan said. 'I just feel like it, that's all. If anybody needs me for anything, I've got my mobile with me. See you later for the run.'

For a moment, Duncan was sure that Micky was going to stand in his way to stop him going, and he felt his muscles tense, ready for fighting. But Micky was looking past him, over his shoulder.

'Duncan.' Luke's voice. 'You going somewhere?'

Just the trace of a smile on Micky's face. 'I was just nipping out for a breath of air,' Duncan said, but he couldn't get any real conviction behind it. Not when it was Luke he was talking to.

'Oh.' Luke passed Micky and stood between Duncan and the lift door. 'Well,' he said, 'Clive's got clients coming in at three-fifteen, and then Pete's got that call from Canada at four. I think we're all free after that. Say twenty past four, here. Any idea where you want to go?'

Very pleasant and reasonable. Duncan felt his strength draining away, as though there was a hole in his foot. 'That's all right,' he said quietly. 'I've just remembered, I've got those stupid Allshapes accounts to sort out. I really ought to get them out of the way, while I've got a bit of spare time.'

'As you like.' Luke shrugged. 'We're all meeting up here at six for the run anyhow. See you then, all right?'

As he pushed through the fire door on his way back to his office, Duncan looked quickly round. Luke was still in position, guarding the exit. So what? The essence of leadership is attention to detail.

I shall have to get myself one of those dear little doggy-beds, like the others have got, Duncan said to himself as he sat down in his chair. Much more comfortable than sprawling over the desk. I'd have no trouble getting to sleep in one of them. He looked round the room and thought, fire escapes. There had to be fire escapes, because of health and safety, but nobody had thought to tell him where they were. It'd be a sensible idea to find out about them, just in case there ever was a fire, or some similar emergency.

He swivelled his chair to face the computer screen. There was a file he'd come across a while back but had never bothered to look at, labelled 'FloorPlan'. Sure enough, it showed him a map of the office. There wasn't any writing on it, but a little experimenting revealed that if you hovered the cursor over the place you were interested in, you got a close-up with neat little words: *closed file store* or *cashier's office* or *Luke Ferris*. He set the cursor dancing like a crane-fly, and before long he found what he was looking for. There was a door next to the library which led to the fire stairs, which came out round the back, in the alley where the dustbins were. He smiled. Somehow, he felt a whole lot better for knowing that – though it did occur to him to wonder why, when he'd asked a few days ago what that door was for, Pete had told him it was where the electricity meter lived.

Flicking the cursor round was fun. Duncan found that he could spin the mouse on its pad with just the very tip of his little finger, and the little spidery letters were pretty as they flashed by . . . Pete's room, Clive's room, Kevin, Luke, Micky; a big room just off the main corridor (not the big or small conference rooms, he'd already found them) which had no label at all. He flicked again, like a kitten batting a ball of wool. Wesley Loop's room.

He paused and frowned. If he'd got the geography of the place straight in his mind, the cursor was hovering over his own office. But it didn't say *Duncan Hughes*. Well, fair enough. Nobody had got around to updating the floor plan yet, megadeal. Wesley Loop; as in Ferris and Loop, presumably. So: he'd inherited the domain of one of the founding partners; pretty cool, right? You don't just stick a man like Duncan Hughes in a broom cupboard, you give him the second-best room in the building. Hah! When he thought of the dreary little coop he'd been banged up in back at Craven Ettins—

Wesley Loop. He hadn't heard the name spoken since his first day. Well, fine. They weren't the chattiest of people, his partners, so it wasn't particularly remarkable that he hadn't heard a load of remember-when-old-Wes-got-his-tie-caught-in-the-shredder type stories. Nothing sinister or first-Mrs-Rochester about that. Presumably, the doggy-bed he'd found in the corner had belonged to him, and maybe he'd chosen the colour scheme and the furniture, although Duncan was inclined to doubt that. There was a general consistency about the decor that suggested it had come as a job lot, chosen by someone who'd looked at the price tags rather than the stuff itself and ordered the most expensive things he could find. After all, money couldn't really mean anything to the Ferris Gang any more.

Four o'clock. He killed the computer screen and leaned back in his chair. He wanted to go and check out the fire escape, but he didn't relish the prospect of explaining his sudden interest in alternative exits to Luke, if he happened to run into him while he was doing it. He could just about understand why they didn't like the thought of him wandering off on his own. After all, the defining characteristic of a pack is that it sticks together. That was how it had been at school. Inseparable, the teachers used to say, usually with grim smiles, as they made a point of making sure the members of the Ferris Gang didn't sit together in lessons. Even so; they split up every evening, didn't they, when the run was over and it was time to go home. Luke didn't seem to have a problem with that. Maybe it was just perfectly ordinary, normal corporate bloody-mindedness. He'd drafted enough partnership agreements to know that the one clause that always gets shoved in is the body-and-soul clause, whereby the new junior partner undertakes to work himself to death so that the seniors can have Mondays off to play golf. Presumably there was something of the kind in the huge great thing he'd signed, just before Luke bit him. What with all the excitement and brave-new-world stuff that had followed, he hadn't given the agreement much thought. It might be an idea to read it, at some point, when he was really bored.

Like now, for instance. He vaguely remembered seeing his copy of the wretched thing in the bottom right drawer of his desk. Sure enough, there it was. It was bigger than he'd remembered; they'd probably had to deforest half of Norway to make enough paper to print the bugger out. It was just as well he could speed-read so well these days.

The usual stuff; in fact, it read like it'd been copied out unchanged from the big grey book of forms and precedents – the lazy man's way, and also, of course, the best. Confidentiality, pre-emption, valuation of assets on dissolution, nothing here he couldn't have recited by heart without needing to look at the page. If anything, an anticlimax; he'd have expected something a bit more flamboyant from Luke Ferris—

9. The incoming partner shall not marry, contract an engagement of marriage, cohabit with any person, initiate, resume or continue any sexual relationship (whether monogamous, polygamous or adulterous), make or reciprocate any flirtatious advances or engage in any romantic or intimate activity whatsoever without the consent in writing of the senior partner.

Fifteen seconds later, he barged through the door of Luke's office, brandishing the document like a tomahawk.

'Oh, that.' Luke shrugged. 'Standard clause, it's in all our contracts. Show you mine if you like.'

'Big deal, since you're the senior partner.'

'There's that, of course.' Luke smiled. 'But I wasn't when I signed it.'

Oh, Duncan thought. 'That's beside the point,' he said. 'And the point is, I'm not having it.'

Luke nodded. 'In that case, the clause doesn't really affect you, does it?'

'Let me rephrase that. I won't put up with it. How dare you interfere with my private life?'

Frown. 'But you haven't got one, you just said. All right,' Luke added quickly, as Duncan opened his mouth to say something uncouth, 'let's be serious. You told me yourself, your wife dumped you. Yes?'

'Yes.'

'And you're not seeing anybody else right now. Yes?'

'Yes, but—'

'Well, there you go. Naturally, soon as you think you're going to get lucky, just drop me a memo, I'll initial it and send it right back, and off you go. Simple as buying a tube of toothpaste.'

Put like that, it did seem fairly reasonable— No, it bloody well didn't, Duncan reminded himself. 'Bugger that for a game of soldiers,' he snapped. 'Look, I don't care if you've all agreed to it. I don't care if it's just a formality. What business is it of yours anyway? What the hell's it got to do with—?'

Luke's frown deepened; not anger, but surprise, as though Duncan had just let slip the fact that he couldn't tell the time. 'I'd have thought that was obvious,' he said. 'After all, you're not a human being any more, you're one of us. *Everything* you do is our business. Particularly if it involves bringing someone else into the pack.'

'Yes, but—' Duncan hesitated. Not something that had occurred to him before. Bearing in mind how lycanthropy was transmitted, you didn't need a particularly lurid imagination— Besides, as and when he met a nice girl, would he *want* to make her a part of all this? Would she have to join the Ferris Gang, and/or Ferris & Loop? He couldn't imagine a stranger being part of the unit; not someone who hadn't been there right from the start, in the playground at Lycus Grove. 'I wouldn't be bringing anybody in,' he said, and if he said it loudly and assertively – maybe it was because he was trying to bustle himself into believing it. 'And anyhow, it's the principle of the thing.'

He knew as soon as he said it that he'd given in; when a lawyer talks about principles and there's nobody else footing the bill . . . 'Fine,' Luke said. 'If that's really the way you feel, then I guess we'll have to call it a day. Pity; I'd sort of got the impression you liked it here.'

Bluff; surely he was bluffing. But Luke didn't bluff, in the same way that cannon balls dropped off church towers don't generally float in mid-air. Panic flooded Duncan's brain. The force of it was far more intense than he'd have imagined possible. Losing the gang, just when he'd found them again after all those years of being apart, would be more than he could bear. *So that's that, then,* he told himself. *That's the price I've got to pay for being able to smell pot noodles three quarters of a mile away.*

Fair enough.

'At least let me think about it,' he heard himself say, and he was ashamed at how obvious the fear in his voice was. 'It's not something to be rushed into, you know?'

'Of course.' Luke had always been magnanimous in victory. It was probably his least attractive feature. 'Take as long as you like.' He nodded, as if to say *dismissed*, and Duncan started to walk to the door. 'By the way,' he added, 'in case you're wondering, in this context, a text message counts as "in writing". If it's an emergency, let's say.'

Duncan smiled as he left the room, but what he really felt inclined to do was roll on his back with his arms and legs in the air. Wasn't that what dogs did when they knew they were beaten?

Duncan jogged back from Putney, where they'd been for their run. For once, he hadn't enjoyed it much. They'd found a fox, its head buried in an upended wheelie bin, and it had given them a good brisk chase. But it gave them the slip in the Waitrose car park, and by then it was too late to look for another one. Actually, he'd been secretly pleased; he hadn't really been in the mood.

He let himself into his flat, thinking *I really have got to find somewhere else; this place is a dump*, and checked the answering machine. Two messages.

Imogen Bick, calling from Crosswoods. Just in case he'd been worrying, Sally was back in the office that morning. Apparently she'd been in Buenos Aires with a (pause) friend. No cause for concern, panic over, sorry you were troubled.

He shrugged. He hadn't actually given Sally much thought, not since he'd formed the hypothesis that Ms Bick had just confirmed for him. Buenos Aires, he thought; well, why not? Probably she didn't get to see much of the place. None of his business, not any more. He deleted the message and went on to the next one.

Sally's voice. One word, four letters, begins with H, rhymes with *yelp*. Then a pause, and then the click.

Duncan stared at the receiver for a moment, stunned, as though Death had thrown him a surprise party, with balloons and poppers and a big cake with a scythe iced on it in steel-grey sugar. Then his brain dropped into gear and he dialled 1471. Number withheld. Thank you so much.

Buenos Aires, he thought. Why would you need a pound of liver to go to Buenos Aires?

He rewound and played it back, this time giving the message the full force of his lupine superhearing. On the fourth replay he fancied he heard a soft clunking noise in the background, which could have been the heavy tread of a sadistic fiend on the stairs, or someone winding up a vacuum cleaner flex. Sod it, he thought; and of course, it would have to be a quarter to midnight, by which time even the eager beavers at Crosswoods would be likely to have gone home—

Home; of course. He still had Sally's home number, somewhere. A quick, frantic skirmish through the jumble of bits of paper, yellow stickies and frayed envelopes that constituted his address database produced the relevant data, and he stabbed it into the phone and waited.

Four rings; then a woman's voice, extremely grumpy and sleepy. 'What?'

Not her. 'Hello,' he said. 'Can I speak to Sally, please?'

'What?'

'Is Sally there, please? Sally Hughes. No, sorry, Sally Moscowicz.'

Pause; then: 'Not here any more.'

'What do you mean—?' He was shouting; not good. 'I'm sorry,' he said. 'But when you say not here any—'

'Moved.' Huge yawn; rather like when Arizona yawned once long ago, not heeding its mother's warning about sticking like it, and that's how the Grand Canyon came to be. 'Bought this flat off her ten months ago. Do you realise what time—?'

'Yes, I'm very sorry. Have you got her new number, by any chance?'

'Huh? Oh, no, sorry. She gave it to me, but I lost it. All right?'

'Are you sure you haven't still got it somewhere? If you could just look—'

Click; implying no, she just couldn't. Furthermore, when Duncan called her right back and started to plead, she got quite upset and used the sort of language you don't find in the pages of Jane Austen. No joy there, then. Have to wait till the morning.

But he couldn't. He undressed, got into bed and turned out the light, but inside his head the dog was howling to be let out. *Help*, for crying out loud. What a singularly useless, unhelpful thing to say, and so typical of Sally, who'd always expected him to be able to read her mind. A sensible, rational creature would've expanded on the theme somewhat: *Look, haven't got much time, trapped in locked cellar with three starving hyenas, Unit 46a on the Springmead industrial estate, carry on down the main drag till you get to the plumbers' merchants, then left and left again*; or *Duncan, get over here right now, there's a huge great spider in the bath*; or even *I seem to be staring into a bottomless pit of existential angst, get your arse over here immediately*. He could've handled any of the above, provided the directions for getting there had been clear and accurate – in Sally's case, that'd be a first, but even so; but *help*, pause, possible muffled thud, click was just so—

Duncan jumped up and turned on the light, although he didn't really need to; superlative night vision was part of the package. His answering machine, he'd suddenly remembered, had all sorts of wizard techie features that he'd never bothered with, on account of human life being too short for standing around prodding little buttons while your brain boils out through your ears. One of the wizard features, he was fairly sure, was something which told you precisely when a call had come in. It wouldn't help all that much, but it would be extra hard data, and any information's better than nothing, unless it's supplied by DEFRA.

First he couldn't find the instruction booklet. Then he could-n't find the right bit (he found it in French, Spanish, Greek and Portuguese, but not English). Then he couldn't make the stupid thing work. Then it told him that the second call had come in at nineteen-fifty-seven, which confused him for a long, tense moment until he realised that the answering machine used the twenty-four-hour clock. Eight in the evening, give or take a morsel of superfluous precision. At eight o'clock, Sally had rung him up and said *help*. Solid facts; scientifically obtained and verified, and no bloody help at all.

He played the message back another six or seven times before he accidentally deleted it, but further and better information proved as elusive as WMD in Iraq. He sat on the floor (might be an idea to get two of those doggy-bed things, one for the office and one for home; ever since the Great Change, he'd found himself feeling unaccountably guilty when sitting on furniture) and tried the analytical approach. Hadn't there been a philosopher once who reckoned he could figure out the whole history of the world just by sitting looking at a pebble for long enough? Well: maybe that explained why *philosopher* didn't tend to show up in the lists of top ten career choices for high fliers. Back to basics. What did he actually know?

From the top. On the day that Luke Ferris had come bouncing back into his life, he'd been talking to someone from Crosswoods on the phone – that Bick woman – and he'd asked if Sally still worked there. A bit later, Sally herself had rung him and told him not to ask after her any more. Then nothing, until the Bick woman called to ask if he knew where she'd got to; at which point the enigmatic pound of liver made its first appearance. Then more nothing; until tonight. Sally, according to the Bick woman, was back from sunny Latin America and all was well. Except that, at eight in the evening, she'd rung up her ex and said 'help'. It was now a quarter past one; oh, and she'd moved house about ten months ago, and the miserable cow who lived in her old flat had lost her new phone number.

All in all, Duncan decided after a while, he'd have been better off with the pebble. He could, of course, fabricate a whole wodge of possible storylines that would account for the pitiful handful of known facts. She'd run off with the client-account money, Crosswoods had hunted her down and were torturing her with cattle prods to find out where she'd hidden it. She was still so completely bombed after her romantic getaway that she thought it'd be amusing to call up her ex-husband on the phone and say 'help' at him, just to worry him to death in the wee small hours. She'd found a spider in her bath, rung for her new boyfriend to come and dispose of it, called Duncan's number by mistake – After an hour of this sort of thing, the only thing Duncan knew for certain was that he wasn't going to get a wink of sleep that night, not if he counted all the sheep in Queensland.

He woke up and found he was huddled on the floor next to the telephone table, with a crick in his neck and sunlight pouring through the living-room window onto the face of the clock, which said nine-fifteen. Curious; a moment ago, when he'd closed his eyes just to rest them for a second, the clock had said 4.45 and it had been as dark as a bag outside. Also, he was late for the office.

Screw the office. He jumped up, lunged at the phone and plunged into the long, gradual slide into brain death that constitutes Directory Enquiries these days.

Eventually: 'Crosswoods solicitors', said a brisk voice. 'How can I—?'

'I need to talk to Sally Hughes,' he snapped. 'I mean Moscowicz. Now.'

'I'm sorry, Ms Moscowicz isn't in the office right now. Can I take a message?'

'No. How about Imogen Bick, is she there?'

'I'm sorry, Ms Bick isn't available right now. Can I take a message?'

'Fine. Get me the senior partner.'

Stupid thing to say; because she stuck him on hold, played Elgar at him for twenty minutes, then cut him off – the way you do, when you get some nut on the phone who won't go away. He should have known better, of course. The telephone is an imperfect instrument, ideally suited for obstructing and frustrating the importunate enquirer. He was just going to have to go there and make a nuisance of himself in the front office.

He got dressed. Duncan Hughes the human being wouldn't have stood a chance on the desperate mission he had in mind; far too diffident, polite, well-behaved. Fortunately, he wasn't that Duncan Hughes any more. Nights spent clambering over people's fences and trampling their flower beds in pursuit of the fox had given him a measure of the arrogant confidence of the true-born aristocrat. If the goons on Reception at Crosswoods tried to play funny games with him, he'd know what to do about it.

He was just about to slam his front door behind him when he remembered his obligations to the pack. He paused and rang the office.

'Hello, is that—?' Needless to say, he couldn't remember the name of the little bald man who crouched by the front desk all day. A muted whimper saved him the bother of having to try. 'Listen, it's Duncan Hughes here. Tell Mr Ferris I'm feeling a bit under the weather, so I won't be in today, all right? Thanks a lot, bye.'

A simple, perfectly straightforward sickie, the birthright of every British worker. So why did he feel so hideously guilty? He scowled, as if he was trying to frighten the guilt away. More important things to think about right now. Besides; he'd make the time up, it wasn't as though there was any work that needed to be done anyway (apart from the Allshapes estate accounts; hah!) and he wasn't a snivelling little employee any more, so if he was stealing time he was in effect stealing it from himself. He slammed the door behind him and set off for the Tube at a long-paced trot.

The address he'd been given turned out to be a large building just off Chancery Lane. The windows, he noticed, were black mirror glass, and the fancy self-opening doors led into a huge reception area where a plaque on the wall told him that Crosswoods's offices were in the basement and sub-basement. He found a lift – very snug, with red velvet upholstery on the walls, though it reminded him a bit of a rather showy coffin – which seemed to go down a very long way before depositing him in the biggest front office he'd seen in his life. Apart from a huge desk, the place was fairly sparse and empty – a few chairs out in the middle, like the Azores surrounded by the vast

Atlantic, and that was about it. Lots of dark red carpet, presumably to match the lift.

The woman behind the desk didn't seem to have noticed him come in, so he walked up to her and coughed. She looked up at him with big, glassy eyes.

'Can I see Sally Moscowicz, please?' he said.

She stared at him vacantly for about two seconds, then shook her head. 'Ms Moscowicz is not available,' she said in a flat, measured voice; not the one he'd heard on the phone that morning. 'Do you have an appointment?'

'Is she in the building?'

Another pause. It was like the delay on a transatlantic phone call. 'Ms Moscowicz is not in the office today. Would you like to leave your name and a message?'

'All right,' Duncan said. 'What about Imogen Bick? Can I see her?'

Just talking to the receptionist was making him feel tired; drained, and oddly cold. He wished he'd worn his coat. The same length of delay, then, 'Ms Bick is occupied right now, can I have your name, please?' Still that same flat, featureless voice; it was like listening to Holland.

'Duncan Hughes.' Saying his name made him feel nervous, as though he was giving away more than mere information. 'Can you ring through and tell her I'm here?'

Pause. In order to prove it he'd need one of those stopwatches they use for timing races at the Olympics, the ones that are accurate to a hundredth of a second; but he was convinced that each of her pauses was precisely the same length. 'Ringing through for you now,' she said, and reached for her phone. 'Ms Bick? A Mr Duncan Hughes is in reception.' Pause. 'Very well.' She put the phone down, then said, 'Ms Bick will be through shortly, please take a seat.'

Duncan felt a bit uncertain about setting out across the carpet desert without a string of supply camels and a compass, but he didn't feel up to explaining why he'd rather stay where he was. He got there eventually, and just had time to sit down before a door he hadn't even noticed opened in the back wall and a woman appeared. She was very tall and thin, with long straight black hair, a pale complexion and bright red lipstick, slightly inaccurately applied, so that she looked as though she'd been eating a toffee apple. 'I'm Imogen Bick,' she said. 'You're Sally's ex, right?'

Duncan nodded. 'I need to see her,' he said.

She frowned. Either she wasn't getting enough sleep or she had poor taste in eye make-up. 'You can't,' she said. 'She's not in today. And even if she was—'

'Is she all right?'

The eyebrows raised, but the eyes beneath showed no sign of surprise; maybe a little annoyance. 'What a strange question,' Ms Bick replied. 'She's perfectly healthy, if that's what you mean. Maybe a little jetlagged still after her trip, but fine otherwise. Why?'

'Will she be in tomorrow?'

'I don't know, I haven't seen her diary. What do you want to see her about?'

Duncan had an imagination, though he used it about as often as he used his appendix. He was relieved to find that it still worked. 'An old friend of hers is very ill,' he said. 'Her daughter rang me up; apparently she hasn't got her new address or phone number. I said I'd find it out for her.'

'I see.' Total lack of belief in her eyes. 'You could have phoned, you know, instead of coming here in person.'

'I happened to be passing.'

'Ah.' The eyes flickered a little, and Duncan found himself wondering how old Ms Bick was. Could be anywhere between twenty-five and fifty. 'Tell you what,' she said, 'leave me this friend's daughter's number, I'll pass it on to Sally and she can ring her tomorrow, when she gets in.'

'So she will be in tomorrow?'

'I assume so. If not, I'll ring her on her mobile.'

'You could ring her now,' Duncan said.

Her smile was like a swim in the North Atlantic in January.

'Bad idea,' she said. 'She's in court. Won't have her phone switched on.'

Duncan nodded. 'You're sure she won't be back in today?'

'Absolutely sure.'

'Fine.' He smiled. 'I don't happen to have that phone number on me right now,' he said. 'I'll come back with it first thing in the morning, all right? Who knows, maybe Sally'll be in then, and I can talk to her myself.'

'It's possible,' Ms Bick said, 'but don't make a special journey. I'm sure your time's worth something.'

'Thank you so much,' Duncan said sweetly. 'Nice place you've got here, by the way. A bit cold and dark for my liking, but definitely not cramped.'

'We like it,' said Ms Bick. 'Goodbye.'

No matter how he looked at it, there was no denying that it had been a defeat. He walked slowly back to Mortmain Street, trying to convince himself that he'd made any progress at all. Additional data gleaned; well, there was definitely something going on, though he couldn't begin to guess what it could be. If everything had been fine and normal, he'd have expected a degree of frostiness and hostility, appropriate for a rejected ex-husband turning up unannounced and making demands, but that hadn't been the thought in Ms Bick's mind. Not fear, because she hadn't seen him as a competent threat, but annoyance that he'd touched on a sore subject, and a great desire for him to go away and never come back. There was also the smell, of course. He couldn't place it, but it had been pretty strong, and it wasn't anything you'd expect to find in a civilised London office. It made him think of school, but that was as close as he could get.

His mind was still locked on to the mystery of the smell when he strolled into the front office of Ferris & Loop. The reception committee, therefore, took him somewhat by surprise.

'Where the hell have you been?' Luke yelled at him.

They were all there, standing beside the reception desk; all except Pete. They surged round him as he came in, and for a moment he was definitely scared. But they didn't bite. Instead, they sniffed.

'Well?' Luke snapped. 'I'm waiting.'

'Sorry,' Duncan mumbled. 'I did phone in—'

'Too bloody right you did.' Micky, this time. 'Said you were ill. You don't look ill to me.'

They were all glowering at him. 'Not ill exactly,' Duncan mumbled. 'Just, well, you know. Under the weather.'

But that just seemed to make things worse. 'We don't get under the weather,' Luke growled (and Duncan felt the hairs prickle on the back of his neck). 'And we almost never get ill. And when we do, it's usually very serious. Which is why I've had Pete running backwards and forwards to that revolting little flat of yours, to see if you're still alive. He's been over there twice already this morning. Poor sod's on his way back there again.'

Aaargh. 'I'm really sorry,' Duncan said, 'it was very thoughtless of me. I should've—'

'I mean,' Luke went on, 'fine, if you want the morning off, just say so. But making out you're ill is not acceptable behaviour, all right? I mean,' he said, scowling horribly, 'quite apart from the fact that we were worried sick about you, because we thought you could be dying and we're your *friends* and we *care*—' (Luke managed to make that bit sound like the list of charges at a war crimes trial.) 'Quite apart from that, just think of the implications, if you're capable of it. One of us dies, when the rest of us aren't there. They find the body, there's an inquest, an autopsy. Have you got the faintest idea what one of us looks like, inside? Well, here's a hint for you. Gray's *Anatomy* wouldn't really be much help. Assuming they could get you open in the first place, which isn't likely. Twenty busted scalpel blades, and then they'd be yelling for angle grinders. We've worked bloody hard for a very long time to make sure that the humans don't believe we exist. All it'd take would be one stupid, careless mistake—' He paused, for breath and to pull himself together. 'You just didn't think, did you? And anyway,' he added, after a long sniff, 'you haven't answered my question. Where have you been?'

Years of law school, vocational training, practice, and Duncan couldn't manage to tell one simple little white lie. Call himself a lawyer? Yeah, right. 'Crosswoods,' he muttered.

'Cross—' Luke's eyes were as wide as dinner-plates. He was *scared*. Just for a moment, until the penny dropped. 'What, you mean sniffing round after that bird of yours? Is that what you've been doing?'

'Yes. No.' Duncan managed to fight back the urge to roll on his back, but only just. 'There's something wrong,' he said, 'if you'd only back off and let me explain.'

Well, he had their full attention, and he did his best to make the most of it. But it's always the same: you tell the story and no matter how hard you try, it comes out sounding silly. It's no good saying *you had to have been there*; they won't get it, particularly if they're furious with you to start with. He knew they believed his data but not the conclusions he'd drawn from them. Well, fine. Screw them.

'Well, it's obvious what's happened,' Micky said, when Duncan had finally ground to an unsatisfactory halt. 'Your ex went off for a week's sun and shagging with some bloke, she's come back worn out and hung over, and the miserable cow in the office doesn't want you to know in case you're madly jealous and you start making trouble. Can't say I blame her, considering how badly you're overreacting. You want to get a grip on yourself.'

'Fine,' Duncan snapped. Micky he could get angry with. 'So what about the phone call, last night? *Help*, remember?'

'Probably not her at all,' Micky said scornfully. 'Probably a wrong number, or someone playing games. Or if it was her, there's bound to be a perfectly reasonable explanation. Besides, no matter what, you shouldn't be getting mixed up with those people—'

Funny thing to say; but before Duncan could ask him what he meant by it, Luke said, 'Look, it's not your fault. You didn't know we don't do sickies like the rest of the British workforce. If you'd known, you wouldn't have been so bloody stupid. Fine. We'll say no more about it. Just don't do it again, all right?'

Those people? Which people? Crosswoods? Women? Humans? 'Understood,' he said. 'I'm sorry if I—'

Luke was scowling at him. 'We'll say no more about it,' he repeated. 'You included.' He paused for a moment, and Duncan realised he was breathing hard, as though he'd been running. 'I've got clients coming in any time now, so you'd all better hop it. Back here, six sharp. I thought we might try Battersea tonight.'

Another unsatisfactory run; not so much as a sniff of a fox, and it came on to rain, suddenly and heavily. Duncan squelched back home in soggy shoes, arrived at his front door and realised he'd come out that morning without his keys.

Not a major setback for a superhuman; he went round the back of the building, shinned up a drainpipe, trudged wearily along a three-inch-wide ledge and found the kitchen window was already open wide enough for him to crawl through. Careless, like forgetting his keys. On the other hand, he had an excuse. He'd been fairly preoccupied that morning. He sniffed, as he always did these days as soon as he got home. No unusual smells. He yawned and put the kettle on.

Help. Would you care to enlarge on that? Maybe Micky had been right, and she'd done it just to wind him up – a pointless exercise, and not in keeping with her character as he remembered it, but maybe she'd changed since they'd split up – correction: since she dumped him, suddenly, without provocation, as though he was a used nappy. Well, quite. That had been out of character too, but she'd done it, hadn't she? So: completely *in* character, once he'd shrugged off Love's rose-tinted welding mask. Just the sort of thoughtless, cruel thing you'd expect—

The click of the kettle switching itself off snapped him out of it, and he made himself a cup of what he'd come to think of as werewolf coffee (instant coffee granules, sugar and boiling water in equal parts by volume), which he took into the living room. If you could call it that; he hadn't done much living in it so far. Much better to call it the dragging-out-a-pointless-existence room and have done with it.

Definitely, he was going to have to move. In fact, he couldn't understand (now he came to think of it) why he hadn't done so already. He could afford better, or at least he assumed he could. Of course, Luke hadn't bothered to tell him the fine details of when, how and how much he was going to get paid – it'd be in the partnership deed somewhere, it always was – but a sixth share of the net had to be a pretty awesome sum, even after overheads. Something large and detached in Walton-on-Thames, maybe (and then he thought, this isn't me thinking, I'd hate Walton-on-bloody-Thames, it's where rich people end up as a punishment for living too long). Anyway, a nice big house somewhere, not that he'd be spending much time there, what with work and then the evening run. He'd be much better off with something small but very central—

There was someone – or something – in the bedroom. Duncan sat up very straight and sniffed, but still nothing out of the ordinary. He frowned. He wasn't quite sure what it was that he'd heard; it had been very faint, almost but not quite faint enough to be dismissed as a figment of his imagination. Burglars? Unlikely, or he'd be able to smell them. Ditto mice and cockroaches. Not that it mattered particularly, though a burglar or two would've been nice. Far from resenting the intrusion, he was delighted by it. Right now, there was nothing he fancied more than flushing out and annihilating something.

The body language of a normal householder preparing to confront a thing that goes bump in the night is a precarious fusion of synthetic aggression and genuine terror. He flattens himself against the wall, flings open the door and shrinks away, a scared rabbit playing at Starsky and Hutch. On this occasion, Duncan wasn't a bit like that. He walked quickly but quietly to the bedroom doorway, opened the door without noise or fuss, and switched on the light.

'Christ,' he said.

He couldn't have been more surprised if his statement had been true. The noise, now he had all the information at his fingertips, could be analysed quite easily. It had been someone shifting very slightly on the bed, probably to relieve cramp.

'Hello,' she said.

Context is everything. Under other circumstances, walking into his bedroom and finding Sally there, sitting on the bed in a decidedly unregenerate black dress, would have been an unambiguously good thing. Instead—

'What the bloody hell do you think you're playing at?' he said.

She smiled. Not, however, *that* sort of smile. 'It's lovely to see you too, Duncan,' she said. 'How are you, anyway? This place is an absolute tip, by the way. When did you last change your pillowcases?'

Oh no, she didn't; not this time. 'How in God's name did you get in here?' he asked.

She shrugged. 'Kitchen window,' she replied. 'Talking of kitchens, are you starting up in the penicillin business, because there's a pot of jam in your cupboard with enough mould on it to cure half of South-East Asia.'

Kitchen window? In that get-up? He leaned back against the door frame, and in the back of his mind a small voice asked, *So how come you can't smell her?* 'Sally,' he said quietly, 'what are you doing here?'

'Stupid,' she replied. The voice she used to say the word with was velvet and chocolate mousse and a sort of dark, soft purple, but the sparkle in her eyes was rather familiar. It was Pete, scenting a cat. The voice put forward a pretty convincing case, but the eyes had it. 'What do you think?'

Something different about how she looked; well, lots of things, but for the moment, let's focus on the lipstick. It wasn't something she'd ever gone in for, back in the old days. It really suited her. 'Haven't a clue,' he replied. 'Look, what was that phone message all about? I've been worried sick. I went round to your office but they told me—'

In a movement so slick that he couldn't remember seeing it, Sally stood up and glided towards him. Presumably she put one foot in front of the other, but from his point of view it was as though the camera had zoomed in, until her face filled his mind's screen. Maybe I'm asleep and this is a dream, Duncan thought, which would account for the fact that I can't smell her. If so, it goes some way to answering the nagging old question of what sleep is actually *for*. Also he thought: definitely approve of the lipstick, but she's using way too much eyeshadow.

Then her arms were round his neck, her grip surprisingly strong. First her hair and then her cheek brushed against his face, so that his eyes automatically closed and he was thinking, really, it's a shame this is only a dream, because it'd be so nice if it was real—

She purred like a cat, or something. And then she opened her mouth and bit him savagely on the neck.

CHAPTER SEVEN

'Ouch,' Sally said. 'Oh shit, I think I broke a tooth.'

Not a dream after all. Duncan snapped out of it, shoved with the flat of his hand and forced her away, or tried to. He pushed quite hard, but she wouldn't budge.

She'd bitten him (so much for twice shy) but of course he was invulnerable: unbreakable skin. He had an idea, though, that it had been a pretty close run thing. Those teeth had been *sharp*—

'Oh,' he said.

She was looking at him. The same sort of profound irritation he'd seen in the eyes of Ms Bick, when he'd shown up uninvited in her front office—

– Which suddenly made sense. 'That explains it,' he said.

'What?'

'Your office,' he replied. 'Why it's underground. No windows. No windows, no daylight.'

The frown deepened, then shattered into a rather nice smile. 'You and South-West Trains,' she said. 'Slow, but you get there in the end. And no, there're no mirrors in the ladies' loo, either.'

'No point?'

'That's right. Look, you wouldn't happen to have a couple of aspirin, would you? Your stupid neck's hurt my tooth.'

'What? Oh, right, aspirin.' He crossed to the cupboard and

found some. They'd gone a bit powdery and soft, but they dissolved in the water just fine. 'So,' he said, taking a deep breath, 'how long have you been—?'

'Never mind me, what about you? Oh, it's OK, I should've guessed as soon as I saw you. The beard suits you, by the way, hides your chin collection. And you've lost weight. All that chasing after cats, I suppose.'

'A fortnight,' Duncan replied, a little hazily. 'Since I joined Ferris & Loop.' He stopped and frowned. 'You know about—?'

She nodded. 'Werewolves, yes,' she said. 'I get the impression you didn't, not till you got—' She hesitated. 'Recruited, or however you'd describe it. Come as a bit of a shock, did it?'

'Yes. Answer my question. How long—?'

Only for a split second it was as though a visor had lifted, and he could just see her in there, behind the toughened safety glass. 'Not while we were married, if that's what you're thinking.'

'I see,' he lied. 'Is that why you dumped me?'

'No.'

Not the answer he'd expected, he realised; then he remembered that she was a lawyer too. 'Is it, like, compulsory? At Crosswoods, I mean.'

Crooked smile. What great big teeth, grandma. 'You didn't do Latin at your school.'

'Well, no.'

'*Trans*, meaning across. *Sylvania*, the woodlands.' Sally clicked her tongue. 'Or so they tell me. They did teach Latin at my school, but I did biology instead. There's a deep irony in there somewhere, probably. Meaning yes,' she went on. 'The entire fee-earning staff at Crosswoods are evolved, if that's what you were trying to ask. I gather it's the same at that outfit you're with now.'

He nodded. 'You remember me telling you about Luke Ferris, the guy I was at school with? Well, it's him and his old gang, which I used to belong to.'

'Oh yes.' She frowned. 'You said you never wanted to see any of them ever again, as long as you lived.'

'Yes.'

'And now you're in partnership with them.'

'That's right.'

She sighed. 'You're going to tell me that that's a classic example of stuff happening.'

'I didn't want—' Duncan shrugged. 'I got fired from Craven Ettins, and there was Luke offering me this job. I said yes, and next thing I knew, I'd been – well, you know.'

'Roughly similar story in my case,' Sally said, gently massaging her jaw. 'Except they hired me thinking I'd be, let's say a suitable case for conversion. Then they weren't sure, and it took them a while to make up their minds. Soon as they'd decided I was their sort of girl, that was it. I was in. I guess it'd have been nice if they'd asked first, or filled me in on the background, but what the hell. On balance, it's been a good thing for me. There are certain advantages.'

A faint click in the back of his mind. 'You really got in through the kitchen window?'

'Yup.'

'You didn't climb up the drainpipe, though.'

'No.'

He had to nerve himself to say: 'You can *fly*?'

Sally nodded. 'Goes with the territory. Not particularly well,' she added. 'I mean, at one end of the scale you've got Concorde, at the other end a chicken. I'm more in the poultry class. I can do vertical lifts and short bursts, fifty yards or so on a good day. But if I wanted to go to New York, I'd have to spend three hours hanging round at Heathrow like everybody else.'

'Even so.' He shook his head. 'That's amazing. How do you—?'

'Search me. It's like wiggling your toes. You decide to do it, and it happens. Show you if you like.'

'Yes, please.'

She nodded again and rose abruptly into the air, stopping just short of nutting herself on the ceiling. She hung there for about ten seconds, then drifted gradually down. 'Landing's the tricky part, of course,' she said. 'Specially in heels. Either you go flat on your face or you nail yourself to the floor. Still, it comes in handy.'

Pause. Duncan knew he had to ask, but he really didn't want to.

'And the other stuff—' he mumbled.

'Yes.' She looked away. 'Mostly we get it from Eastern Europe these days, black-market medical supplies. There's a sort of running joke in the office. Group O is Ordinaire, A is Appellation Contrôlée . . . You think wine snobs are a pain in the arse, you wait till you hear blood snobs.'

Duncan breathed out slowly. 'And sunlight?'

Sally shook her head. 'Not so much of a problem these days, thanks to the advances in barrier-cream technology. A good all-over daub with factor thirty and a pair of wraparound shades, and we're practically normal. Practically,' she repeated, a little wryly. 'I mean, beach holidays aren't a good idea. But so what, we're lawyers. We know that the secret of attaining happiness lies in starting off with a realistically achievable definition. Only want what you know you can get.' She grinned. 'OK, as universal truths go, it's pretty banal. I mean, it's a bit like discovering the Holy Grail and finding it's got *33cl please dispose of tidily* written on the side.'

Whatever, Duncan thought. 'Can I ask you something,' he said. 'Well, two things, actually.'

'You can ask.'

'All right, thanks.' He took another deep breath. 'First, why did you dump me like that? Second, what was that phone message all about? I've been worried sick.'

She laughed. 'Oh, that. Sorry. The truth is, I got absolutely pissed out of my skull.'

'Ah.'

She nodded. 'At my gran's. It was her eightieth birthday party, and I had a small sherry. It's a metabolism thing, when you're evolved – something to do with blood sugar. Anyway, I got home, started feeling very sorry for myself, picked up the phone, and that's all I can remember. I gather I must've said something annoying.'

'Yes.'

'Go on, then. What did I say?'

'Help.'

'Oh.' She pulled a face. 'Sorry about that.'

'It's OK.'

She clicked her tongue again. 'About the other thing,' she said.

'Well?'

'It was—' She looked away again, noticed a cobweb in the corner of the ceiling, frowned. 'Losses are a bit like diamonds. You've got to be very careful about cutting them, or you end up doing a lot of rather expensive damage. I should've been a bit more sensitive, maybe.'

'Oh.' But, Duncan thought, doing the mental arithmetic; in that case: 'So why did you come over here and try to—?'

Sigh. 'Isn't it obvious? You come round to our place asking questions; Imogen, bless her, was absolutely positive that you'd rumbled us, so we thought, there's only two guaranteed ways of shutting you up, and really, we aren't all that keen on cold-blooded murder. No pun intended,' she added. 'Of course, we didn't know you're one of *them*.'

Something Micky had said: *mixed up with those people*. A good case could be made for saying that most of the unhappiness in the world comes from people thinking in italicised pronouns. 'So,' he said. 'What are you going to do now?'

'Don't need to do anything. I mean, you may be an ambulance-chaser rather than a bloodsucker, but we're all in the same profession. Nothing to worry about any more, we apologise for any inconvenience.'

'Oh.' He thought about that for a moment. 'You're sure that's all there is to it?'

'Hardly a grey area.' Sally glanced over his shoulder in the direction of the wall clock. 'Good heavens, is that the time? I must fly. So to speak. Got an early court appointment.' She stood up straight, almost started to move. 'So,' she said, 'is it fun, being one of your lot?'

'Yes.'

'Good. I'm pleased for you. And it was sort of sweet of you to be worried, I guess.'

'Right,' Duncan said. 'Why the pound of liver, by the way?'

She blinked. 'What?'

'Your mate Ms Bick said you nipped out for a pound of liver, just before you went AWOL.'

'Oh, right. Well, I could spell it out for you, but I seem to remember you're a bit squeamish around words like *dripping* and *oozing*. Just think of it as the equivalent of a flask of coffee, all right?'

'So who did you go to Buenos Aires with?'

'Nobody. One of my aunts lives there, if you must know. I'll see myself out.'

A moment later, she'd gone. Through the door this time, like a human being.

Luke was standing by the front desk when Duncan walked in next morning. Not, he decided, a chance meeting.

'You look rough,' Luke said.

'Yes.'

'Trouble sleeping?'

'Yes.'

Luke nodded. 'Figures,' he said. 'Maybe I should've mentioned it. Nothing to worry about, it's quite normal.'

Duncan looked at him. 'What's quite normal?'

'Not being able to sleep the night before a full moon,' Luke replied. 'It's never bothered me, but I know Pete doesn't even bother getting into bed, because he knows it's a waste of time trying. Takes different people different ways. Clive reckons he sleeps like a log, but he always gets dreams about drowning in tapioca pudding.'

The night before full moon; what with Sally disappearing and then materialising in his bedroom when least expected, Duncan had clean forgotten that he had that particular thrill to look forward to. Nonetheless, a side issue. He looked at Luke, braced himself and said, 'Have you got a moment?'

'Several.'

'I need to ask you – well, tell you something, and then ask. If that's all right.'

Luke frowned. 'Let me guess. Girl trouble.'

He made it sound like something contagious and antisocial. 'Sort of. You see, last—'

'They can be a pain in the neck sometimes, can't they?'

Duncan nodded slowly. 'You know about it.'

'Follow me.'

The small interview room was only small in comparison with the large interview room. You could have held a concert in there, or a slightly cramped football match. In the middle of all that empty space was a table and one chair. Duncan sat in it; Luke perched on the edge of the table.

'What we need,' Luke said, 'is strong black coffee and some Viennese fingers.' He stuck two fingers in his mouth and whistled. A few seconds later, the little bald man who worked the front desk appeared, holding a tray.

'Sugar?' Luke asked.

'Two.'

Luke raised his eyebrows. 'If you're sure.' It was, Duncan noticed, a very small teaspoon. 'All right,' Luke went on, gnawing the chocolate off the end of a biscuit, 'let me save you the embarrassment. Last night your ex-wife came to see you.'

'She flew in through the bathroom window.'

Luke didn't seem to find anything worthy of comment in that. 'She tried to recruit you to their side. Didn't work, of course. She gave you some sort of explanation, then went away. All right so far?'

Duncan dipped his head slightly in acknowledgement. 'Is that what Micky meant yesterday, when he said I shouldn't get mixed up with those people? He knew she's a—'

Luke laughed. 'She works for Crosswoods, right? That's all we needed to know.' He leaned forward a little. 'It's my fault, I suppose. Me and the rest of us, we've been through this whole thing together, from the start. We found all the stuff out as we went along – there wasn't any need for briefings and putting anybody in the picture. Now you've joined us, not having a clue about any of this. I guess I should've taken the trouble to fill you in.'

Pause. If Luke was expecting him to say something, Duncan didn't know what it was. 'Maybe it would've been nice,' he said.

'Well, there you go,' Luke said briskly. 'Listen, there's something you need to understand, about their lot and our lot. We don't get on. I'm not saying we're the good guys and they're the baddies, it really isn't like that. It's more a case of cats and dogs. Bats and dogs would be more appropriate, but anyhow: it's a feud, basically. I imagine that at some point, a long time ago, one of us pissed off one of them, or vice versa, God only knows what about. Ever since, there's been bad blood, if you see what I mean. We don't like them, they don't like us. It's not exactly open war – I mean, we don't go looking for a fight, nor do they, mostly – but if the opportunity comes along, naturally we do what we can to screw them over, so long as it doesn't lead to serious escalation.' He sighed. 'It's stupid, really. It'd be much better if we could all just get along peacefully. I mean, all that hatred and intolerance stuff, it's so *human*, we should be above that kind of thing. On the other hand,' he added, with a trace of a grin, 'when we do manage to get one over on them, it's sort of fun.'

'Fun,' Duncan repeated.

'Fun,' Luke said firmly, in an and-that's-an-order kind of a voice. 'Relieves the boredom a bit, which is always welcome. Probably why we do it. Anyway, that's beside the point. What you need to remember is, Romeo and Juliet and star-crossed lovers are all very well for teenagers, but we're grown-ups now; so if you're still carrying a torch, I suggest you switch it off and bury it somewhere. All right?'

Not a good time to argue the toss with the alpha. 'Sure,' Duncan said. 'It was all over a long time ago.'

'Really. Which explains why you go off the rails as soon as she whistles for you.' He twitched his nose. 'You realise you were set up.'

Duncan looked up sharply. 'I don't—'

'Use your intelligence. Come on, you're one of us now. Or maybe you're too close to it to see, I suppose that'd be understandable. All right, I'll spell it out.' Luke took another biscuit and ate it before continuing. 'There you are at Craven Ettins, and in the ordinary course of business you get a call from some tart at Crosswoods. In conversation, you ask after your ex. Fair enough: you don't know their dark secret. They don't want humans taking an interest in them, also understandable. It's obvious she left you because she was about to be recruited; even you can see that, I'm sure.'

'She said that wasn't the reason.'

'I bet she did. The sad fact is, though, that sometimes people don't tell the truth. Even lawyers.' Luke grinned. 'So,' he went on, 'they start figuring that if you've got it into your head that you wouldn't mind giving it another go, and you start hanging round her, calling her, all that – needless to say, her bosses wouldn't be happy. Fine; they tell you to piss off, they get her to tell you, in no uncertain terms. Problem solved. But then they find out you've left Craven's and joined us. And they know what we are, goes without saying.'

'Oh.'

Luke smiled. 'It's a small community, we all know each other. So, it's suddenly a different ball game. Now they do things a bit different, their lot. We recruit straight away – well, you know that, Day One and we go straight for the jugular, no messing about, it's the canine way. Their lot like to take things a bit more slowly. You start off on probation: they let you in on the secret, and then you've got to prove you're worthy for a week or so before they actually sink the teeth in. I'm assuming that Crosswoods assumed that we do something similar; in which case, there'd be a fair chance that we wouldn't have bitten you yet. Hence their cunning plan: to piss us off by snatching you from under our noses, so to speak. Get you before we can, turn you into one of them. I don't know if they just wanted to be annoying or whether they had something sneakier in mind – have you as some kind of undercover agent or whatever. It's a bit technical, but basically, they don't have the invulnerability thing that we do. It's swings and roundabouts, because they're completely immortal unless they get the old two-by-four through the heart or they go out in the sunlight without the special make-up. Anyway: if they'd recruited you first, I could still have bitten you without needing a trip to the dentist afterwards, but it wouldn't have had any effect. Result: we'd have thought you were one of us, but you'd really have been one of them. Just a theory,' Luke added, 'and it's entirely possible they weren't planning anything so devious. But it's what I'd have done in their shoes, if I'd thought of it. But there're other explanations. Like I said, it could just be spite, or maybe the girl's still fond of you and—' He shrugged. 'No matter. The phone call and the cry for help were just bait, of course. Probably she never went missing at all, that was just to snag your attention. Anyhow.' Luke stood up, stretched his legs and appropriated the last Viennese finger. 'Now you know the score, and the bottom line is, stay well clear. We may decide that honour calls for reprisals at some stage – I haven't made my mind up yet – but as and when we do them over, it's got to be a pack decision and organised entirely by me. It's too complicated an issue for lone wolves. All right?'

Even if he'd had the courage, Duncan wasn't sure he'd have been physically capable of displaying dissent. A voice that, by a process of elimination, had to have come from him said, 'Understood.' And that, apparently, was that.

'Fine. Glad we've cleared that up, and like I said, maybe I should've put you in the picture right from the off. Anyway: serious talk now over, the rest of the day's your own. Oh.' Luke stopped, and frowned. 'Nearly forgot. There's a punter to see you. I parked her in the big interview room, you'd better get down there sharpish before she starts climbing the walls. Something to do with that funny estate of yours, the one where the accounts won't balance.' Grin. 'In your shoes I'd be inclined to anticipate a bollocking, unless you've got the clients really well trained.'

Shit, Duncan mused, as he darted back to his office for the files. He really wasn't in the mood for anything to do with Bowden Allshapes deceased right then. Volcanoes had been erupting right across his world lately, heaving up new mountains and submerging the familiar, old continents under the sea, and all the maps he'd carefully drawn of his life over the years were now just so much waste paper. There were serious issues to be addressed urgently, matters of identity, self-image and quite possibly true love. He simply didn't have the time or the energy to be bothered with silly old *work*.

'Sorry you've been kept waiting, I was in a—' Duncan's words had preceded him into the room. But as soon as he saw the person sitting opposite the door, on the client's side of the table, something seemed to happen to his mouth, or possibly his brain. He stood and gawped for a good five seconds.

'Hi,' she said. 'I'm Felicity Allshapes. Are you Duncan Hughes?'

He nodded.

'Great to meet you at last. I love being able to put a face to a name.'

The Australian accent helped, a bit. Australia is a wonderful country, just coming into its glorious prime as a nation, but its inhabitants, when they speak, do tend to sound rather as though they're chewing toffee. They don't immediately put you in mind of goddesses or angels. To a certain extent, this helped break the spell. Duncan was just about able to speak.

'Um,' he said.

'Sorry to barge in like this,' she went on, 'I know how really busy you are, and it's so kind of you to spare me a few minutes. But I had to come to London on business at literally an hour's notice, and I thought that while I was here—'

'Fine,' Duncan croaked. 'No problem.'

Felicity Allshapes smiled. Of course, you can't analyse smiles.

You can't measure them with micrometers and Vernier callipers and say, if the left upper corner of the top lip had been twelve-thousandths of an inch lower down, it'd have been completely different, no big deal at all.

'That's so nice of you, I really appreciate it. And we're all so grateful to you for agreeing to carry on acting for us, what with you changing jobs and all. You've done so well for us already, it's such a comfort knowing you're here looking after us.'

Something's wrong, Duncan thought. 'Oh, it's all part of the service,' he said vaguely, and managed to load himself into a chair without falling over. 'What did you want to see me about?'

'Well.' She bit her lip, and Duncan had to try very hard not to think about pearls on a bed of rose petals. 'I've got to say, we're all really sorry about this and we do hope it's not going to mess everything up, not after all the hard work you've put in already. The thing is, there's some more assets of the estate we've only just found out about: stocks and shares, building land, a small block of flats in Canberra, stuff like that.' Her face clouded up, and for a split second Duncan wanted to burst into tears. 'Is that bad? I mean, is it going to make all sorts of problems for you?'

While she was saying that, Duncan was setting himself a test. Look away, he ordered himself, and see if you can tell me what colour her hair is. He looked away. He couldn't.

'Well yes, actually.' It was a sort of deep chestnut brown. His favourite hair colour. 'You see, it's the duty of the executors to make a full declaration of the assets when applying for probate, so the Revenue can calculate the amount of tax payable—' Luckily, the speech came out automatically, no thought required. He couldn't be bothered to listen to himself making it. Instead, he tried the test again, this time with the colour of her eyes. They were green (he'd always had a thing about green eyes) but he had to look.

Query: had the hair been chestnut and the eyes green when she came into the room? Would they be those colours if there wasn't anybody there to see them?

'Oh.' He must've come to the end of the speech, because she

was gazing at him, all guilty and sad. 'So what you're saying is, you're pretty much going to have to start all over again.'

Duncan nodded. 'Not quite as bad as that, but we'll have to submit a corrective account, and it's going to have a knock-on effect because of reassessing all the other property, not to mention the income-tax implications. There may also be penalty charges from the Revenue, if they don't believe it was an honest oversight. And then there's the problem of some of the new assets being located overseas—'

Now he knew what it was, the thing that was so wrong. He wondered how he could've been so stupid. 'Excuse me,' he said, cutting the foreign-domicile speech off in mid-flow, and made a show of looking at his watch. Then he frowned, took it off his wrist and shook it before dropping it in his pocket.

'Very sorry about all this,' he said. 'Can you possibly tell me the time? My stupid watch has stopped, and I've got these clients coming in at ten-fifteen.'

'Oh dear,' Felicity said, 'it's nearly that now.' He knew that, of course. ' Look, would it be all right if I came back to see you at half past nine tomorrow morning? I really would like to get this wretched mess sorted out, otherwise I'll be worrying myself to a frazzle about it.'

Duncan smiled warmly. 'That'll be fine,' he said. 'If you could bring the rest of the papers with you, that'd be a great help.'

As soon as he'd shooed her off the premises, Duncan scuttled back to his office, dropped into his chair like a dead weight, and lay back with his eyes shut for five uninterrupted minutes. Then, with a long sigh, he opened the file and pulled out the great fat bundle of correspondence.

He hadn't been able to smell her. That, of course, was what he'd noticed, but hadn't realised he'd noticed until the penny finally dropped right on top of his breeze-block-thick head. On the other hand, he'd taken a good long look at her reflection in the shiny stainless-steel back of his watch, so she wasn't one of *them* (shit; *he* was doing it now). In which case, what the hell was she? And why was she suddenly at risk of worrying herself to a frazzle over a transaction she'd cheerfully allowed to go to sleep for well over a year?

Most of all, though: why *now*?

There was some work to be done: post to be answered, the missing information he needed to finish off a couple of complex inheritance-tax returns, a few grossing-up calculations, a handful of apportionments of income . . . He tore through them like a wild boar in brushwood, not stopping to check his results (he knew they were perfect), devouring them like a starving man eating. When he'd finished he felt a great pang of regret, because now there was nothing to stop him turning his mind to the important, impenetrably bewildering shit that had showered down on him over the last forty-eight hours. Trying to remember how Luke had done it, he stuck his fingers in his mouth and whistled. The first two attempts sounded like a live duck in a blender. The fourth was exactly right, and a moment later the little bald man appeared with a tray. Duncan nodded, not looking up, and reached for the sugar bowl, which he emptied into the cup until it started to slop over.

Vampires exist; well, if werewolves are real, why not? If he'd heard it on the news, he'd have been able to get over it and put it away in the none-of-my-business folder, along with earthquakes in the Philippines. But he didn't have that luxury, because she was one, and she—

All right, fine. He admitted it. Duncan Hughes and the guy who starts off the Olympics: outstanding torch-carriers of our time. Needless to say, Luke had spotted it within minutes of meeting him again. Probably he'd been able to smell it, with that superbly sensitive nose of his. The question – the only question that actually mattered in the whole wide world, now he came to think of it – was the one he'd asked her. Had she dumped him because she'd joined Crosswoods, or because she didn't love him any more? He'd heard her answer and Luke's views on the matter. Presumably, one of them was right. A typical Ferris throwaway line: *or maybe the girl's still fond of you.* Oh, and by the way. The world's going to end in ten minutes, and you'll end up in heaven or hell. One or the other. Does it really matter which?

Bloody Ferris: self-centred as a drill, sensitive as tank armour, but what if he was right? If Sally still loved him, the world was a road that led somewhere. If she didn't, it was just the playground at Lycus Grove, ruled by the Ferris Gang, evolved superhuman hooligans. Simple as that.

He was grateful for the clarity, at any rate. There were side issues, of course. Just his bloody luck that there was a stupid feud between his lot and her lot. Romeo and Juliet: another of Luke's maddeningly perceptive asides (except that it went further and deeper than that; Romeo, proverbially, wasn't built in a day). And there was Luke's alternative explanation to consider: the mole theory. (Could you be a mole and a werewolf at the same time?) If there was any truth in that – actually, it wouldn't make a hell of a lot of difference. Political issues between the furry Montagues and the pointy-toothed Capulets didn't really interest him. All that mattered was the question, to which he kept coming back like a driver going round in circles in the fog; no matter how much distance he tried to put between himself and it, everywhere he looked, there it was.

Hopefully, he reached out for the counter-irritant. The curious behaviour of the gorgeous, completely unmemorable, odour-free Felicity Allshapes. Not a vampire, not a werewolf, definitely not human, and he couldn't get the fucking accounts to balance. Furthermore, he was going to have to redo the whole bloody thing practically from scratch, because of these new assets that had decloaked like Klingons in front of him. Well; he tried, but he couldn't muster up much in the way of interest for that, either. Clearly the Allshapes clan were some kind of weird non-human, but he was just their lawyer, peripherally involved and getting well paid for it. Didn't matter a toss what kind of life form they were – goblins, angels, leprechauns – so long as they approved the bills. Just work, that's all.

Most of all, though: why *now*?

He glanced at his watch; eleven-forty-five. In a little under eight hours, the full moon would shine (assuming it wasn't cloudy). Sally's lot used barrier cream to keep the sunlight off; would it work with moonlight as well? But he daren't even try it, for fear of Luke and the rest of the gang. They hadn't actually talked about it much, but he'd got the impression that That Time was far and away the biggest thing in their lives, the greatest pleasure, the thing they lived for. Not wanting to think about it, he'd sort of assumed he'd enjoy it too, while deliberately keeping it at the back of his mind, so he wouldn't dwell on it. *I don't want to turn into an animal, thank you very much*, he confessed to himself. So maybe it was like parties when he was a kid – *you'll enjoy it once you get there*, his mother had assured him, and that was how he'd come to learn the truth about lies. He hadn't enjoyed parties, in spite of his mother's solemn promises; but when he told her and said he didn't want to go to any more of them, she'd either not believed him or chosen to ignore him, as if that would somehow make her promise come true. The intriguing thing was that, up to a point, it had worked. He'd gone to more parties, hating them, persuading himself that he was having loads of fun. Maybe that was when he'd realised he had a career as an advocate; believe something enough and you make it true. Like religions. Or lawyers.

Or, he thought, I could slip out of the office right now on the pretext of buying socks, book a one-way flight to New Mexico and spend the rest of my days peacefully hunting javelinas through the sage-brush. He didn't know an awful lot about New Mexico, but he had an idea it was big and empty, and the locals were pretty relaxed about harmless eccentrics, so long as they paid their bills and didn't eat anybody who'd be likely to be missed. Yes, he had that option; and who knows, he might meet a nice girl out there, settle down, buy a house and a Toyota. He could do that, if it wasn't for the question.

Talking of the Americas: while Sally and Duncan had been married, he'd met an insufferably huge number of her relatives and heard all about a thousand or so others, none of whom had been an aunt living in Buenos Aires. He'd have remembered something like that.

He grunted, and clicked his mouse to print out the letters he'd written. Less than eight hours, and he wouldn't be even remotely human any more. A quotation floated into his mind – Dr Johnson, or one of those people: something to the effect that someone who makes a beast of himself gets rid of the pain of being a man.

Which would be fine, if it actually meant something. But quotations and aphorisms are generally just verbal Christmas presents; enticingly done up in pretty paper and ribbon, but once you get them open they generally turn out to be just socks.

I'd like to go home now, please.

Well, at least he'd had the courage to admit it to himself. The trouble was, of course, that as far as he knew it wasn't possible. Whether he liked it or not, he was stuck like it. Going back to being wimpish, feckless Duncan Hughes, assistant solicitor with Messrs Craven Ettin and general all-round loser, wasn't an option. It was like his eighth birthday, when he'd have given anything to be seven again.

The door opened, and Pete looked in. 'Come on,' he said.

'What?'

'Pub. We're waiting for you.'

'Oh.' Duncan closed his eyes. 'Actually,' he said, 'I really don't feel like—'

But Pete had gone, leaving the door ajar. More compulsory fun. As he dragged himself to his feet, Duncan felt the weight of the ludicrous irony of it all. One quick nip in the side of his neck had given him everything he needed to be *free* – extraordinary senses, freedom from fear of injury and sickness, mental abilities that could make him rich, secure, independent; but it had also bound him to the pack, so that his life for the foreseeable future consisted of silent group lunchtime drinking that didn't even get him drunk, of evenings spent chasing animals through alleys, over garden fences and dustbins, followed by a few hours of sleep, followed by the same again, endlessly repeated. At some point, he remembered, Luke had called it evolution, and he'd been partly right. He'd evolved into a superior form of life, better than a human. At the same time, he'd regressed to being an adolescent, and tonight he'd slip back one stage further and turn into an animal. He was playing on a board on which the ladders were the snakes and the snakes were the ladders (let's consolidate: not snakes and ladders, just adders); where every step forward was also a step back, and the good stuff and the bad stuff were all the same. And come sunset, it was all going to get just a bit more serious. Something to look forward to.

Lunchtime drinking: twelve pints of strong beer, no effect whatsoever, and he didn't even have to pay for the drinks. The Ferris Gang was even more taciturn than usual, and Duncan had an idea that they were staring at him when he wasn't looking, as though they suspected him of having done something, or being about to do something. But he wasn't quick enough to catch them at it, or else they weren't doing it and he was imagining the whole thing.

'Busy afternoon?' Luke was talking to him.

'What, me? No.'

'Clients coming in?'

He shook his head.

'Just as well.' Luke nodded, as if he'd decided not to press charges. 'Your first time, you'll want to take it easy, save your strength. It can be a bit intense.'

Oh, wonderful. 'What do you mean, "intense"?'

Luke shrugged. 'Don't worry about it, you'll be fine. Put your feet up. Take a nap, if you can. Oh, and it's probably best if you don't eat anything.'

'Right.'

'Don't worry, it's not important, just— That's not your best suit, is it?'

'What? No, it isn't.'

'Good. Shoes?'

'Huh?'

'What've you got on your feet? Let me see.'

Very unwillingly, Duncan lifted his left foot off the floor and rested it on the edge of the table. Pete frowned; Micky made a sort of tutting noise.

'Laces,' Luke said. 'Not a good idea. Slip-ons are better, something with elastic in the sides. You might want to nip out at some point this afternoon, Kevin'll go with you. Where's there a shoe shop around here?'

'John Lewis,' Micky grunted. 'Or isn't there a sort of sports place in Ludgershall Square?'

'Better off going to Oxford Street,' Clive said. 'Oh, and what about curare?'

Luke shook his head. 'Won't need that.'

'Just to be on the safe side?'

'Hang on,' Duncan interrupted. 'What the hell is curare?'

They looked at him, as though they'd forgotten he was there. 'Muscle relaxant,' Luke said. 'But you won't need it. That whole approach went out years ago, along with aconite and the Lord's prayer written out backwards.' He smiled. 'Don't worry,' he said. 'You'll be fine.'

Back in his office, Duncan did a Google search for curare; also aconite, and the Lord's prayer written backwards. Then he tottered as far as the men's toilet and threw up.

Not that he was scared about the physical implications; even though curare turned out to be a medicine to control lethally violent muscle spasms, and aconite was a poison derived from the wolfsbane plant (go figure), and as for the Lord's prayer written out backwards . . . But what the heck: if the Ferris Gang went through this shit once a month and survived, it couldn't be too big a deal, purely in terms of bodily pain and suffering. Probably no worse than toothache, or breaking your leg (which he'd never done; never had bad toothache, either). All right, so what if it hurt like hell? That really wasn't what was eating his mind. But the thought of changing, turning into an animal—

'Duncan?'

Kevin was gazing thoughtfully at him from the doorway. Of

course, the partners of Ferris & Loop never ever knocked before entering someone else's room. As far as they were concerned, the word 'private' meant a foot soldier.

'You ready?'

'Sorry?'

'Are you ready? Shoes, remember?'

By and large, on balance, he'd always quite liked Kevin, in much the same way as people like big clumsy pieces of furniture. He was inoffensive, sometimes he came in handy, and when he wasn't needed for anything he just stood there. Occasionally you felt an almost overwhelming urge to dust him, but that was all right. He probably wouldn't mind.

'Shoes,' Duncan repeated. 'Oh, right, yes. Did he really mean all that?'

Kevin frowned slightly. 'I guess so. Or he wouldn't have said it, would he?'

On the other hand, Kevin was big. He'd been six feet tall at fourteen, and by the time he'd stopped growing he'd become a definite menace to door frames, lampshades and low-flying aircraft. He'd been co-opted into the Ferris Gang because, from time to time, when diplomacy or personality failed, Luke had needed to have somebody thumped. Kevin was good at thumping, although he'd always done it in a rather dreamy, absent-minded way, like someone not quite awake swatting at a fly. That, presumably, had something to do with why he'd been appointed as Duncan's escort. A gentle, six-foot-eight hint.

'Fine,' Duncan said, standing up. 'Timothy White's, was it?'

'John Lewis, Micky said. Or we could try Oxford Street. Up to you, really.'

So they went to John Lewis, and Duncan bought a pair of light tan slip-ons and (he wasn't quite sure why) a change of underwear. On the way back, he decided to ask:

'Kev,' he said. 'What's it like?'

'What's what like?'

'You know. Changing. What we're going to do this evening.'

'Oh, that.' Kevin frowned and was silent for ten seconds. 'It's hard to describe, actually. I don't know, it's not like anything, really.'

Well, he *was* talking to Kevin. 'Does it hurt?'

'Nah.'

Duncan nodded. 'Does it feel – well, funny? Strange?'

'Mm, a bit.' Another long, grave silence. 'I suppose it's a little bit like getting into clothes that're way too small for you, only the other way round. Or you know when you're driving and you go over one of those humpbacked bridges too fast? You don't actually feel anything, mind.' Kevin paused, bit his lip, actually looked over his shoulder before whispering, 'Don't tell Luke, but I've got a cousin who's a chemist.'

'Your secret is safe with me.'

'He gets me these super-strong sleeping tablets,' Kevin went on, as if Duncan hadn't spoken. 'You're only meant to have one at a time, but I take three, round about teatime. Then, when I wake up, it's happened.'

'Ah.'

'Micky says he enjoys it,' Kevin said. 'Pete's got an old leather belt he bites into. I think Clive does some sort of yoga thing. You know, like those blokes in India who walk on red-hot coal.'

'I see. What about Luke?'

Kevin shrugged. 'He's never mentioned it.'

'Figures.'

'Sorry?'

'Nothing.' Not making the most of a rare opportunity. 'So,' Duncan pressed on, 'what exactly happens, then? From the beginning. I mean, do you start sprouting hair all over your face, or what?'

Something had gone wrong. Kevin didn't answer, and this time it wasn't because he was thinking. It proved to be the end of the conversation, and they shared the taxi back to the office in cold, dead silence.

Back in his room, Duncan tried the shoes on again. Kevin had insisted that he get a pair that was two sizes too big for him; the girl in the shop had tried to point this out, until Kevin had looked at her. After that, she mumbled once or twice but that was all. Duncan walked round the room in them a couple of times, feeling like Charlie Chaplin, then flopped into his super-comfy chair and leaned his head back as far as it would go.

Have a nap, Luke had said. Yeah, right. With his head buzzing the way it was, even a heaped handful of Kev's cousin's zonk pills wouldn't do any good at—

She was looking down at him, which suggested he was lying on the floor or something. She was just as stunning as he remembered, except that he couldn't quite focus on her. Also, the lid was in the way.

'It's how he'd have wanted to go,' she was saying, to someone he couldn't see. 'Running, hot on the scent. It's the only time they really feel alive.'

'Ironic.' A man's voice. 'He wouldn't have felt anything, would he?'

'A bit,' she replied. 'Not a terrible lot. His heart just stopped.'

'Ah. Cholesterol. Too many choccy biccies.'

She shrugged. 'Anyway,' she said, 'he's ours now.' She unfolded a sheet of paper. He couldn't see any of the writing on it, but he recognised it as the CV he'd sent in when he applied for the job with Craven Ettins. 'A bit out of date,' she said, 'but it doesn't matter. He never did anything during the last five years.'

'Let's see.' She moved the paper out of his field of view. 'Oh dear. Not much here, is there?'

'Oh, I don't know. Seven GCSEs. Three A-levels. Clean driving licence.'

Offstage tongue click. 'Yes, but they died with him, didn't they? What does it say under *other interests*?'

'Nothing.'

'Sports and hobbies?'

'Nope.'

'Well, fine. So all he's good for is basic non-skilled, then.'

'General clerical?'

'That's even worse. We've got 'em stacked up six deep in the stockroom, you can't hardly walk about in there.' Sigh. 'How come we never get a wheelwright? Or a silversmith? There's a worthwhile vocation, we could use all the silversmiths we can lay our hands on.'

She frowned. 'Maybe he's got hidden talents.'

'Balls,' sneered the unseen voice, 'he's a lawyer. Bloody professionals, all they do is take up space.' He laughed, whoever he was. 'And this one can't even add up.'

Apparently, that was a joke, because she laughed. 'Oh well,' she said. 'Waste not, want not. And you've got to say one thing for werewolves, they're always in pretty good shape.'

The man he couldn't see lifted off the lid, and she leaned forward. She was holding something; a bit like a croupier's rake, except that it was made of chunky steel and glowing red hot. There were letters embossed on the side of the blade facing him; letters the wrong way round, like mirror writing—

BA
Made in England

The glowing metal came closer and closer, until he could feel the heat—

Someone was shaking him. Duncan opened his eyes, and saw Pete, staring down at him with a strange blend of concern and fury in his eyes. 'For fuck's sake,' Pete said, and Duncan noticed something sticking out of his jacket pocket: the end of an old leather belt, much chewed.

'Sorry,' Duncan mumbled. 'Did I doze off?'

'You could say that,' Pete grunted. 'For a moment there I thought you were dead, till you snored. You idiot,' he added, 'do you know what time it is?'

Over Pete's shoulder, through the window, it was dark except for the orange haze of street lamps. 'Oh,' Duncan said. 'That time.'

'Yes. You ready?'

'As I'll ever be.'

'You'll need to drink this.' Pete was holding out a test tube, filled with clear blue liquid.

'Will I?'

Pete nodded. 'Medicine,' he said. 'Stops you turning back into a human every time you step out of the moonlight. Good for twelve hours, then you need to have some more. Don't ask me what's in it, and it tastes like shit.'

Pete was wrong there. Much worse. 'Finished?'

'Mm.'

'Then get your arse up out of that chair. Luke's waiting for you in reception.'

'Pete.'

'What?'

'I don't want to.'

For a tiny fraction of a second, a unit of time that only specialised equipment could have registered, the look in Pete's eyes seemed to say *me neither*. But it passed. 'Don't be such a fucking wimp, Duncan,' Pete snapped. 'What you want or don't want—'

'If I stayed indoors, with the blinds drawn, it wouldn't happen, would it? I could just stay here, I wouldn't be letting anybody down or anything like that. The rest of you don't need me, you got on perfectly all right before I joined. I'll just be in the way.'

Pete shook his head. 'It isn't like that, Duncan mate,' he said. 'Look, you've got a good life. A bloody good life. Great job, loads of dosh, no stress, hardly a crippling workload, and you're with your mates all day. Be reasonable. Is one night every month really so much to ask? Besides,' he added, momentarily breaking eye contact, 'it's a good laugh. You'll enjoy it once you're there.'

Duncan glanced down at the belt-end. It was strong leather, a full quarter-inch thick, but in a couple of places it had been bitten right through. Kevin had said it didn't hurt, and unless he was in court or drawing up a bill, Kevin rarely made the effort to lie. But he got those tablets from his cousin, even though it was completely painless. Of course, there's more than one kind of pain.

'You've got to,' Pete said.

New Mexico, Duncan thought; I haven't got to do anything I don't want to. That's the whole point of being one of them. One of us.

'I'm scared,' he said.

Pete closed his eyes for a moment. ''Course you are,' he said, 'you're not a complete moron. But it's OK. You'll come through it all right, I promise you.'

Pete, who'd wanted to be a teacher. 'Fine,' Duncan said, and the strength leaked out of him. 'Sorry. I didn't mean to—'

'Whatever.' Pete glanced down at his watch. 'Shit, look at the bloody time. Come on, move.'

Out of his nice, safe office into the corridor, through fire doors, round corners, into reception. They were all there, dead silent, not looking at each other. Kevin was flopped in the chair behind the front desk, his head forward in his lap. Fast asleep. *Don't tell Luke*, he'd demanded, but Luke wasn't stupid, he must've realised long ago. It hadn't occurred to Duncan that he'd have to undergo this terrible experience in front of other people – not just other people, in front of *them*, his oldest and closest friends, who could be relied on to pick up on the slightest nuance of weakness in his conduct and hold it against him for ever. He tried to comfort himself with Kev's tablets, Pete's chewed-up belt, Clive's transcendental meditation or whatever it was, but it was no good. He was going to make a bog of it, he knew it, and they'd be watching him like hawks. They might make allowances, feel sympathy, forgive him, but they'd never, ever forget—

The backs of his hands were tickling. He glanced down, expecting to find them covered in hair, like welcome mats, but there was nothing unusual he could see. Crazy expression, to know something like the back of your hand. He'd never really given them much thought, certainly never taken the time and trouble to memorise them to the point where he'd know at a glance if something about them had changed. They were just hand-backs, as far as he was concerned. There were a couple of small scars that he could call to mind, but that was it. If he ever needed to claim them from the lost-property office, he'd have a devil of a job describing them convincingly.

'Fuck,' Pete said. He said it as though answering a tedious but entirely legitimate question. Duncan looked at him, and saw that he was standing perfectly still, apart from his left hand, which was feverishly trying to tease the leather belt out of his jacket pocket. It was hard to see what could possibly be difficult about it, but Pete was fighting a losing battle. So, it must be about to begin—

Except, they were indoors. No moonlight. Surely—

'Ready?' Luke, sounding maddeningly calm. Nobody replied, and he leaned forward and stabbed at something with his index finger: pressing a button on a console, presumably. There was a whirring noise, which seemed to be coming from the ceiling. Duncan looked round for its source, and saw a flat panel slowly opening a few inches from the electric-light rose. It struck Duncan as a bit too James Bond to be true, but Luke was pressing another button. Then the lights went out.

But it wasn't dark. A silver beam, like a searchlight, shone down through the open hatch, and Luke stepped into it.

Looking back on that moment, Duncan was prepared to admit that his expectations had been coloured somewhat by the movies. He was anticipating a state-of-the-art special effect, a morphing sequence that would've set George Lucas back a year's wages, even at cost. It wasn't like that. A human silhouette stepped into the beam, but the pale silver light illuminated a wolf; a wolf on its hind legs, as if it had just tried to catch a bird in flight, or was trying to get its nose into a particularly tall wheelie bin. It stayed like that for a moment with a puzzled look on its face, as if trying to figure out what it was doing standing on its back legs. Then it dropped to all fours, swished its tail and walked – swaggered – out of the beam into the shadows.

Shit, Duncan thought, there's a fucking *wolf* loose in the room. But then he found the new scent. One less human in the room, but we've been joined by one of us.

Pete and Micky had grabbed the arms of Kevin's chair. They lugged it under the beam and jumped clear, and suddenly there was a wolf in the chair, curled up with its nose buried in its tail. It lifted its head, sniffed and jumped down. Two wolves.

Micky went next. He stepped forward impatiently: *my go now.* His tail was wagging as he left the silver circle. Pete left the beam with the belt still in his mouth. Clive got as far as *om mane pad*—, but his wolf trotted out with its tongue lolling.

My go now.

He was very acutely aware of five wolves, grouped around him in the shadows. The scent was fine: strong, friendly, reassuring, *normal*, like coming home after a trip abroad. But the five restless shapes communicated a rather different message. There's a human in this room with us, they seemed to be telling him, and our self-control isn't perfect.

I don't want to do this, Duncan thought. On the other hand—

A small step for a man, a giant leap for inhumanity. As soon as his right foot breached the circle, he felt the light more intensely than he'd ever felt anything before. It didn't hurt. On the contrary, it was *wonderful*. It was the most amazing thing ever, it was so much better than being human, it was—

As he completed the stride and the light fell on him, Duncan suddenly realised exactly what it was that Pete and Kevin and Clive were so afraid of. Not the pain. The pleasure.

CHAPTER EIGHT

The biggest wolf lifted its head and howled.

There were no words in the sound. Thinking about it later, Duncan decided that it was wordless in the same way that there aren't any bits in clear soup. All the words had been mashed up in a blender until they were puréed, the solid lumps reduced to a flow of tiny particles of meaning. It was language improved, evolved into what language ought to be: pure communication without ambiguity or approximation. What it said was, *Right, let's be having you.*

It had been dark, with the lights off; but now it was as bright as day. Duncan noticed that his senses had somehow run into each other, and he realised that that was how it should be, of course. Poor bloody humans have senses that know their place; you see sights, hear sounds, smell scents and so on. Demarcation, like the unions back in the 1970s. He wondered how on earth humans coped. He had just one sense – one-stop perception – and it was so much better.

So. Luke's voice, in his mind. *What do you think of it so far?*

Duncan looked at them. They were five grey-and-black wolves, thick-furred, red-eyed, their tongues hanging out, but they were also Luke, Micky, Pete, Clive and Kevin, looking exactly like they always did; every nuance of profile and proportion exactly the same – Luke's strong chin and exaggerated nose, Pete's heavy jowls, Micky's small, sharp eyes, Kev's rather unfortunate ears, Clive's weak forehead and tree-trunk neck. *There's a mirror on the far wall,* Micky's voice said, and Duncan started to move towards it, then stopped.

'Can you read my mind?' He intended to say the words, but no sound came out.

Yes.

He found the mirror. In it— He froze, bewildered. Shouldn't he have turned into a wolf, like the others? The reflection didn't seem to be any different: it was just him, same as usual. Or rather, he looked like a big vicious dog, with a hairy snout and a button nose and two pointy ears lying flat against the side of his head, and will you check out those fucking *teeth* – but anybody would know it was Duncan Hughes, entirely the same as always, nothing important changed. That's me, he thought; that's how I've always been, except until now, for some unaccountable reason, I've chosen to dress up as a monkey derivative. Bloody silly thing to do, because it didn't suit me. This is much better. So much more *me*—

The urge was irresistible; he threw his head back until he was staring at the silver square in the ceiling (his head went so much further back on this neck) and howled.

He wasn't entirely sure what he was trying to say, because he'd never had the capability to express anything so complex before. It was his whole life, basically, compressed into one loud stream of sound; in particular, it was everything that had been wrong with his life, all its frustrations and disappointments, shortcomings, failures, missed and denied opportunities, and of course the special, miserable and bitterly, bitterly unfair pain of being *him* rather than somebody else, all blended and sieved into a compressed burst of noise. It was also the wild delight of being free of all that, but still himself. It was being very pleased indeed, for the very first time ever, that he was who he was: the one and only Duncan Maurice Hughes, werewolf-at-law, proud partner in the Ferris Gang, the best bunch of werewolves on the whole frigging planet. It was *yetch* and *yes* at the same time, and terribly, delightfully loud.

You're pleased, then. Luke was grinning at him, and Duncan felt his tail wag like a rotor blade. (Talking of which, how the hell had he managed all those years without one? It was amazing, you could say so much with it, just think what Shakespeare could've achieved if only he'd had a tail.) *That's all right, then. Come on, we're wasting time.*

Which was when the sadness hit him; because, of course, this ecstasy was only temporary, brief as moonlight, once a month when the moon was full and the sky wasn't overcast. He heard himself whimper, and the others laughed at him inside his head. He growled, which made them laugh even more. Then Luke jumped up against the wall and pressed the lift button with his front paw, and Duncan understood how unbearable it was to be cooped up inside a building on a night like this. The lift doors sighed open and the pack shuffled inside, demure as a junior-school outing. He took careful note of the order of precedence: Luke first, naturally; surprisingly, Pete next, ahead of Micky; then Clive, Kevin and finally himself. The doors closed. It was rather a tight fit for six wolves; he felt warm fur and hard muscle pressing against him, bodies that weren't his own but weren't foreign, either. Very faintly, he could hear a mind mumbling *om mane padme om*, but not with any real conviction.

The entrance hall was deserted, and the tall glass street doors were slightly ajar. Outside, the glow of street lights mixed uncomfortably with the moonshine, like orange juice in milk. Luke stopped to sniff; there were human scents, but tolerably far away. There's never anyone much around in the City after going-home time. Even so—

Don't worry about it, a voice told him; Pete's, at a guess, although he wasn't quite sure. Only Luke's voice in his head was completely unmistakable; the others, he realised, sounded a bit too much like his own voice to be instantly recognisable.

They were out on the street now, running briskly along the

pavement, close in to the buildings, where there was a decent bit of shadow. Of course, he could see perfectly in this light, and what he couldn't see he could smell. It was as though he was replaying in his mind CCTV footage of everybody and everything that had passed that way since it rained last, on a huge bank of monitors that allowed him to watch every minute of every day simultaneously. Every detail, apart from a few trivial things that only the eye could record, was sharp: age, sex, height, weight, diet, lifestyle, everything you really needed to know about people, as opposed to their mere appearance. He'd read somewhere about some scientific tests that proved that the difference between beauty and ugliness was generally no more than twenty-five thousandths of an inch, the breadth of a propelling-pencil lead. Move the eyes that much closer together, or widen the mouth, or exaggerate the uplift of the nosetip, and drop-dead gorgeous turns into water-buffalo's-arse ugly; as total and decisive a change as, say, that between man and wolf. Smells don't deceive the way looks do. They aren't susceptible to subtle advocacy, the manipulative persuasion of the deceitful lawyers of the mind that make us want to like pretty people and hate ugly ones.

Luke had stopped, for no apparent reason. He lowered his head and snapped at something on the ground. It proved to be the inset handle of a manhole cover. He got his teeth hooked round it and began to pull, his back arched, feet thrusting at the ground for leverage. The cover lifted, then rolled back as he released it and it fell with a clang. Luke looked up, scanned the area for potential threats and witnesses, and jumped down into the hole.

That's dangerous, Duncan thought; I can't jump that far, I'll hurt – *No, you won't.* The answer was entirely satisfactory and when his turn came he jumped into the dark hole without a moment's hesitation.

He landed hard and skidded a few inches, thinking *piece of cake*. Then he followed the others. It was darker, sure, but there was still plenty of light. The overwhelming strength and richness of the smells was rather disconcerting; a bit like an art gallery with the pictures hung much too close together. The sheer complexity of the tones of decay made him long to stop and drink them in, tracing each one, like unravelling a huge tangle. *Don't dawdle.* He quickened his pace to a smart trot, following the tail in front until the pack broke into a wonderful, exhilarating run. He'd have been quite happy if it had lasted for ever, and of course his sense of time had changed along with everything else – no more seconds, minutes or hours, just blissfully elastic moments that contained as much as you cared to cram into them. You could live the rest of your life in the glory of one second breathing in a new scent; it could expand to crowd out the hour of standing motionless that followed, or squash down into nothing to make way for the next scent or sight or sound. He needn't have worried after all. This night could be the whole of his life, if he wanted it to.

After a while Luke stopped, sniffed, jumped up suddenly and braced his front legs against a spot on the roof. It gave way, and orange light flooded into the tunnel. Luke sprang up into the light and vanished; the others followed. This time, Duncan didn't even bother to think *I can't jump that high* as he peered up at the lip of the manhole. If the others could do it, so could he. He jumped, only just made it, scrabbled with his paws until he'd got his balance, and looked round.

It could have been a park: too big for a city garden, and they hadn't run for long enough to get out into open country. The grass he stood on was politely short, and the trees carefully arranged, like decorations on a cake. He saw Luke throw back his head and howl. For ten seconds or so the sound filled the world; then a short tense silence, followed by a distant echo – no, very slightly different. A reply. And, since there aren't any natural wolves in Britain any more, that could only mean another pack of Us, a long way away. He remembered what Luke had said, about territories and boundaries, some other gang whose turf covered Kew, or was it Sutton? Hearing them, however, was rather different to hearing *about* them. It was as though he was the first man on Mars, and someone had stopped him as he vaulted from his landing module and asked to see his passport.

Just letting them know we're here. A vague intonation he couldn't quite isolate told him the voice in his head was Pete's. He understood. The two packs bore each other no ill will, but if they happened to meet, they'd have no choice but to fight it out until one or the other was annihilated. Perfectly reasonable, like China getting stressy if the USA violated its airspace. You can understand most things, even nuclear war, when you're a wolf.

Luke was sniffing again. He was the nose of the pack, sniffing on behalf of all of them. He turned his head and the other five heads moved with his; Duncan felt his tail bristle, and although he didn't know why, he understood that he didn't need to, so long as Luke did. It briefly crossed his mind that at some point in the recent past he'd contemplated rebellion – leaving the pack, going to New Mexico or somewhere equally improbable. He could have been angry with himself if his understanding wasn't so perfect. Silly human. Clueless.

Luke had started to run and, as he followed, Duncan caught the scent. At once it filled him, as though he was an engine filled with petrol. With a scent to follow, he was alive.

Fox; splendid. But it didn't last. He'd barely warmed up his lungs when Luke stopped, jumped up on his hind legs, twirled round in a circle, dropped down to all fours and growled horribly. Duncan realised they were standing on a tarmac road; Luke was dancing round the body of something, and the scents told the story. Some idiot car-driver had run their fox over, and it was lying on the kerb, all flat and useless, like a burst balloon. Stupid, pointless waste; the frustration was almost more than he could bear, for about five seconds. Then Luke started running again, and he'd forgotten all about it.

Cat. Cat? Thought we didn't do cats. *Yes, but time's getting on, can't be all night looking, must chase something. The pursuit of happiness, remember?* That made sense. Besides, there had to be some justification for cats, or else a person could lose faith in the universe.

It was a big, fat, black moggy, and Duncan heard it clearly: *badbadbadbad*, its funny little brain broadcast as it scampered away from them. Luke stretched his back and shoulders into an impossibly long stride, his nose almost brushing the cat's absurdly fluffy tail; but then the cat jumped, landed on the side of a tree and ran straight up it. The pack stopped, slamming into thin air as if hitting a wall. There was the cat, simply reeking of delicious fear, but it was eight feet off the ground. Pete was trying to climb the tree, jumping with his back legs, scrabbling with his front paws, his jaws snapping like castanets. Micky was running round the tree in a tight circle, as if he couldn't believe the chase was over. Duncan could hear the cat mewing, *Nyanyanyanya*, and caught himself leaping at it like a dolphin. For a split second he hung in the air, just long enough to close his jaws on a patch of air no more than six inches from the fucking cat's fucking tail— He landed on all fours and tensed his legs to jump again, so full of anger that he believed for a moment that it would float him off the stupid, gravity-ridden ground.

Leave it, Luke commanded. It was as though a valve had opened. Duncan felt his ears go back and his tail wag. *Good effort, though.* That made him glow; praise from the pack leader, like having his tummy rubbed, pure joy. He let out a short, sharp bark, like a stick breaking. Something Jenny Sidmouth had said once came back to him, hard and fast as a returning lunar module: *it's only when you start thinking as a part of the team that you can really call yourself a lawyer.*

The cat was still taunting them, but it didn't matter now. He understood; by climbing a tree, cheating, the cat had admitted its basic and incorrigible inferiority. Besides, they didn't do cats. Wouldn't dirty our teeth on a cat. They climb trees, after all. Might just as well chase squirrels.

Then Luke howled again. There was a slight but all-important difference about this howl: not command, not authority, but a deep, unquenchable longing for something that could never be attained. Duncan didn't need to sniff. This wasn't a scent you had to hunt out of the air. It was itself a predator.

Leave it, Luke ordered, and Duncan thought, quite right. Hadn't he had one lucky escape already, the night of his first run with the Ferris Gang, when he'd actually seen it on the railway lines? The scent flooded all his senses, and he could see it perfectly, as though it was there in front of him: the white unicorn, with silver hooves and a golden horn. He understood without even having to think. Chasing the unicorn while in human form was stupid and dangerous, but chasing it as a wolf would undoubtedly be fatal. A human being would probably pass out and fall over, just this side of terminal exhaustion; a wolf would keep going until his heart stopped and his brain burst.

Do you know why there're no wolves in Britain any more? Luke was talking, just to him. *They'll tell you it was humans, hunting them to extinction. Bollocks. The truth is, they ran themselves to death, following Her. That's what happened to—* Pause; the data stream broke up for a moment. *Well, anyway. Just leave it, all right?*

He could feel the pain in Luke's mind, of course. Everything he'd ever wanted, everything he would ever want, lay at the end of that scent trail. Duncan understood, and a terrible desire to catch the unicorn for him ripped into him like claws. Luke couldn't go, because the pack needed him; if he ran himself to death they'd be leaderless, a living body with a dead brain. But they could spare me, Duncan thought; they managed all right without me before, and if I could catch her—

No. Leave it. Heel. Bugger this for a game of soldiers, let's go on up the bypass and chase lorries.

For a few seconds, Duncan understood. The unicorn was out of bounds. Chasing lorries was almost as good, since they'd have a bloody good run and scare some stupid human shitless without the embarrassment and consequences of a genuine kill.

It was a neatly crafted human-wolf compromise, very middle-way and Liberal Democrat, and it was what they always did under the circumstances, even though it wasn't what any of them really wanted—

In which case, Duncan thought, why do it?

The pack stopped dead in its tracks. Someone growled, almost certainly Micky; whereas from Pete he felt a great and focused sadness, like that you'd experienced on being shown the draft of your own obituary for your approval.

Sorry, Duncan thought; he was thinking aloud, of course, because he had no choice. It was frightening, but liberating as well. Sorry, Luke, but actually that thought came from you. I was just agreeing with you, that's all.

Well, don't.

But you're right. Why the hell should we have to go chasing stupid lorries, when She's out there? So, maybe we'll all die, so what? Where's the point in staying alive if we can't chase the stuff that's worth chasing? I wouldn't have dared (he added quickly, as the pack started to growl), only it's what you were thinking. Wasn't it?

Silence; not just outside, but in his head, too. It went on so long that Duncan was scared he'd gone deaf, physically and (immeasurably worse) mentally. Then Luke said: *How did you know that?*

Duncan knew that the others couldn't hear them. They were standing perfectly still, ears pricked up, tails motionless, alert and deeply disturbed. They hated him, of course.

I heard you, he replied.

You weren't supposed to.

Oh. Sorry.

Luke was staring at him. *You shouldn't be able to.*

Really? I didn't mean to, honest. I mean, I can't help hearing what I hear. It's not like I did it on purpose.

Are you challenging me?

Effete urban westerners in the twenty-first century don't really know what fear means. They think they get scared when they nearly drive into a parked car, or come within an inch of being flattened by a breeze-block falling off a scaffolding tower. They think a sudden sharp twist in the guts and not being able to breathe for ten seconds or so is fear; which is like looking at a forty-watt bulb and telling yourself you're staring directly at the sun.

No, of course not, you *know* I'm not. Come on, Luke, you can read my mind, you'd know if I was—

Maybe. But maybe I would and you wouldn't.

Luke was coming towards him. His ears were back and his tail was down; his jaws were open. As he approached, Duncan remembered a long-forgotten RE lesson at school, when they'd been taught about how Lucifer and the fallen angels rebelled against God. At the time he remembered he'd thought, how stupid can you get? What part of *omnipotent* didn't they understand? And what utter plonkers they must have felt, when they realised what they'd done.

So. Luke was so close he could feel the heat of his breath. *You're not challenging me, then.*

No, really. Really really.

(He was sitting in something wet. Three guesses.)

That's all right, then.

Four more seconds of concentrated staring; then Luke broke eye contact and walked away. It was wonderful to be alive, Duncan realised; and the thought that he'd have been prepared to risk this amazing thing called life just to chase some stupid horse with a spike on its nose seemed so ludicrous that he couldn't understand it. But it hadn't just been fear of death. What had scared him was fear of—

Sin? The ultimate crime, rebellion against the alpha; worse than death. Worse, like murder's worse than parking on a double yellow. To think that he'd apparently come within an ace of the biggest Thou-shalt-not of all; he was shaking all over, and the cold was unbearable.

But you did think it. Really you did.

I know. Just . . . Don't keep on about it, all right?

Duncan stopped trembling. The others were still looking at him, but they didn't hate him any more. In fact, as far as they were concerned, something may or may not have happened, but if it had, they'd forgotten all about it. *Why are we all standing about here like prunes?* Kevin asked. *Let's go and chase lorries, like Luke said.*

So they trotted down the road until they came to the bypass. As luck would have it, there was no traffic to be seen, but the rumble of approaching wheels hummed up through the tarmac. Micky lifted his head, suddenly tense. The others did the same, all except Luke; he was rubbing behind his ear with a freshly licked paw.

All right, yes, it's pointless. But at least it's running. You want to go back to the office and chase a rubber ball round the closed file store till daybreak?

Not a lot in it, Duncan thought. And the same goes for chasing cats. Or foxes, for that matter. You know that better than I do. You were the one who put it into my mind.

Did I? I wouldn't know.

Having a lie inside his mind was like trying to swallow a fir cone. You did, you know you did.

Maybe. But if I'd known you could hear me, maybe I'd have kept my head shut.

Headlights. Kevin barked; Clive was making that yappy, whimpering noise that Duncan's Aunt Chrissy's red setter used to make when it was begging at table. This is silly, Duncan thought, grown men getting frantic at the prospect of running behind a petrol tanker. And so what if you can all hear me, I don't care.

They can't. I can. Now shut up.

Mind you, he thought, as the tanker blasted by in a roaring haze of light, noise and stench, for an inanimate object it does have a certain crude allure. Like, it's big, and—

The others were off; Luke in front, not just because he was the leader, mostly because he was the strongest and the quickest. Kevin pulled easily ahead of Pete and Micky, but he couldn't catch Luke – he wanted to, more than anything in the world; the ambition streamed out of him, like oil from a Norton, but he didn't have the muscle, or the will. Micky next, with the tip of Pete's snout at his front shoulder – issues between those two, Duncan realised: they keep them down all the rest of the time, but tonight they can't quite manage it – then Clive, resigned to bringing up the rear. Then—

Then nobody. It was only when Duncan saw the white of Clive's tail vanishing into the dark that he noticed that he himself hadn't moved. For a moment he was stunned. What had got into him? Why was he sitting there, when the chase was on and the pack was committed? The answer was simple. He hadn't felt the tug, like a hook in a fish's lip. Lorries didn't cut it for him after all. There was no passion, no desperate need to catch and reduce into possession. If he wanted a lorry, he realised, he'd go to a Volvo dealer and buy one.

Something occurred to him and he froze. He couldn't hear the others' thoughts. Maybe they'd already run out of range, or perhaps it was his blatant act of defiance. Whatever it was, it had cut him off from the pack. He was alone.

Instinct prepared a wave of terror to flood his mind, but it refused to break. Free will, he thought, and his jowls contorted into a grin. Free will: not a concept a lawyer could ever come to terms with. Lawyers are pack animals too; unless followed by the words *with every house purchase*, the phrase has no meaning for them. It's a contradiction in terms, like the pursuit of what's-its-name, thingy. The prosecution of happiness, now; that was perfectly reasonable. But to chase something you could never hope to catch—

Like a lorry. Or, come to that, a unicorn.

Even as Duncan's mind selected the word, the scent hit him. It was close, fresh; it was *coming towards him*. He froze. Something told him he wasn't the only predator out hunting on the bypass that night. Or, come to that, the most dangerous.

He looked up, and she was there. Light from a distant dot-matrix sign shimmered on her white coat, her silver hooves, the ludicrous and impossible horn in the middle of her forehead. She was standing perfectly still, looking at him with huge eyes, big, round and as red as blood.

He closed his own eyes, but it made no difference. Her scent, the sound of her rapid breathing, the feel of her pulse, practically pounding up through the asphalt into the soles of his feet. The only sense lacking was taste – her blood, in his mouth, on his tongue, the most delicious thing. Desperately he tried to hear her mind; he found it, but it was locked. He knew that if she moved, so much as a shiver, he'd be lost. Please, he begged her, please don't run. Just stay exactly where you are until dawn, when I can get out of this stupid dog and back into me—

Her spring was perfect, a miracle of fluid grace. Her pace, as she collected it, was unbearably beautiful. He felt the hook, not in his lip but his heart. He had no choice at all.

If I survive this, I'm going to be in so much trouble. He wasn't running; he was reaching out to her with his front legs, each stride a desperate appeal, like a drowning man grabbing for a rope just out of reach. He could feel each bound like a kick in the ribs as his feet thudded on the hard road, sending a jarring shock up his tendons. She seemed to float, her hooves' contact with the ground so brief that it was nearly impossible to see. She ran the way a hummingbird flies, and with no perceptible sign of effort.

After three hundred yards she left the road and set off across some open ground, a common or something of the kind: grass underfoot, no trees, a kind of silver desert. He'd studied maps, he should have been able to figure out where this patch of open land was, the direction they were headed in, the tactical considerations – likely obstacles (roads, canals, built-up areas) that could be a hindrance or a possible source of advantage. Or maybe he didn't know the area at all; maybe what he'd thought was his own knowledge was just a data feed from the pack, without which he might as well be in the Sahara. Scents were no help either, because her smell drowned them all. No; cleverness wasn't going to help him, it'd all be decided by sheer speed of foot, and he knew just by watching her that she was holding back, running just fast enough to keep a healthy distance and still force him to follow. He thought about Luke's assertion that she was the reason why Britain's a wolf-free zone. At the time he'd assumed it was a sort of sideways joke.

She ran, and as he followed, he wondered: when I die, assuming it's before dawn, will I stay a wolf after I'm dead, or will I turn back into a human? Intriguing point; pity I won't be there to find out, because I might be able to take another fifteen seconds of this, but no more than that. Should've listened to Luke. Shouldn't have been such a complete fool. He watched her immaculate stride. Why do fools fall in love?

The pain in his chest was past ignoring now. Every lungful of air came wrapped in coarse sandpaper, and tore at his throat as he dragged it in. His legs were numb, which was a blessing, and his back crackled with pain each time he heaved it. But the scent was burning inside him like petrol vapour, powering the piston that drove him, and stopping was as impossible as taking another stride. She was still there, exactly the same distance ahead of him, hardly exerting herself. Any minute now, he promised himself, she'll put on a little burst of speed and leave me behind (leave me for dead, even) and that'll break the chain. But she didn't. It was, he reflected bitterly, something like chasing lorries – pointless, because you never catch them. Well.

She picked up her pace; just a little, just enough to force him to find strength he didn't have, to keep up. The pressure of his blood against his eardrums was unbearable, and he could taste it in his mouth, sweet as chocolate and rich in nutritious iron and other valuable trace minerals. No more natural wolves in Britain, and pretty soon one less unnatural one. Natural; selection was natural, it filtered out the idiots and the losers, leaving only those sensible enough to chase lorries instead of unicorns as the breeding stock. Which was eminently fair, he could understand that. It was just unfortunate that he'd turned out to be one of the rejects—

Something hit him very hard, and he went to sleep.

She was kissing him. No, not quite. He opened his eyes, and saw a golden spike.

The scent. He growled, but the point of the spike tickled his throat. His muzzle was wet. The unicorn had been licking it.

'You ran into a tree,' she said, in a voice that left no doubt about how hard she was having to work to keep herself from laughing. 'In the dark, easily done. Are you all right?'

Her voice was – well, familiar, yes. Duncan knew it from somewhere. The awkward part was, he was sure it was his own. Except—

'Dizziness? Nausea? Blurred vision?'

Except he wasn't a girl, and it was a girl's voice. Maybe he'd heard it in his dreams; in which case, it was a real bummer that he could never remember them when he woke up.

'Who—?' he mumbled. It came out, he was pretty sure, as human speech.

'We meet at last, Duncan Hughes.' Her sweet, comical face – practically Disney – twitched into what a hopeless anthropomorphiser would have declared was a smile, though of course, horses don't, not even horses with golden horns sticking out of their heads. 'You're probably all right,' she went on. 'Werewolves don't tend to get concussion, unless you drop large mountains on top of them. The tree's a write-off, I'm afraid. It's been there for over a hundred years, actually. Sweet chestnut, though I don't suppose you're interested.'

He was talking to – no, being talked to by – a unicorn. And under ordinary circumstances, he'd have been fairly relaxed about that, because you get to chat with all sorts of interesting imaginary people when you've had a nasty bang on the head, if you're human, and then they go away and the headache starts and sooner or later you get well again and go back to work. But he wasn't human and she wasn't imaginary. He could feel her breath; he could taste it, as rich and smooth as the proper hot chocolate you get in France or Belgium. He could feel the point of the horn, as she carelessly let it rest for a split second against his jugular vein. Just enough to tickle.

'Are you going to kill me?' he asked.

She snickered. 'Sorry,' she said. 'Private joke. No, of course not, don't be silly. Not unless you try and bite me, but you're not going to do that.' She backed off a step and lifted her head. 'I trust you,'she said. 'After all, if you can't trust a lawyer—'

The urge swelled inside him, snatching control of his nerves and muscles away from him, but he fought it. Not just a wolf, after all, a werewolf, which means half-human. You don't eat people while they're talking to you. Terrible bad manners.

'You know me,' he said. Partly a question, partly a statement.

''Course I do, silly,' she said. 'We've known each other for ages; and you've taken such good care of me, even though I've driven you batty ever so many times. I don't deserve you.' Her nostrils flared, and her fat pink tongue licked her lips. 'I had an idea you were the one for me, way back when you first joined Craven Ettins. Don't ask me why, I just knew. Affinity, I think the word is. I've been aware of you for ever so long – ever since Lycus Grove, actually. Maybe it was because you were the last one to join the gang. It made you different, somehow.'

Just when you think you're all bewildered out. 'You've been watching me since I was at *school*?' He shook his head; not the shrewdest of moves. 'That's creepy.'

She nodded. 'Actually,' she said, 'you have no idea how truly creepy it is. If you had, you'd be on your feet and running so fast— But don't let it worry you,' she added pleasantly. 'I'm not going to hurt *you*. Perish the thought.' She lifted her head, and her ears waggled in different directions. 'Just a taxi,' she said, 'on the bypass. You think your hearing's amazing, you should try living with mine. Where were we? Oh yes. Craven Ettins; I have a little confession to make there. It was me got you fired, actually.'

The words were English and more or less grammatically correct, but the sense— 'You got me fired.'

Nod. ''Fraid so. And I fixed it so Luke Ferris came back into your life. Have you ever wondered about his name, by the way? Ferris? Well, Ferris *and* Loop, come to that.'

'What? No.'

'Really? I'm surprised, a bright young man like you. Loop: as in the French word *loup*, meaning wolf. Ferris is, of course, derived from *Fenris*, the great sky-wolf of Norse mythology who eats the gods after the battle at the end of the world. Then there's Lycus Grove – *lycus*, Greek for wolf. It's been raining clues all your life, great big heavy ones with hobnail boots on, but it seems that somehow you've managed to avoid getting any of them. If you'd been doing it on purpose, I'd have said it was really clever of you.'

Great sky-wolves. Duncan most definitely wasn't in the mood for great sky-wolves. 'You got me fired from my job?'

'Only because I knew you were so unhappy there, and your next job would be so much better. Which is true, isn't it? I mean, there's no comparison. Not just the money; the people, the hours, the office furniture, not being treated like shit all the time, everything. Yes, I had a word with that cow Jenny Sidmouth. Told her that unless she got rid of you pronto, I'd take all my business elsewhere. Actually, she didn't need a whole lot of persuading; said she only kept you on out of force of habit, which was a bit mean of her if you ask me. I mean, you weren't exactly dynamite, but you were competent.' She lifted her head again, and her front offside hoof lifted and pawed the air. 'Helicopter,' she said. 'I can feel the slipstream from the blades a fraction of a second before I hear the noise, which is odd, don't you think? Anyway, talking of names—'

'You got me *fired*,' Duncan persevered. He knew perfectly well that the point wasn't in dispute, but he wanted to make it. He wanted—

She nodded. 'An apology, of course. Right, I'm sorry. Bit of a cheek, and no, I wouldn't have liked it myself if I'd been in your shoes. But you've got to admit, it's all been for the best. Not to mention the fact that I got you that job in the first place.' Pause. 'Well, when I say *me*— But that's another story, and of course, your poor head, you don't want me jangling your brains with all this difficult stuff at once. I'm being inconsiderate, and I hate that.' She breathed out through her nose. 'The others are looking for you,' she said. 'They chased a sixteen-wheel Scania practically into Hampton Wick before they noticed you weren't there. Your friend Luke's going to be a bit stressed out, but don't worry. His bark's worse than his bite. I've been dying for a chance of working that in,' she added. 'I have a rather sad sense of humour. No, don't worry about Luke. He feels threatened, that's all. He's been the alpha so long, ever since dear Wesley joined us, he can't bear the thought of being forced into second place. Especially by you. Of course, you never knew Wesley, he was before your time.'

It had taken a split second to seep through. 'By *me*?'

'Well, naturally,' she said. 'Just think, senior partner before you're thirty-five. That'll wipe the grin off Jenny Sidmouth's face, won't it? Just be patient, it'll come. Oh, and one more thing.' He hadn't seen the movement, it was so fast; but the point of her horn was tucked under his chin, to the extent that he realised that breathing wouldn't be good for him just then. 'Stay away from that ex-wife of yours, will you? She's no good for you. Not a very nice person. She'll tell you they made her join, or they tricked her into it, and then they made her dump you because of what she'd become. Don't believe a word of it. She'll only break your heart again.' The horn-point withdrew, and Duncan gulped air. 'After all,' she went on, 'there's plenty more fish in the sea. And even if she really did still care about you, there'd be no future in it. They aren't like your kind. I mean, without getting too gross about it, there's certain things that your lot and her lot simply can't do— And think what it'd be like living with one,' she went on. 'At night, you get into bed, she hangs upside down from the pelmet. You fancy steak and kidney pie, she won't touch anything except raw liver and black pudding. Holidays would be a complete disaster, what with her –' she snickered '– unfortunate skin condition. All that cream they've got to wear, it'd be like hugging a bacon sandwich, all oily. No, really, you're better off. One day you'll meet a nice little bitch, someone who likes running and chasing things, and you'll be grateful I warned you in time. Not that it's any of my business, of course, but—' She tossed her mane; it fluttered for a moment like falling snow. 'It's entirely up to you, of course, what you do. But if you're sensible, you'll take my advice. After all, I'm on your side. You'd do well to remember that.'

Up till then he'd been struggling, he'd have been the first to admit. But this time she'd said something that was demonstrably untrue. It made him feel better, in a way. 'No, you're not,' he said.

'Beg pardon?'

'You're not on my side.' It sounded odd when he heard himself say it, but it was so obvious. 'That's not possible,' he said. 'I mean, I'm the hunter and you're the prey. That's—' He searched for the word. 'That's *nature*,' he said, though it wasn't quite what he'd been looking for. 'Red in tooth and claw,' he added. 'Our lot chase your lot, your lot run away. I mean, I'm all for greater understanding and world peace and stuff, but I'd have thought that pretty much ruled out friendship.'

Her deep, dark eyes sparkled. 'I didn't say we're friends,' she said. 'You don't have to be friends to be on the same side. Look at the EU. And while I think of it, Luke was quite right about why there're no natural wolves in Britain. No great loss,' she added casually. 'They were a nuisance. Worried sheep. But I meant what I said. When you come right down to it, there're only two sides that matter, us and them. You're us. They're them. Focus on that and you'll be all right.' She yawned, in that uniquely horsy way, lips drawn back from her teeth. 'It's getting late,' she said. 'So late it'll be early any moment now, and you'll want to be back under cover before sunrise, believe me. It's been such a treat, talking like this. See you around, Duncan Hughes.'

She turned away and broke into a smart trot. With a snarl he tried to jump up and follow, but the movement made him horribly dizzy and he flopped down in a heap. Mist had come down, quite suddenly, as though someone had turned a tap on; she was turning into a fuzzy white glow on the edge of his vision. 'Who are you?' he shouted after her.

Extra-special hearing. He could just make out the words 'Three guesses' before she faded completely away.

CHAPTER NINE

'My Uncle Charlie,' the sad-looking man said, pushing a fat blue folder across the desk. 'Well, actually my great-uncle, that's my grandad's brother. Ninety-six, he had a good innings. It's all in there.'

Duncan nodded and opened the folder. You never knew, when you started off the administration of a new estate; not till you actually got your paws on the documents – title deeds, share certificates, building society books, policy documents. Even now, there was just a hint of the small child on Christmas morning when he opened one of these folders. If he'd been nice, there'd be reams of blue-chip holdings and a street of houses in Fulham. If he'd been naughty, coal.

Apparently he'd been nice. Great-uncle Charlie had been loaded when he went. The crisp crackle of Shell shares; the soothing thick buff of land certificates; a library of blue and red Deposit Account books; bank statements with balances that read like population statistics. Every probate lawyer has the soul of a vulture, and the sheer scale of what Great-uncle Charlie hadn't taken with him should've been enough to give Duncan cramp suppressing a happy grin. Instead, he flicked through, did the mental arithmetic and launched into his customary lecture on What Happens When Rich People Die. The sad man nodded – they always nod; they're genuinely upset, sometimes, but there's a subtle magic in a lawyer's voice when he's talking about inheritance tax nil-rate bands, capital gains tax exemptions and vesting *in specie* that makes even the sincerest mourner start to think a bit. Duncan had come to think of it as that Death-Be-Not-Proud moment, the point at which the tears dry up and the drool begins to gather.

He gave the lecture, but his mind was far away. He was thinking about the night before, and his mind was troubled. Understandably.

The sky had started to pinken alarmingly at the edges when Luke and the gang had eventually found him. He'd babbled, about scenting a fox, chasing it, getting hit by a car, wandering in a dazed state. It was perfectly obvious they hadn't believed a word he'd said; perfectly obvious, too, that they weren't equipped to cope with a pack member telling deliberate lies. Either they'd have to ignore it and pretend they believed him, or else there'd have to be an enormous row, probably ending in blood; they'd hesitated for maybe a whole second, but the issue hadn't been in doubt. What had decided it, he knew, was that it was nearly dawn and they had to get back to base before the sunlight caught them out. No time, therefore, for the truth. They'd asked him if he could run, and he'd murmured, 'I think so,' in a brave, wobbly voice. They'd made it back to the office with a maximum of five minutes to spare.

They could read his mind, of course. So why—?

'All things being equal,' Duncan heard himself drone, 'we should be able to obtain probate within two months, on an undertaking to the Revenue to make full disclosure of assets at a later date. Of course, this involves the executors in personal liability—'

If they could read his mind, why hadn't they seen the lie? Answer: they'd seen it and chosen to pretend they hadn't. No, that just wasn't possible. They must have been able to see her. She was burned into his mind's eye like a cattle brand, and all the let's-not-fall-out-over-this goodwill in the world couldn't overlook something like that. He'd defied Luke, the pack leader, to chase after the white unicorn that couldn't be caught. He'd survived, and she'd filled his poor brain up with an overload of bizarre shit that leaked potentially disastrous implications like Chernobyl. It occurred to him that she'd quite probably done it on purpose, to break the pack up; at best, force a civil war, and, more likely, sign his death warrant. But they'd heard his lies, his mind had presumably been wide open, and all they'd had to say for themselves was *Do you feel up to running?* And after that – well, it was a bit hazy. He remembered riding up to their floor in the lift, everybody stony silent; the lift doors opening, sunlight through the still-open roof hatch, the change back (he'd hardly noticed it) everybody dispersing to their own offices without a word. He'd dropped like a stone into his chair and woken up feeling like road kill with the sunlight blasting through the windows and the phone telling him that his eleven-fifteen appointment was waiting for him in reception.

So far, so agonisingly unresolved. Just as well the lecture delivered itself, and all he had to do was look solemn. For once, that was no bother at all. Poor dead Great-uncle Charlie, he thought. Each man's death diminishes me, as what's-his-name so beautifully put it back in sixteen-something, but right now he reckoned that if the old geezer had to fall off the perch, he couldn't have picked a better time. Werewolf or not, Luke had to observe the basic decencies; which meant that, as long as Duncan was in the interview room with a client, Luke couldn't come bursting in and rip his throat out with his teeth. In which case, the sad man could take as long as he liked. That and the fact that lawyers charge by the hour, of course.

'Naturally, we want everything done properly,' the sad man was saying, 'and of course we've all been knocked for six, poor Uncle Charlie going so suddenly and everything. But I just happened to glance through the share prices in the *Telegraph* this morning, and I noticed that Kawaguchiya Integrated Circuits is up six on takeover rumours, so if we've got to wait for this probate business before we can—'

Cue for another lecture (Dead Men's Shoes And How To Keep Them Shiny), affording Duncan four good minutes in which to panic at the thought that Luke might be crouched outside in the corridor right now, sharpening his teeth on a bit of pumice. (Or was that budgies?) He listened, sniffed. No; Luke was in his office, talking to some accountant on the phone. Luke was saying that in his opinion, Schumacher had lost his touch and Honda hadn't cured the tyre problem, so it was going to be anybody's guess until Monaco. If anything, he sounded unusually relaxed and at peace. Very odd.

The sad man left, eventually, leaving behind a faint taste of greed and a job of work, which took Duncan six minutes. As the printer spooled out the letters, he sat back in his chair and did his best to brace himself. He didn't really believe that Luke would actually kill him, but that was about all the optimism he could scrape together. It wasn't going to be one of his best-ever mornings.

Luke got off the phone. He dictated an attendance note and two letters, put something away in his filing cabinet, ate a raw-steak sandwich, drummed his fingers on the desktop (it sounded like cannon fire), stood up and paced round his office a few times, went back to his chair, turned round three times, sat down, stayed put for four endless minutes, stood up again, walked to his office door, closed it behind him. Heading this way. He was coming.

New Mexico, Duncan thought, but it was much too late for that. He caught himself checking his office out for hiding places; fatuous. There weren't any, and even if there had been he couldn't hide from Luke's nose. The sound of Luke's feet in the corridor was deafening. Duncan swivelled his chair to face the door.

Knock. Since when did anybody knock before coming into a room in this place?

'Come in,' he squeaked.

Luke was looking well, as though he'd just come back from a good holiday. He was wearing a smart grey suit, a white shirt that practically bleached the eye, and a pearl-grey tie. He was smiling. 'Morning,' he said.

'M,' Duncan replied.

'How are you feeling?'

'Oh, fine.'

'Head all right?'

'Mphm.'

'Splendid. Usually, after the first time, you get a sort of hangover; I think it's because there're traces of chemicals left over in the bloodstream that aren't there the rest of the month, if you get me. Also, there's the chance you might have eaten something that a human might have trouble digesting. We change, the contents of our stomachs don't. But if you're feeling all right—'

'Yup.'

'Delighted to hear it.' Luke came closer, perched on the edge of the desk. 'Right, then,' he said pleasantly. 'Tell me how you did it.'

Always, throughout Duncan's life, that infuriating feeling that he'd missed something everybody else knew. 'Did what?'

'Duncan, my dear old mate.' No expression on Luke's face, unless you counted the look in his eyes. 'Let's not muck about. You lied to me, all right?'

'Um.'

'You told me a load of old rubbish about getting run over by a car. Now, I know it can't have been true,' Luke went on, 'because if a car had hit you, the result would've been one insurance write-off and you standing there with a big smirk on your face. So, whatever it was that knocked you for six last night, it wasn't a pissy little tin box on wheels. Would you like to tell me something at this point, or shall I go on?'

Duncan shook his head.

'Please yourself. Actually, I'm not stupid, I know what you did. You chased the unicorn. Come off it,' he added as Duncan made a feeble attempt to protest. 'I could smell the bloody thing. I told you to leave it alone, but you chased it anyway. I'm assuming that's what happened to you, and all I can say is, you're lucky to be alive. I hope you realise that.'

Pause. Something was wrong. This wasn't the pack leader talking to the subordinate who'd defied a direct order. Duncan maintained eye contact and said nothing.

'Note the word *assuming*,' Luke went on. He was getting tense; Duncan could smell it. 'I'm having to assume, you see, because I don't know for certain. Which brings me back to my question. How the *hell* are you doing it?'

'Doing what?'

For a moment, Duncan was sure that Luke was going to spring. 'You know perfectly well,' he hissed instead. 'Closing your mind so I couldn't see into it. You lied to me, but how do I know that? Because I worked it out, and because it was a bloody stupid lie that any fool could've seen through. I couldn't read it in your mind, though. I looked, and there was just this blank wall. *Nothing.*' Luke spat out the last word as though it was something disgusting. 'And the others,' he went on. 'What the fuck did you do to them? They didn't even realise there was anything wrong. When you told us all that crap about getting hit by cars, they *believed* you. And that's—' He shook his head and watched Duncan silently for a moment, the way a dog watches its prey when it's frozen stiff with terror. 'I'm a good alpha,' he said eventually, 'I know all the stuff. I know how this werewolf business works. But for the life of me I can't figure out how you're able to do all this. Do you want to take over from me, is that it?'

Now there was a question. If Duncan said yes – well, he'd be lying, for a start. More to the point, it'd be like pressing the button that launches the nukes that start off World War Three. Inevitably, immediately, there would be a fight to the death.

'No,' Duncan said.

So far, so good. Luke stayed where he was: no spring, no growl, no teeth meeting in Duncan's throat. 'OK,' Luke said slowly, 'that's nice to hear. All right: if you won't tell me how you're doing it, perhaps you'd care to tell me why. Is it because of her?'

Duncan was about to reply when the little cartoon light bulb flickered inside his head. By *her* he didn't mean the unicorn. He was thinking about Sally, and the vampires. 'Of course not,' he said. 'Look, I told you everything about—'

'Quite. Flew up to your window, like a cross between Romeo and a Harrier. At the time, I was sure you were telling the truth. After all, I thought, he can't lie to me, I'd know straight away if he was. But maybe it's not as simple as that any more.'

'I promise.'

Luke thought about that. 'Sure,' he said. 'Cub's honour, and all that. Fine, so it's not about her. In which case, if it's not your loathsome vertical-take-off ex and it's not ruthless ambition, then what the fuck's got into you?' Now, at last, he was allowing himself to get angry. 'Just doing it for the hell of it, are you?'

'No, of course—'

'Hierarchy means nothing to you, I suppose. You think ethics is a character out of the Asterix books.'

'Luke—'

'Don't "Luke" me, you bastard.' A snap, but a controlled snap. To his astonishment, Duncan realised that Luke was afraid of him. Well, not actual fear. There was only one thing in the world that Luke was afraid of: it was white, with silver hooves and a highly improbable growth on its forehead. But wary, as of something unknown and as yet unassessed; something that needed to be observed and gauged before it could be tackled. 'God, you're an ungrateful little shit, Duncan Hughes. You were stuck in a fucking miserable job, right down at the bottom of the heap, people pissing on you like you were a lamp-post. I brought you back, made you a partner, made you one of *us*, and this is how you say thank you. What the hell did I do to deserve that? Well? Come on, I'm listening.'

What Duncan wanted to say (so much that not saying it practically hurt), was, *you sound just like Sally. Or my mother.* In which case, he realised, he'd won – though it wasn't a contest he'd started, or a victory he wanted. He wasn't even aware of having fought. Luke had backed down, acknowledging that, if they fought, he wasn't sure he'd win – hence the unsheathing of the emotional claws, rather than the onslaught with the physical teeth. From werewolf to cat; evolution in reverse.

'Nothing,' Duncan said; and a great urge came over him to tell Luke everything – about the unicorn, what she'd said, the bewildering stuff about getting him fired from Craven Ettins, and Lycus Grove; about Ferris being derived from the great sky-wolf; and by the way, what—?

'What happened to Wesley Loop?'

He hadn't intended to say it aloud. It just sort of slipped out, like a goldfish when you're changing the water in its bowl. He nearly reached out with his hand, as though trying to snatch the words back before they reached Luke.

'Ah,' Luke said.

Oh well. 'He died, didn't he?'

Luke had gone all quiet: werewolf to cat to hedgehog curled up in a ball. 'That's a good question,' he said.

'Well?'

'I think so.' It had taken Luke a lot of effort to say that; it was like watching a hen laying a pyramid-shaped egg. 'I know what you're going to say, dead or alive, it's not usually a notorious grey area. In Wesley's case, though—'

'Tell me about it,' Duncan said. It was, he noticed after he'd said it, an order.

'Wesley.' Luke seemed to shrink a little. 'Well, it was just after I left school. Round about the time you must've made your mind up that you didn't want to know us any more. We've got to talk about that at some stage, by the way; but all right, yes, I'll get on with it.' He licked the back of his hand and rubbed behind his ear. 'I met Wesley Loop at a Christmas party. Actually, that's misleading – I'd known him for years. He's sort of my third cousin twice removed, or something complicated like that. Family, at any rate. But he was just one of those bland, boring people round about your own age who you see at big get-togethers and do your best to avoid, because you know that if you get to know them better you're really going to hate them. Anyhow, that was Wesley. All I knew about him was that he'd just finished law school – everybody was very proud, why can't you be more like your cousin Wesley, all that stuff. But we were trapped at this really boring party, and he came up to me and said hello.'

Luke paused, and it was obvious that he'd forgotten Duncan was there. He was talking to himself.

'He was telling me about law school,' Luke went on. 'About how great it had been, and how much he was looking forward to starting work, and how utterly fabulous the legal profession was; and, naturally, I wanted to stick my arm down his throat and rip his lungs out just to make him stop, but you can't, not at a Christmas party, with your gran there and everything. So I stood there and nodded and mumbled "Hey, that's great," until I just couldn't take any more. So I said, 'Wesley, excuse me a second, I'm going for a piss.' I scuttled off to the bog, and I'd just got my fly open when the door opened – I'd locked it behind me – and Wesley came in. Well, you can imagine. I was just about to explain that I was fine with that, broad-minded as the next guy and really pleased for him, but if he didn't get out in one second flat I'd break his neck in six places; and then he bit me.'

'Bit you.' Duncan heard himself say. 'You mean, like—'

'Yes.'

It seemed for a while as though Luke didn't want to continue with the story. At some point he'd folded his arms; now he was sitting on the edge of Duncan's desk, staring at his shoes, his mind evidently a long way away in space and time. It was, of course, inconceivable that he was regretting what had happened. Wasn't it?

'And that,' he said, abruptly breaking the silence, 'was that.' He looked up, and he was smiling. 'Wesley told me afterwards that he'd been bitten by one of the lecturers at law school. Crazy old bugger, by the sound of it; he had this idea of recruiting the finest minds and the fiercest spirits, and he'd got it into his head that the best place to find them was kids who wanted to be lawyers when they grew up. The way he saw it, the country's run by lawyers anyhow – look at how many politicians started off as barristers, he said – though, if you ask me, that proves the old boy was on the wrong track. He thought – well, anyhow. That was how Wesley got his start; and thanks to his werewolf super-powers he'd done amazingly well in his exams, got a cracking job already lined up, but what he really wanted to do was start his own firm – and, more to the point, his own pack. That was why he'd had his eye on me, it turned out. He knew I was the leader of a gang at school. Apparently, Wesley had always been the archetypal fat-kid-with-glasses, so he didn't have any friends of his own. Then he heard about me, and reckoned that there was a ready-made pack just waiting for him to take over. That was the deal, basically. I'd go to law school, convert the rest of the gang and persuade them to come too. By the time we'd quali-fied, Wesley'd have served his time and got his practising certificate, so he'd be able to set up his own practice; we'd all join, and there we'd go. Sounded all right to me, and the others were quite happy to go along—'

'After you'd bitten them.'

'Afterwards, yes. Pete was a slight problem.' Luke frowned. 'He did so want to be a teacher, the stupid sod. Even after I'd recruited him he made a hell of a fuss, to start with. I told him, regardless of his personal feelings in the matter, that now that he was one of us the one thing he most definitely couldn't do, in all conscience, was work with kids. Well, obviously. He had to admit I was right about that, though he did get rather pissy when I explained it. But anyhow; that's how Ferris and Loop came about. It was Loop and Co to begin with, until we'd all done our two years and were ready to join the partnership. But already by then—' Luke sighed, and shook his head.

'Problem?' Duncan asked.

'You could say that.' Luke clicked his tongue. 'Poor old Wesley. It was always meant to be *his* firm, *his* pack. But the plain fact was, he wasn't alpha material. Not a born leader. Clueless. I stuck it out as long as I could, out of simple respect, but it couldn't go on. He was making a bog of everything, both in the office and – well, once a month. He annoyed the clients,

nearly started a turf war with the Dulwich pack, and he was getting on all our nerves. Also, he was obsessed with—' Pause.
Deep frown. 'He was obsessed with a certain horse-like creature,
to the point where he only survived because he was too weak and
feeble to run long enough to kill himself. We were going
nowhere as a pack, and the others made it pretty clear that I had
to do something. So I did.'

Another pause. Duncan took a deep breath.

'You challenged him, then,' he said quietly. 'You killed him.'

'Fucking hell, no.' Luke's horror was genuine enough. 'After
all he'd done for me? Absolutely not. No, I took him on one side
and told him, straight out: Wesley, you can't cut it as pack
leader, you know that as well as I do. And we both know who
ought to be doing your job; so let's quit screwing around and
face up to it. Credit where it's due, he didn't make a fuss; just
hung his head, looked sad. To save his face, we kept his name at
the top of the notepaper: him and me, joint senior partners.
Ferris and Loop. And he was nominally Number Two in the
pack, though it was pretty clear he wasn't up to it. We carried
him, though, in work and fun. It was the least we could do. And
he was very nice about the whole thing, very realistic. Wasn't
long before everything found its own level, so to speak, and we
were able to carry on with our lives and not think about it.'

Again he fell silent, and Duncan had to cough quite loudly to
snap him out of it. 'So,' Duncan said, 'what happened to him? In
the end, I mean.'

'He died.'

Duncan knew that already; but the way Luke said it shocked
him. He'd expected a matter-of-fact, law-of-the-jungle, Darwin-
knew-best tone of voice. Not bitterness. Not anger.

'Oh,' he said. 'What happened?'

Luke stood up and walked to the window. With his back to
Duncan, he said, 'He was chasing the unicorn. Like I told you
just now, he was obsessed. I'd warned him often enough. I told
him, she's out of your league, she'll be the death of you. And he
said, yes, I know, I'll be more careful. But he couldn't help it,

poor bastard. One sniff of the scent and he'd be off. But I wasn't all that worried. He'd chased her before, and we'd found him, all crumpled up in a heap, passed out from exhaustion. So I told myself, he won't come to any harm, he's a wimp. Wimps can't run themselves to death even if they want to. And so, when he picked up the scent, I let him go. Oh, I told him not to; but I didn't stop him. I mean, I didn't grab him by the scruff of the neck and hold him down on the ground, like I should've. I know the others couldn't understand why I let him get away with it, disobeying a direct order; thought I'd gone soft, I guess, which isn't so far from the truth. But it's hard when you start off thinking someone's the leader of the pack and it turns out he's not meant to be – you are. There's always that mental block. And so I persuaded myself that he couldn't come to any serious harm. And you know what they say. Spare the tooth, spoil the pup. Only, he was five years older than me. It shouldn't have been my responsibility, it wasn't fair.' Suddenly Luke laughed. 'Fair,' he repeated. 'Not a word I have a lot of use for, except when I'm being ironic. I let him chase the unicorn one night, and he died. We found him, flaked out, dead as a doornail, on Ham Common. Of course, soon as he died he turned back into a human. I can picture him now, lying there in the moonlight with this really comical look on his face, glasses hanging from one ear, white as a sheet. We had to leave him for the humans to find. I mean, we couldn't very well carry him – no hands, go figure – and eating him would've been *tacky*. The local paper said he'd been jogging and had had a heart attack. Death of prominent local solicitor. He got a whole inch and a half, jammed in between a planning application and a flower show. I loved him dearly, but honestly, it was about what he deserved. Rule number one in our little community: don't bite off more than you can eat. And that's the Wesley Loop story,' he added, shaking his head. 'Very sad, but in all fairness you couldn't call it tragedy.'

Duncan let it sink in. Very sad – Luke was right about that. Certainly no tragedy. But that wasn't the important point. The crucial thing was – and maybe Luke hadn't realised – it was only half a story, if that. There was more to it, Duncan was absolutely sure, but he had no idea—

'What about her?' he said.

'What? Oh, you mean the unicorn.' Luke shrugged. 'Who knows? She's been around since the year dot—'

'How do you know that? And about her having killed all the natural wolves in Britain . . .'

'Not all, obviously.' Luke frowned. 'I mean, some of them died of mange or getting run over by stagecoaches, or old age, whatever. But she finished them off, when there were just a handful left. Someone told me—' He tailed off, looked blank for a moment, then went on: 'Someone from another pack; the Epping Forest lads, I think, or the Hornchurch lot.'

'And how did they know?'

Clear from his face that Luke hadn't stopped to consider. 'Dunno,' he said. 'Maybe it isn't true, at that. But all the other packs I've talked to over the years know her. They've had bad experiences with her, too. Does it matter? She's trouble, that's all you need to know. Stay clear. Maybe next time you won't be so lucky.'

That bit of advice seemed hard to find fault with. Still, Duncan couldn't help wondering—

'All right,' Luke said. 'I've answered your question, now would you mind answering mine? Keeping us all out of your head. I rather fancy you're about to tell me you don't know how you do it.'

Duncan nodded. 'I didn't even know that was what I was doing till you told me.'

Luke yawned. 'Well,' he said, 'that's possible, of course. I've heard of cases, though they're bloody rare. Sort of like a natural inbuilt ability. Probably you can also bend spoons. The thing is,' Luke went on; he was trying to be quietly terrifying, but he wasn't succeeding. 'There's a time and a place for bending spoons, right? On a prime-time TV chat show, excellent. Having dinner with the Duke of Westminster, not such a good idea. He may be impressed by your uncanny abilities, but he's going to be really pissed off about all the buggered-up antique silverware.'

Duncan looked at him. He seemed a little smaller than usual. 'Fine,' he said. 'Tell me how to stop doing it, and I'll stop. Right?'

He'd watched dogs having this kind of staring match. They growled, too, but in this case there was no need of a soundtrack. It wasn't that Duncan felt stronger. It was Luke who was being diminished. After a second or two Luke looked away.

'You suit yourself,' he said quietly. 'After all, we're supposed to be *friends*. Like, you know, on the same side and everything. But you go ahead and do what you want. Just don't expect us to be there every time you wind up half-dead on the common.'

He started to walk out of the room. 'Luke,' Duncan heard himself say, but obviously he'd said it too softly for Luke to hear. Odd, considering.

The door closed, and Duncan flopped back into his chair as if he were a test pilot pulling twenty Gs. There had been a question in there at the end of the scene that he couldn't answer, and it was bothering him like toothache—

– Because, yes, they *were* supposed to be friends. That was the natural choice of word to use for the Ferris Gang, wasn't it? Friends, mates, buddies, ever since Year Ten. If there was anybody he should feel comfortable with, it ought to be Luke and Pete and Clive and the others. They'd grown up together, done it all together, heard the car alarms at midnight together; and yes, people change when they grow up and go their pathetic little separate ways. But always, buried deep inside under the cave-in of experience, there's the essential sixteen-year-old still alive, still keeping the faith, waiting for the others to come back and for things to be right again. So why hadn't he told Luke about the unicorn? Properly told him: all the weird and unsettling stuff she'd said, including the very pertinent stuff about Lycus Grove and their joint origins? If anybody could shed some light on all that, surely it'd be Luke. Instead, he'd faced him down (his pack leader; a retrospective chill froze his blood for a moment) and sent him away with his tail between his legs. Why, for crying out loud? Didn't make sense.

It was me got you fired, actually. And then she'd gone on to say something even stranger. *I fixed it so Luke Ferris came back into your life.* But that was simply insane. According to Luke (and if the story of Wesley Loop was true, he was quite right) the unicorn was their mortal enemy, their greatest and only natural predator. Why the hell would she go to all that trouble—?

More to the point, *how* had she done it? Solicitors are fairly broad-minded people, but he had difficulties with the mental picture of a white horse with a horn in its face prancing into Jenny Sidmouth's office and saying *I demand you sack Duncan Hughes immediately.* What had she said about that? Something about blackmail, taking all her business away from the firm. Even more surreal: exactly what would a mythical deformed horse need solicitors for? And where (more pertinent still) would she get the huge sums of money needed to pay them?

You know how it is with toothache. Unless you can take your mind off it, the pain grows until you can't think about anything else. Duncan sighed, and picked up the phone.

'Yes, hello. Jenny Sidmouth, please.'

Reception didn't seem to have recognised his voice. On the other hand, she hadn't asked who was calling, either. That wasn't standard operating procedure.

'Duncan.'

Who'd have thought so much spite could be packed into a name. 'Jenny,' he said. 'Sorry to bother you—'

'Really?'

'What?'

'Are you really sorry? No offence, but I'm a bit sceptical about that. Bastard,' she added, by way of clarification. Precision is everything in the legal profession.

'Sorry to bother you,' he repeated quietly, 'but I was wondering. Could you spare me a few minutes? Lunch, say.'

(Get him; chatting so casually to Jenny Sidmouth, the five-foot-two-eyes-of-blue Darth Vader of Craven Ettins. He was almost proud of himself.) 'Are you serious?'

'There's something I need to ask you about.'

'You are serious, aren't you?'

'Oh, come on.' He was turning on the charm. Query: since when had he had any charm to turn on? 'You're the one who sacked me, not the other way around, and I'm not holding any grudges. I take it something's happened that's ticked you off a bit, since I left.'

He'd forgotten the particular noise that only Jenny could make. A bit like a snort or a laugh; also a bit like a lion roaring, or a saw cutting bone. 'You could say that.'

'Fine. Come to lunch and tell me about it.'

'Like you don't bloody well know. You bastard,' she added (repetition is sometimes necessary in the interests of absolute clarity). 'Talk about vindictive, treacherous, sneaky – How long did it take you? You were hardly out of the door five minutes, and you stole my best fucking client.'

Puzzled. 'Excuse me?'

'No explanations. Didn't give me a chance. Just a one-line letter: *kindly forward all files and documents to our new lawyers, Ferris and Loop, FAO Duncan Hughes*. Wouldn't take my calls. After all the years I spent on them. Gone, just like that.'

'Excuse me,' Duncan said mildly. 'Who are we talking about, please?'

'Oh, don't. Please don't pretend that you don't know. Oh, and while you're at it, rot in hell. That's after we sue your arse into the ground for seduction of trade and breach of restrictive covenant. I trust you've briefed your insurers, because by the time we've finished with you—'

'Seduction of trade?' Duncan asked, curious. 'Don't think I've heard of that one.'

'Well, no, I just made it up. But we'll have you for it, whether it exists or not. You know what you are, Duncan?'

'A bastard?' he hazarded.

'You're a disgrace to the profession,' she snarled, and slammed the phone down on him.

He raised a stately eyebrow and put the receiver back. Threats aside (and putting aside a lawyer's threats is like plucking a chicken; what you're left with is scrawny-looking and much smaller than you'd expected) he wasn't particularly bothered, but the implication that was left sticking up out of the mud after the flood-waters had rolled back was pretty bloody fascinating.

Duncan tried to remember how you went about getting a cup of tea in this place. There was a protocol, he knew, but it had slipped his mind, so he stuck two fingers in his mouth and whistled. He was still drying his fingernails on his tie when the door opened, and the little bald man scuttled in: tray, china teapot, cup, saucer, plate with two digestives, two Rich Tea and a Viennese whirl. He smiled; the little man cringed, dumped the tray on the desk and fled as though every wolf ever whelped was after him.

He frowned. He wasn't all that fond of Viennese whirls.

Jenny Sidmouth was upset with him because he'd stolen a client. *Hardly out of the door five minutes*: straight away after he'd left, therefore. Duncan didn't need to think long and hard about that. There was only one client who fitted the criteria: the file that had come swooping in after him like a homing pigeon, much to his disgust. His least favourite too-difficult file; the client who'd had enough clout to get him fired; the client who was also, apparently, a unicorn. Not to mention dead.

Bowden Allshapes.

CHAPTER TEN

The unicorn was saying his name.

He stopped dead. Inertia hit him like a truck up the bum, jerking him forward so that his feet skidded. She'd stopped too. She was only a few feet away; less than that, even, mere inches. He tried to spring, but his feet were stuck in something. He looked down. Icing – he was ankle deep in white cake icing. Well, he'd never liked the stuff much at the best of times.

He strained against the air, like a carthorse pushing against its collar. No chance; because it was one of those dreams, the sort where you can almost get there but not quite. He growled.

'Duncan,' she said. 'For fuck's sake.'

Not her usual style; and part of him was aware that it wasn't really her talking. It was Pete, shaking him by the shoulder and telling him to wake up. But only part. The other part could almost feel the tickle of her fur on the tip of his nose, it was so close. It pushed—

'Silly,' said the unicorn. 'I'm not the one you're after, am I?'

That didn't sound like the sort of thing Pete would say. He strained a little more, until the pain in his ankles broke his concentration.

'When she comes for you the second time,' the unicorn said, 'remember where you put the sausage roll. Got that?'

'Sausage roll,' he repeated. 'Yes, got that.'

'Then basically you're ready,' she said. 'And I think your hairy friend is trying to attract your attention. You'd better wake up before he dislocates your shoulder. Oh, and by the way—'

('Wake up, you dozy bastard,' Pete was bawling in his ear. 'There's a client in reception for you.')

'Yes?' he said.

'The reason why the accounts won't balance is that you've forgotten to add the—'

He opened his eyes. His field of vision was full of Pete. No unicorns anywhere.

'Forgotten what?' he mumbled. 'Fuck it, Pete, what've I forgotten?'

Pete scowled at him. 'The client you've got coming in at three-fifteen, presumably,' he said. 'Which is why the poor git's been sitting out in the front office for the last ten minutes.'

'No.' Duncan sat up sharply and nutted himself on Pete's chin. 'No, the accounts—'

'What?'

'Forget it.' He sank back in his chair. 'What time is it?'

'Twenty-five past three, and you've got a client—'

'I must've fallen asleep.' Not, Duncan realised, the most perceptive thing he'd ever said. 'But hang on,' he went on, 'what about the pub trip? You know, lunchtime drinking except we don't get—'

'We didn't go today. Luke said he didn't feel in the mood. Look, what's that got to do with anything?'

'Nothing.' Duncan yawned and stretched. His knee collided with the desk, jarring something off it onto his lap. A tape-measure: how had that got there? He scowled at it, as if everything was its fault, and shoved it in his inside jacket pocket.'Who did you say was in the front office?'

'Client.' Pete was sounding volcano-about-to-erupt patient. 'It's in your diary, you pillock. Look.' He stabbed a chunky forefinger at the diary open on Duncan's desk. 'Three-fifteen,

Mr Bois d'Arc. Pull yourself together, can't you? You're supposed to be a lawyer.'

'Ah, but I'm a disgrace to the profession,' Duncan replied. 'Still trying to work out if that's a bad thing, in context.' He yawned again. Ninety per cent of his body ached. Last night, presumably, catching up with him. 'Sorry,' he said. 'Must've dropped off. I hate sleeping in chairs, it always gives me a cricked neck.' He glanced down at his diary. The entry was there all right, but not in his handwriting. He couldn't remember anything about it, and the name itself rang no bells. 'I suppose I'd better go and see this bloke,' he yawned.

'Yes,' Pete snapped. 'And get rid of him as quick as you can, will you? I saw him, he's a fucking weirdo.'

Coming from a werewolf, that was strong terminology. 'All right,' Duncan said mildly. 'In what way a weirdo, though?'

'I don't know, do I? I didn't hang about. Gave me the creeps.'

Intriguing. To someone who'd talked to the unicorn, the creeps didn't come easily, but anybody who could freak Pete out must be interesting, to say the least. 'Fine,' Duncan said. 'And thanks for—' But Pete had withdrawn, slamming the door behind him.

Weirdo, Duncan thought, quickly straightening his tie. His trouser legs, he noticed, were caked in mud. No idea how they'd got that way, but probably he ought to be grateful for small mercies. He sniffed, but he couldn't detect a stranger.

The little bald man in reception struck him as even more terrified than usual; he nodded in the direction of the waiting area, and fled into the back room, where the franking machine lived. Duncan shrugged, put on his being-polite-to-punters smile and looked round for his visitor.

Weirdo, he thought. Yes.

In appearance, the man was so utterly nondescript that he was scarcely there at all. He was medium and middle everything, his only remotely distinguishing feature being a rather pale complexion. Even his suit was impossible to describe – could've been grey, blue or black. His shoes were brightly polished, his hair neatly combed. But 'weirdo' was exactly the right word.

It was the smell. Partly the smell he didn't have, partly the smell he did. The scent that even a human couldn't have helped noticing was embalming fluid. What was quite palpably lacking was anything human, or even remotely organic. No sweat, breath, methane; none of the myriad bacterial squatters that camp out in the digestive system; no blood.

'Mr Bois D'Arc?' He pronounced it Bwadark, the eternal hopelessness of the Englishman trying to get his tongue round French.

'Boycedarch,' the man said pleasantly. No accent.

'Sorry to have kept you waiting.'

''Salright.'

Mr Bois D'Arc stood up and extended a medium-sized hand, for shaking purposes. Duncan really didn't want to touch it, but what could you do? As he'd rather suspected, it was cold. Not refrigerated; more like last night's pizza.

'Follow me,' Duncan said, but the man didn't move.

''Salright,' he said again. 'I just got a message for you.'

'Oh.' Duncan said. 'Fire away, then.'

Mr Bois D'Arc nodded, and braced himself. A moment later, he opened his mouth. The voice that came out was quite different, and very familiar.

'Duncan,' she said. 'I haven't got much time. If they find out I'm doing this – well, I got in so much trouble for the last time, you wouldn't . . .' Mr Bois D'Arc closed his eyes for a moment. Then she continued: 'Look, you've got to help me. There's nobody else, and I'm really scared. The instructions are on a bit of paper in his top pocket. For crying out loud, don't be late; got that? Oh Christ, is that the time? See you. Bye.'

The voice stopped. Mr Bois D'Arc stood quite still, looking at the far wall. Duncan realised he hadn't drawn a breath for quite a while, and gulped some air. Either this strange man (weirdo; the perfect word exists, so why not use it?) was the world's greatest impressionist – Rory Bremner and Mike

Yarwood nowhere, Mr Bois D'Arc number one – or else the voice he'd just heard belonged to his estranged wife, Sally.

'Excuse me,' he said.

'Yes? Hello? Who are you, please?'

Oh, Duncan thought. 'Can I have it, then?'

'By all means. Have what?'

'The piece of paper.'

Mr Bois D'Arc frowned, looked about him, saw the stack of elderly magazines on the table, and ripped the front cover off the *Sunday Times* colour supplement for 17 April 1983. 'Here you are,' he said, holding it out with pride. 'Will that do?'

'The piece of paper in your top pocket.'

Mr Bois D'Arc was concentrating. His lips moved silently for a moment or so. Then he felt in his top pocket and produced a folded yellow Post-It. There was fluff all over the sticky bit. 'This one?'

'I imagine so, yes.'

'Right.' Mr Bois D'Arc's cold fingers pressed it into Duncan's palm. 'I used to be a dentist, you know,' he said, with a hint of great sadness in his voice. 'It wasn't much, I suppose, but it was helping people who were in pain.'

'Is that right?'

'I think so. Is there anything else I can do for you?'

'No, I don't—'

'I could look at your teeth,' said Mr Bois D'Arc hopefully. 'Please let me. It'd be like—'

'No,' Duncan said, as though talking to a naughty dog. 'No, I don't— Stop it,' he added, but Mr Bois D'Arc was surprisingly quick and exceptionally strong. Before Duncan could move, the weirdo had grabbed the top of Duncan's head with one hand and his jaw with the other. A little twist, like opening an oyster. 'Bit of plaque there,' Mr Bois D'Arc said, 'and I don't like the look of that filling. Would you like me to see to it? Only take a moment.'

He said it casually enough, but somewhere deep down he sounded like a man pleading for his life. Then, suddenly, as though he'd been switched off at the mains, he let go and took a step back. 'So sorry,' he said, 'old habits. Well, I suppose I have to leave now. Where's the door?'

''Hind you,' Duncan mumbled, rubbing his jaw. 'Look—'

'Yes,' said Mr Bois D'Arc, turning through a hundred and eighty degrees precisely. 'Yes, I can see it, thank you. The pleasure was all mine.'

'Yes, but—'

Mr Bois D'Arc lifted his left foot and marched stiffly across the front office into the small stationery cupboard, shutting the door firmly behind him. Four seconds later he emerged, retraced his steps, pivoted through seventy degrees and disappeared into the lift, which had opened its door for him. Duncan sagged, and lifted his right hand to his nose. It reeked of formaldehyde.

Well, he thought. Pete had warned him, and he hadn't listened. He carefully unfolded the Post-It note. Sally's handwriting.

Moondollars, Lower Beowulf Street, 4.15. Carry copy today's Financial Times.

Fine, he thought. Perhaps she felt in dire need of a little financial advice: should she offload those Kawaguchiya Holdings shares now, or wait and see if the Dutch offer was just a fishing expedition? Possible; but so is England winning the World Cup. The one sure and certain thing was, he shouldn't go. Not under any circumstances whatsoever. He checked his watch. Lower Beowulf Street. He could just make it, if he ran.

Just as well he was good at running. He burnt shoe leather down Kingsway, skidded round the corner of Saxony Lane and barged through the heavy glass doors of Moondollars coffee shop with fifteen seconds to spare. She wasn't there, of course. That, however, was nothing unusual. He scanned the room to make sure she wasn't hiding behind a pillar or something, then sat down at the only empty table. A waitress materialised and asked him what he wanted; he ordered a coffee, a sausage roll and a slice of caramel shortbread.

Ten minutes later, his order arrived, but still no sign of Sally.

Explanations, he thought, as he tore open one of those stupid paper tubes of sugar: she's in deadly peril and got intercepted before she could escape and come here; the message was a hoax and the whole thing's a wind-up; Luke and the gang have set me up and, any second now, Trinny and Susannah are going to come bouncing out of the kitchen and start criticising the cut of my jacket. He checked the Post-It note again, just to make sure he'd got the right place and time. Then he shrugged, stirred his coffee and opened the newspaper.

Duncan was halfway through a mildly interesting article about capital gains tax indexation when he heard a pop: something like a champagne cork, something like a loud spit. He looked up, and noticed that he could see the opposite wall, in spite of the fact that the front page of the *FT* was in the way. He frowned. There was a hole in his newspaper, about three-eighths of an inch in diameter, that he was sure hadn't been there a moment ago.

Odd, but not worth bothering about. He moved his arms to turn the page and in doing so, happened to glance down. There was another hole, about the same size, in his jacket, between the bottom of his top pocket and the base of his lapel. He sniffed, and caught a very faint whiff of burning.

Moths with plasma torches? He didn't think so. But he had a working hypothesis that wouldn't be hard to test. With the butt end of his coffee-spoon, he probed the hole in his jacket. It tapped against something solid, the contents of his inside pocket. He searched and took out the tape-measure that had fallen off his desk, soon after Pete had woken him up. He pursed his lips. True, he'd only given it a cursory glance before pocketing it, but he was sure he'd have noticed if there'd been, say, a shiny bullet embedded in its chrome-plated casing. As there now was.

He stared at it. A bullet. That'd explain the holes in his jacket and the paper, but—

Fuck me, he thought. The popping noise. Somebody's shooting at me.

Just in time, Duncan managed to stop himself jumping up. If whoever it was intended to take another shot at him, he'd have done so by now. Besides, it didn't matter. They could hose him down with machine guns, and his werewolf skin would turn the bullets into so many flat copper discs. True, it was annoying, mildly disturbing even, to be caught in somebody's crossfire; but it wasn't his best suit and as for the newspaper—

So many flat *copper* discs. He remembered something and took another look at the tape-measure. The protruding back end of the bullet wasn't copper-coloured. More kind of silvery.

Jesus, he thought, and dived under the table.

One, two, three seconds passed. No popping noises. He peered round a table leg. Everything seemed normal. People were drinking coffee, eating doughnuts; he watched their reflections in the big, no-longer-fashionable etched-glass mirror that covered the back wall. Nobody taking aim at him, or hurriedly reloading a gun, unscrewing a silencer or trying to hide something under a coat while scuttling furtively for the door. Just a bunch of office workers drinking coffee and eating stuff. He counted, and frowned; then, as he moved his head a little, he saw the lower half of the waitress approaching.

'You all right?'

He scrambled back into his seat. 'Dropped my fork,' he mumbled.

'Would you like a refill?'

'What?'

'Coffee. Would you like—?'

'Just the bill, please.'

You can send an Englishman cryptic notes, carried by crazed ex-dentists. You can lure him to inexplicable trysts and stand him up. You can shoot at him with silencers and silver bullets. Waste of time, if you're hoping to shatter his imperturbable Saxon calm. The only way you'll achieve that is to try and stick him for six pounds seventy-nine for a coffee, a sausage roll and a slice of caramel shortbread.

'Excuse me,' he said, 'but are you sure this is right?'

The waitress looked at him, and then at the bill. 'Mphm.'

'Oh.' He glanced at the sausage roll and the shortbread, both untouched. 'Oh, all right, then.' He gave her a ten-pound note and she went away.

Explanations, he said to himself; but what remained of his mental faculties were getting bored with that game. Could be any one of a number of possibilities – she'd set him up, someone else had set him up, the bullet had been meant for someone else entirely, or else it was a novelty tape-measure designed to look like it had a bullet blasted into it, and he hadn't noticed when he picked it up. Did it, he asked himself as he scooped his change from the saucer and stood up, fucking well matter? No, it didn't. What mattered was getting the hell out of there before it happened again, perfectly rational explanation or no perfectly rational explanation. Also worth bearing in mind: the next time he got a life-or-death urgent summons from That Bitch, he was going to lock himself in the toilet with a good book and not come out for at least twelve hours. The only sensible course of action, really.

One last glance at the coffee-shop clientele: no masked gunmen to be seen. Thanks to his trusty tape-measure, no harm done. Even so: nearly seven quid for a coffee and a couple of snacks. Scowling horribly at the world, Duncan stuffed the caramel slice in his mouth, wrapped the sausage roll in a paper napkin, pocketed it, and left.

Back at the office, after he'd had a nice sit-down and a delayed fit of the shakes, he dropped by Luke's office. Luke was on the phone, talking loudly about Mareva injunctions, so he sat down and looked at the pictures on the wall: wildlife photographs – deer, antelope, gazelle, zebra. There was also a shiny brass photograph frame on his desk, but it was empty.

'Duncan.' Luke had finished his call. 'You look funny.'

Duncan fished in his pocket for the tape-measure. 'This yours?'

Luke examined it. 'No. Hang on, isn't that a—?'

Duncan nodded. He noticed that the sight of the silvery butt-end seemed to bother Luke. 'Yes,' he said. 'I was having a coffee in one of those Moondollars places. I think someone shot me.'

'With—' Marked reluctance to say the words. Understandable, Duncan conceded.

'I think so,' he replied. 'It looks like sil— I mean, it's not a normal bullet, is it? They're made of copper or something, aren't they?'

'Lead with a copper coating.' Luke was practically squirming away from it. 'Which that isn't. What were you doing in a coffee place in the middle of the afternoon?'

Duncan could feel the truth inside him, hammering to get out. 'Just felt like going out for a few minutes,' he replied, wondering if he sounded convincing.

'So you weren't meeting anybody. I mean, nobody knew you were going to be there.'

Not so long ago, Duncan had believed that lying to his pack leader wasn't possible. 'Wouldn't have thought so,' he said.

'And was there anything odd going on? Apart from someone shooting at you.'

'Well, they charged me seven quid for a coffee and a bit of cake.'

He'd meant it as a joke, but the look on Luke's face suggested he was more surprised about that than the murder attempt; not just surprised, more like disturbed. He scowled, crushing his eyebrows together (a duel to the death between two champion fighting caterpillars). Then he shook himself, smiled and said, 'Well, anyhow, no harm done. Any assassination attempt you can tell your friends about can't be too much of a problem. It was probably mistaken identity. Turf war between crack gangs, something like that.'

Duncan looked at him. 'Silver bullets?'

'We're only assuming it's silver,' Luke replied briskly. 'More likely it's some kind of nickel alloy. Like the crap they make tenpence pieces out of. After all,' he added, with a quick sideways glance, 'if nobody knew you were going to be there, it can't have been a planned ambush aimed at you specifically.'

A fat lot of help, in other words. Duncan slouched back to his office feeling vaguely betrayed, though he couldn't think of a logical reason for taking it that way. Of course, if he'd been a sensible, loyal pack member, he'd have told Luke the whole story; in which case, Luke would almost certainly have been able to tell him exactly what was going on and what to do to make it stop. But—

But.

But the fact was – uncomfortable, but needed to be faced – there wasn't anybody in the Ferris Gang who he felt he could talk to, and he was fairly sure he knew why. Luke had said it out loud to his face, and the others would be sure to take the same line: stay away from that vampire ex-wife of yours, she and her kind are nothing but trouble. Which was true, he didn't need to be told that. Excellent advice, but impractical; a bit like saying that the best way of avoiding death is not to be born in the first place.

Nobody here he could talk to, but he had a file. As soon as he was back in his office, he lugged out all the Bowden Allshapes files, stacked them up on his desk until they formed a barrier more than adequate for keeping the Picts out of Northumbria, and started to read.

Bowden Allshapes, deceased. According to the death certificate, Bowden Emma Allshapes, female (all that time he'd been plagued with the bloody file, and it had never occurred to him to wonder whether the dear departed was a he or a she) was born on 17 January 1912, and died on 5 November 2002. Cause of death: old age. Turning to the schedule of assets: just as well she hadn't been able to take it with her, because she'd have needed a fleet of lorries. The late Ms Allshapes had been seriously loaded: land, securities, furniture and art, cash money. Her heirs were all off-relations, scattered across the globe (Australia, Canada, New Guinea, Wisconsin, Penang; name a time zone, there was an Allshapes in it). What else, for crying out loud? She'd lived in a zonking great big house in Surrey; for a moment Duncan caught his breath, but it proved to be a false alarm. The address was on the Surrey-Hampshire border, a long way away from where he'd met the unicorn.

This was getting him nowhere, and Duncan was thirsty and hot. Biting the heads off a few pencils helped a little. He threw the corpses in the bin – all but one, which he pocketed. Of course (he reflected, chewing wood splinters) it hadn't been his file to begin with. He'd inherited it from Petula de Soto, who'd been sacked the year after he'd joined Craven Ettins. She'd done most of the actual work, pretty much everything bar drawing up the accounts. Accordingly, she might just have met some of the family. He checked the correspondence clip, but there were no notes of meetings. It had all been phone calls, letters and e-mails; hardly surprising, given the wide dispersal of the Allshapes clan.

Yes, but at the very least there must've been a funeral, which at least some of the Allshapes must've attended. Splendid. Now, where there's a funeral, there's always an undertaker's bill. He wasn't quite sure what it could tell him, but he might as well check it out. He pulled out the documents folder and began to riffle.

'Busy?'

He hadn't heard Pete come in. 'Nothing urgent,' he muttered. 'Was there something?'

Pete looked away. 'Thought I'd drop by for a chat, that's all. If you're in the middle of something, I'll clear off and leave you in peace.'

Said almost hopefully, as though Pete didn't want to be there and would be pleased to be told to go away. Duncan stuffed the papers back in the folder and closed the lid.

'I gather you had a bit of an adventure.'

Surprised, no; disappointed, a tad. Not Pete's fault, really. If Luke had ordered him to investigate, he'd have had no choice but to obey. *Duncan's hiding something, go and find out what it is.* 'Sort of,' Duncan replied casually. 'Though the more I think about it, the more I'm inclined to think I've got hold of the wrong end of the stick. I don't think Luke believes anyone was actually trying to kill me,' he added casually.'I rather got the impression he thinks I was being paranoid.'

Pete nodded slowly. 'That's what he told me,' he said.

'Well, there you go. I mean, if there was somebody out to get us, Luke'd know about it, wouldn't he?'

'Bound to.'

Duncan yawned ostentatiously. 'He seemed more surprised that they charged me seven-odd quid for a tea and a sausage roll.'

'Well, he would be.' Pete was frowning curiously at him. 'We don't pay for drinks, remember.'

Years ago, Duncan had been dragged along to visit some boring old relative who built model steam engines in his garage. He recalled the tedious explanation of how the stupid things worked: a wheel went round and round, driving a shrubbery of little cogs and gears. If you pressed a little lever, the mechanism dropped into place and the piston started buzzing up and down, like the back legs of a demented grasshopper. The lever made a distinctive click; and while Pete was talking, Duncan was sure he'd heard that same noise in the back of his mind. It was perfectly true: they went to the pub each lunchtime, drank several gallons of beer, munched at least an outer of pork scratchings and dry roasted peanuts, and nobody had ever asked them for money.

'I thought that was just pubs,' he gabbled.

'And restaurants, pizza places, chippies; anywhere that does food and drink.'

'Even Moondollars?'

'Yeah, why not?'

Duncan ransacked his mind for a justification for that last question. 'Well,' he said, 'they're American, aren't they?'

'Yes. What's that got to do with it?'

Nothing, obviously. 'Do they have werewolves in America?' he asked. Not that he cared, but he desperately wanted to buy thinking time. 'I suppose they must do, if we've got them over here. I never thought of that; werewolves all over the world.'

Pete looked at him suspiciously. 'You're hiding something,' he said.'You shouldn't be able to do that.'

Not you as well. 'Me? No. Open book, honest. After all,' he added, much too quickly, 'if I was in some kind of trouble, you lot'd be the first ones I'd tell.'

'Not if it was something you didn't want us to know about.'

Go away. 'Sure. Like what?'

'Something to do with – oh, I don't know. Money, girls, some nasty personal habit. The point is,' Pete went on, 'it shouldn't be possible. We share stuff, OK?'

'Sure, Pete. Of course.'

'Good. So, how are you doing it?'

'I'm not.'

There are such moments; you're lying to someone, he knows it but can't quite bring himself to accuse you. There shouldn't be, but there are. 'That's all right, then,' Pete grunted. 'In that case, I'll let you get on with what you're doing.'

'Estate accounts. Very boring stuff.'

'Enjoy.' Pete stopped at the door. 'See you at the run tonight.'

Oh, that. He wasn't in the mood; maybe he could make an excuse . . . And then he realised. It was still full moon. All that to go through, all over again—

Well, his mother had been right all along. Never sticks to anything, gets bored so easily; one minute it's model trains, then it's computers, next week it'll be something else. So: he was tired of being a werewolf, after so short a time. He didn't want to play any more.

No, he argued with himself, it's not the magnificent heightened senses and superpowers and all that stuff. It's not even the changing into an animal, because that's great. It's them: Luke, Pete, the bloody Ferris Gang. I was right to leave them and wrong to come back. If only I can get away from them for good; New Mexico—

But that wouldn't be possible, would it? Your wolf is first and foremost a pack animal. He's part of a group. He *belongs*. Now, belonging is a wonderful thing, as opposed to being isolated and lonely and nobody in the world giving a damn. But like everything else, it depends. Above all, it depends on who you belong *to*.

Duncan put his foot on the desk and pushed, driving his chair back until he could stretch his legs out comfortably. Let's think about this, he decided. When I was a little kid, I belonged to my parents, which was fine. Then I belonged to the Ferris Gang: not so fine, but it kept me from getting beaten up in the playground. Then I belonged to Sally, even after she dumped me. Now I'm back with the old crowd, body and soul, and according to them for ever and ever. Now, wouldn't it be fun, just for a change, to belong to me?

Not possible. But, if what the pack wanted him to believe was true, neither was thinking so that they couldn't hear him. Come to that: if he really belonged to them, even wanting not to wouldn't be possible either. It'd be like those love potions in fairy stories: he'd be in love with the pack for ever and ever, whether he wanted to or not.

He sat up. All right, then. New Mexico. Just reach for the phone – Directory Enquiries, travel agent, one-way trip. It was so easy, even humans could do it. Go away, don't come back. Simple.

He hadn't moved. Why was that? Fear is always a good place to start. But he wasn't afraid of Luke any more. If anything, it was the other way round; and although that was no guarantee that Luke wouldn't try and tear him apart (quite the opposite), that thought didn't reduce him to a cringing jelly, like it should have done. If he wasn't afraid of Luke, he certainly wasn't afraid of the others. In that case, it wasn't fear.

Inertia? So set in his ways he couldn't make the effort? Definitely not. His whole life had changed completely over the last week or so. Ties, something holding him back? Family? Not likely. Couldn't be that, then, since he didn't have anybody else in the whole wide world . . .

It's like when you're lost in some huge, complicated building.

You wander up and down stairs, up and down corridors, trying to find the way out. There's nobody around to ask, and your sense of direction's completely shot. You find a door; it's plainly marked *This Way Out*. You grab the handle. It's locked.

Sally, then. In spite of everything. But that was ridiculous; it'd been a long time since she'd dumped him, and had he gone around moping and pining, not sleeping, thinking about her night and day? Hell as like. It was only since all this werewolf stuff had happened – well, almost. Round about that time, anyway. And what about the crazy vampire business? Rather than try and get his head around that, he'd left it well alone. It had served a valuable function, in a way, because it made her even more unattainable than before. Their kind and our kind. A state of undeclared war between the bloodsuckers and the ambulance chasers. Simply not possible; like so many other things.

So, Duncan said to himself, I'll need to stick around for now, until I can sort that out. Once I'm free of her for good, I can get my US visa and slip quietly away into the desert, be a coyote instead. Until I've dealt with it, though, I'm wasting my time.

He felt in his top pocket and found the folded yellow sticky. Her handwriting: he'd know it anywhere. Rounded, clear and inelegant; if letters could talk, her handwriting would be shouting all the time. What the hell was so special about her, anyway?

He leaned forward to reach for the phone, but stopped himself. He'd had enough of Crosswoods's receptionist to last him a lifetime. Getting past their front desk wasn't an inviting prospect, either. He even toyed with the idea of trying to burst his way through – superhuman strength, after all, he wasn't the weedy little nerk he still thought of himself as. But a whole office full of vampires made that a non-starter. In which case he'd have to be patient, and cunning.

He told the little bald man in the front office that he was just nipping out for a packet of chocolate biscuits, and took a taxi to Crosswoods. The street was unusually empty, and he felt uncomfortably conspicuous standing in the middle of it as he tried to figure out a grand strategy. He'd hoped there'd be an alleyway or something that he could lurk in while he waited, but no such luck. The best the geography offered was the doorway of the next building but three on the right. The thick mat of cigarette butts he found there suggested that that was where the buildings' smokers escaped to when the craving got too much to bear. In which case, the sight of a sad, hunched figure standing there looking furtive wouldn't be anything unusual. Fine. He leaned against the doorway, adopting the guilty-casual crouch of the inveterate health-criminal. Perfect camouflage.

He was in for a long wait, he knew that. To occupy his mind, he played at making up perfectly rational explanations for the bullet in the tape-measure that didn't involve conspiracy, malice or the supernatural. As a form of mental exercise it was better than crosswords or sudoku, and some of the solutions he came up with were splendidly ingenious and almost plausible, but they didn't convince him for a moment. It was like being an art forger in a picture gallery, looking at one of his own products hanging on the wall. Just because a hundred experts thought it was a genuine Vermeer didn't change anything. From time to time, people came out of the door and stood next to him for a while, looking hunted and wreathing him in blue smoke.

Quarter to six. By now, the Ferris Gang would've realised that Duncan was absent without leave. He'd taken the taxi in the hope that it'd mask his scent trail, though he wasn't entirely sure it'd be enough. Would they figure out where he was likely to be and come looking for him? He considered the odds. More likely, if they were going to come after him, they'd try his flat first. Not enough daylight left for them to go out there, come back, come round here; and they wouldn't split up to form separate search parties, not this evening. He didn't feel like dwelling on what they were likely to be saying about him, and there was bound to be a certain degree of fun and games when he showed his face in the office tomorrow morning. He decided that he could cope with that.

Quarter past six; half past. It was worryingly dark now, but mercifully the sky was overcast with heavy cloud. Nobody had come out of the Crosswoods building; clearly they worked late there. At Craven Ettins, timekeeping was a competitive sport, with every member of staff determined not to be the first to leave. On any given evening you could tour the offices and see solicitors doodling, phoning their relatives in Australia, playing *Empire Builder* on their PCs, reading the Bible, any damn thing rather than incur the shame of leaving the office while their rivals were still there. Colin Abrams in Conveyancing had been building a scale model of the *Enterprise-D* out of matchsticks when Duncan left; chances were he'd have finished it by now. Was it the same at Crosswoods, or were they actually doing paying work in there? Anything was possible.

Quarter to seven, and Duncan started to worry. He hadn't actually given much thought to what he was going to do later on; undergoing the change alone wasn't something he wanted to think about, but he'd sort of assumed he could dash back to his flat, lock himself in and be very, very brave and self-controlled until dawn. He glanced nervously up at the sky; still enough cloud, just about, but hardly a skyful. All it'd take would be one stray moonbeam, and he'd be screwed. He'd be safe on the Underground, of course, but there was the walk from the station to home. He'd be cutting it fine if he left now. If she didn't show in the next five minutes—

He'd always been able to spot her at long range, presumably because every detail of her was stored in his memory, a full biometric record, like an identity card: the ratio of height to shoulder width, the speed she walked at, everything that was slightly different about her. Therefore he knew, as soon as the glass door slid open, that she was there – her, not some irrelevant other person; her, the genuine article. The hunter's instincts he'd acquired ordered him to stay still, keep quiet, let the quarry come to him. They were good instincts for the job in hand, but he resented them. *Not cut out to be a predator*, he admitted to himself; probably why he'd never really cut it as a lawyer, before Luke Ferris ram-raided his way back into his life. He watched as she came into sharper focus. At fifty yards he could make out the profiles and radii of her face; at twenty-five yards, the effects of light and shade on the curved planes of her cheeks. Subconsciously he ran a check of how she'd changed, how she'd stayed the same. Something had hardened her a little; he hadn't really noticed it before, when he'd seen her in his flat. Maybe it was the difference between artificial light and daylight. Under the moonlight, now – things didn't look the same at all by moonlight, not any more.

When she was fifteen yards away, he got ready to move; at ten yards he straightened his back, balanced his weight on both feet, tried to find the right words—

'Sally.'

(Well, he'd tried; not his strongest suit.)

She turned her head sharply and found him. 'Duncan? What the hell are you doing here?'

He was pleased, absurdly, to hear terror in her voice, rather than anger. 'I need to talk to you.'

'Go away.'

'It won't take a moment.'

She'd stopped. No more than twenty-four inches away. 'Duncan, you fucking lunatic, do you know what time it is?'

Yes indeed. He'd glanced up at the sky just before he moved out to meet her. Cutting it very fine indeed. 'We can go some-where if you're worried about that,' he said.

'Are you out of your skull? In your condition?'

He couldn't help grinning at that; she wasn't impressed. 'So what're you going to do?' he said. 'Call a policeman?'

'No, I'm going back to the office. You can't follow me there.'

'Can't I?'

'You wouldn't want to try.'

He shrugged. 'Go on, then.'

She looked at him. 'The Underground,' she said. 'But you're on your own after that.'

'Fine.'

She started to walk; he remembered that deceptively brisk pace. 'You're being incredibly stupid,' she said, 'you know that? Soon as you get out the other end, you'll – it'll happen, and then you'll really be in the shit. They'll kill you for it, you know that? When one of the pack goes rogue, it's a sort of sacred duty. They hunt him down and—'

'Balls,' Duncan said. 'Got to catch me first.'

That made her stop dead. 'You've left them, then.'

Apparently he had. 'Yes.'

'Oh.'

So it made a difference, did it? 'I don't like what it's done to me,' he said. 'And I don't want to be in their gang any more. Truth is, I never liked them much anyway.'

They walked on in silence for a while, until they were in sight of the Tube station. As soon as they were underground, standing at the top of the stairs leading down to the platforms, she stopped and faced him. 'You complete, utter shit,' she said.

Bit of a non sequitur. 'Why?'

'You know perfectly well why.'

He couldn't help sighing. 'This isn't another of those telepathy things, is it?' he said. 'You know, where I've done something wrong but you won't tell me what it is so I've got to guess? I hate those. I thought that since we aren't actually married any more—'

'You do realise,' Sally said, 'how much trouble you've got me into?'

Yes, one of those telepathy things. 'What trouble?'

'Oh, don't be so *stupid*. They'll have seen you come up to me, us walking away together. They'll think I'm up to something; betraying them—'

Big melodramatic word, *betraying*. Maybe these days he lived the sort of life where big melodramatic words were no big deal, tools you needed in your everyday work, like dynamite in a mining camp. 'Why?' he asked.

'Now you're being deliberately stupid. Because your lot and our lot—'

'It's nothing to do with that, is it?' The insight came to him as he said the words. She gave him a startled look, then frowned.

'No.'

Oh my God. He nodded, to give the impression he had some vague clue about what he was saying. 'It's about her, isn't it?'

Now he'd lost her again. 'Her? Who are you—?'

'The unicorn.'

'Are you mental or something? There's no such thing as—'

'Bowden Allshapes.'

He'd said the name without really thinking; thrown it at her, the way you'd throw mugs and boots and other small, handy items at a burglar. The effect was spectacular. She stopped doing everything, as though he'd switched her off.

Then, 'Yes,' she said.

Oh.

Didn't take her long to get going again. He'd always known she had her own independent power source. 'How the *hell* did you find out about—?'

Duncan laughed. Really, it was quite funny. 'Bloody Bowden Allshapes,' he said. 'The hours I've spent, faffing around with two hundred quid here and nineteen pounds fifty there, just trying to get rid of it and get it out of the door, and now it turns out to be fucking *important*. Like, my whole bloody life—' He pulled himself together. No good seizing the high ground if you trip and go sliding down the slope on your arse. 'At Craven Ettins I handled the Allshapes probate file,' he said. 'Estate accounts. Never could get the rotten things to balance.'

'Hang on.' She was staring at him. 'Estate accounts. That's when someone's died, right?'

'Come on, Sally, you went to law school. It's the final stage in winding up an estate, when you figure out—'

'Bowden Allshapes isn't dead.'

Well, she must be, or we wouldn't have been . . . He was about to say that, but he didn't. It was like shrill white noise inside his head, drowning everything out. She's right, he thought. Because if she's right, it makes *sense*.

'How would you know?' he mumbled.

'Because I spoke to her just this morning.'

– Because if Bowden Allshapes was still alive, still spending her money – pair of tights here, loaf of bread and packet of ham there, nothing much, just a few quid now and then – it'd explain why the fucking accounts never stayed still from one day to the next. Not that that was possible; the banks and building societies and company registrars had closed all her accounts and transferred her shares into the names of the executors; nobody could touch a penny without Duncan Hughes, solicitor in charge of the file, knowing about it. And Duncan Hughes would know straight away, like a shot, because the accounts wouldn't balance—

'Shit,' he said. Not anger or despair. More a kind of reverent awe, inspired by the majesty of his own stupidity. 'But hold it a moment,' he said, more to himself than her. 'It doesn't have to be her, it could just be the executors or someone fiddling the books. No,' he corrected himself, 'because all the money's frozen in our client account, I'd have to sign a pink slip, so it can't be that.'

She was looking at him again. 'Duncan,' she said. 'What are you talking about?'

Then his delayed-action memory finally clicked into place. 'You saw her this morning?'

'Yes. She's Jacky Hogan's client. Divorce. Messy. So she can't be dead—'

'You're sure it's a woman?'

'Well, yes. Long hair, tits, the works. I notice stuff like that.'

'Bowden Allshapes is *dead*.' He waved a furious, ineffectual hand. 'It says so on her death certificate.'

'No, she isn't.'

My patience is infinite, he told himself, my patience is infinite, my patience . . . 'Look,' he said. 'Are we talking about the same person?'

Shrug. 'I don't know. You were the one who brought her up.'

'Yes, but—'

'Then it can't be the same person, can it?'

Except – except that the unicorn had been female. No question about it. Female voice, big soft eyes, habit of buggering up people's lives for them. Sally wasn't the only one who noticed things. And now she was kebabbing him with her sharpest stare. 'All right,' she said. 'Tell me what you know about Bowden Allshapes.'

And why not? So he did; and people trying to get down to the platforms had to squeeze round them for quite a while. They muttered quite a lot, but went unheeded.

He told her about the unicorn (single-handedly responsible for the extinction of British wolves) and how it was the only thing on earth that Luke Ferris was afraid of; how he'd met it twice, chased it, talked to it. He told her about the accounts that wouldn't balance, and how Felicity Allshapes had come to see him in the office—

'Describe her.'

He thought. 'I can't.'

'Why not? Official Secrets Act? Cat got your tongue?'

'Can't remember what she looks like,' he admitted. 'I mean, all I can remember is she was quite nice-looking. But—'

'That's her, then. Same woman.'

Much the same effect as a slap round the face with a mackerel. 'Excuse me?'

'That's her,' Sally repeated. 'That's Bowden Allshapes. You know it's her because you can never remember what she looks like. Two minutes after she's left the office, you can't even say what colour her hair is, or her eyes, or anything. All you can say is, *God, I wish I looked like that.* But that's all.'

All. Allshapes. All manner and every kind of shape: now a unicorn, now a pretty girl, and possibly even a dead woman, for the benefit of a doctor and possibly Her Majesty's coroner. 'So if that was her, pretending to be her own cousin or niece or whatever,' he said slowly, 'then who's the dead woman with all the money?' But of course, she wasn't dead. Any of her. 'Screw that,' he said angrily. 'That's me all explained out. What's it got to do with *you*?'

She tried to close up, like the window at the Post Office after you've been queuing for half an hour, but something made her hesitate. 'She's a client of ours, like I said just now. Divorce. Her husband's huge in mobile phones, it's a nice fat—'

'Client,' Duncan repeated. 'Yours? I mean, are you handling the file?'

She opened her mouth, closed it and nodded. 'I inherited it from a girl who left,' she added quickly. 'It was just a case of sorting out the finances—'

'You know her. By sight.'

'Yes, though if only you'd listen to what I tell you occasionally, you'd know that that's pretty well meaningless. I've met her dozens of times, but I wouldn't recognise her if I passed her in the street.'

'All right.' There was a hell of a lot more that she wasn't telling him, for some reason, but time was short. Next item. 'Why did your lot try and kill me?'

Finally he'd done it; left her speechless.

'I know it was your lot,' he went on, casual as he could manage. 'It was in a Moondollars coffee shop. You sent me this note.' He fished out the yellow sticky, unfolded it and held it where she could see but not quite reach. 'Your handwriting. I went along, just like I was told. Someone shot at me with a silver bullet.' I know it had to be one of your lot who shot at me,' he added airily, 'because I looked for the shooter in a big mirror nailed to the back wall. Of course, I didn't see anybody with a gun; but there were twenty-seven people in the café, not counting me, and twenty-six reflections.'

Sally was looking at him with eyes big and round as saucers. 'Oh Christ,' she said. 'Duncan, I'm so sorry. I never meant—'

'What?' He hadn't meant to grab her shoulders. People were staring. 'What didn't you mean?'

'It wasn't my fault. Nobody ever tells me anything. Anyway,

how could you be so utterly stupid, to walk straight into an obvious ambush like that? If you can't be bothered to look after yourself, why the hell should I have to? You know what, you've got no consideration for other people.'

That was Sally; never more ferocious than when in the wrong. 'Just tell me,' he said. 'Why do your lot want to kill me? Is it because of Bowden—?'

'I don't know, do I? I was just doing as I was told.'

Also typical Sally; when she was lying, she went pink. 'That's not true.'

'Look.' She'd raised her voice. Several passers-by had stopped to watch. 'I haven't got time right now, and neither have you. Have you got any idea how you're going to get out of—'

Of course he hadn't. 'Of course I have. Easy. All I've got to do is stay underground till it's daylight again. It'll be a bit boring, but no big deal. I can ride round on the Circle Line, like the tramps do.'

'You can't.'

''Course I can. The trains run all night, don't they?'

'No.'

Oh, Duncan thought. Fancy me not knowing that. You can live in a city all your life, and not know the most basic things about it. 'Well, I expect I can find somewhere. I mean, I've got the whole bloody Underground network to hide in, must be thousands of places. Don't change the subject.'

'For crying out loud, Duncan, it's not that easy. They've got guards, security patrols—'

'I'll smell them long before they see me.'

'CCTV.' She scowled at him. 'Dogs.'

'Ah. The company of like-minded life forms.'

'Be serious for just ten seconds, can't you?' Sally was practically shouting now. 'If you get caught, it could be really bad.'

'Nah. I can take care of myself.'

'Oh really? They arrest you and take you outside to put you in a car. One second in the moonlight, that's all, and then there'll be bits of minced-up policeman all over central London. I don't know about your lot, but mine prefer a rather lower profile.'

He'd never liked Sally much when she was in the right. 'Let me worry about that,' he said firmly. 'All I want from you is a straight answer. Bowden Allshapes. What exactly—?'

'Oh *shit*.' She gave him a glare that would've stripped varnish, then threw her arms around his neck and kissed him.

Opinions differ. Even among the songwriting community, there's a sharp divergence of opinion. Some practitioners reckon a kiss is just a kiss, others would have you believe it can be a blow-your-head-off spiritual experience. If he was honest with himself, Duncan would have to have admitted that he hadn't collected enough hard data to form a reasoned opinion. Certainly, when they were married, kissing Sally had been mostly quite nice, but not—

More to it than met the lips. Duncan couldn't put it into words, and anyhow he was far too preoccupied to try; but suppose Captain Kirk had landed on a planet where writing and speech were unknown and they could only communicate by snogging; and suppose the prettiest girl on the planet had been assigned to recite to him the whole of their version of the *Encyclopedia Britannica*, complete with footnotes, index and alphabetical list of contributors, in three seconds flat. Something like that. Nice, but confusing.

'All right?' he heard Sally say; and then, while he was still struggling to snap out of it, she was walking away. That made no sense whatsoever. He started to run after her, but she was on the stairs that led to the street; a few more steps, and she'd be out of cover and exposed to the full fury of the moon – he called her name, but she couldn't have heard him. She'd gone.

Duncan looked round. To say that people were staring at him would be an understatement; in fact, his viewing figures were so high, he wouldn't have been surprised if major companies had come rushing up pleading to be allowed to advertise on him. He growled and moved away towards the ticket barrier.

All in all, then, a failure. He hadn't found out what was going on, or how Sally fitted into it; he'd managed to drag out a few tantalising scraps of information, but really, they just made things more confusing than ever. In return, he was in deep, possibly permanent shit with the rest of the pack, and he had somehow to get from the Tube station to his flat without turning into a wolf and killing somebody. Even by his standards, a poor evening's work, and he had every right to feel unhappy and depressed. Odd thing was, he didn't.

Why not? Three guesses.

Only took one, didn't it? Because Sally couldn't have kissed him like that if she hadn't, at some fundamental, subatomic level, meant it. In which case – well, there may be troubles ahead, but while there's moonlight and laughter and love and romance, he was entirely prepared to face the music and run like buggery.

Duncan should've been formulating a plan of action all the way home. Instead, his mind insisted on deconstructing every aspect of the kiss – a foolish exercise, but every time he tried to be worried or scared, a little voice kept telling him that it really didn't matter, everything was going to be just fine, because . . . and there the little voice tended to mumble, so he couldn't make out anything specific. But it sounded like it knew what it was talking about, and the stress melted like blowtorched snow. So Luke was going to be a bit vexed with him in the morning. So what? Besides, that'd only happen if he went into work, and when you thought clearly about it, he didn't have to do that. So they might come looking for him at the flat. No big deal. London's a big place, and even their noses couldn't track him through its vast polyodorous crowds. As for getting from the station to his own front door – actually, he'd have liked to hear what the know-it-all little voice had to say about that, because he didn't have a clue. Furthermore, it had just occurred to him that not only are wolves inadequately equipped to turn keys in

locks, but also (if last night was anything to go by) his clothes
and other portable possessions had simply gone away somewhere when he transformed, and returned automatically when
he changed back. Even the little voice had to admit that that
was an awkward one; he'd have to stop just inside the station
entrance, put his key on the floor, go outside in the moonlight,
change, come back, somehow pick the key up in his mouth—

But what the hell, it'd be all right. Even if it wasn't – even if he
had to spend the whole night slinking around in the shadows of
parked cars, trying very hard not to bite anybody or anything –
he was somehow reassured that it must be possible, and if it was
possible he could do it. It was only impossible things (like getting
someone to be in love with you when they didn't want to be) that
merited worrying about, and right now, if he was asked to com-
pile a list of impossible things he desperately needed to do, he
wouldn't be able to think of anything to put on it.

She kissed me, Duncan thought. True, she swore at me first,
but if memory served that wasn't unprecedented. She didn't
have to do that, but she did it anyway. In which case—

The train stopped. He looked up, saw the name of the station, and scrambled to get out before the doors shut. In which
case – he carried on musing – the really big, important question
was how could he get to see her again, and when? There was no
doubt in his mind that one more interview was all that was
needed to do the trick. Damn this stupid werewolf thing,
because otherwise he could go round to her place right now,
bash the door down if needs be – no, couldn't do that, didn't
know her new address. But it had to be possible to find it;
policemen and private investigators find out people's addresses
every day, so it can't be all that hard. So: once he'd got that, it'd
just be a case of—

He stopped dead. The pavement under his feet was pale,
almost milky, and the air felt cold and a bit damp. He sniffed:
diesel. Fuck it, he thought, I'm outside. I must've left the station without realising it.

Very reluctantly, he looked down at the backs of his hands.

No thick grey fur. Also, he was standing upright, rather than being down on all fours. And he was still wearing his suit, and wiggling his toes told him that his shoes still contained feet, not paws. He looked up and stared straight at the round, bright silver disc in the sky. Full moon. It hadn't happened.

Duncan closed his eyes for a moment, then opened them again. No change.

For all of two seconds, he couldn't move or breathe. Then, as soon as normal service had been resumed, he threw his head back and howled – not from lycanthropy, but for sheer joy.

CHAPTER ELEVEN

Not, Duncan realised, the most sensible thing he'd ever done; because if the Ferris Gang were looking for him, anywhere within a five-mile radius, he'd just told them where he was. Couldn't be helped, though, and he'd have to face them sooner or later, unless he was serious about New Mexico; which he wasn't, not any more, not unless Sally fancied going there with him.

Talking of which: coincidence? Unlikely. It had to have been the kiss. How that could have been possible he neither knew nor cared, in the same way that he didn't have the faintest idea how computers work but was only too happy to use them. More important still than the fact that she apparently had the power to save him was that she'd used it. You don't save someone's soul with a kiss unless you quite like them, at the very least. Yippee, he thought.

A sudden noise made him jump; he realised it was a dustbin falling over, half a mile away. He still had the superpowers, then; that was nice, but he wasn't really fussed. He yawned. God, he was tired. A long and weary few days.

Brief pause for thought. If Luke and the gang were after him right now, they'd be here already. Since they weren't, he was prepared to bet they were off persecuting small animals or chasing traffic, in which case he didn't have to worry about them until the morning. A few hours' sleep, therefore; then pack a few things in a bag and find somewhere to doss down for a while until he'd forced some kind of resolution.

The stairs to his flat seemed painfully steep tonight. Duncan hauled himself up to his landing as though he was carrying a hundredweight of coal on his back, and rummaged in his pocket for his keys. No need. Door already open.

Oh come on, he thought, why's it got to be tonight? Whatever it is – unicorns, vampires, beautiful but unmemorable girls, accounts that won't balance – couldn't it wait till the morning and give him a chance to get some sleep, a bath and a bacon sandwich? Apparently not. With a deep sigh, he shoved the door open and walked in.

When he saw the mess he was relieved. Cupboards ripped open, drawers pulled out, stuff scattered all over the floor: just plain, ordinary, comfortingly normal burglars again. He smiled and waded through his jumbled possessions to the kitchen. They wouldn't have nicked his kettle. You couldn't give it away.

The kettle was still there, but they'd scattered the tea bags all over the floor and torn the door off the fridge. Big deal. Chances were, he wouldn't be coming back here again, at least for a while, and a fridge is just a fridge. He found a stray tea bag that hadn't been shredded (strangely meticulous burglars, these. What had they imagined he could have hidden inside his tea-bags?) dropped it into the one unbroken mug and filled the kettle with water.

'I'm sorry about the mess.'

Duncan froze. The voice (nondescript male) sounded like it had come from right next to him, but he couldn't see anybody. He sniffed: no scent but his own. He held still for two minutes, listening carefully. Nothing but the soft whimpering of the kettle as it slowly persuaded the water to think about boiling. Oh well, he thought.

'You don't know me, of course.'

He dropped the kettle on his foot. After he'd done a little

dance, he burst out of the kitchen into the living room. Nobody there; nobody in the bedroom or the bathroom, either. But definitely not just his imagination. What little self-esteem he had left assured him that if he was going to hallucinate voices, they'd have to be more interesting that that one. He slouched back into the kitchen, and heard a faint muffled cough.

'Oh, sorry.' A patch of air directly ahead of him seemed to shimmer, as though God was playing with the vertical hold, and out of the blur stepped a man. He was short, bespectacled, podgy, a bit thin on top. 'Forgot,' he said. 'It's a nuisance, being invisible. I mean, you don't tend to look at yourself, do you, so it's easy to let it slip your mind.'

Duncan heard a rather terrifying growling noise, and realised he was making it. Bad manners, of course, but never mind. The back of his neck was itching like crazy. 'Who the hell are you?' he said.

'Wesley Loop,' the man replied. 'I was going to clear up a bit before you got back. Is it all right if I sit down?'

'Wesley —?'

'Loop.' The intruder looked round, tutted and perched on the edge of the smashed-up worktop. 'You know – or hasn't Luke told you about me? I used to be his partner. Ferris and—'

'You're dead.'

Mr Loop frowned. 'Well, yes,' he said, sounding mildly offended. 'Look, would you mind not glaring at me like that? I'm really sorry about the furniture and stuff, but you know how it is. Time of the month and all.'

At that moment Duncan happened to catch sight of the bedroom door. It had been ripped off its hinges, and something had taken a bite out of it, just above the handle. It occurred to him that, whatever Mr Loop's reason was for being there, it wasn't to steal his DVD player.

'I got the curtains drawn as quickly as I could,' Mr Loop went on. 'But it was awkward without hands, and I suppose I got a bit carried away. I'll write you a cheque in a minute, if you tell me how much for.'

'But you can't,' Duncan said. 'You're dead, he repeated.'

Mr Loop sighed, and when he spoke again, it was a bit slower and louder, as if Duncan was a small child, or a foreigner. 'That's perfectly all right,' he said. 'It'll be a company cheque. Crosswoods's office account. You won't have any problem with it at the bank.'

'I don't care about the stupid cheque. What the hell are you doing in my flat?'

He could tell that Mr Loop was a sensitive sort of person, the kind who gets upset when people raise their voices. 'I came to see you,' Mr Loop explained, martyred-patient. 'And obviously I couldn't call on you at the office. What are you doing home so early, by the way? I didn't expect you back till the early hours. Shouldn't you be out with the rest of them?'

'What are you doing in my flat *alive*?'

Puzzled frown, followed by the clunk of the dropped penny. 'Oh, I see,' said Mr Loop. 'You don't know about—' He paused. You could almost see the tip of the dilemma horn poking through his shirt. 'I don't think I'm supposed to tell you, actually. It's a bit of a delicate situation, and—'

Grabbing him by the throat had seemed like a good idea at the time; the only thing to do, in fact. As Duncan flew through the air and splatted against the wall like a fly on a windscreen, he had a fraction of a second in which to reflect on that; and yes, if he had his time all over again, he'd still try and strangle the bastard, because if there was one thing he hated more than anything else, it was *bloody not knowing*—

'Are you all right?' asked Mr Loop anxiously.

Duncan sat up and felt the back of his head; then he turned half round and looked at the wall. The plaster was all smashed up, but he felt fine. Hooray for superpowers.

'Please don't try that again,' Mr Loop said. 'Really, if I'd known there was going to be all this violence, I wouldn't have got involved to start with. Honestly, all I wanted was to acquire new skills that'd help me be the best possible lawyer I could be. Throwing people into walls—' He shuddered. 'The idea was, eventually, when we'd built up a good, solid practice, that Luke would look after the bread-and-butter work, leaving me to handle the more abstruse and intellectually challenging cases. Copyright,' he added sadly, 'intellectual property. Internet jurisdictions. Ecclesiastical law, even. As it turned out, though—'

'Excuse me,' Duncan interrupted mildly, 'but presumably you know all about this stuff. If I attack you again and you throw me against this wall really hard, what's the worst that could happen?'

Mr Loop furrowed his brow in careful thought. 'There could easily be significant structural damage to the building,' he said. 'Which would inevitably render you liable in damages to the landlord – I'm assuming this property is leasehold?' Duncan nodded. 'In fact,' Mr Loop went on eagerly, as though he'd finally found something in all this dreary unpleasantness that he could bring himself to take an interest in, 'depending on the nature and degree of the damage, the landlord could be entitled to forfeit the headlease, thereby depriving you of all and any interest you may currently hold in the property, regardless of any premium you may have paid to your predecessor in title. In which case, a court might be inclined—'

Duncan threw a chair at him. It smashed over his head like a Hollywood prop, but with no sign of having hurt him. 'Really,' Mr Loop said. 'What on earth did you do that for?'

'To shut you up, mostly,' Duncan replied. 'Also, I want you to hit me again.'

'Good heavens. Why?'

'To see if it hurts, of course. Because if it doesn't, I'm going to pull your head off, or at least I'm going to have a bloody good go at it. Presumably I won't succeed, but what the hell, it'll be fun trying.'

'Mr Hughes. Duncan,' Mr Loop added; then, 'Can I call you Duncan?'

'Sure. If it's with your dying breath, so much the better.'

Mr Loop bit his lip. 'I seem to have annoyed you,' he said. 'What did I do?'

Just when you think you're way past gobsmacked, somebody says something like that. 'What, apart from trashing my flat, you mean?'

'I've already said I'll pay for—'

'Why did you do it, incidentally?'

A guilty look washed over Mr Loop's face. 'I was still in my other form at the time,' he said wretchedly. 'I'm afraid that when I'm a wolf, I have no respect whatsoever for other people's property. I was hoping you would understand,' he added resentfully, 'since you're—'

'Oh, forget about it,' Duncan said, with a rather grand wave. 'It was all junk anyhow, and I'm leaving here in any case.'

'Ah.' Mr Loop looked genuinely relieved. 'That's a very mature attitude.'

'Whatever. No, the reason why I'm going to smash your face in is because you won't fucking tell me what's going on.'

He launched himself across the room at Mr Loop, who sidestepped and clouted the side of Duncan's head like a tennis pro returning a volley. Duncan flew a short way through the air and crash-landed against the frame of the kitchen door.

'This is really quite inappropriate,' Mr Loop said. 'Listen. If I tell you what you want to know, will you please stop this dreadful behaviour?'

'Sure,' Duncan replied, and spat out a mouthful of splintered wood. 'I was starting to get bored with it anyhow.'

'Very well.' Mr Loop paused and watched him, as though he didn't trust him not to launch another attack. 'So, what's on your mind?'

'Oh, nothing much,' Duncan replied and, astonishing himself with his own speed and dexterity, lunged at Mr Loop with his arms outstretched. This time, either he was a fraction quicker or Mr Loop was a little slower – the left hook missed the side of Duncan's head by at least twelve-thousandths of an inch, and Duncan contrived to get hold of the end of Mr

Loop's tie. He jerked hard, and was delighted to watch Mr Loop sailing through the air and landing awkwardly on top of the cooker.

'Ouch,' said Mr Loop. Then he rolled off and landed on the floor. Duncan charged at him, aiming to drop-kick him into oblivion, but his hurtling shoe met air and then, regrettably, the edge of the cooker. To his surprise, it hardly hurt at all. The pasta jar hurt even less when Mr Loop broke it over his head – an ill-considered move, since it gave Duncan a further and better chance to do his Johnny Wilkinson impression. His toecap caught Mr Loop millimetre-perfect in the groin and the little man lifted off his feet like Peter Pan on wires in a pantomime, shot through the air and disappeared through the kitchen window in a shower of glass and wood splinters.

It occurred to Duncan that he might have gone a bit far this time, bearing in mind that his flat was on the fifth floor. Not that it mattered, of course. Wesley Loop was dead, Duncan had Luke's word on that, and they couldn't have you for killing a dead man, not even if David Blunkett was still Home Secretary. Nevertheless—

He picked the kettle up off the floor, refilled it and plugged it back in. He really was going to have to leave soon. Even if Luke and the gang didn't show up, sooner or later someone was going to notice Mr Loop's spreadeagled corpse and the curtains blowing through the smashed window five storeys above it. Never mind. There was too much rushing about in modern life, leading to all manner of stress-related disorders. A nice cup of tea, therefore, and then he'd go on the run.

He'd fished out the tea-bag and was stirring in the milk when he noticed something on the back of his hand. A pale silver stain. Moonlight.

He frowned. He was looking at a hand, not a paw. So: if his earlier theory was right, how long would it be before the effects of the kiss wore off, or was he cured for good? He wished, not for the first time, that lycanthropy had come with a handbook or manual, something you could look stuff up in, rather than having to rediscover the wheel every five minutes. Of course, he thought with a mild pang of guilt, Mr Loop could probably have told me the answer if I hadn't kicked him out of the window. Why did I do that, he asked himself, and why aren't I curled up in a ball on the floor whimpering with terror and guilt? Fuck's sake, I just *killed* someone. That's got to matter, surely?

The doorbell rang.

Oh, Duncan thought. Didn't take them long, did it? Well: he could resist arrest, probably successfully, if he didn't mind damaging a copper or two. Or he could go quietly, cooperate, explain. He was a lawyer, after all, and although he'd managed to skive off doing any criminal work while he was training, he reckoned he could still remember the basics of what they'd told him at law school about standard when-someone-gets-busted protocols. Thanks to his ace in the hole, he was confident that it'd only be a temporary annoyance at worst. They'd go away, check the records, find out that the ironed-looking corpse was Wesley Loop, who'd died years ago in a park in Surrey and therefore couldn't have been murdered that night in north London, and let him go. Simple as that. The worst thing he could do was complicate matters by mangling law enforcement officers. He nodded to himself, went into the hall and opened the door.

'You'll notice I rang the bell this time,' said Mr Loop.

Not a mark on him, by the looks of it. 'You're alive,' Duncan said.

'No,' Mr Loop replied. 'Can I come in, please? I'll wipe my feet and everything.'

'Of course,' Duncan said. The anger had evaporated, he noticed. Probably just as well. 'The kettle's just boiled, if you—'

'Not for me, thanks.' Mr Loop passed him and walked into the kitchen. 'I don't eat or drink nowadays.' He paused, looking round for something to sit on. 'Can we agree a truce, please?' he said. 'Believe me, I do understand your urge to sublimate your bewilderment and anxiety into acts of reckless violence, but really, it's completely pointless.' He picked a shard of broken glass out of his ear. 'I hope we've established that beyond reasonable doubt.'

Duncan nodded. 'No more playing ping-pong with each other, promise,' he said. 'And I don't usually lose my temper like that. It's just been a rough old couple of days, that's all.'

'Quite.' Mr Loop hitched up his trouser knees and sat down on the broken remains of Duncan's telly. 'I think we can make allowances for each other at this time. It must be particularly trying for you, since I gather it's your first—' He caught sight of the smashed-out window frame, and the silvery-grey shimmer. 'Would you mind,' he added nervously, 'if we went into another room? Somewhere darker.'

'What? Oh, I see.' Duncan got up and led the way into the bedroom, having first checked that the curtains were drawn. 'So, you're still—'

'Yes, essentially.' Mr Loop sat down on the bed, while Duncan perched on the edge of the overturned wardrobe. 'Like yourself, I do well to stay indoors and in the shade until this current phase of the moon is over. Luckily under the circumstances, I have the knack of – becoming invisible would be an overstatement, but let's say I can discourage people from noticing me. Accordingly, when I fell out of your window and became a wolf in mid-air—'

'Is that because you're dead?' Duncan asked. Then, without waiting for an answer, he added, 'You are, aren't you? Dead.'

'Yes.'

'Oh.' At least he managed to keep himself from saying *I never met a dead person before*. For one thing, he had an uneasy feeling that it wasn't actually true.

'I'm sorry if that makes you feel uncomfortable,' Mr Loop went on. 'Quite understandable if it does. We go to great lengths to conceal our true nature, but in your case, of course—'

'Was he one of yours?' Duncan broke in. 'The man who brought the note from Sally. The dentist.'

Mr Loop looked at him for three seconds, then nodded. 'Norman Standwell,' he said. '1946 to 2002, dental surgeon. Cardiac arrest. Though I wasn't aware that you'd met him. You say he brought you a note.'

'He's a—' Duncan hesitated. He couldn't help thinking the word sounded silly. 'He's a zombie, then.'

Sharp intake of breath. 'I'm sorry,' Mr Loop added, 'you weren't to know. But we don't use the Z-word. We find it pejorative and insulting. Instead we say "revenant", or "after-walker". "Undead" is an acceptable colloquialism, but properly speaking it refers to our colleagues in the vampire community, so it can be confusing.'

Duncan nodded slowly. 'Anyhow,' he said. 'That's what you are. You and that dentist bloke.'

'Yes.'

'And Bowden Allshapes.'

Mr Loop smiled. 'Oh, assuredly Bowden Allshapes. Though again,' he added, 'that might be construed as misleading.'

'Misleading?'

'Like referring to God as a vicar.'

That one went over Duncan's head like a cruise missile. He waited for a moment, to make sure it had gone away, then said, 'What happened?'

'Excuse me?'

'To you. And the dentist bloke. And you make it sound like there's more of you.'

Mr Loop smiled. Not quite like a shark; not exactly like the jaw of a skull lolling open. But not cuddly, either. 'Oh yes, there are more of us. Quite a few, in fact.'

'How many?'

This time a laugh, somewhere between a cough and a snigger. 'I can't give you an exact figure,' Mr Loop said. 'But a substantial number. Not as many as the Liberal Democrats, but loads more than UKIP, if you follow me.'

'Oh. More than werewolves?'

'Heavens, yes. More than werewolves and vampires put

together. Using the same frame of reference, compared to us you and your sister community are the Lord's Day Observance Society. You're fringe,' he added, just a little smugly. 'We're starting to matter.'

Something about the way he said that. 'That sounds like you're – well, *for* something.'

Mr Loop nodded. 'Oh, quite definitely. Actually, that's a good way of putting it. We're for something, in the sense that we serve a purpose. Also, we're for something as in having an agenda. I suppose that would make us the National Trust, though in time we hope to become the RSPCA, or something like that. But yes; most certainly we're for something. All thanks,' he added, 'to our mutual friend Bowden Allshapes.' A sort of fond smirk showed on his face. 'I little thought when she killed me that I'd be saying this one day, but Bowden Allshapes is all right. And I believe you'll come to think so too, in time. Actually, that's why I'm here.'

Duncan stood, and Mr Loop tensed up, watching him closely. No trust there, then. 'You didn't answer my question,' Duncan said. 'What happened? I mean, I was always told that when you die, that's it. But you're saying you can sort of – well, opt out, like a pension scheme or something. Are you saying that you've found a way of—?'

'We didn't find a way. The way found us. A bit like a fox finding a rabbit.'

That sank in, and Duncan thought for a moment about the dentist. 'Now you're making it sound like it's – like it's not a nice thing,' he said awkwardly. 'But a moment ago you were saying, go out and prepare for government. Which is it?'

Mr Loop shrugged. 'Like everything in this life – no word-play intended – a bit of both. Like getting a job and working for someone, I suppose. You go along to the interview all nervous and trying your best to impress. You get the job – and six months later you're longing for the parole board to come along and get you out of there. Let me ask you the question: who's the predator? You think you are – warily stalking the job through the long grass, careful not to make a loud noise and startle it away. But it's the job that catches you, and next thing you know, you're a prisoner in a chain gang. I suppose the moral is, be careful what you hunt.' Mr Loop sighed. 'People throughout history have yearned for eternal life. Those of us who've achieved it find out it's not quite what we imagined it'd be. No, it's not a nice thing, as you put it. There's an entity,' he went on, his voice hardening. 'I'm not quite sure how you'd define it; somewhere between a god and an insurance company, maybe. When I encountered it, the form it took was a white unicorn with silver hooves and a golden horn in its forehead. It killed me. Like you, I assumed that I'd reached the end of the road. I was wrong. What I mistakenly thought was death turned out to be a form of recruitment. At the time, after I'd got over the blind relief of still existing, I was bitter, resentful. The entity doesn't bring people back from the dead and then set them loose. It harvests them. Sustainably, of course,' Mr Loop added. 'Fortunately, the living aren't yet an endangered species, although we shall have to be careful as time goes on. In my case, I was unhappy about it. You see, I believed that by becoming a werewolf, I'd got as close as I could reasonably expect to perfection, given my aims and aspirations. I wanted to be rich, powerful and respected; that was why I became a lawyer, and a werewolf. Having achieved my aim, I resented being killed and having everything I'd won for myself taken away. As a revenant, I had to start at the bottom again, work my way up, prove myself all over again—' Mr Loop stopped for a moment. He looked as though he was thinking back over what he'd said, in case he'd been indiscreet. 'We all have to start at the bottom, you see,' he went on. 'Your Mr Standwell, for example. In life, he was a well-respected dentist with a flourishing practice in Worthing. Now he runs errands. I was a solicitor, founder and senior partner of my own firm, leader of my own pack of werewolves. I, by contrast, am still a lawyer. What's more, I'm doing far better as I am now than I could ever have done if I'd stayed running Ferris and Loop. Excuse me if this sounds like boasting – well, it *is* boasting. These days I head up the legal department of Allshapes International – whereas my former partner Luke Ferris is still battling along in private practice and chasing lorries on the Kingston bypass on his day off. Oh, Luke and I are still in the same profession, but that's like saying a whale and a clownfish are both in the same ocean. To die is an awfully big opportunity, you see. I'm one of the few people it brings out the best in.'

This lecture sponsored by the Death Marketing Board. Duncan gave himself a mental shake, like a wet dog. 'Allshapes International,' he said.

'That's right.' A faint, Gollum-like glow lit up Mr Loop's eyes. 'Essentially we're an employment agency. We supply staff. When our clients approach us, they know we'll be sending them a cheap, docile workforce; men and women who'll get the job done quietly and efficiently. No unions, no health and safety, no National Insurance, no statutory coffee breaks, no employers' liability insurance. No wages. We charge twelve pence an hour a head for our people. As far as labour costs are concerned, that's it.' Mr Loop smiled. 'At the moment, of course,' he went on, 'we're limited to sectors where they want workers with no skills and no motivation. But there's plenty of work like that about. Call centres, cleaners, agricultural, that sort of thing. We make all the difference to employers struggling to compete against China and Eastern Europe.'

'You're a public service,' Duncan said quietly

'As a matter of fact, we are. Really, it's just a logical extension of current practice. Outsourcing your customer service department to Calcutta or Bangalore is all very well, but even Indians have got to be paid *something*. You need to look at it from the employer's point of view,' Mr Loop went on, and the passion began to build in his voice. 'When an employer takes on staff, all he wants is a certain amount of work done adequately and on time, as cheaply as possible. If he hires a traditional worker he may get that, but a whole lot of other stuff comes with the package. You hire a living, breathing human being – it's such an intimate relationship that you might as well marry him and have done with it. You've got to consider his health and welfare, take account of his feelings, coax him along with little incentives. There he is, a fellow creature, your equal in the eyes of the law; making demands on your time and energy, needing to feel he's loved and wanted. It's just like a marriage – and all you wanted was the floors swept and the empty pallets stacked. We give you what you want: no less and definitely no more. And at sensible prices, too. You can see why we've got to be responsible with our expansion programme. If we aren't careful, we'll put the living out of a job.'

Duncan realised that he'd had about as much of Mr Loop as he could take. 'Fine,' he said. 'Thanks. Now I know. What's any of this got to do with me?'

Mr Loop didn't answer straight away. The expression on his face was hard to read, until you broke it down into its component parts. He looked a bit like a thoughtful man in a restaurant: eager, because he was hungry; guilty, because an animal had had to die just so he could eat steak; angry, because the steak was well done instead of medium rare. 'It's got everything to do with you,' he said. 'Apparently. I don't know why. I'm just the messenger.'

Mr Loop took a step forward. Duncan matched it with a step back.

'Bowden Allshapes wants you,' Mr Loop went on. 'What for, I don't know. Not my place to know, I'm only a lawyer. For lawyers, as you well know, there's no right or wrong, just winning. The words *dead or alive* were mentioned, though that may have been intended as a joke. I wouldn't know. I don't really do humour.'

Duncan stepped back again. 'I'm not going anywhere with you, you lunatic,' he said.

'Lunatic.' Mr Loop smiled pleasantly. 'Interesting choice of word; originally meaning one whose behaviour is influenced by the phases of the moon. If you'd care to step outside, we could settle this quite easily, wolf to wolf. Or I could throw you against the walls a few more times, I suppose, if that's what you'd prefer. It'd be pointless, though. We both know who'd win. Personally, I could never see the point in fighting a losing battle. The most that can be said for it is that it's good exercise, but I'd far rather do ten minutes on the rowing machine.'

'You think you can make me go with you? By force?'

'Yes.'

Duncan tried to step back again, but a wall was in his way. Stupid, stupid wall. 'Bit crude, isn't it? After all,' he added hopefully, 'you're a lawyer, not a thug.'

'Crude? Not a bit of it.' Mr Loop advanced again. 'All law is based on force. All our writs and court orders and injunctions are founded on the fact that if you disobey the court, policemen will come and take you away. If you resist them, they'll hurt you. If you resist them a lot, they'll kill you. We trade our subtleties and quote the decision of Lord Justice Lane in *Peabody v Smallbridge*, but really it comes down to which one of us gets to impose his will on the other. In this instance, me.' He frowned. 'And honestly, you can't believe you'd stand any chance against me, even if you insist on being really boring and fighting to the death. Think about it. Even silver bullets wouldn't hurt me, because I'm already—'

'All right.' Duncan raised his hands. Just the faintest sound, but loud as next door's angle grinder on a Sunday afternoon to someone with super-hearing. The question was, had Mr Loop heard it too? 'Point taken. I'll come quietly.'

'Excellent.' Mr Loop smiled with genuine warmth. 'I'm so glad. Otherwise, I'd probably have had to kill you, and then I'd be faced with the chore of lugging you back to headquarters gripped in my jaws. When you're ready, we'll be going.'

Duncan went to the front door and opened it. Nothing there. Of course, he could have been mistaken, but who else sniffed like a cross between a pistol shot and tearing calico?

'Once we transform,' Mr Loop went on, 'we'll have to be careful not to be seen. I have a certain advantage over you in that respect, but—'

'I won't transform,' Duncan interrupted. 'I'm cured, hadn't you noticed?'

'Cured?' Mr Loop looked at him. 'That's not possible.'

'Ah,' Duncan said cheerfully, and stepped out into the moonlight. Mr Loop bounded after him, and as soon as the moonlight touched him, he vanished. In his place stood a huge grey wolf. 'Heel,' Duncan chirruped, as a couple of passers-by gave them both an anxious stare. 'There's a good boy. Walkies.'

Mr Loop growled, then fell in beside him. 'You ought to wag your tail a bit,' Duncan whispered. 'Just while there're people about.'

The red glow in the wolf's eyes said *don't push your luck.* Duncan smiled. If he could keep Mr Loop feeling annoyed and irritable, maybe he wouldn't notice the smell. 'If I'd thought,' he said, 'I could've brought along an old belt or something, for a lead. Or a rubber ball, perhaps.' He felt in his pocket. For some reason there appeared to be a sausage roll in it; then he remembered. Moondollars, the bill. He broke off a corner and held it just in front of the wolf's nose. 'Here, boy,' he said. 'Treats for good dogs.'

The wolf paused for two seconds, then lifted his snout and snapped. It was probably just as well that Bowden Allshapes wanted Duncan intact, with the full set of fingers. 'Wooza good *boy*, then?' Duncan said desperately; because at all costs he wanted to keep Mr Loop from noticing the almost overwhelming smell, or look round and see the four shapes that had separated from the shadow of the bus shelter on the corner. He snatched a pen from his top pocket, threw it into the darkness ahead and yelled 'Fetch!' The wolf looked up at him with disgust and loathing in its eyes, as the four shapes came into the amber circle of the light of a street-lamp. Pete, Clive, Micky and Kevin – so where was Luke?

'Good dog,' Duncan said. '*Kill!*'

Mr Loop stared at him, sniffed and spun round, jumping in the air as he turned. Pete sprang before he had a chance to land, reaching out his muzzle and snapping at the revenant's throat. He missed, but Kevin crashed into Mr Loop and closed his teeth on the loose skin over his shoulders, pulling him down, while Micky and Clive went for his flailing paws. Mr Loop caught Clive's ear in his teeth and shredded it, but Pete was there now, going for the throat again. All of them were snarling, yipping, growling. It was a strangely captivating sight, but Duncan had seen enough. He left them to it, and ran.

Where was Luke? He hadn't anticipated any sort of tactical subtlety. As he turned the corner he could hear claws scrabbling on paving stones, and smell fresh blood. It wasn't working out the way he'd hoped, when he'd first heard Pete's distinctive sniff and had known that the pack was coming to find him. He'd expected the battle to take place on the stairs, allowing him to double back to his flat, nip across the landing and vanish down the fire escape. From there he'd have had only a short way to go before he reached the station approach, with its life-saving cluster of pubs, late-night convenience stores and other people-magnets. Instead he was heading in the opposite direction, down streets that were empty at this time of night, where taxis never cruised. With Luke unaccounted for he felt desperately exposed. He lengthened his stride, running fast. (But could he outrun Luke Ferris, particularly tonight? Be realistic – no chance.) There was a pub around here somewhere. Would Luke risk making a scene in a crowded pub? Duncan grinned ruefully. There were certainly precedents.

As he ran he tried to listen. The dogfight was apparently still going strong, though it was hard to make out who was winning. If he'd been a betting man, he'd probably have had to favour Mr Loop, in spite of the odds. He sniffed: if Luke was nearby he couldn't smell him, but that didn't really mean a lot. Someone as smart as Luke would think to disguise his scent . . .

There was a thought. Frantically, he tried to recall his local geography. This was Huntingdon Street, he was fairly sure; in which case, the next left was Skinners Lane, leading to Fife Avenue, which carried on down to—

Oh joy – to the canal. The dirty, yucky, smelly, neglected canal, with its floating crust of soggy cardboard and styrofoam burger boxes. The smell hit his heightened sense like a slap across the face. Nobody in his right mind would want to go paddling in that, let alone swim in it. Not unless he had a werewolf on his trail. Duncan looked both ways, to make sure that nobody was about, then closed his eyes and jumped in.

It tasted worse than it smelled, which was quite an achievement for a mere chance accumulation of water molecules. He spat out a mouthful of the revolting stuff and kicked up his heels in the briskest doggy-paddle he could manage.

He kept it going for just under five hundred yards, to be safe, then ploughed across to the opposite bank and hauled himself out. He was soaked through, of course, but the water was probably the least of his problems; at a guess, there was enough oil in the canal to keep Europe independent of the Middle East for a month. But oil smells; and so do all the other revolting things that wind up in city canals. Luke's nose, precision instrument that it was, would have trouble finding Duncan's scent under all that, even if they were standing next to each other. He grinned, shook himself hard, and trotted away up the nearest side street.

The road name was unfamiliar. Duncan was off his small patch, with only a vague idea of where he was, but since he had nowhere to go until Crosswoods opened its doors in the morning it really didn't matter very much. He felt painfully hungry and thirsty, but he dared not set squelching foot in a pub or a chippie smelling like that. It occurred to him that (if he was really lucky) when he'd hauled himself out of the canal he'd walked into a completely new life: werewolf- and zombie-free, maybe, but he couldn't actually lay claim to anything from his past except (possibly) the only girl he'd ever really loved and a suit of wringing wet, oil-soaked clothes. That thought would have depressed him if he hadn't caught sight of a patch of silver light on the pavement ahead. He glanced up at the full moon, staring down at him like an angry headmaster, and came to the conclusion that there are worse things in life than being wet.

He followed the alley until it came out into a wide shop-lined street, where he paused beside the front steps of a bank. Just for fun, he took a cashpoint card out of his wallet and stuck it in the slot. The machine flashed a green light at him and switched itself off. Bowden Allshapes, presumably: he was impressed. There were security cameras built into these gadgets, weren't there? In which case, his presence there was now recorded, time-franked and visually confirmed. Probably a good idea to be somewhere else as quickly as possible.

Far away in the distance, a wolf howled. He quickened his step.

Now, if only he could find a change of clothes . . . If this was a nice old-fashioned neighbourhood, with rows of back-to-back houses, each with a little snippet of garden just wide enough to accommodate a washing line, he might be in with a chance. (Though that would mean stealing, and he wasn't sure he'd ever stolen anything in his life; not from a stranger, anyhow. Some desperado he was turning out to be.) But he was in flat-and-bedsit country, so he could forget that idea. Every step he took sounded like a rotten tomato hitting a Cabinet minister, and he was leaving a trail of oily footprints.

Duncan walked for fifteen minutes or so, just to put as much distance as possible between himself and the end of his scent trail, then flopped down on a low wall. Delayed panic, he assumed: he was shaking as though he'd got the flu, and his head hurt. He tried to collect his thoughts, but they wouldn't hold still. They kept scampering in all directions, like chickens. Mr Loop and Bowden Allshapes; vampires; where was Luke; the kiss. Ah yes, the kiss, which had cured him of lycanthropy but generously left him those amazing superhuman senses. But he couldn't really bring himself to be interested in any of that stuff. The kiss . . .

In films, when the hero and heroine are escaping from the

bad guys, dodging machine-gun bullets as they leap from exploding buildings or weave cars through traffic at breakneck speeds . . . In films, just as the chase is getting desperate, and any sane person in such a situation would only have room in their mind for panic and terror, there's always a lull, a pause in the headlong chase and special-effects barrage, while the boy and the girl take time out to discuss and untangle their relationship, declare everlasting love. Those bits always spoiled the film, as far as Duncan was concerned, because it stood to reason that when hot lead filled the air and the wolf pack was on your trail, you simply wouldn't be in the mood for any of that stuff, it'd be the last thing on your mind. So unrealistic, was Duncan's view. So untrue to life.

Just goes to show; truth stranger than fiction. Sure, his old life was irredeemably over now, one way or another. He'd gone AWOL from the pack, the undead were after him with a butterfly net and a killing bottle, vampires were shooting at him in coffee shops. If this was a movie, it was one of those lemons where the producers haven't been able to make up their minds which big action sequence to go for, and have therefore compromised by including them all. But here he was, a fugitive hunted by terrifying monsters whose existence he'd have refused to believe in a few weeks ago, and all he could think about was whether she still—

'Excuse me.'

A long black car had pulled up beside him, and the back window was winding down. Mirror glass all round, he noticed, very Californian; wasn't it illegal in the UK, though? A smart-looking middle-aged woman was looking out at him. He raised his head.

'Excuse me,' the woman repeated, 'but is this Van Helsing Avenue?'

Duncan shrugged. 'Sorry, no idea,' he said. 'I'm sort of lost myself, actually.'

'You poor thing. And you're all wet. Has it been raining?'

'No, I don't think so. Actually, I fell in a canal.'

'Good heavens. No wonder you're soaked. Why don't you go home and get changed, before you catch your – oh, I forgot, you said you're lost.' She frowned sympathetically. Nice woman, Duncan thought. 'You're not having a particularly good evening, are you?'

He laughed. 'Not really, no.'

'Well.' The woman's voice became brisker. 'Tell me where you want to get to, and we'll find it for you on this satnav thing; that's if George can get it to work. He's only had it a week, and – yes, dear, I know, the handbook doesn't make sense. What was the name of the street?'

'Thanks, but really,' Duncan said. 'I'm fine.'

'Nonsense. It's no trouble.'

There was, of course, no street in London where he wanted to go – quite a few he wanted to stay well away from, but he could manage the navigational side of that perfectly well without any help from technology. But he couldn't very well say that, could he? 'Harpers Ferry Road,' he said (he had no idea where that was, but he'd seen the name somewhere and it had stuck in his mind). 'If you can just give me directions—'

'Hang on. Is that – ah, here we are, well done, George, you're getting the hang of it at last. I told you it was just a matter of not hitting the little box thing. Oh,' she added, a moment later. 'I'm afraid it's rather complicated. You'd better come here and take a look at it for yourself. I don't understand these funny little pictures.'

Duncan really didn't feel like moving from his nice comfortable wall, but he'd got himself tangled up now. He stood up and squelched over to the front passenger door, which swung open.

'Hop in,' a man's voice said.

'No, I'd better not, I'm all wet.'

'Don't worry about that, I've got seat covers on. Washable.'

Some people are so nice it's annoying. He climbed into the front seat, looking for a screen of some sort. There wasn't one. The car door slammed.

'What—?' he said stupidly, as the engine fired and the car

264 • Tom Holt

started to move. He would probably have gone on from there, but something small and hard was digging into the back of his head. If this was one of those stupid films he disliked so much, it'd be a gun.

'Silver bullets, naturally,' the woman said. 'Did you know that we have to get them individually hallmarked, by law? It's true. They've all got a little lion and some numbers stamped on them. Ridiculous, isn't it? Oh, would you mind terribly putting your seat belt on?'

The car tore round a corner, throwing Duncan hard against the window. He straightened up again. The driver, he noticed, was a short, bald, round-headed man who reminded him of someone. The hard, cold pressure on the back of his head was still there.

'Suit yourself, then,' the woman said. 'Only George does so like to drive fast. Of course, you're practically indestructible, so it doesn't matter terribly much. Talking of which: Wesley's fine, in case you were worried. A few broken bones, and one of his feet came off, but nothing that can't be put right in a jiffy.'

Wesley. Wesley Loop. In that case—

'We've met,' he said dully. 'Haven't we?'

'That's right,' the woman chirruped. 'And this time it's me chasing you, which is rather fun, isn't it? Not that it makes any difference in practice. Oh, while I think of it, I'd just like to say thank you for all your hard work, looking after our legal business. Now I really don't want you to think, just because it was all a bit of a sham and there was no way you could ever have got those silly accounts to balance, that we don't really appreciate all your effort on our behalf. In fact, it was your sheer perseverance—'

'It's dogged as does it,' the driver muttered.

'Be quiet, George. It was your perseverance that convinced us that you were just the person we were looking for; which is why you're here now, of course. Though we were just a little bit surprised when Wesley said you were – well, like that. We assumed you'd have transformed, but clearly you haven't.

That's really very clever of you. George, did you *really* tell Wesley dead or alive? You know what he's like. No sense of humour, but he does so love to show off.'

The kiss, Duncan thought, hold on to it. If he could believe that the kiss was the only real thing he'd experienced that night, he felt sure that somehow he'd find a way out of all of it – wake up and discover it had all been a dream, something like that. But the kiss was slipping away, and instead he was being made to understand that reality was being driven way too fast in a car with a shape-shifting zombie gangmaster who probably didn't mean him well. In a reality like that, kisses and everything they stand for couldn't really exist, could they? You could want to believe in them with all your heart and soul, but deep down you'd always know that they were imaginary, as mythical as werewolves or unicorns. There are kisses at the bottom of our garden, you'd say, and your mother would smile faintly and say, That's nice, dear, now go and wash your hands, tea's nearly ready—

Without really knowing why, except that it was all make-believe anyway so it didn't really matter what happened, Duncan shot out his hand, grabbed the driver's elbow and shoved it hard. The car swerved violently. He smelled burning rubber and the noise of metal meeting concrete and losing a short but nasty fight was so loud that it hurt. His head shot for-ward, only very briefly delayed by a sheet of toughened glass, and he sniffed blood as his head emerged through the shat-tered windscreen into the fresh air. And the moonlight.

'*George*!' Her again. But George couldn't move. He was sit-ting with the windscreen round his neck like an Elizabethan ruff. 'George, I've dropped the stupid gun – do something.'

Oh well, Duncan thought, and he threw himself at the scrunched remains of the windscreen. He felt little mosaic tiles of glass patter round his shoulders like snowflakes as he sailed through the air, and then he landed, on all fours, on the tarmac. There was a loud noise behind him; from context, he guessed it was probably a gunshot. He ran half a dozen strides, to the cover of a parked van, and ducked down. No more shots. He crept round the side of the van and sprinted away up the middle of the road. He'd cleared fifty yards before he realised he was still on all fours, and that it wasn't hindering him at all. In fact, he couldn't run any other way. Also, his hands were paws, and he knew without having to look round that at some point in the past few seconds he'd acquired a tail. He'd transformed.

CHAPTER TWELVE

He couldn't help it. He lifted his head and howled.

Why the hell did I just do that? Duncan asked himself. But now he came to think of it, why shouldn't he? After all, he was a wolf, he was entitled: freedom of expression, a fundamental lycanthropic right. Likewise, what was he doing skulking behind parked cars just because some prat of a human (or ex-human – like it mattered) was taking pot-shots at him with, yes, all right, silver bullets? But it was dark and the bloke hadn't looked like the sort of human who possessed the considerable skill needed to hit a moving target with a pistol. And he only had their word for it that the bullets really were silver. And he wanted to bite somebody, a lot, and they did seem to be the obvious candidates—

He trotted round the car onto the pavement, so as to come up on their blind side. It was a pity he didn't have opposable thumbs, since getting a car door open would be tricky, but there were other ways of getting humanoid bipeds out of their metal boxes. He debated the relative merits of getting his snout under the sills and turning it over like a hedgehog and simply crashing his way in through the back window. Both were entirely possible, of course, for a werewolf with superlupine strength, and both struck him as potentially enormous fun. Pity he had to choose between them, really.

In the event, he didn't need to decide. They'd opened their doors and climbed out, the silly creatures; the man saw him and pooped off a shot from his little gun. It went high and left, and before he could waste another shot, Duncan leaped. The man collapsed under his impact like a flat-pack coffee table; Duncan heard the chunky thud of his skull on the pavement, as his teeth met in the loose, flabby skin of his throat. A quick sideways jerk of the head, and that one'd keep. He looked round quickly for the female.

'Mr Hughes, don't be annoying.' She didn't sound the least bit worried. He stood still, waiting for her to move so that he could attack. She looked down at him and smiled.

'In case you're feeling torn apart by remorse,' she said, 'George'll be just fine. Of course, he won't be able to talk much until he's been fixed up, but really, that's not a problem. In fact, I may just leave him that way, at least for a day or so. There, that's your mind set at rest. Now hop in the car and sit still.'

There was such a terrible, casual authority in her voice that for a split second Duncan felt an urge to obey her. Probably, if she'd just kept to '*Sit*' or '*Here, boy*,' he wouldn't have been able to resist. As it was, he tore himself free just in time. She frowned, as though the thought that he wouldn't obey hadn't crossed her mind. Then she gave a slight shrug, and turned into a unicorn.

Oh, Duncan thought.

Dead or alive, the annoying Mr Loop had said; to her, obviously, it made no odds. He growled, and the fur on the back of his neck was as crisp as the bristles of a hairbrush. She was keeping perfectly still, winding him up; she knew perfectly well that he couldn't start chasing her until she moved, just as he couldn't stop until he caught her or died trying.

'Last chance,' she said cheerfully. 'It'll end the same way, but you can save yourself a run.'

I like running, he thought. She nodded her head just a little, arched her back and leaped off the pavement into the air.

At one point, Duncan tried to get a car to run him over, but it swerved and hit a concrete bollard. He tried to dislocate his shoulder by jumping a wall that was obviously far too high, but he cleared it easily, landed smoothly and hardly missed a stride. He tried to get people to notice him, so they'd call the RSPCA or some other paramilitary organisation, someone with black helicopters and steel nets to haul him in with. But the few people who weren't looking the other way as he thundered past them must've assumed he was just an unusually big dog and they walked on by. When she crossed the canal, he could have sworn that she bounded over the surface of the water, her step so light that the meniscus bore her weight. He plunged in, doing his best to take his eye off her so that when he reached the other side she'd be long gone and there'd be no scent trail to follow. But as he grimly doggy-paddled through the treacly black water to the far bank, he saw her waiting for him, standing under a street lamp whose amber light blazed on her horn and hooves. It was punishment as well as execution, and he had no more choice in the matter than a car being towed.

After a while, when his lungs were beginning to cramp and the roaring in his ears was drowning out every other sound, he realised that she was running him round in a circle. That, he couldn't help thinking, was simply taking the piss, as though she was getting him to chase his own tail. The Paradise Garden Chinese restaurant flashed past the edge of his vision for the sixth time; he'd gone there once, with some of the Craven Ettins people – what were their names? Chris and Nina and Dave and Ramesh and Pauline; he'd got on well with them, but they'd all found better jobs and moved on, leaving him behind just as this stupid white unicorn was doing, running himself to death trying to keep up with yet another effortless front-runner . . . There comes a point when you've simply got to stop, even if it's only because you're about to die—

Something crashed into Duncan from the side, lifting him off his feet into the air. He landed badly and scrabbled to his feet, desperate not to lose sight of the unicorn, not really caring what had hit him. He sniffed for the scent trail, but before he could move after it a stunning weight landed on his back, smearing him onto the road surface like butter. He heard growling, loud enough to make itself audible over the thudding of his heart, and felt something sharp pressing against his throat, unable to penetrate his skin but determined to try its best. Teeth—?

It was Luke: a huge grey and black wolf tearing at his throat, grappling at his face with its claws, trying to flip him over onto his back and pin him down. Duncan was amazed at how much of a fight he managed to put up against it, in spite of the over-whelming weariness that was numbing every muscle in his body. He twisted his spine like a rubber band and bit back, catching Luke's nose between his jaws and grinding down on it. Luke yelped and clamped his teeth on Duncan's ear; Duncan tried to jerk his head free and felt tearing, like a frayed sheet. *Luke, you arsehole, let go, I'm busy*, he thought furiously, but the pressure grew rather than slackened; Luke was forcing his head down onto the tarmac, and Duncan didn't have quite enough strength left to resist. It was pretty close, all the same – if he wasn't so miserably tired, he realised, he'd be winning – and he knew he had no choice but to keep fighting until he'd definitely lost. *Get off me, Ferris, you fucking lunatic*, roared his hidden voice inside his head. *She's getting away, don't you—?*

Yes, Luke's voice replied calmly. *Isn't she?*

It was as though Duncan was an engine and some small but essential component had broken. He stopped fighting and froze. The pressure from Luke's jaws didn't increase but stayed at the same constant level.

Better now?

Duncan tried to nod, but Luke's grip meant he couldn't move his head. *Yes*, he thought back. *It's OK, you can let go of me.*

No chance. Luke was laughing, somewhere under all that fur and spittle. *If I let go now, the first puff of air with her scent on it and you'll be off again. Oh and by the way, I think you've cracked a couple of my ribs. Don't know your own strength, that's your trouble.*

Duncan's head felt like a stream when you disturb the mud at the bottom and it turns all cloudy and yuck. His throat was raw and full of blood and bitter goo, as though he'd just thrown up. One of his eyes didn't seem to want to open, and his nose—

He couldn't smell her.

He panicked and tried desperately to throw Luke off him. The pain in his ear increased sharply, then faded away.

I'm going to let go of you now, Luke's voice murmured in his head. *Don't even think about following the unicorn, it's long gone. Now, when I count to three; one, two—*

As the force applied to him waned, Duncan felt himself tense like a spring and then gradually relax. She'd gone, there was no point. No point to anything any more.

(Now there was a familiar thought—)

Fuck you, Hughes. Luke's voice in his mind sounded relieved, almost joyful. *Always chasing after women, that's your problem. Anything female, even bloody horses. You want to get a grip.*

Well, yes, Duncan thought. Yes to both. *Where did you come from?* he asked.

What? You called me.

Duncan was about to deny it when he remembered the howl. But that had been sheer reflex, an instinctive reaction to the transformation. Lucky, though. *Thanks,* he thought quietly.

You're welcome. Apart from the cracked ribs, of course. And now, for crying out loud let's get out of the bloody road before we're seen. I really don't want to spend what's left of my holiday dodging police marksmen.

He had a point there, of course. *Sorry.*

Whatever. Your place is nearest, and the others might still be there—

No. Definitely not there. *If it's all right with you, I'd rather go somewhere else.*

Why?

Well, it's in rather a mess.

Oh, for – All right, please yourself, just so long as we get out of sight. Follow me.

Luke limped as he ran, which made Duncan feel painfully guilty. However he chose to look at it, Luke had just saved him from a painful, ridiculous and distressingly non-terminal death, and in return he'd busted Luke's ribs and done something unfortunate to his friend's front left leg. It could've been worse, but it wasn't good.

There was a sort of shed in a Tesco's car park. Luke smashed the door in as though it was one of those paper jobs you get in traditional Japanese houses. Inside, it was pitch dark: no windows. They huddled in a corner, well away from the moonlight leaking through the remains of the door. It was too dark to see anything, but Duncan felt himself change back, and a long, sad sigh from Luke suggested that he'd done the same.

'You complete bastard, Duncan,' Luke said. 'Where the hell did you get to? And what's Wesley fucking Loop doing walking about not dead?'

Duncan closed his eyes. It was, after all, a fair question. 'You've seen the others, then.'

'Yes, what's left of them. No, it's all right, they're not hurt. Not permanently. Clive's left ear looks like a helping of coleslaw, Pete's nose is a right old mess, Micky's got a broken leg. Kevin's more or less in one piece; it's just as well his love life is a total zero, because he wouldn't be much use on that score for a week or two. But they'll mend OK.'

'What about Loop? Did they—?'

'He got away. Knew he'd been in a fight, though. Duncan, where the hell did he suddenly spring from? He's dead. I know he's dead, I was the one who found him. Your lady friend with the unusual forehead jewellery did for him.' Luke paused for a moment, and Duncan heard him shudder. 'This is serious, Duncan mate. There's something scary going on. So what—?'

In the end, it came down to knowing who your friends were. True, the kiss had cured Duncan – for a while. But it had worn off, because a kiss is just a kiss. Luke, on the other hand, had saved him from Bowden Allshapes, when nobody or nothing

else could have done. He felt his resolve crack, and immediately
the pain started ebbing away. If he told Luke, told him everything, his wise, strong friend would put it all right.

'Truth is,' Duncan said, 'I haven't got a clue what's going on.
But if I tell you, maybe you could make sense of it.'

Luke growled, and at the same time Duncan heard his voice
in his head: *I knew there was something you were keeping from me.*
'That'd probably be a good idea,' Luke said aloud. 'Go on,
then. It'd better be worth hearing, though. You realise you've
screwed up my night off. The others are all right, they've had a
nice fight. All I've done is trotted around looking for you.'

So Duncan told him all about it; from the first phone call
from the Bick woman at Crosswoods, all the way through to the
revelations of Wesley Loop and the nasty few minutes with
George and the silver bullets.

When he'd finished, Luke said: 'That's it?'

'Well, yes.'

'Nothing you've left out? Like, how come you didn't transform when you got off the train?'

Oh, Duncan thought. I forgot to tell him about the kiss – silly
me. 'There *was* one other thing,' he said.

'Thought there might be. Involving some bird, right?'

'My wife, actually.'

'Your ex-wife.'

'Yes, well.' Duncan realised that when he'd left off the prefix
it was because, at some level in his mind, he was already regard-
ing the problem they represented as solved. That was stupid,
though: a kiss is just a kiss. If he wanted to get rid of that problem as well as all the others, he still needed help. 'It's like this.'

So he told Luke about that as well; and when he'd done that,
Luke looked at him for a moment, then lifted his chin an inch
or so and barked. Duncan glanced behind him. There were
black shapes moving outside in the moonlight.

'I was right,' Luke said, and he wasn't talking to Duncan.
'He's the traitor.'

There was a wolf in the doorway, standing on the very edge

of the silver stain like a border guard. *Pete?* Duncan asked, but the wolf only growled.

'Not here,' Luke said. 'We'll deal with him back at the office.'

Duncan shot to his feet, but Luke was too quick; Duncan felt his thumb sticking into the hollow at the base of his throat, and his hand wrenching his arm up behind his back. He fought back, not caring if his arm broke, but Luke pushed him forward. He stumbled, and the moonlight took him.

As soon as his front paws touched the ground the pack was on top of him, crushing him flat and holding him down. He'd seen Wesley Loop fighting all four at once, but he made no effort to resist: the attack was too quick, too shocking. His *friends*—

'And I always reckoned I was such a good judge of character.' Luke was still inside the hut, as though he couldn't quite bring himself to join in. 'But he left us, and that's when the rot set in. Of course,' he added sadly, 'it's not his fault, it was that bloody woman.'

Luke. What did I do?

'You let us all down, Duncan.' Luke stepped out into the moonlight; just before he changed, Duncan felt sure he caught sight of silver light flashing on a drop of moisture at the corner of his eye. *Really, I'm not blaming you, not entirely. After all, you didn't even know you were doing it.*

The pack growled. Luke walked slowly towards where Duncan lay and lifted his head, staring at the sky. *Doing what, for God's sake?* Duncan thought at him. *Look, whatever it is I'm supposed to have done, I didn't mean it.*

Luke gazed down at him, his eyes more than usually red. *I know, I know. You wouldn't hurt us on purpose. But –* He looked away. *You're a lawyer, Duncan, you know what strict liability means. It doesn't matter if you didn't do it on purpose, or even if you didn't know. You did it, and that's all that's needed for a conviction: no proof of malicious intent required. Personally, I've always thought strict liability's barbaric; just because you are something or you've got something or someone's done something to you, even though you*

*never meant anybody any harm. But there. Fairness doesn't enter
into it. The law's just violence in fancy dress, Duncan. Wesley Loop
always used to say that. He never meant to betray us either, but that
wouldn't have stopped me ripping his throat out for it.*

They lifted him with their shoulders, pressing hard against
him so he couldn't move: Pete, Micky, Clive and Kevin, his best
mates. *We're going to have to chance it,* Luke was saying to them.
*We can't muck about going the back way. If people see us, they see us.
We'll head for the Westway flyover, we'll be under cover there a lot of
the way, and after that—*

Clive's ears pricked up. *We'd be better off taking the Cromwell
Road extension and then carrying on to the Embankment, traffic'll
be all right at this time of night, and—*

Can't do that, Micky interrupted, *there's temporary lights at
Earls Court, you'd get caught up in all the slow-moving stuff.*

(Which proved, Duncan reflected, that in spite of everything,
deep down under the fur they were still men. Not that that was
likely to do him a lot of good . . .)

Something shrieked. Five pairs of ears went back, and Luke
reared onto his back legs, staring up at the sky, growling deeply.
Quick, he broadcast, *back into the hut thing before they see us, and
don't let him give you the slip.*

They pressed hard against Duncan, lifting him off his feet,
and started to run in a half-circle to get back to the hut. More
shrieks, and Duncan felt a violent down draught of air, as
though there was a helicopter directly overhead. He tried to
look up but they wouldn't let him. They were squeezing him so
hard that he couldn't breathe, trotting as fast as they could go
with him wedged in between them. He heard Pete yell '*Look
out*,' and the pressure suddenly faded. He felt the tarmac under
his paws, shook his head and lifted it.

They could have been enormous black birds, crows or whatever – Duncan was no twitcher. But birds didn't glide quite
like that, with their wings held out straight and stiff, and
besides, there aren't any birds with bodies as big as people, or
not in this country at any rate. Pete snapped at the nape of

Duncan's neck but he dodged easily and, seeing a gap, shoul-
dered Kevin out of the way. He expected to get bitten for that,
but Kevin didn't seem all that interested in him; he was growling, his ears were flat to his skull, and a moment later he
launched himself in the air, snapping wildly at the nearest of the
flying things. He missed and dropped down again, by which
time Duncan was past him; but Luke was blocking his way.
Still, even Luke seemed preoccupied with whatever those creatures in the sky were.

His curiosity got the better of him, and he glanced up in
time to see a black shape swooping right at him, going unbelievably fast. Luke barked and hurled himself into the air; his
teeth caught in something trailing from the creature's wing and
he hung suspended by his jaws for a moment, until the creature
flapped wildly and fell to earth. Its wild screech nearly drowned
out Luke's deep, guttural growling; they were fighting on the
ground in a tangled ball of movement and noise. Another of the
creatures materialised out of the darkness and soared up
directly over Duncan's head, hovering motionless for a split
second before putting its wings back and swooping down. Kevin
hurled himself at it and they collided with a thick, solid noise
that was painful to hear. *Bugger this, get out of here*, Duncan
shouted to himself. But something flew low over him, washing
him all over in a soft bath of cool air. He felt something like fingers clamp onto his shoulders. All four of his feet left the
ground. He was flying.

Or rather, being flown. Staring down, he saw Clive leaping
up at him like a dolphin, heard the snap of his jaws closing on
thin air an inch or so below Duncan's trailing paw. Then the
scene below him panned back and grew small, as the werewolves dwindled into unreliable shapes and blended into the
darkness. He tried to look up, but all he could make out was
black cloth billowing in the slipstream. He remembered that he
was shit-scared of heights, and shut his eyes.

The flight was no fun at all, worse even than Virgin Atlantic,
but eventually he felt something hard bash against the soles of

his feet, first the back pair and then the front. The grip on his shoulders went loose, and he didn't go tumbling through empty space. He opened his eyes, and found that he was looking up at a woman.

Actually, she was quite nice-looking, if you were into Goth. Her face was very pale and she'd seriously overdone the eye-shadow, but— Fuck you, he yelled at himself, you've been snatched from the jaws of death by vampires, you don't know where you are or whose side these people are on, and you're actually *checking her out.* Deeply ashamed of being himself, he rose slowly to his feet.

'Happy landings,' the vampire said.

And that was another thing: vampire. That, quite definitely, was what she was. He took a step back. It brought him out of a patch of shadow, and moonlight fell on his face.

'I wouldn't get carried away with the walking-backwards business if I were you,' the vampire said pleasantly. 'Thing is, we're on a roof.' She smiled reassuringly, then glanced over her shoulder. 'I don't know what's keeping the others, but they should be along in a moment or so. They won't have hurt your friends, by the way, not unless they really had to.' She shrugged. 'Assuming you still care,' she added. 'My name's Veronica, by the way, Veronica Zhukov. I'm mostly maritime law and con-flicts of jurisdiction, though I like to dabble in intellectual property when they'll let me.' She shivered. 'Would it be all right if we went inside now?' she asked. 'Only it's a bit nippy out here, and time's getting on.'

She led him down a ladder through a trapdoor. 'In case you were wondering,' she said, 'this is the Crosswoods building. But you'd guessed that, I'm sure.'

As soon as the trapdoor closed, shutting out the moonlight, Duncan changed back. His paws became hands just in time to grip the rungs of the ladder and save himself from falling twenty feet onto hard concrete—

'Oops,' Veronica Zhukov said. 'Sorry, wasn't thinking. You all right?'

'Fine,' Duncan replied. 'Are you going to kill me?'

She looked shocked. 'Heavens, no,' she said. 'What a strange thing to say. Besides, if we'd wanted you dead, we'd simply have left you with your furry friends.' A serious look reshaped her face. 'I can see why you're suspicious about us,' she said. 'But there's no need, really. I want you to look on us as the good guys.'

Like a fish-hook: not easy to swallow. 'Really?' he said. 'But you tried to kill me.'

'I don't think so,' she said. 'We've only just met.'

'Well, maybe not you personally, but your lot. You shot at me in a coffee shop.'

'Good gracious.' Veronica's eyebrows rose. 'I honestly don't think that could've been us. After all,' she added, 'we're lawyers. Which isn't to say we don't do nasty, spiteful things sometimes, but not shooting at people. It's so *gauche*.' She sighed. 'If we're going to be melodramatic, we might as well do it in my office, or the interview room. I hate standing about in draughty corridors.'

She led him to a door which opened onto a plushly carpeted landing, down a flight of stairs into a passageway, the most startling aspect of which was its normality. It reminded him of the top floor at Craven Ettins – industrial-grade Wilton underfoot, woodchipped walls, plywood doors with aluminium handles. Junior-grade employees and support staff lived here: real people, as opposed to executives and bosses. He felt almost at home. Trainees, clerks and secretaries, he felt, don't get to turn into wild animals at the full moon, or swoop in through windows on fluttering black wings. That sort of caper would inevitably be reserved for the graduate-entry types.

'I thought your office was in the basement.'

She grinned. 'That's just PR,' she said. 'We like people – in the trade, I mean, not the *public* – to believe we can't get about much in daylight. Actually, so long as we've got our barrier cream on, it's no bother. Let's have a coffee,' she added brightly. 'The kitchen's just through here.'

And a kitchen was what it turned out to be: lino-floored, with battered-looking chairs retired from front-line service. There was a handwritten note Blu-Tacked to the wall urging everybody to wash their mugs up before leaving, and when she opened the fridge for the milk he saw a cardboard fish-fingers box, twelve bottles of something red with labels marked with letters of the alphabet, and a tub of strawberry ice cream.

'Sugar?' Veronica asked.

He nodded. 'Two,' he added. 'Thanks.' It came in a Piglet mug. He grabbed it and held it, savouring the warmth.

'If you don't mind me abandoning you for a bit,' she said, 'I'll nip down and see if the others are back yet. There's biscuits somewhere,' she added, 'if the girls haven't eaten them all.'

Biscuits. The door closed behind her, and he sat still for a while, catching his mental and spiritual breath. Biscuits: he remembered them, vaguely. They belonged to a world where people were people, rather than werewolves, zombies, vampires or unicorns; a place he might once have taken for granted, but never again. The events of the last two days suddenly rushed up around him, like flood water, and he huddled in his chair, his face in his hands, as though his memories were a cloud of buzzing flies.

He tried to concentrate his mind on what had Luke said. *I was right, he's the traitor.* What the hell was all that about?

The door opened. He looked up, but it wasn't that nice-looking Veronica, and it wasn't Sally, either. It was just some middle-aged dark-haired woman in a sort of gown thing, like students wear when they get their degrees.

'Well?' she said.

Duncan decided he really wasn't in the mood. 'Well what?' he snapped.

'What've you got to say for yourself?'

Duncan considered for a moment. '*Help!*' he suggested. 'Or *Leave me alone, you bunch of weirdos.* Take your pick.'

The woman raised both pencilled eyebrows. 'That's a funny attitude from a man who's just been saved from being torn apart by wild dogs.'

He shook his head. 'Wild lawyers,' he corrected her. 'Dogs is just what they do in their spare time. Can I go now, please?'

She looked at him as though he was burbling. 'You want to *leave*?'

'Yes.'

'With them still out there, hunting you?'

'Well, yes. Why shouldn't I?'

'Oh.' She shrugged. 'But you were the one who came to see us,' she said. 'We assumed you'd got something for us.'

'Me? No.'

'Oh,' the woman repeated. 'But you were so persistent. First you came to the front desk. Then you were hanging about for hours earlier on this evening. We thought—'

'I wanted to speak to Sally,' he said. 'Sally Moscowicz. My ex-wife.'

'Yes, but—' She frowned. 'You mean it was personal, rather than—'

'Yes.'

'Oh.' The frown deepened. 'I'm Caroline Hook, senior partner.' The woman stuck out a hand, and without thinking Duncan shook it. Very cold skin. 'It seems like we've been at cross purposes, then. No matter.' She clicked her tongue. 'In that case, yes, you can go whenever you like. The rescue's on the house, by the way.'

He nodded. 'You wouldn't have done it if you hadn't thought—'

'If we hadn't thought you had something for us. Frankly, no.'

'I see. So it wasn't Sally who—'

'No.'

'Fine.' Duncan stood up. 'In that case, thanks ever so much, sorry for any inconvenience.' He hesitated. 'I'm really free to go, am I?'

'I just said you were, didn't I?'

'Anywhere I like?'

'Yes.'

'New Mexico?'

Caroline Hook looked vaguely startled. 'I suppose so. Why?'

'No reason.' He took a long stride towards the door, then paused. 'Just out of interest.'

'Well?'

He furrowed his brows. He had to ask. 'If I had had something for you,' he said, 'what sort of thing would it've been?'

'I beg your pardon?'

'What *sort* of thing? Secrets? Troop movements, encryption keys, home addresses, formulas? The thing is, I don't *know* – bank account numbers? Or would it not have been information at all: an actual thing, like a key or—?' He looked at her. 'You aren't going to tell me, are you?'

She shook her head. 'What seems to have happened is a simple case of mistaken identity,' she said. 'We assumed you were the traitor. Our bad judgement. You get a free rescue out of it, compliments of Messrs Crosswoods. Just think: services from a lawyer that you don't have to pay for.'

The T-word. 'So there is a traitor,' he said.

Suddenly Ms Hook was interested in him again. 'Yes,' she said. 'Do you happen to know—?'

'Sorry. Betraying what, exactly?'

He'd lost her. 'It's a quarter to two in the morning,' she said. 'Sunrise is at seven. If I were you, I'd find somewhere dark.'

'All right.' He walked past her, then stopped in the doorway – like Colombo used to do, except he'd have figured it all out by now. 'There *is* a traitor, though,' he said again.

'Yes,' she repeated.

'A traitor to who?'

She smiled. 'Client confidentiality,' she said. 'You know better than that, Mr Hughes.'

'Fine. I had to ask. How do I get out of the building?'

'Out of here, turn left, down the corridor to the end, brings you to the main lift.'

'Thanks.' He nodded politely, then added: 'And thanks for the rescue. Do the same for you some time.'

Ms Hook smiled frostily. 'I doubt that very much. You see, I don't get into messes like that.'

'No,' Duncan replied, 'I don't suppose you do.'

Out of the door; he paused, sniffed, and turned right. When they'd been married, Sally had never worn perfume or anything like that. But earlier that evening, when he'd been talking to her in the Tube station, she'd practically reeked of the stuff. Camouflage, he guessed: to mask the smell of the barrier cream, or caked blood on her breath, whatever. Following the scent trail was like being given a guided tour. He went down two flights of stairs, down one corridor, up a flight of stairs, along another corridor, left, left again, right, through a fire door, through a room full of computer monitors – he stopped and wiggled a mouse on its pad, waking the screen up out of its flying-stars screen saver; what he saw there was interesting but by no means unexpected – down another corridor, across a landing, up more stairs, across another landing. He hesitated in front of the door he'd come to and listened. Then he smiled. He'd know that snore anywhere.

Not actually a snore, strictly speaking; more a sort of popping noise, like a demijohn of home-made wine peacefully fermenting. It came from a large, long black box lying in the middle of the office floor. Only one kind of box is made in that very unusual shape. It was lined with red velvet, which showed a touching respect for tradition. Duncan peered down into it.

Sally had always looked her best when she was asleep. Something to do with her eyes being closed; there was always that fierce, brisk, not-suffering-fools look in her eyes when they were open. Snuggled on her side in the velvet-lined box, her cheek resting on her hand, she looked like a party girl who'd flopped down to sleep as soon as her head hit the pillow, with all her make-up still on. But each time she breathed out there was that little *pop*, like a raindrop hitting the surface of a pool, and you couldn't help smiling.

Tough.

Duncan rummaged in his pocket until he found the expensive sausage roll – minus the fragment he'd used to distract Mr Loop – that he'd doggy-bagged from Moondollars. It was flaking up into crumbs and bits of pocket fluff had ground themselves into it, but he wasn't planning on eating it. Instead, he crumbled it to bits until he was able to retrieve the ice-cream stick he'd inserted into it for safe keeping, a lifetime ago. Once he'd got it out he binned the handful of sausage-roll debris and looked round for a sharp edge.

In the end, he had to sacrifice a pencil-sharpener. It was one of those cheap plastic ones; he put it between his teeth and crunched down on it, spat out the flakes of chipped plastic and fished the tiny blade off the tip of his tongue. As cutting tools went it was pretty pathetic, but it'd do. He perched on the edge of Sally's desk and slowly, carefully whittled the end of the ice-cream stick into a point. Then he picked up a ruler and measured it. Four inches. Not having the handy paperback edition of Gray's *Anatomy* on him, he couldn't be sure it was long enough, but since he hadn't got anything else it was going to have to do. Finding the big heavy thing to go with it was no problem at all - the bookshelves were lined with them. In the end he chose Kemp & Kemp's yellow bible of personal-injury damages; apt, he thought, and it weighed three pounds if it weighed an ounce.

With Kemp & Kemp in his left hand and the ice-cream stick poised behind his ear like a carpenter's pencil, Duncan used his right hand to nudge Sally very gently onto her back. She stirred and made a growling noise, like a sleepy lion-cub, but didn't wake up. Fine. He teased the ice-cream stick out from behind his ear, balanced it sharp end down over where he guessed her heart must be, rested Kemp & Kemp as lightly as he could on the blunt end, and cleared his throat.

'Hi, sweetie,' he whispered. 'Time to wake up.'

She made that cute little snarling noise he remembered so well. It meant a variety of things, depending on context: your feet are cold, I want more covers, no, I'm too tired. This time it meant, it's too early, let me sleep. He hardened his heart and applied a few more foot-ounces to Kemp & Kemp.

'Wake up, my little fruitbat,' he murmured. 'I want a word with you.'

Her eyes opened, and she looked at him through the 1960s-style bead curtain of sleepiness.

'Duncan?' she mumbled.

'Hello.'

Her eyebrows cuddled up to each other. 'What you doing here?'

Well, she'd never been a morning person. 'I need to talk to you.'

'Wass time?'

He glanced at the clock on her wall. 'Two-thirty a.m.,' he said.

'For crying out—' She stopped. Maybe she'd noticed the slight but nagging pressure of the ice-cream stick. 'What the fuck are you playing at, Duncan?'

Duncan smiled. 'I know,' he said. 'As wooden stakes go it's pretty pathetic. On the other hand, never underestimate the effect of Kemp & Kemp slammed down hard with a good wristy action. It might work, it might not. Do you want to find out?'

Sally's eyes were wide open now. 'Are you out of your tiny mind?' she said, and he felt a certain satisfaction when he heard the fear in her voice. 'For Christ's sake put that thing down, before you do me an injury.'

He shook his head a little. 'You know what?' he said. 'You're such a hard person to pin down figuratively, I reckoned my best bet was to give literally a go.' He sighed. 'I know, I'm lousy at threats, I haven't had the practice. But I mean it. Either you give me a straight answer or you get my Buffy impersonation. Entirely up to you. Five seconds. One—'

'Duncan, you lunatic. You can't just go around murdering people.'

'People, no, I grant you. But you're not people any more, are you? I'm prepared to go to the House of Lords with this one if

I have to. I suppose they could have me under the Wildlife and Countryside Act, on the grounds that bats are a protected species, but that's a risk I'll just have to take. Two.'

'Duncan—'

He sighed, tightened his grip on Kemp & Kemp, and lifted it a foot in the air.

'All *right*.' It came out as a furious squeal. 'All right,' she said, 'I'll tell you anything you want. Put that fucking stick down, right now.'

Just as well, he thought, as he lifted the point off her. There was a five per cent chance he might actually have done it if she hadn't caved in. Of course, the stick would've snapped off before it had even punctured her jacket.

'How the hell did you get that thing in here anyhow?' she demanded, wriggling sharply away from it. 'We've got scanners, they're supposed to detect stuff like that.'

Duncan grinned. 'Thought you might have,' he replied. 'So I hid it. In a sausage roll, as a matter of fact. You might want to recalibrate your sensors.' He took a deep breath, and said, 'It was something in the lipstick, I take it.'

'What?'

'When you kissed me. Some sort of fiendishly clever lycanthropy suppressant. You wanted me not to be able to change into a wolf, so your friend Mr Loop wouldn't have any bother bringing me in.'

Sally had squirmed her way as far up the box as she could get without sitting up. 'I can't believe you're doing this,' she said. 'I mean, I know there's a whole lot of things wrong with you, but I never thought you'd turn *violent*.'

'Just getting in touch with my inner cub, I guess,' he replied. 'For crying out loud, Sal, I'm a *werewolf*. Something like that, the changes aren't just fur-deep. But you should know,' he added. 'You did this to me.'

Her eyes flashed. But the anger had a little-girl quality to it: a furious rage at being found out. 'Balls,' she said. 'It was your nasty friend Luke Ferris—'

Duncan shook his head. 'Oh sure, Luke had a lot to do with it. Luke was the reason you chose me. It was that way around, wasn't it? At the time I thought it was me chasing after you, but—' He grinned suddenly. 'I've learned a thing or two about chasing lately,' he said. 'Courtesy of Bowden Allshapes. Sometimes, it's the quarry who does the chasing and the predator who does the leading-on. Otherwise,' he added, scowling quickly, 'why the hell would you have married me in the first place?'

'It wasn't—' It wasn't like that, she'd been about to say. Well, maybe not; but that wasn't the issue under discussion. 'Let's leave *feelings* out of this, shall we?' Duncan said firmly. 'Let's stick to what you were told to do.'

'I don't know what you—'

'Law school.' He frowned. 'Should've wondered about that at the time. Expensive business, going to law school. Now, your mum couldn't afford to pay your fees and living expenses. Your dad buggered off when you were small and was never seen or heard of again. I don't remember you ever getting a part-time job or anything like that.'

'I got a grant.'

'Really? Clever old you, because they stopped giving them three years before we started the course.'

'I mean a loan, not a grant.'

'Ah, right. That clears that up, then. And there was me thinking that someone else had paid your fees for you. A relative, maybe. Or a prospective employer.' Duncan moved his head a little so that he couldn't see her so well. 'It's what the army do, I believe, and big corporations: they pay your college bills and in return you've got to work for them for a certain number of years. Sort of like indentured slavery, only you get to keep the bit of paper saying you've passed all your exams.'

Sally was looking at him, though he wasn't looking back. He could feel it, like the little spot of light from a magnifying glass. 'Duncan,' she said, 'what are you talking about?'

He wasn't sure why that was too much to bear, but it was. He

turned back sharply, suddenly aware of the weight of Kemp &
Kemp in his left hand. One tap, like knocking in a nail. 'It was all
about the Ferris Gang, wasn't it?' he said. 'Right from the start.
I imagine they picked up on Wesley Loop first. I'll bet he wasn't
as discreet as he should've been, at law school or wherever. They
found out what he was, and that he was planning on starting up
his own pack; they found out or figured out that he'd be most
likely to start recruiting with his cousin Luke, who already
had a pack of his own. So they started studying us; and they
focused on me, because I was the weak link. I didn't want to
hang out with Luke's gang any more. I quit, which made me the
perfect target. I'd detached myself from the pack, but they
knew that if they applied the right sort of pressure, I'd go
back like a shot. Presumably that's when you got your orders:
get in there, secure him for us, so that when the time's right
we can reel him in. I honestly thought you loved me, but—'
He paused, waiting for a contradiction. No dice. 'I hope it was
worth it, from your point of view. What was it? The price of
your admission to the sisterhood?'

'Something like that.'

'And the phone calls? *Help* and all that; and your sidekick Ms
Bick warning me off. To make me think you were in trouble, so
I'd come running.'

'More or less.'

Duncan hadn't really been expecting a confession. Quite definitely it wasn't what he'd wanted to hear. It was just the
miserable old truth; and the whole point of lawyers is so you
don't have to make do with the truth if you don't want to. She
might at least have done him the courtesy of lying.

'Fine,' he said. 'So when Luke said I'm the traitor—'

'Clever old Luke.'

'Oh.' He frowned. 'In that case, I owe your boss – Caroline
something, nice woman . . .'

'Hook.'

'That's it, Caroline Hook. I owe her an apology. I told her I
wasn't the traitor after all.' His frown deepened. 'But hold on a

moment,' he added. 'If she's the senior partner of this outfit, she'd have known, surely—'

Sally didn't say anything. Not like her at all. Then bits of stupidity began to flake off the inside of Duncan's mind, exposing what passed for his intelligence. *You mean it was personal, rather than*— That nice Ms Hook: she'd told him everything he needed to know, and he'd been too stupid to notice.

'Sorry,' he said. 'Typical Hughes, brain like a tea bag. Someone got you this job, right? Like they got me mine at Craven Ettins. An important client put a word in for you; the sort of client you don't say no to. Your boss Caroline doesn't know the half of it, does she?'

Sally's face froze over, like a lake in winter. 'You know what, Duncan?' she said. 'You're a complete waste of time and resources. If you're going to stab me with that lolly stick, go ahead. If not, I'd like to go back to sleep. It's been a tiresome day – it's had you in it.'

He nodded, and laid Kemp & Kemp carefully down on the desk. 'Sorry to have bothered you,' he replied. 'It was a tape-measure, by the way.'

'What was a tape-measure?'

'In my inside pocket. At that coffee-shop place. It stopped your bullet. Otherwise it'd have been a nice shot. Do you practise a lot?'

She shook her head. 'Enhanced hand-eye coordination,' she said. 'Comes with the puncture marks on the side of the neck. Our office darts team's been top of the Law Society south-eastern area league for the last twenty years. Thanks for telling me that, I couldn't believe I'd missed.'

Duncan nodded a couple of times. 'I see,' he said. 'Only, that nice Veronica sounded so sincere when she said it wasn't your lot who tried to kill me, I actually believed her. Which only left you.' He dragged up an excuse for a winning smile. 'Dead or alive, that's what they told Loop – which suggests that they don't care which: it's as broad as it's long if you're in the zombie-making business. Presumably if you'd managed to kill me in the coffee shop, they'd have resurrected me and—' He clicked his tongue. 'Don't suppose you feel like telling me why. For old times' sake, or whatever.'

Sally shook her head. 'You've suddenly come over all insightful,' she replied. 'Figure it out for yourself.'

'Already did that,' Duncan sighed. 'Dead or alive, says it all. No, I just thought you might like to tell me yourself, in case you were feeling, oh, I don't know, guilty, something like that.'

'What would I be feeling guilty about? You just told me I didn't actually miss. And it wasn't my fault you'd got a tape-measure in your inside pocket.'

'Fine.' He stood up. 'Will they be awfully cross with you when you tell them you failed?'

'Have I?'

'Well, it does rather look that way,' Duncan said. 'I've been slung out of the wolf pack and they're out to kill me, so whatever it is I'm supposed to do to betray them, I can't do it now. I've sussed out what your game is, so I won't be trusting you again, and you didn't manage to kill me. I'd have said it was as comprehensively fucked up as it could get.'

And then she smiled. 'You're right, of course,' she said. 'Oh well, never mind. So.' She yawned. 'I guess this is goodbye for ever, then.'

Duncan nodded. 'With luck.'

'In which case,' Sally said, 'I'd just like to say that you're the most annoying, immature, self-centred, inconsiderate, shallow-minded, feckless, pathetic man I've ever met, and sex with you was like listening to the shipping forecast. Apart from that, no hard feelings.'

'Thank you,' Duncan replied gravely. 'And, since we're being so refreshingly frank with each other—'

'Yes?'

He grinned. 'You're the only girl I ever loved, or ever will,' he said. 'Silly me.' He started to walk backwards, towards the door. 'Just one last question, something that's been really bugging me all along. If I ask you, promise you'll tell me?'

290 • Tom Holt

She shook her head. 'No promises. You can ask.'

'All right.' He paused. The door was right behind him – he could feel the handle in the small of his back. 'How do you and your mates manage to put all that eyeshadow and stuff on if you can't see yourselves in mirrors? It must be a real—'

Sally was scrabbling for something in the lining of her coffin. No prizes for guessing what. Duncan dived for the door, opened it and hurled himself through, pitching forward onto his face as soon as he could. He heard the bang and felt the slipstream as the bullet whizzed by overhead.

CHAPTER THIRTEEN

Down the stairs Duncan went, bump-bump-bump like Pooh being dragged by Christopher Robin, ever so grateful for his near-as-dammit-invulnerability as he crashed his knees into steel banisters, or missed steps, stumbled and finished the rest of the flight slithering down on his back or his face. Three landings down he stopped by grabbing onto the rail (it came away from the wall, but it had done its job as far as he was concerned) and looked back up for signs of pursuit. None, apparently. Either Sally'd given up, or she'd been sensible and taken the lift.

The hell with that, he thought. He hopped up onto the banister, glanced down into the cavernous stairwell beneath, and dropped.

After a short but interesting fall he landed on his feet, wobbled for a moment and looked all round. As far as he could tell, he had the entrance lobby to himself. Then he heard the *ting* of a lift bell and saw the light over the lift door starting to glow. As the doors slid open, he dived like a goalkeeper at the front desk and scrambled behind it.

There was a clock on the wall facing him, which told Duncan it was five past three in the morning. He stifled a groan. Three and a half, four hours before the sun came up. If only he had a jarful of the stuff that Sally had doctored the lipstick with, the

292 • Tom Holt

stuff that kept him from transforming. Or he could go back and ask nicely for another kiss. Well, perhaps not.

Still, out of the building would be a start. In which case, since he was cornered and outgunned, he really had no option other than the modern urban equivalent of a good old-fashioned cavalry charge. He didn't have a horse, but he did have (he suddenly noticed) Megarry and Wade.

The best thing about Megarry and Wade's book on the law relating to land transfers, from a tactician's perspective, is that it's big. Compared to Megarry and Wade, Kemp and Kemp wrote in haiku, pruning away every superfluous word, rationing the adjectives as though they were fattening. Megarry and Wade, by contrast, believed passionately in the full expansive flow of language. Fortunately, Duncan's werewolf super-strength allowed him to lift the thing off the floor, where it was providentially lurking, without wrecking his elbow tendons. He hefted it and listened carefully to the woodpecker tap of court shoe heels on laminated wood flooring. Sally's movements were easy to reconstruct. From the lift shaft, she crossed the lobby until she could see that the main door hadn't been smashed or unlocked; then she turned and looked round, assessing the merits of the various hiding places that the front office offered. Since the desk was pretty much all there was in the way of useful cover, he anticipated that it wouldn't take her long to figure out where he was. Accordingly—

Megarry and Wade's *The Law Of Real Property* (seventh edition) flew through the air like a fat, chunky owl, air resistance flicking it open. It hit the side of Sally's head with a muffled splatty sort of sound, bounced off her shoulder and flopped to the floor. For nearly a whole second she stood looking confused. Then her knees gave way, and she folded onto the floor like a suit of clothes whose owner has been teleported out of them.

Victory, Duncan thought. Except—

He jumped up from behind the desk and dashed halfway to where she lay sprawled. Nearly victory, he amended. Good improvisation, perfect timing, excellent throw, but the stunned woman lying at his feet wasn't Sally.

Bugger. He leaned down to peer at her face, and recognised her: Veronica something, Russian-sounding name. The nice-looking one. He sat down on his heels, feeling extremely stupid until it occurred to him that, whether or not he'd just knocked out the wrong woman, there was nothing to stop him slipping the catch on the front door and getting away. Fine, he thought; he stood up, turned and saw Sally standing between him and the door. She was pointing something small and shiny at him, and he was prepared to bet money it wasn't a stapler.

'Cooperation,' she said.

Oink? 'Cooperation what?'

'You asked how vampires put on make-up,' she said. 'We don't. We get our friends to do it for us; and then we do theirs back. I suppose you could say it's a bit like monkeys and com-munal grooming, but I prefer to think of it as a symbol of unity and mutual support. You know – I got all my sisters and me, that kind of thing.' She frowned. 'What've you been doing to Vee?'

'I hit her. With Megarry and Wade.'

'Oh. Bit uncalled for, wasn't it?'

'I thought she was you.'

'Fine. I wouldn't bother,' Sally added, as Duncan surrepti-tiously reached for the book. 'I mean, you can try if you like, but I'll only duck out of the way, and then you'll die feeling a right prat instead of an innocent victim. Your choice,' she added rea-sonably. 'I'm just trying to be considerate.'

Duncan looked at her, then slowly and deliberately picked up the book.

'Suit yourself,' she said testily, and pulled the trigger. She fired four times before running out of bullets, and when Duncan lowered Megarry and Wade from in front of his heart, there were four neat holes in the front cover, forming a rectangle no bigger than a matchbox.

'Werewolf reflexes,' he said, with a grin. 'I figured if that ditzy little gun of yours couldn't shoot through a tape-measure—'

'Bastard,' she said.

'That's it, isn't it? You haven't got any more silver bullets.'

'That's right, be all smug about it. Hardest thing I ever did, staying married to you for a whole year.'

'At least I don't pop.'

She scowled at him. 'What do you mean, pop?'

'In your sleep. You make this sort of popping noise with your mouth. Makes you look like a goldfish.'

'That's not true – you're making it up.'

'I am not. Pop, pop, pop. Kept me awake for hours. I'd just lie there, waiting for the next pop. Enough to drive you mad.'

'I don't—'

'How would you know? You're asleep at the time.'

'Well rid of me, then, aren't you?'

Yes, Duncan thought. I suppose I am. 'Are you going to try and stop me leaving now?'

Sally shook her head. 'Not try so much as succeed, actually. I'm faster than you, and stronger, and I can fly. Also, the others'll be here in a moment. I don't know what it's like at Ferris and Loop, but around here you can't go letting off guns without attracting a certain amount of attention.'

He took a step backwards. 'You surprise me,' he said. 'I wouldn't have thought you'd have wanted your friends around right now.'

'What on earth makes you say that?'

Duncan grinned. Not his best effort ever. 'You know what your boss asked me, that Caroline? She asked me if I knew who the traitor was. At the time, of course, I hadn't got a clue, but it's sort of come to me, like a revelation or something. Next time I see her, I must remember to tell her. I'm sure she'll be interested.'

Silence. Duncan could hear Sally's heart beating, the faintest creak from her shoes as she shifted her weight just a little. 'Nice try,' she said. 'Wrong traitor, actually. Besides, she won't believe you.'

'Well, if she doesn't, no harm done as far as you're concerned. Let's try it and see what happens.'

'You please yourself,' Sally replied. 'Anyway, it's not true.'

He raised an eyebrow. 'Is that right?'

'Yes. You're the traitor. You have been all along, you just didn't know. Oh, you were quite right about Bowden Allshapes putting me through law school and getting me a job here, but I was only ever just a way of getting to you. Ironic, really,' she added bitterly, 'because I'm quite bright, though I say it myself, and you're just a dead loss, no wordplay intended. But no, it was you they wanted, and I was just an eyelash-flutterer with a law degree.' She scowled. 'I got my partnership on merit,' she went on. 'I worked bloody hard and I'm good at my job. You'd still be a miserable little assistant solicitor at Cravens if Luke Ferris hadn't wanted you to complete his collection. Of course, that's men for you. It's not how good you are, it's who you happened to be at school with.'

Duncan nodded. 'I see,' he said. 'So I'm the traitor. What am I supposed to be betraying? Your boss knows,' he added quickly, before Sally could speak. 'That Caroline, she knows but she wouldn't tell me. So why don't you—?'

He hesitated. Sally was smiling, but he was prepared to bet she wasn't aware she was doing it. Habit of hers, one he remembered; small recompense for the heartbreak and misery, but if he hadn't been married to her, he wouldn't have known about the habit, and a tiny little light bulb wouldn't have started to glow in his head. Looked at from that perspective, it'd been a small price to pay.

'Why don't you tell me what it is?' he went on. 'And then at least I'll know if I've actually done something to deserve all this. Not that it matters—'

'No, it doesn't.' A goodness-is-that-the-time look flickered across Sally's face. 'What matters is delivering you, dead or alive. I know it's the most appalling cliché, but there's a hard way and an easy way. Your choice. Five seconds.'

He had to admit, she did melodrama really rather well. Not many people could've said that without making him want to snigger, because it was something people only said in movies, and he didn't watch that kind of movie. But she said it with a kind of eyes-wide-open sincerity that almost made it sound like a genuine choice. Bloody hell, they were trying to *kill* him . . . A surge of irritation swept through him, because it was really nasty of her to put him in a situation where someone could come out with a bloody stupid line like that and expect to be taken seriously. He reached behind him, grabbed hold of the plain wooden chair provided for the Crosswoods receptionist and swung it over his head, bringing it down as hard as he could on the edge of the desk. It flew apart, leaving him holding one splintered leg, ending in a nice sharp point where it had split along the grain. One improvised wooden stake; and in the other hand, the wrist-numbing weight of Megarry and Wade.

'I've chosen,' Duncan said.

But Sally just sighed. 'You and your male ego,' she said. 'You really think you can fight your way out. With a chair leg.'

He shrugged. 'You talk like a bad film, I think like one. I guess we're all victims of American popular culture.' (As he said it, a strange but pleasing thought occurred to him: *she may be a vampire and trying to kill me, but I'm not afraid of her any more. When we were married, she scared me stiff. I was always afraid I'd do something wrong and she wouldn't love me any more.*) 'Well, go on, then,' he said wearily. 'If you're going to try and kill me, go ahead. If not, I'm leaving. No offence, but I've had just about enough of you to last me.'

'Oh for crying out loud,' she said, and flew at him. Literally: both feet off the floor, arms spread like wings, she lifted into the air, hovered for a moment, then swooped like a diver, straight at his face.

There are some things you can never really prepare yourself for, and one of them is seeing your ex-wife zoom at you through the air like a huge black seagull. Duncan ducked just in time, dropping the chair leg and the book as he instinctively shielded his face with his hands. As she shot by overhead, he felt the hem of her sort-of-cape-thing flick the corner of his eye, and noticed that she was wearing perfume. That, and make-up too. Being

undead had clearly helped her express her long-repressed femi-
nine side.

Sally banked a foot or so from the wall and came by for
another pass, sending Duncan scuttling under the front desk. He
banged both his head and his knee but neither of them hurt. She
screeched – it was the cry of a pterodactyl or a Nazgul or a huge
killer bat, but it was also unmistakably *her*, the same tone of
voice she'd always used for telling him he had to grow up and
start taking this relationship seriously (which generally meant it
was his turn to Hoover the lounge) – and came down for another
pass, grabbing the desk with both hands, lifting it off the floor
and hurling it across the room. Well, he thought, she always did
throw things when she was in a strop.

All in all, it was an inopportune moment for a sudden blinding insight. But intuition is a bit like your mother, it always
tends to call when you're in the middle of something else. So
absolute was the revelation that he clean forgot about the fight,
his history with his opponent and the very real prospect of being
killed. Not that they weren't very real issues, but this was simply
much more important. He stood up, and said, 'Wait a second.'

Sally braked in mid-air; it must have been his tone of voice.
'What?' she said, hovering, her cape barely fluttering, so that she
looked like a five-foot-five killer hummingbird.

'I know what the thing is,' he said, less than brilliantly. 'The
thing,' he repeated. 'What I'm supposed to betray to you.'

She smiled. She'd always had a nice smile. 'No, you don't,'
she said. 'You just told me you don't.'

'Ah, but I've figured it out.' Didn't he ever feel pleased with
himself. The way you do. 'I know why it had to be me, and why
I was able to stand up to Luke instead of backing down with my
tail between my legs—'

'You know, I have trouble visualising you with a tail,' she said.
'Especially between your—'

'And that's what your lot want from me,' he said, as much to
himself as her. 'You reckon you'll be able to use it, like a command code or something; make us do what you want, use us—'

He frowned: not a nice idea, werewolves at the beck and call of vampires, a ferocious and expendable workforce. And they wouldn't be rounding up sheep or carrying newspapers home in their mouths. It'd be '*Good boy, kill*' – 'I'm right, aren't I?' he said defiantly. 'Your lot want it – the vampires, I mean. And your other lot, too: Bowden Allshapes and Wesley Loop and all those nutters. You want to be able to say "Heel" and we'll all do exactly what you tell us to—'

'Not bad.' Sally nodded approvingly. 'That's half of it, anyway. It's all right, we don't need you to be able to figure out the other half. In fact, it'd fuck up everything if you did. Right,' she said briskly, 'we can get on now. You see, there'd be no earthly point killing you if you didn't know the secret.'

Oh, Duncan thought. Sod it. Should've kept my face shut. Except it wouldn't have made any difference. There was no way out of there except over her undead body.

She took her time: careful, meticulous, hallmark of a good litigation lawyer. She drew herself up in the air, studying him like a golfer considering a long putt, and he discovered that he was suddenly too scared to move. *Fine wolf you turned out to be*, he told himself, and waited for the moment.

Which didn't come. She was all ready to swoop when another black-caped figure flew at her, catching her round the neck and pulling her down to the floor. Catfight, he thought; at least, change that C to a B and you'd be nearer the mark. It was that nice-looking Veronica. She must've come round out of her Megarry and Wade-induced slumber, and maybe she assumed it was Sally who'd clobbered her, or maybe they just didn't like each other much. In any event, they were fighting it out in fine style, though it was all happening too fast for Duncan to catch the finer points. It was mostly wrestling, with some karate, kickboxing and biting thrown in. A bit like having an episode of *Xena Warrior Princess* filmed in your living room, and the production people had forgotten to tell you about it in advance.

Duncan was ashamed to admit it, but he knew quite a few people who'd have paid money to watch. Not, however, his cup of tea. As quietly and unobtrusively as he could manage, he started to creep on all fours towards the door.

For a while, he thought he was going to make it. He paused three times and glanced up, and they seemed to be getting on just fine without him. The main problem appeared to be that no matter how hard they bit each other, they couldn't break the skin; it didn't stop them trying, though, and no matter what your views might be on violence in the workplace, you had to admire their perseverance and dedication. But, when he was no more than seven feet from the door and wondering whether a quick lunge might carry him through, he heard a noise like someone gargling custard, followed by a heavy thump. He wanted to ignore it and make his dash anyway, but somehow he couldn't. He looked over his shoulder.

Nice-looking Veronica was hanging in the air as though she'd got her cape caught up on an invisible coat hook. Beneath her on the floor, Sally lay in a heap, like some bulk commodity tipped off the back of a dumper truck. He stared at her for a moment, wondering if she was—

'It's all right.' Veronica's voice sounded unbearably weary. 'She'll be OK.' She looked at him, and added: 'You still care, don't you?'

'Yes. Well, no, actually,' he added. 'Not like that. What've you done to her?'

'Throttled her till she blacked out.' Long sigh, as of someone completely fed up. 'She'll have a hell of a sore throat for a day or two, and I doubt I'll hear the last of it for a long time. But never mind. Going somewhere?'

Duncan nodded. 'New Mexico,' he said.

'Oh.' Veronica sounded disappointed, which was— Although she wasn't nearly so nice-looking now. Her hair was tangled like a bramble patch and there was spit dribbling down her chin. 'Why? Got relatives there or something?'

'No. That's the point,' Duncan said. 'I suppose I shouldn't have told you,' he added, wondering why he had.

She shrugged. 'To be honest with you, I'm feeling too tired to care. Properly speaking, I ought to stop you, but—' Slowly, like a drifting leaf, she let herself glide gently to the floor. 'If you want to go, go. I'll tell the others that we fought and you won. Which is probably what'd happen, seeing how knackered I feel. Well, go on, then.'

Duncan didn't move; which was bloody odd, he had to admit. He blamed it all on curiosity, but that was only a very small part of it. 'What was all that about?' he said.

'What? Oh, you mean—' She grinned. 'I was saving your life,' she said. 'I'd rather assumed you'd figured that out for yourself, which was why I hadn't mentioned it.'

'Oh,' he said. 'Thanks,' he added.

'Thanks,' she echoed. 'Well, that makes it all worthwhile, doesn't it? Sorry,' she added. 'Uncalled for. After all, I didn't rush to your rescue out of a high-minded regard for the value of canine life.'

(Or because I like you, she didn't add.)

'It's because your lot needs me. Because of the secret, right?'

Veronica nodded. 'I overheard a bit of your conversation,' she said. 'Dreadful manners, but I was too woozy to move. Was it you who bashed me, by the way? I remember something whirling towards me, but that's about it.'

Duncan nodded guiltily. 'I thought you were Sally,' he said.

'Ah, fine. Anyway, I heard what you two were saying about Bowden Allshapes, and Sally not really being on our side all along. Actually, we had our suspicions, but it seemed so hard to believe: one of us, working for the enemy. The other enemy, of course, not your lot.' She sighed. 'It's all a bit confusing, if you ask me. Still, she as good as admitted that she wanted to hand you over to the zombie people. It had to be that, or why was she trying to kill you? Dead, you'd be no earthly use to us, but of course it's as broad as it's long to them.' She smiled. 'Once I'd worked that out, I didn't really have any option. Hence the unseemly display of energy. That cow,' she added, frowning, 'has broken two of my fingernails. I've a good mind to do something spiteful and vindictive in return, like giving her a purple rinse while she's still out cold. Everybody'd assume she'd done it herself, and it could be days before she found out. Happy thought,' she said, 'but I suppose I'd better not. I've got to work with her, after all.'

That one hit Duncan like a slap across the face. 'What, after you've found out – well, that she's a mole for Bowden Allshapes and she was going to—'

Veronica shook her head. 'It's not like we've got any choice,' she said. 'Like it or not, we're stuck with each other. Even if she wasn't a partner, even if she was just, you know, *staff*, we couldn't just fire her. She's one of us. Trouble is, not all of us are nice.' She paused for a moment, then clicked her tongue. 'No, I imagine Caroline'll give her a thorough talking-to – and don't pull faces, you've never heard Caroline when she really gets going. Given the choice between an earful from our senior partner and being buried at a crossroads with a stake through my heart, at the very least I'd have to give it some serious thought. After that, I guess we'll just have to keep a very close eye on her, for ever and ever. Tiresome, but that's how it is. Besides,' she added, 'she's the only one who knows how to make broadband work. That's a giggle, by the way, it really is; for us, I mean, being in on the secret. I mean, imagine what it's like calling the twenty-four-hour helpline and *knowing* that the voice at the other end is an unnaturally resurrected corpse, instead of just suspecting—'

Duncan resisted the urge to frown. Was she *flirting* with him? He wished he knew a bit more about the subject, but he'd had precious little experience. Sally hadn't flirted, in the same way fish don't climb mountains. But if she was, then why? Not because she liked him, so it had to be some dark and devious tactic, part of all this stuff he was supposed to be running away from. It occurred to him that he hadn't done much running away lately, even though it should've been the Christmas fairy perched on the very top of his agenda.

'I'll go now,' he said. He didn't move, though.

'Oh.' Veronica looked at him. 'You sure? Wouldn't you be better off staying here? What I mean is, out there you've got the werewolves, who were trying to kill you, and the zombies, ditto.' She looked away. 'Whereas we've got a vested interest in keeping you alive.'

'Have you?'

She nodded. 'You were saying. After she started throwing the furniture about, but before she went in for the kill. You'd figured it out. The secret.'

'Oh, that.' He'd forgotten; in fact, he had to ransack his mind for the residues of that sudden flash of enlightenment. Fortunately, they were still there. 'It's just a theory,' he said. 'Nothing concrete. I mean, it's not really something I could trade with.'

She shrugged; a bit too couldn't-care-less-one-way-or-another to be entirely convincing. Did vampires get to meet a lot of men, he wondered. If werewolves were anything to go by, grim comradely celibacy was the general rule. *Stop thinking about all that stuff*, he ordered himself. 'You may as well give it a go,' she said. 'Unless you've got scruples about betraying your pack, even though they did turn really nasty on you.'

His turn to look away. 'Should I have?'

'God, no. I mean,' she went on quickly, 'by the looks of it they're convinced that you've already double-crossed them, and I doubt there's anything you could say that'd change their minds. So, in that case, you've got nothing to lose by it, have you?'

He pulled a face. 'I can't stay here for ever,' he said. 'Can I?'

Veronica looked thoughtful, as though it hadn't been a rhetorical question. 'We can always use another probate lawyer,' she said. 'But I guess it might be awkward, you working in the same building as Sally. I don't think Caroline'd go for it, no. Pity, though. It'd have been – well, interesting. I mean, they're a great bunch of girls and we get along pretty well most of the time, but—' She shook her head. 'No, it wouldn't work. Forget I suggested it.'

'Right. In that case—'

'But maybe you should stay here for now,' she said, rather quickly. 'Regroup. Figure out your next move. We'll help you.'

Odd effect those three words had. Four, if you counted the ellision. 'Would you?'

'I will, yes.'

Strange thing to say, Duncan thought. Still, it had to be better than going out into the werewolf-and-zombie-filled night. He didn't know a lot about the persistence levels of zombies, but he knew Luke and the gang. Not quitters; and they must have a pretty good idea of where he'd ended up, after that spectacular rescue. At the very least, it'd be sensible to stay out of their way till moonset and sunrise.

'Fine,' he said. 'In that case—' Suddenly he grinned. 'You know,' he went on, 'there's something I've always wanted to say and I never thought I'd ever have the chance, but this situation is absolutely tailor-made for it. May I?'

Veronica gave him a puzzled look. 'Sure.'

'You won't sigh or click your tongue or anything?'

'Not if you don't want me to.'

'Splendid.' He stood up, smiled, and took a deep breath. 'In that case,' he said, 'take me to your leader.'

She blinked. Then she sighed and clicked her tongue. 'That's it, is it?'

'Yes.'

'All done now?'

'Yes.' He scowled at her. 'You promised you wouldn't—'

'Caroline's office is this way,' she said.

Stairs, landings, corridors. They arrived at a door. She knocked, then went in without waiting for an answer.

There are strict and universal rules about the expression of status by means of office furniture, even when the furniture in question is a coffin. Sally, he remembered, had had light oak with brass handles. Caroline the senior partner, by contrast, had exquisitely figured burr walnut with silver handles, resting on a pair of trestles of turned rosewood. The effect was slightly spoilt by the fact that, when Caroline sat up, she had a grey mud pack on her face and curlers in her hair.

'Sorry to barge in,' Veronica said, fooling nobody. 'We'd like a quick word.'

Her choice of pronouns wasn't wasted on Caroline. When she

peeled the slices of cucumber off her eyes, there was a quizzical look in them. 'He's still here, then,' she said.

'Yes. Sally tried to kill him. You were right, by the way. She's working for the Allshapes consortium.'

Caroline sighed, as if to say how very tiresome. 'Where is she now?'

'Front office. Asleep. I, um—'

Caroline did a quick lift of the eyebrows that said *how many times have I told you girls not to play rough games?* 'I suppose we'd better put her in disgrace till the morning,' she said. 'The key's in my desk drawer.'

Veronica nodded and went to the desk. With the key she unlocked a big old-fashioned safe. From it she took first a pair of rubber gloves, tongs and a thing like a welding mask, second (using the first) a string of garlic. Holding it at arm's length, she left the room.

'Now then,' Caroline said. 'To what do we owe the extended pleasure?'

'What?' Duncan recalled his attention from the direction of the doorway. 'Oh yes, right. You know what we were talking about earlier?'

She nodded. 'You told me you didn't know.'

'That's right, I don't.' Deep breath. 'But I think I may have figured it out.'

He had her attention. 'This is – well, a guess, right?'

He nodded. 'But, um, she thought—'

'Veronica,' Caroline said promptly. 'Vee, not Ronnie. Go on.'

His face felt annoyingly warm. Perceptive bloody woman. 'Veronica thought you might want to hear it anyway. In return for . . .'

Caroline nodded. 'Asylum,' she said. 'Which is a pretty fair description of this place during office hours. It's a deal. Well?'

It'd have been nice, Duncan thought, if she'd asked him to sit down. The omission, he felt sure, wasn't accidental. 'I suddenly remembered,' he said, 'about something that happened when Luke Ferris and I were at school together.'

'I see.' Very slight frown, signifying that he still had most of her attention, but if the building caught fire or got ripped out of the ground by a freak tornado she'd probably notice. 'Feel free to reminisce,' she said. 'Try not to be too long about it, because Veronica'll be back in a few minutes, and I'd rather keep this between ourselves for now.'

Duncan nodded, and tried to order his thoughts; a bit like taking someone else's seventeen greyhounds for a walk through a free-range chicken farm, but he did his best. 'We had a homework rota,' he said. 'It was based on good Marxist principles: from each according to his abilities. Pete did all our French and German, because he was good at languages; Mickey did all the science, Clive did the geography and the—'

'You, of course,' Caroline interrupted, 'know who all these interesting people are.'

'Sorry, they're other members of the gang. Luke didn't actually do anything except organise, which meant looking very fierce if it wasn't done on time. When I joined the gang, they elected me maths specialist, because all of them hated maths. I told them I was no good at it, but—' He shrugged. 'Anyhow, the first time we were set maths homework, I went away and did it all, and brought it in so that everybody could copy it out, and then we handed it in.'

Duncan paused for a moment. 'Well?' Caroline said. 'Straight As, I trust.'

'Not exactly, no. Actually, it was more like Finland in the Eurovision Song Contest. The thing was, it was equations, and since I was doing them for everybody, I took real care over it. And with equations, as you know, you can check them afterwards to see if they've come out right, and I was sure I'd got a hundred per cent. I was really pleased. But when we got our books back, we'd all scored zero. Luke was not pleased—'

'Is this story going somewhere, or are we still doing background and character development? Because—'

★

'Useless,' Ferris shouted, kicking the nearest chair over. He sounded like a dog barking. 'Completely fucking useless.' He slammed his maths book down on the desk as if he was trying to put it out of its misery. 'And bloody Whitworth's going to know we cheated. How could you be so *stupid*—?'

Ferris was scary enough at the best of times. That was the whole point. Nobody was going to give you a hard time if someone as scary as Ferris was your friend. This, though, wasn't the best of times for a scariness masterclass. For one thing, it was just the two of them. The rest of the gang had been sent away, told to wait by the tennis court while Ferris dealt with the situation. There was, of course, no point trying to argue the toss. You might as well plead with a mudslide or a volcano. But it's hard to stay still and quiet when the most terrifying boy in the school is coming towards you with that terrible, efficient look on his face.

'I did my best, honest,' Duncan said. 'I checked them over, three times. They all came out just right. Look, I'll show you if you—'

Not the right thing to say. 'I don't care about the bloody equations. I couldn't give a stuff about them, otherwise I'd never have let *you* do them for me. That was coursework, you cretin, it goes towards our exam grades. Thanks to you—'

Duncan retreated behind a desk. All that achieved was to make it possible for Ferris to act very scary indeed. He picked the desk up and threw it an impressive distance across the room. Duncan had never seen him actually hit anybody; nothing had ever been allowed to get that far. Being hit hurts, sometimes quite a lot, but fear controls you.

'I'm sorry,' Duncan said. 'Really, really sorry. But—'

He'd backed up as far as he could go. There was a wall behind him, and it wasn't going to get out of the way just to let him escape. Ferris took the step that brought him within arm's reach.

He hesitated.

It was one of those moments . . . Once, when Duncan's dad had been driving them all home from gran's house, he'd swung out to overtake a slow lorry, and there'd been a car coming straight at them on the other side of the road. Duncan could remember the moment quite clearly. He'd thought, *we're going to hit the other car, very hard; probably we'll all be hurt or even killed. Oh well.* In that fraction of a second, before dad hauled his wheel one way and the other driver hauled his the other, and the two cars scraped past each other and the swearing started, Duncan had faced death and seen it for what it was: the end of everything, certainly, but so what? Because it had come briskly, efficiently, not dragging out or playing the scene for all it was worth, he'd understood what it actually meant; that tomorrow there'd be a world without the Hughes family in it, or there might not be a world at all. But if that was the worst that could happen – well, not so scary, after all. It was only later, when mum screamed and dad started yelling at her for screaming, and Duncan had burst into tears, and they'd pulled over onto the verge and there'd been several minutes when nobody was under control at all, that he'd been frightened. But then he'd been very frightened indeed, mostly because his parents were acting like lunatics or wild animals, which wasn't supposed to happen. It was as though they'd changed, from humans into something else. Monsters—

Simple lesson. Fear is worse than death. We have nothing to fear but fear itself. And scary things, of course.

Ferris was looking at him. Then he said, 'I ought to smash your stupid face in.'

– Which was, by all meaningful criteria, an admission of defeat. It said, *I should do this but I'm not going to.* Or, *but I can't.* Maybe Ferris had seen it in Duncan's eyes, the Oh-well moment, the great comfort and reassurance that comes from knowing that this is as bad as it gets and things can't get any worse. In other words, the fast, dribbling puncture of fear.

I've won, Duncan thought. *I've beaten him.*

And he was just congratulating himself on standing up to the bully, or at least having the good instinctive judgement to back up against an immovable wall so he'd had no choice but to stand up to him, when Ferris swung back his right arm and punched him extremely hard in the solar plexus.

It had been a bit like being a fish. There was nothing he could breathe. He was drowning in air, and he could feel his eyes trying to push their way out of their sockets. He swayed for a moment, feeling slightly bemused but not particularly panicky or anything, and then dropped to the floor. The opposite wall became the ceiling. His head bashed hard against something solid. A bright light came on at the opposite end of his head from his eyes, which was odd. It was so bright that it flooded everything for a moment. Then it switched off, and he was looking up at Ferris, who was staring down at him with a look of utter, wet-underpants terror.

Strange, Duncan thought, it's not like he's got anything to be afraid of. But he really didn't look good at all. His face was as white as paper, and he was shaking. Like a bad dose of the flu, except it didn't come on as quickly as that, surely. Duncan decided he didn't like the look of it. What if Ferris was really ill? Shouldn't he be doing something?

'You all right?' he asked.

For a moment, Ferris opened and shut his mouth like an albino goldfish. Then he said, 'Am I all right?'

'Yes.'

'Fine. What about you?'

'Me?' Funny question to ask, when you've just thumped someone. Would it be rude to say, *Yes, I'm fine*? (The implication being that Ferris couldn't hit for toffee.) 'Sort of,' he hedged.

Ferris was looking past him, at the wall, with a gormless-stunned expression on his face as though he'd seen a ghost. Duncan sat up (no aches and pains, so nothing broken) and looked over his shoulder to see what was so fascinating. First, he noted that the solid thing he'd hit his head on was an iron water pipe that supplied the radiatior. Second, there was blood.

He reached up and felt the back of his head. Wet and sticky, like the glue they used in the art room. He looked at his hand, which was red.

'Cut myself,' he said. Then his brain clicked in, and he realised why Ferris was so upset. If someone came in, a teacher, and saw all that mess everywhere, they'd be in dead trouble. Detention, probably. 'We'd better get it cleared up,' he said.

'What?'

'The blood,' Duncan said. 'We'd better clean up the blood before anybody sees.'

For a moment or so Ferris had stared at him, as though he was having trouble understanding what he was saying. Then he nodded sharply, the decisive leader. 'Get the board-rubber thing,' he said, quickly kneeling and pulling out his handkerchief. Duncan hurried to obey. This was better: Ferris giving orders, him carrying them out. The thing about Ferris was that he always knew what to do. They'd managed to wipe off all the blood, and nobody ever said anything . . .

'That's it, isn't it?' Duncan said. 'Luke killed me. By accident, of course. I bashed my head on that pipe and it killed me. Only I didn't die.'

Caroline nodded slowly. 'That would make sense,' she said, and he could tell she hated herself for having to say it. 'You died for a fraction of a second – when the bright light came on in your head – and then you shook it off somehow and came back to life.' She frowned. 'The tape-measure,' she said.

'What?'

'The tape-measure. The one that stopped the silver bullet. Can I see it, please?'

Obviously someone else who knew how to give orders. He felt in his pocket, found it and handed it over. Caroline looked at it briefly, then gave it back. 'Would you mind,' she said, rather quietly, 'taking off your jacket and unbuttoning your shirt? Pretend I'm a doctor, if it'll help.'

Orders are orders. Wishing (not for the first time) that he wasn't quite so habitually scruffy, Duncan did as he was told. She looked at his chest, then nodded.

'There,' she said, pointing.

Duncan looked down. There indeed: on the skin of his chest, on the left-hand side, about where his inside jacket pocket would be, a small round red scab, about the same diameter as the bullet hole in the tape-measure.

'She fired two shots,' Caroline said.

'Oh.'

'I wouldn't have thought she'd have missed. She's very good at anything involving aiming, things like that. Did she tell you she's on the darts team?'

Duncan looked down at the scab, then back at her. 'She shot me and I didn't—?'

'Apparently not.'

'Oh.'

It was maybe a full half-second before the dam broke inside his head. When the roaring and the turbulence had died down a little, he said, 'Did I tell you about the unicorn?'

Caroline shook her head. 'But I assume you're talking about Bowden Allshapes,' she said. 'It's the body she uses when she wants to kill werewolves. It's a hobby of hers, I don't know why she does it. Probably she just doesn't like your lot very much. We all have a good laugh about it—' She stopped. 'You've met her,' she said flatly.

'Yes.'

Suddenly, it was hard to imagine her ever laughing again. 'You met her and chased her,' she said. 'But she didn't kill you. Or at least, you didn't die. Do your shirt up, by the way, you'll catch your death.'

'Well, I was pretty well out of breath—' No wordplay intended, he thought. 'That's right,' he said. 'Actually, I kept chasing her till I hit a tree.'

Caroline nodded. 'And I suppose everything went white for a moment, and then you had a nice little chat. In other words, you did it again. Like with the water pipe. Bashed your head in, but no lasting harm done.' She shook her head, as if it was a watch that had stopped. 'You know what this means. You're—'

The door opened, and in came nice-looking Veronica. Vee, not Ronnie. She was still wearing the rubber gloves, and the welding mask hung from her wrist. 'She was just waking up when I got there,' she said. 'She wasn't happy.' She looked at Duncan, then at Caroline (note the order). 'Have I missed something?' she said.

Duncan wanted to run away and hide, for some reason. 'We were just chatting,' Caroline said. 'Guess what. Mr Hughes here is going to join us.'

'Really?' Genuinely pleased; then – 'But what about Sally? Won't that be a bit awkward?'

Caroline's face had that Mount Rushmore look. 'I don't think so. Sally may well be leaving us soon. A better offer, as I understand it.'

No, something yelled inside Duncan's head. But when it looked round for support, it realised it was in a very small minority and resolved to keep its mouth shut in future. 'Oh,' Veronica said. 'You mean, the dead people—'

Caroline nodded firmly. 'I think Sally believes she has a future with them. Well,' she added briskly, 'we've all got a future with them sooner or later, if you see what I mean, but—' Pause, slight frown. 'Nearly all of us, anyhow. But yes, I don't think Sally will be a problem. Now, since Mr Hughes's speciality is probate, tax and trusts, we'll have to do a bit of reshuffling. I suggest you take over matrimonial finance from Sally; Rose can do your commercial litigation and personal insolvency, I'll do Rose's commercial landlord and tenant; that leaves a bit of a gap in product liability, but we'll all have to huddle together like willows aslant a brook and cover it as best we can. Does that seem all right? Vee?'

'Fine,' Veronica said brightly. 'Well, this is a—'

'Hold on,' Duncan said.

Really, he didn't want to cause difficulties. It would have been so nice, so neat. After all, he couldn't go back to the Ferris Gang, not now that he'd actually committed the crime they suspected him of, and he needed somebody to protect him against Bowden Allshapes, he was pretty well convinced of that.

Apparently, these people were prepared to do that. Which was odd: hadn't Wesley Loop offered to pay for his damaged furniture with a Crosswoods office account cheque? Didn't that mean—?

But instead, he said, 'I don't want to seem ungrateful, but what about the – well, let's call them cultural differences. No offence, but I sort of got the impression that my lot and your lot don't get on terribly well.'

'Fight like bats and dogs, you mean?' Caroline shrugged. 'You know what the watchword of the twenty-first century is, Mr Hughes? Diversity. The melting pot.' She looked at Veronica, then back at Duncan. 'Cross-pollination,' she said, with a face so straight it was practically obscene. 'I think it's high time we challenged these outmoded species stereotypes and embraced an environment where skin, fur and feather can coexist in mutually beneficial harmony.' She frowned. 'Strictly speaking it should be membrane rather than feather,' she added, 'but it hasn't got that ring. Look,' she went on, 'the bottom line is this. What choice have you got?'

New Mexico, protested the little voice that had made itself so unpopular a short while ago. It didn't get a noticeably better reception this time. 'Fine by me, then,' Duncan heard himself say. 'So long as your people—'

'You can leave them to me,' Caroline said firmly. 'Though to be honest I don't think they'll have any objections. You might find things a bit strained for a while,' she added, and Duncan noticed a curiously resolute expression on Veronica's face, 'but I'm sure it'll all shake down soon enough. The important thing,' she added, 'is getting the work done. Looking after our clients, especially the old and valued ones.'

Oh, Duncan thought. Like that, then. And for a moment there, he'd imagined they wanted him for his legal acumen. 'Of course,' he said. 'Though I should point out,' he added hopefully, 'I think there may be a bit of aggravation about my existing clients following me here. I'm thinking of, you know, the big, long-drawn-out probate jobs.'

Caroline nodded. 'Me too,' she said. 'Just the sort of work we need to attract here.'

'Ah. You think they'll want to come?'

'I don't think they have any choice.' The smile Caroline gave him was all eyes and teeth, proving beyond question that there are worse things that kindly old grandmothers can turn out to be than disguised wolves. 'The work's got to be done. You're – well, the only man for the job. You know that, don't you?'

Eek, he thought. 'Yes, but I really don't think it'd be—'

'Just a second,' Veronica broke in. 'Are we talking about Bowden Allshapes?'

'Yes. Be quiet, Vee.'

Didn't work. Maybe vampires were stroppier with their leaders than werewolves, or maybe she had some other motivation. 'But that's crazy,' she said. 'You know they're out to kill him. It'd be—'

'Not such a big deal as you might think,' Caroline interrupted smoothly. 'And no, I'm not being cruel and heartless. Am I, Mr Hughes?'

For some reason, Duncan blushed. 'Actually, no,' he said. 'At least, it's possible that—'

'Oh, I think it's been proved. To my satisfaction, anyway.'

Duncan looked hard at her, trying to get *So are we not telling her about the me-being-unkillable thing, then?* into one slightly simpering frown. But she wasn't looking at him, so it was a complete waste of time. 'Don't worry your pretty little head about it, Vee,' Caroline said. 'It's important for this firm that we build up our substantial private client base with long-term high-yield ongoing— Don't look at me like that,' she snapped. 'All right, so you fancy Dog Boy here. Fine.' Duncan didn't see the expression on Veronica's face, because he was too busy staring very hard indeed at the carpet. Nice carpet. Good thick weave. Years of wear in a carpet like that. 'As far as I'm concerned, he's our chance of getting the Allshapes people. That's an awful lot of money, for ever and ever. Apparently they want him, very badly. Don't know why, but it takes all sorts. My guess is they want to cut costs by getting him –' she paused to relish the words '– in house. Fair play to them, we're all in business to make money, not spend it. But they won't get the chance, I'll see to that. In return, we're going to look after Mr Hughes. We're going to cherish him – that can be your job, if you want – and make sure that no nasty big dogs or dead people push him around. He's got nowhere else to go, so he's happy with the deal. We're happy; we get Bowden Allshapes, plus a nice bonus which I won't go into now. Is there anything there that you – either of you – have a problem with?'

Before Duncan could say, *well, actually, yes*, Veronica stood up. She was still wearing the gloves. 'I'd better go and check on Sally,' she said. 'I had to use all the garlic just to keep her quiet – she may be having a bad reaction to it or something.'

Caroline didn't look at her. 'No, don't do that,' she said.

'But she might get really sick. She could—'

'Well.' Caroline shrugged. 'Think about it, Vee. She's in bed with the dead people. As far as they're concerned, it's just something you do; like a christening or a bar mitzvah, only without the reception and the buffet lunch. Might as well let her get it over with in peace and quiet, don't you think? She hates any kind of fuss.'

Which was true; fuss being defined as parties, occasions, things she had to put on uncomfortable shoes and a frock for. Weddings. Funerals.

'You can't just let her die,' said his voice. There were times when he hated the sound of it.

Caroline frowned. 'If you feel so very strongly about it, we'll do a deal. Be *quiet*, Vee. You join up with us, the garlic goes back in the safe. Well?'

This time, Duncan glanced at Veronica. She was watching him (now there was a coincidence); she was looking at him as though he was the envelope containing her exam results, pass or fail. No pressure. Lose one, get another, apparently. Plenty more hammerhead sharks in the sea.

'Deal,' he said.

There are moments when the world stands still; and you notice, but nobody else seems to. Caroline, for instance. She nodded, smiled pleasantly, said, 'Splendid. Vee, go and see to poor Sally. Mr Hughes – actually, I think I should start calling you Duncan, if that's all right. Come with me, and I'll show you your new office. Of course,' she went on; she'd stood up and was walking out of the door. He snapped to it and followed her, like a dog. 'Of course, you'll need somewhere to stay for a day or so; from what the girls told me, you won't want to go back to your flat in a hurry, even once the moon's waned. You can camp out in your office for as long as you like, we haven't got a problem with that. In fact, we do it all the time. After all, anywhere long and wide enough to put a box in – and no windows, of course . . . Now, here on the left you've got the computer room – don't touch anything in there, ever, even if you are immortal – and next door to that's the secretaries' room, where they have their coffee. That's the lavatory. We haven't actually got a dedicated men's loo, so a certain degree of discretion . . .'

He was listening, because this was the sort of stuff that governs every aspect of office life and only tends to be told you once, at great speed, when you haven't got anything to take notes with. But he was also thinking: well, love again. Thought we'd seen the back of that particular hazard, but apparently not. She's nice-looking, mind. Very nice-looking. Only . . .

'Here we are.' Dammit: he'd let his attention wander and forgotten how he'd got here. Caroline pushed the door open, revealing a small, bare room, empty except for a—

'As I was saying just now,' she went on blithely, 'you can stay here until you've found somewhere to live. Of course, you aren't used to sleeping in one of these, but I promise you, it won't take you long to get used to it. Much less trouble than a hammock, for example; and in Tokyo I believe the average apartment is smaller than one of these beauties. Lined, of course,' she added. 'You may find red velvet a bit unrestful, so feel free to change it.'

'Um,' Duncan said. 'Thanks.'

Actually, the biggest problem was getting into it. Came with practice, he supposed. It was like climbing into a narrow, steep-sided bath. The previous occupant, whoever she'd been, must've been quite short; he had to lie with his feet up on the bottom end and his arms crossed over his chest. All in all, red velvet was the least of his problems.

Dwelling on the discomfort did help take his mind off the other stuff – for a while. But it had been a very long day, and pretty soon his eyelids began to slide shut. Goodbye Sally, apparently, and what about nice-looking Veronica? The perils of the rebound hadn't really figured much in his life up till now, but rushing into something in his frame of mind – not to mention the vampire thing. He didn't really know anything about vampires; in spite of which, he'd just accepted a job from them, a job involving Bowden Allshapes. Talking of which, what about that other thing, the one he'd been carefully leading his mind away from ever since it had splattered itself all over his mental windscreen? Couldn't really be *true*, could it? Had he really died – several times, apparently – and then carried on as though death was no more than a sneeze? It was all too . . .

Duncan opened his eyes. At first he thought the light was old Mister Sun leering at him through the window; then he remembered where he was, and what he was in. Pins and needles in both feet, incidentally, plus cramp in his knees. Even hard-as-nails werewolf joints couldn't take that kind of abuse.

Just a moment, though. If the light wasn't the sun (because of the room being windowless; and he distinctly remembered turning off the light before he started the getting-in-this-stupid-fucking-thing manoeuvres) then what was it?

He looked up. It was soft white light, the gentlest of glows, a bit like photonic face cream, and it was coming from the magnificent white unicorn standing over him.

CHAPTER FOURTEEN

'Hello, you,' said the unicorn.

He should have recognised the scent, of course. It was everywhere, as soft and all-pervasive as the light. Instinctively he tried to jump up, but his feet weren't working, and an infinite number of tiny stabs of pain bustled up and down his nervous system like commuters on an escalator.

'You,' Duncan said.

'Me.' The unicorn nodded her head gravely. 'We meet again, Duncan Hughes. How are you settling in, by the way? Aren't you a bit uncomfortable in that shoebox thing?'

'How did you get in here?'

She tossed her silver mane. 'I can get in anywhere, any time,' she replied brightly. 'No bother at all. If you're interested, I turned myself into a cold germ and floated in through the air-conditioning. All shapes, see? Oh, but you do look funny lying there, like a man in women's clothes. For two pins I'd tie a great big pink ribbon round you.'

Duncan tried his feet again, but no good; all that happened was that he felt like he was dancing barefoot on broken glass. But he remembered something—

'You can't touch me,' he said. 'I can't die. Can I?'

The unicorn dipped her head. 'The second statement is true.

However, it doesn't follow on logically from the first, which is false. You're coming with me, Mr Hughes, whether you like it or not.'

'Really.' Not so deep inside him, something with red eyes and big teeth started to growl. 'You're going to drag me with you down the ventilation shaft.'

'I could,' the unicorn replied. 'If I absolutely had to. But I don't. I can make you get up out of that silly box and come with me quite voluntarily. I can even make you open doors for me.'

'Is that right. How?'

The unicorn rubbed her nose against her left foreleg. 'Quite simple. If you come with me – I won't press the point about opening doors – I'll spare the life of your ex-wife. She belongs to me, after all, and I was going to convert her, now that her cover's blown. But instead, I'll let her go. I'll even stop her being a vampire: she can lead a normal, happy life, get old and fat and die of old age in a nursing home, like regular folks. There, you see? An offer you can't refuse, as the saying goes.'

Duncan took a deep breath. This wasn't going to be easy.

'No,' he said.

For a moment he wondered if she'd heard him. Then her beautiful soft nostrils flared, and she said, 'Really? Are you quite sure?'

'Yes.'

'You surprise me,' she said, in a slightly harder voice than he'd heard her use before. 'I had you figured for the decent, honourable type, the sort who always does the right thing. Consider carefully, please. A human life hangs in the balance. This is a genuine, twenty-four-carat moral dilemma. Your response should be as predictable as a scientific experiment.'

Duncan grinned. He enjoyed the grin; he'd earned it. 'Balls,' he said. 'Bloody woman screws up my life, then she tries to kill me. Twice,' he added. 'That I know about. No, you can have her. She wants to come and be one of your zombies, who am I to stand in her way?'

'Heavens.' The unicorn lifted a hoof and pawed at the carpet.

'What's got into you, I wonder? Could it possibly be a backbone, or are you just bluffing? What if I were to bring her in here right now and kill her, on the spot? Do you think your iron resolve could handle that?'

Duncan shrugged. 'I'd rather you didn't,' he said. 'But if you choose to murder someone, it's hardly my fault.'

The unicorn gazed at him for a while out of her soft blue eyes: swimming-pool colour, Duncan decided, and you could drown in them if you got out of your depth. 'You are bluffing,' she said. (Admiration? Possibly, coming from her.) 'But you're doing it so well I'll have to let you get away with it. You've guessed that dear Sally's more use to me as she is. Now, you're far more valuable, but I can't be doing with waste. I'll just have to try something else. How are your poor feet, by the way?'

He'd forgotten about them. 'Better,' he said.

'Ah. Well, in that case—' She turned to face the door. 'Can't catch me,' she chirruped, and trotted out into the corridor.

Fuck, Duncan thought. But he was on his feet, and he was running. The scent was like a wire loop round his throat; if he didn't keep up, it'd tighten and choke him. Of course, she'd planned this all along—

He sprinted into the corridor, but she'd gone. He flared his nostrils and caught a whiff of her scent, enough to give him directions. He lunged.

Down the corridor, fast as he could go, until he came to a T-junction. He stopped and sniffed again. The scent was there, leading him left, but it was surprisingly faint. There were other scents (damp, mildew, formaldehyde) that crowded it out, trying to smother it. Logic suggested she'd be taking the most direct route to the main exit; trouble was, he hadn't paid attention when Caroline was showing him round, and he hadn't got a clue where the main stairwell or the lifts were. In fact, he was lost. Sod it.

Or, rather, joy.

I'm lost, he thought. In this bewildering maze of corridors, stairs, landings and passages, I'm completely lost. Hooray!

Hooray for my shitty sense of direction, and the rich pong of preservatives and decomposing textiles, which can drown even her scent.

Which way now? Can't give up (grin), wouldn't be playing the game. How about left? Well, why not?

Duncan turned left, running fast, and sprinted down a long corridor lined with bookshelves crammed with musty-smelling volumes of law reports and obsolete editions of Halsbury's *Statutes*. He sort of recognised this corridor: there's one in every law office, and when you find yourself in it, you know that the only way you'll ever find Reception again is either outrageous luck or a search party. A smile the width of the M25 snaked across his face and he ran faster.

The corridor ended in a flight of stairs (they always do) which led to a landing (*that* landing) on three sides of which were identical unmarked fire doors. Duncan nearly wept for joy, because he knew that whichever door he took, it'd be the wrong one. He'd spent weeks, maybe months, trailing up and down passageways like these, searching for the way out, an ounce of trial for a hundredweight of error. The sheer delight of running flooded through him as he burst through the left-hand fire door. Not running to anywhere or away from anything; just running. He took a racing line into the bend, accelerated out of it, and crashed into something immobile and extremely solid.

Werewolves, as previously noted, are tough as old boots, even in human form. But running into a horse's bum at close on thirty-five miles an hour takes it out of anybody – it, in this context, being every molecule of breath in his body. He stopped dead, teetered for a split second on entirely numb feet, and fell backwards like a chainsawn tree.

Duncan's last thought before blacking out, and his first on coming round a second or two later, was *Horse? What's a horse doing in—?* Then it occurred to him that horses aren't the only creatures with horses' backsides. *Bowden bloody Allshapes*, he thought, and sprang to his feet, just in time to get the full force of a bucking kick in his solar plexus.

Predictably he sat down again, grabbing instinctively as he folded for something to hang on to. He hadn't really expected to connect with anything, but his flailing hands closed on hair. Tail, he thought, as the world swirled round and round inside his head like the fake snow in an old-fashioned glass paperweight. *Tail—*

He hauled.

It was like those world's-strongest-man TV shows that used to be so popular at one time, where the competitors had to tow a lorry by means of a strap gripped in their teeth. He kept hauling. The horse (the *unicorn*, for crying out loud) tried to kick again, but couldn't get a firm footing and stumbled, allowing him to drag her back a full eighteen inches. She rallied, and for a moment Duncan reflected on why tractors and other such machinery are rated in horsepower. But the mere fact that she was at least five times stronger than him simply didn't enter into it. All the anger and frustration of every werewolf who'd ever hunted the white unicorn, every canine who'd ever run after something too fast for it to catch, raged white-hot inside him and compelled him to hang on. Let go? Are you out of your tiny mind? *Never* let go, not ever; not even if they drag you off your feet or bash you on the nose with a rolled-up newspaper.

And then: *Just a second*, he thought, and let go.

Interesting and unforeseen consequences. The unicorn, striving with all its considerable might to get away from him, shot forward like a cannon shell. She didn't get far, though. There was a thump and a splintering noise, and she stopped, her horn embedded up to its base in a substantial, meets-all-relevant-British-Standards plywood fire door.

For maybe as long as three seconds Duncan stood rooted to the spot, looking from the bunch of long, fine white hairs in his right hand to the comprehensively stuck unicorn vainly trying to wrench itself free. Then the fog lifted and he knew exactly what he had to do, and how little time he had to do it in before Bowden Allshapes realised that her best bet was to transform herself into some other life form that didn't have a great big spike sticking out of its nose. He grabbed blindly at the nearest bookshelf and felt his fingers tighten on something suitably wide and thick. As he swung it up to shoulder height he noticed in passing that it was Whitehouse and Stuart-Buttle on Revenue Law; not as chunky as Kemp and Kemp or Megarry and Wade, but formidable nonetheless and (thanks to its shiny cover) marginally more aerodynamic. He took a quick instinctive aim and let fly.

Tax statutes have put many people to sleep over the years, but never more efficiently or opportunely. The unicorn staggered, sort of came apart at the knees and folded up like a pasting table. Before she'd hit the ground, Duncan pounced. She was hanging by her horn, her head and neck off the floor, the rest of her messily flumped like used laundry on a teenager's floor. He landed on her ribcage with a soul-satisfying thump and reached out to grip her bottom lip with his left hand, while his right scrabbled to unbuckle and pull free his trouser belt. A simple loop through the buckle; a bit of a job getting it round her neck, but he got there in the end. When he was reasonably satisfied with the security arrangements, he dug his nails into the unicorn's lip and twisted—

'Ouch,' she squealed, and opened her eyes.

Cue to let go of the lip and hold on tight to the belt with both hands. Sure enough, the unicorn vanished, to be replaced a nanosecond later by a huge and very hairy humanoid, presumably some variety of troll. But it had a neck, and Duncan jerked on the belt as hard as he dared without solid data on the breaking strain of leather-look plastic. The troll made a peculiar noise, choked and turned into—

Duncan rarely forgot a face, especially one capable of launching the regulation thousand ships. The face of the woman he was lying on was rather familiar, though of course he couldn't remember having seen it before . . .

'All right,' she rasped. 'Stop it, you're hurting.'

Not that lying on top of women had featured all that much in his life to date; but if this was typical, it was an overrated pastime. For one thing, their elbows dig into your solar plexus. He opened his mouth to say, *No, I'm not, you're dead, dead people don't feel pain*. But he didn't, for some reason. Instead, he slackened off the weight on the belt just a little.

'We meet again, Bowden Allshapes,' he said.

He'd expected it to sound rather better than it did. She didn't seem particularly impressed. She just gurgled, 'Get *off* me, you clumsy idiot, you're squashing my arm.' Curiously, it was one of the things Sally had said to him more than once during their married life, but all in all he was prepared to accept it as a coincidence.

'No,' he said. 'And don't go changing into a hedgehog or anything. It takes you just over two-thirds of a second to do a transformation. Think how tight I could get this belt in two-thirds of a second.'

A good argument clearly presented: the secret of successful advocacy. She called Duncan a very vulgar name and became perfectly still. Good old brute force, he thought. Trial by combat: an unjustly neglected branch of litigation, in his view, since it's invariably cheaper, quicker and fairer than the usual forms of dispute resolution used in the UK, not to mention a damn sight less traumatic for the participants.

'All right,' she grunted. 'Just think, though. If that Veronica happened to wander past right now, what do you think she'd make of us?'

'Good point,' Duncan said, and stood up, dragging her to her feet with a brutal jerk of the wrist. 'Attention to detail. I approve of that.' She yelped, and for a split second he grinned the relieved smile of the man whose theory has just been proved right. 'Let's find an empty office or something and discuss this like civilised monsters,' he said.

As if on cue, he noticed a half-open door. It led into a sort of boardroom, with a long, shiny table and lots of chairs. He wrestled her into one of them with a couple of yanks of the belt, and sat down next to her.

'Cosy, this,' he said. She gave him a look, but it bounced off.

'Just to clarify before we get started. You do anything that makes me think you're about to change shape or something like that, and I'll pull hard on the belt and throttle you.' He paused and looked at her. 'You don't like pain, do you?'

She raised an eyebrow. 'Well,' she said, 'it hurts, you see.'

'Quite. But you *really* don't like it. Which is odd, isn't it?'

'No, actually. I think you'll find it's pretty unpopular generally. Like rice pudding, or the government.'

Duncan shook his head. 'When Wesley Loop and I were beating the shit out of each other – actually, it was a bit more one-sided than that, but on the few occasions when I managed to land one on him, he hardly seemed to notice. And that bloke you were with earlier, your driver. George. I don't think they really felt anything, either of them. I mean, Wesley got annoyed when I threw him against walls, but it was just the inconvenience rather than agony or anything. I think they didn't feel it because they're dead. Or undead, or whatever the technical term is. I think pain's the body's way of warning you that you're about to come to harm. If you're dead already, why bother? It's just discomfort which serves no purpose. Well?'

She frowned, then nodded. 'One of the perks of belonging to our organisation,' she said. 'Like a health plan, only better, I think.'

'But you—' He smiled. 'You still feel pain, don't you? Because you're not like them. You're still alive.'

Her so-what shrug was nearly perfect, but not quite. 'You make it sound like it's unusual,' she said. 'But loads of people are alive every day.'

'Not people like you.'

A slight glow of irrepressible pride as she answered, 'There are no people like me. I'm unique.'

Duncan nodded. 'Let's hear it for small mercies,' he said. 'And don't even think about trying to change the subject. You're alive. You're this sort of incredibly rich and powerful zombie gangmaster, but you're not one of them. You never died. Did you?'

'Oh, all right, then, if it means so much to you.' She pulled a face. 'No, I never died. Call me an old stick-in-the-mud if you like, but—'

'Sh.' She stared at him, but she shushed. 'Now then,' he went on, 'Luke Ferris told me that it's directly because of you that there's no natural wolves in Britain. Is that true?'

'You say it like it's a bad thing.'

'So it's true. Interesting. I don't know the exact date offhand, but according to the History Channel or David Attenborough or whoever I got it from wolves have been extinct here for over four hundred years. So if it was you who wiped them all out—' He hesitated, in case she denied it or something, but she just sat there trying to look bored. 'I was going to say, four hundred years old, you've worn well, almost as well as Joan Collins. But then it occurred to me that I haven't got a clue what you look like. And I'm sitting here next to you.'

The bored look got a little colder and harder. 'You do say the sweetest things,' she said. 'Would you like to see me as I really am, Mr Hughes? Just say the word.'

'Not really, no,' Duncan said very quickly, but too late. It was well over a second before he managed to snap out of it, jerk hard on the belt and look away. Strange, how something natural, like a human head, could be so much more repulsive than vampires or werewolves.'Would you mind terribly —?'

'Sissy,' she said viciously. 'I hate people who judge by appearances. It's all right,' she added. 'The scary monster's gone now – you can look.'

He relaxed the strain on the belt, but didn't look back just in case. 'As I was saying,' he croaked, 'you're still alive. Unlike,' he added, 'most four-hundred-and-somethings. The question really is, how?'

She sighed. 'Oh, the usual,' she said. 'Healthy diet, plenty of fresh air and exercise, five fresh fruit and veg a day. That sort of thing.'

'That sort of thing,' Duncan repeated. 'And a little bit of creative bookkeeping as well.'

He heard a hiss, as of breath sucked in sharply. 'What's that supposed to mean?' she said.

Duncan turned to look at her. Mercifully, she'd gone back to being lovely and instantly forgettable. 'It's where I come in, isn't it?' he said. 'Because you're not the only one who's unique around here. Me too, in my own highly specialised way.'

Synthesised yawn. 'There're all sorts of ways in which you're different from other people,' she said, 'all of them either annoying or embarrassing or both. Simple tact—'

'Also,' he went on, 'it's how Luke got dragged into all this – him and the rest of the gang. I guess Luke must've said something about it to Wesley Loop, and he told you, and it all spiralled out of control from there. And there was me always assuming that Luke was the centre of the universe and I was just some sort of pathetic little moon or asteroid or something in orbit around him. And all the time, it was the other way round. It was all me, wasn't it? From the start.'

She didn't bother contradicting him. Instead, she looked at him with a lack of expression so complete that he could feel it dragging him in, like a black hole. 'More than once I've asked myself,' she said, 'why did it have to be you? Why couldn't it have been somebody *tolerable*? Possibly with some tiny vestige of a personality.'

That annoyed Duncan, and he scowled. 'Wasn't, though, was it? It was me. Because I was the only kid in the school, the only human being on the whole fucking *planet*, who could've done that maths homework and got precisely that particular set of answers. Nobody else, not all the Nobel prize-winners and professors of pure maths and quantum-nuclear-astrophysicists. Only me.' For a moment, the unfairness of it all surged over him and left him speechless. Then he blurted out, 'They were right, weren't they? My answers, to those questions. I got all the sums right.'

She made him wait a very long time before she said, 'Yes.'

'Not right for anybody else, of course,' he added bitterly. 'Just for me.'

'Well, of course. After all,' she added, 'you're the only person in the world who does his sums in Base Ten Point One instead of boring conventional old Base Ten.'

Duncan looked up sharply. 'Is that all it is?' he said, astonished in spite of himself. 'One rotten decimal place out, and all this shit ends up happening to me?'

Her eyes were like the empty space between galaxies. 'One decimal place is all it takes,' she said. 'Just a very slight variation, so small you'd never notice under normal circumstances. Anything larger and it'd show, you see. It was essential that whoever I chose should look completely normal and ordinary, so nobody would ever notice. Ten-point-one instead of ten was pretty well perfect.'

Duncan sat very still and quiet for a second or two. Then he said, 'And that's why I didn't die. That day in the classroom, when Luke bashed me and I hit my head on the pipe. Because of one decimal place.'

She sighed, as if he was being tiresome. 'Be grateful,' she said. 'The fact that you're point one out of phase with the rest of humanity saved your stupid life. I'd have thought only getting a B in maths instead of an A was a small price to pay for twenty years you wouldn't otherwise have had.' She slid a finger between the belt and her neck. 'Look, is this really necessary?' she said. 'I think we understand each other now. And if you understand, you'll see that your only possible future's with us. Certainly not with Luke Ferris or these—' She grinned. 'These *people*. They may be colourful and mildly amusing for a while, but they can't help you. Only I can do that. You do see that, don't you?'

Duncan shook his head. 'Other way round, though, isn't it?' He pressed his little finger against the belt, applying a very slight pressure. 'You need me, I'm the only one who can save you.' Then he pulled a face. 'Because of this – what did you call it? Variation? Out of phase? All sounds a bit *Star Trek* to me.'

Her voice became calm and businesslike. 'It's perfectly simple and straightforward, actually. The thing about you is, you exist just a tiny bit out of step with everybody else. Basic, fundamental quantum theory; when the boffins get around to discovering it, in about twenty years from now, it'll all seem so blindingly obvious that we'll all wonder how we could've been so stupid as not to have figured it out before. Honestly,' she added with feeling, 'scientists. Clueless, the lot of them. No imagination; they can't make the intuitive leaps. If you want them to think just a weensy bit out of the box, you've got to climb up a tree while they're snoozing and pelt them with apples.'

It took Duncan a third of a second to work out what she meant by that. Oh, he thought. 'So that was you,' he said. 'Sir Isaac New—'

'Yes, that was me.' She sounded too bored to talk about it. 'And a load of other stuff, too. A few nudges here and there, when the pace of research had slowed down to a pathetic snails-overtaking-on-the-inside crawl. Mostly, though, my part throughout history has been providing the funding. With what I give those useless nerds each year, I could buy South America. And after all that, they're still lagging way behind. Which is why—'

'Which is why you need me.'

Nod. 'Yes, it's why I need you. Sad, isn't it? Until they find out the true significance of the anti-clockwise gravitic semi-quark – and they haven't even discovered it yet – all that expensive science is useless, and I've got to rely on *you*. Which is exactly why,' she added brightly, 'your prospects with me are so dazzlingly bright. For twenty years, you know you're completely indispensable to me. If that's not an invitation to fleece me blind, I don't know what is.'

But Duncan wasn't interested. 'And it's not because I can't be killed—'

'Actually, you can.' The businesslike voice again. 'But only by someone or something that's out of alignment by exactly the same degree that you are: point one of a degree. You'll be pleased to hear that there're only two other people on Earth who meet that criterion, and they're both Buddhist monks living in a monastery in Nepal; so stay clear of the Himalayas and you're laughing. Apart from them, there's a washing machine in Tierra del Fuego and a pot-bellied pig somewhere in the Solomon Islands, and that's it, as far as we know. Nobody and nothing else can kill you.'

'Not even you?'

'Not even me. Yet. In twenty years, mind you—'

'Thanks for the warning.'

'Token of good faith,' she said airily. 'My pleasure, glad to have been of service. Of course,' she added, 'death's not everything. For instance, you could be buried twenty feet down in solid rock. You'd still be alive, but after the first ten years you'd probably get a dreadful dose of the fidgets.'

Duncan grinned. 'Ah,' he said, 'but if I was buried alive, I'd be no good to you, would I? I wouldn't be able to do that special thing that only I can do.'

Click of the tongue, loud and sharp as a ringmaster's whip. 'Don't fanny around, Duncan,' she said. 'You know perfectly well what it is, so don't try pretending you don't. I was hoping we were on the same wavelength, you and I.'

'All right.' Duncan closed his eyes for a moment. 'Tell me if I've got this right. You exist because you're not legally dead—'

'Oh, I'm *legally* dead,' she corrected him. 'But I'm also illegally alive, if you follow me. I was a lawyer once, you know. Well, my father was a lawyer, and I married a lawyer; women weren't allowed to be lawyers in the sixteenth century, so I did all the work and we had to pretend it was them. I was brilliant, though. Utterly brilliant. Oh, you're looking at me and giving me that come-off-it look, but it's true. Never lost a case. All my clients got off. I even,' she added calmly, 'got myself off death, on a technicality.'

Duncan played that back in his mind. Still didn't make sense. 'Death?' he queried weakly. 'But that's nothing to do with – I mean, you can't talk your way out of death. It doesn't listen.'

Smuggest grin ever. 'Listened to me. Everybody listens to me. No, it was a logical progression, from bending man-made law to the laws of nature. That's what lawyers do, after all. We bend the truth. Just a little heat and pressure at the right place, applied just so, and we change the world. We take a reality in which our client was in the house helping himself to the loose cash and the DVD player into a slightly different reality in which he was down the pub with twenty-seven witnesses. We do it every day; and it's not lying. It can't be lying if twelve honest citizens believe it, because what a jury believes is by definition the truth. We change reality. One moment things are one way, the next they're completely different; and everybody accepts it, so it must be true. Truth is what everybody accepts, it's the only definition that makes sense. Oh sure, there're a few dissidents who refuse to fall in with the majority; eyewitnesses who saw the defendant steal the car or beat up the old lady. They won't accept it when he gets off, but that's their problem. They're at variance. Out of phase, just like you.' She sighed, and smiled. 'It's not magic or anything like that, it's perfectly normal, happens a million times a day all over the world. It's just that people don't realise that's what's happening. Like people didn't know about gravity until I nutted Sir Isaac with the apple. Like they don't yet know about the anticlockwise gravitic semiquark. Yet.'

Duncan opened his mouth to object, because of course it couldn't be true. Then he remembered that he was a werewolf. At some point he'd accepted that, and now he believed it. What people accept is the truth.

'Anyhow,' she went on, 'the law's a bit fuzzy on what death really is. You die and your body stops moving, but until all your affairs have been put in order and your bills have been paid and your money's been shared out and your relatives have all fallen out with each other over who gets the ormolu clock in the dining room, you're still sort of there, what the law calls a legal person. It's a bit like being a ghost, except of course,' she added with a broad grin, 'there's no such thing as ghosts. As far as the law's concerned I died years ago, but I don't actually stop being a person, in the eyes of the law, until my estate's finally wound up.

Till then, I'm kind of betwixt and between: Bowden Allshapes, deceased. And thanks to you—'

Duncan nodded; he felt strangely grateful to her for saying it aloud. 'Thanks to me,' he said, 'your estate can't be wound up, because in order for that to happen, the estate accounts need to be drawn up and signed. And that can't happen, because no matter how many times I add up the figures, they always come out slightly wrong.'

She beamed at him. 'In Base Ten, yes. Really,' she added, 'I'm stunned you hadn't realised earlier. All you had to do was calculate the mean error over, say, fifty attempts, and then draw a simple Venn diagram—'

'Bugger Venn diagrams,' Duncan said forcefully. 'I keep you alive by not being able to get the accounts to balance. And that's *all*—'

She drew out a thin smile. 'That's all,' she said. 'Just a small thing, but so's a six-millimetre Billinghurst reed valve, and you try running a faster-than-light engine without one. Oops,' she added, 'not invented yet, on account of Jason Billinghurst is still at school, just about to do his maths GCSE, actually. I'm paying for him to get special coaching. But in eight years' time—' She moved a hand in a vague gesture, like a queen trying to wave to cheering crowds with her eyes shut. 'Like I said,' she continued, 'perfectly simple. And you were quite right, by the way. Luke Ferris happened to tell Wesley Loop about that maths homework you did; about how you swore blind you'd checked it all thoroughly but it still came out completely wrong. Don't ask me how the subject happened to come up. Just making conversation, most probably. And because of it, your life, and Luke's, and all the other boys in your gang—'

Duncan was sure he hadn't meant to drag on the belt, because that'd have been spiteful and he wasn't a bully; or at least, he hadn't meant to drag that hard. Just a twitch was all he'd intended, probably, to remind her who had the upper hand at that particular moment. Possibly he'd forgotten his own strength; just conceivably possibly, he was upset about something.

Anyhow – she yelped and made a strange gagging noise, and then the belt broke. Actually, it was the stupid little pop rivet that held the buckle on; it tore through the fake leather, and suddenly she was free. A nice example of reality changing because of one little thing, if you cared to look at it that way. Or—

She vanished, and her chair kicked sideways to make room for a white unicorn. Before Duncan had drawn the lungful of air he needed to swear with, she'd barged past him and shot out of the door. He fought it long and hard this time, the desperate, compelling urge to chase her. He dragged out every last scrap of human rationality. He told himself, you know what it's all about now; you know what she really is and what you really are. You don't need to chase her, and you sure as hell don't want to. This is her way of hunting you, and if you play by her rules you'll lose. Whatever you do, stay here and don't run after her.

He put the case well, and he wasn't the same weak-willed easily led no-self-confidence loser he'd always been ever since he joined the Ferris Gang. He'd grown a hell of a lot over the last few weeks. He was stronger, wiser, more able to fight back. As a result, Duncan held out for a full two seconds before jumping off the chair and racing out of the room.

Maybe she'd done something with her pheromones, or maybe the cleaners actually got as far as this part of the building before giving up in terrified despair. The scent was much stronger than it had been, far too strong to ignore. Cursing himself for his stupidity, Duncan ran. The carpet provided excellent traction underpaw. Query: can a unicorn run down stairs?

Apparently, yes. He clattered down two flights to a landing, stopped to sniff and tore down the first turning on the left. At school they'd told him, no running in the corridors. Another of life's crucial lessons he'd completely failed to learn.

I could run into a wall, he thought, or straight through a window. Wouldn't do me any harm, even though I'm six floors up, I'd just land, smash a few paving slabs, no sweat at all. But I'm just kidding myself. I couldn't do it, because I can't ignore the scent. Enslaved. No free will whatsoever. Situation normal, in fact. It's a dog's life.

Round another corner, like a greyhound after an electric hare. And then he stopped. It wasn't at sudden as that, of course. There was a degree of skidding as his shoe heels failed to grip on the wool pile, and rather a lot of static electricity, and an encounter with a wall that would've spoiled an ordinary human's day. He just bounced off it, though, and sat down heavily on the floor.

It wasn't that the scent wasn't there any more. It was so strong he could feel it tugging at him. But there was another scent now, and it was stronger. For a moment he felt like he was being pulled apart. Then something broke, just like his stupid belt had done, and he turned his head like a horse on a leading rein. Another scent. Not that he knew much about that sort of thing, but he fancied it was mainly violets.

'Hello,' said Veronica. 'Why are you sitting on the floor?'

'Hunggh,' he replied, because he'd been neglecting his breathing lately. 'Unicorn,' he added. 'Chasing. Bowden Allshapes.'

'Oh.' She looked at him. 'I thought—'

'Your smell,' Duncan said. 'Scent,' he amended quickly. 'It—'

'Do you like it?' She smiled. 'I can't remember what it's called, it's just some stuff I bought at Gatwick last time I went on holiday. Usually I don't bother much about that kind of thing but . . . ' She paused and her brow furrowed. 'Are you all right?' she said. 'You look funny.'

'I'm fine.' Not, perhaps, one of those lies that change the nature of reality he'd been hearing so much about. Just a lie gradually turning into the truth as he got his breath back. 'Thanks,' he added.

'For what?'

'Saving my life.'

Veronica raised both eyebrows. 'Did I?'

'Not sure.' Duncan pressed his back to the wall and stood up. Feet just about working. 'At least, you saved me from a fate worse than death, which is kind of the same thing, only more so,

I suppose. Look, have you got any more of that stuff? The scent, I mean.'

'Yes, in my desk drawer. Did it really—?'

He nodded. 'Stopped me chasing her, yes. One moment I was a complete goner, the next I was just crashing into walls. Which,' he added, noticing the cracked plaster for the first time, 'is absolutely fine by me. Sorry about the wall, by the way, but—'

'Don't worry about it, we've got loads of them.' For a split second Veronica froze, with that characteristic did-I-really-just-say-that look on her face. 'I mean, it's all right, nobody's going to notice. If they do, I expect they'll just hang a picture over it or something.'

She's gabbling, Duncan thought. Reminds me of something. Actually, reminds me of me, when I used to try and talk to girls, before I met Sally. He turned down the corner of that reflection so he wouldn't lose the place. 'Anyhow,' he said, 'definitely it seems to have done the trick. By rights I should be chasing after that horrible bloody unicorn. But, well, here I am. That's marvellous, really.'

She nodded. He had the feeling that, at that moment, she'd have agreed with him if he'd told her he was a trouser press. Very curious indeed; but for once, here was something weird and inexplicable he was quite comfortable with.

'Absolutely,' she said. 'What was she doing in here anyway?'

Duncan smiled. 'Came to offer me a job.'

'Oh. Did you—?'

'Not likely. Actually, at one stage I was trying to strangle her with my belt. But it broke.'

'Ah.'

Just to tempt providence, he sniffed. The unicorn scent was still there, but for some unaccountable reason he felt no urge whatsoever to chase after it. So instead: 'Could you possibly show me where the kitchen is again? I know you showed me earlier, but I'm afraid I've forgotten. No sense of direction.'

'Of course.' Beautiful smile. 'I was just headed that way myself, as it happens.'

At four o'clock in the morning, wearing scent? Anything's possible. 'That's lucky,' he said. 'Only I could really go for a strong cup of coffee right now.'

There's always that stage, when speech dries up, the brain blanks out, and suddenly your feet become so unspeakably fascinating that you spend the next twenty minutes staring at them, rather than, say, at the person of the opposite sex sitting in dead silence next to you. Presumably there's a good reason for it, or else evolution's time-and-motion experts would've done away with it back in the early Neolithic era. You've just got to be patient, sit it out. Counting the lace-holes on your shoe uppers helps pass the time. Eventually, she asked, 'Is the coffee all right?'

For the record it was bitter black treacle with thick chewy chunks of undissolved instant granules floating about on top. 'Fine,' Duncan replied. 'Just how I like it.'

'Oh good. I used to like coffee, but ever since – I mean, it doesn't really agree with us, for some reason. We tend to have tea instead. Earl Grey or lapsang, without milk.'

You can tell when mere attraction is starting to coagulate into a Relationship when she tells you what she likes to eat or drink, and instead of saying 'Yech' or 'You really like that muck?' you smile inanely and say 'Yes, that's my favourite too.' Interestingly, this is one of the few lies that not even the cleverest lawyer can bend into a new reality.

'Is it really? I mean, that's rather unusual. I thought all men liked their tea extra strong with tons of sugar.'

'Not me,' Duncan replied, and all around him the universe stayed grimly the same. Oh well. 'Strong coffee and weak tea, that's how I like it. About the unicorn.'

He hadn't really meant to press Veronica for information. It was just that he felt the need to break the silence, and he didn't want to trash the fabric of reality by continuing the hot-drinks theme. But she looked up at him, as though this was something she'd been expecting.

'She's Sally's client, really,' she said. 'Mainly. But you know how it is, we all do bits and pieces of work for her. I mean, if she needs some conveyancing done, Rose or Matilda does it, because Sally's strictly litigation. I did a couple of leases for her a while back. Would you like a slice of Battenberg cake? We bought one for Rose's birthday on Tuesday – there should be some left.'

Vampires eating Battenberg cake? Well. A small, rebellious part of his brain did the maths (Tuesday: by now it's probably so stale you could sharpen scythes on it) but got no support. 'Yes, please,' Duncan said. 'That'd be nice.'

'I expect you think we eat nothing but raw liver and black pudding,' Veronica went on, as she opened a cupboard and fetched out a big Tupperware cake box. 'Actually, most of us have a sweet tooth. And no, before you ask, it's not long and pointed.' Her fingers lifted the lid, and a few stray molecules drifted out; enough for a werewolf's nose to detect a familiar but unexpected smell . . .

'No,' he yelped. 'Don't open—'

Too late. She'd opened the box. The smell of fresh garlic wafted up, hitting her like a truck. Her mouth dropped open, her eyes glazed like fogged-over glasses, and she slowly fell backwards onto the floor. The sound of her head hitting the lino was—

Duncan was on his feet, standing over her, but of course he hadn't the faintest idea what to do. He grabbed the box, of course, and looked round for somewhere to dispose of it. But no window to hurl it out of, naturally, and chucking it in the bin would be rather like stuffing a pinless grenade under a sofa cushion. A choking, gargling noise at his feet started him shivering with terror. He was stranded in an ocean of cluelessness.

'Bit like kryptonite, really,' said a familiar voice. 'Only cheaper, of course. Also organic, biodegradable and produced from renewable resources. Hello, Duncan. Bet you weren't expecting to see me.'

Luke Ferris straightened up from an empty space under the worktop. He was in human shape, which was something. He looked rather as though he'd just spent twenty minutes trying to climb out of a running combine harvester. His clothes were comprehensively ripped, his hair was full of dust and grit, and the sole of one of his shoes was lolling out like a rude boy's tongue.

'Rescue time,' he said. 'Come on, I haven't got all night.'

Duncan stared at him. He didn't say anything, because they don't make words that can handle that kind of strain. Luke took a step forward, then looked down at Veronica, who was beginning to twitch.

'You have no idea,' Luke said, 'how hard it is to get hold of a simple string of garlic at three in the morning when you're a wolf. I had to ram-raid a greengrocer's in Islington for that lot. It says *produce of more than one country* on the label, which doesn't exactly inspire confidence, but it seems to have done the trick. Well? You coming, or not?'

There was one word that Duncan could just about manage. 'No,' he said.

Luke had never been top of the class in English at school, but you'd have thought he could understand 'No.' Apparently not. 'Don't muck about, Duncan,' he said irritably. 'I think our best bet is to make for the roof and see if we can jump across to next door. It's about thirty-five feet, but we'll be transformed so we should make it. Unless there's a fire escape, but—'

'Fuck you,' Duncan said. 'I'm not going.'

This time, it sank in – rather like a JCB in a swamp. 'What the hell do you mean, not going?' Luke scowled at him, then made one of his trademark Oh-for-pity's-sake head gestures. 'Look, if you're worried we're going to beat you up or tear you limb from limb, forget it, all right? Yes, you've got a certain amount of explaining to do, and yes, the atmosphere may be a trifle fraught around the office for a day or so until we've got a few issues ironed out, but – sod it, Duncan, we're your mates. We'll get over it somehow and everything'll be fine, you'll see. Now get your arse in gear and let's leave. This place gives me the creeps.'

'No,' Duncan said. 'And it's not that. I don't want to go. And I don't want to be in your gang any more.'

On the floor, Veronica had stopped moving. Duncan wasn't a doctor, or a vet or an undertaker or whatever was appropriate in the circumstances, but he was pretty sure that wasn't good. But he didn't know what to do.

'I've got to get someone,' he said. 'You go away.'

'*What?*' Luke stared at him as though he'd just burst into flames. 'Just a moment,' he said. 'It's her, isn't it? That *thing*. Oh, for crying out loud, Duncan, you don't mean to say—'

'Yes,' Duncan replied. 'And if anything bad happens to her, I'm going to kill you. Now, unless you happen to know what to do, I suggest you go away, because in ten seconds I'm going to yell for help, and you may not want to be here when it arrives.' He looked up, and a spurt of anger filled his brain. 'You think it's funny, right? Well—'

'Duncan.' For a moment, he felt the tug of the old authority. 'You're wasting your time, mate. That much garlic – she practically *touched* it. You can get the whole lot of them in here and there's bugger-all they'll be able to do for her. Sorry, mate, but she's had it.'

CHAPTER FIFTEEN

So your best friend has just murdered the girl you love. What are you supposed to do about it?

Well, it depends. You can go on the Trisha Goddard show and get helpful advice from a lot of strangers, and maybe even a publicist and some useful product-endorsement deals. You can check out *Yellow Pages* for an all-night silversmith who'll run you off half a dozen .357 magnum bullets while you wait, so you can kill your best friend and have two corpses to stare blankly at instead of just one. You can forgive your best friend (she was a nice girl but there's no point crying over spilt blood, plenty more bats in the belfry, &c) and go back to working for him with the rest of your boyhood chums. Or you can stand perfectly still with your mouth open, while what's left of your heart and brain howl *No—*

Rewind a bit. The girl you love: when had that happened? Duncan couldn't say. Didn't seem to matter. Now that she was lying on the floor gagging up her last few breaths, the chronology of it wasn't all that relevant.

Just to complicate matters further, Luke did something he'd never done before, something Duncan wouldn't have thought was possible. He cleared his throat nervously, like an Englishman about to speak French, and said, 'Duncan, I'm sorry.'

'What?'

'I'm sorry. I had no idea. Sod it, I thought I was rescuing you.'

'Oh,' Duncan said. 'Right.'

'I mean, last I knew, you were being abducted by vampires. You know, the Undead, our natural enemies. It didn't seem likely they were bringing you here so that you could find true love.'

Duncan remembered something. 'You were just about to kill me,' he said. 'For being a traitor.'

Luke conceded the point as though it was a minor typographical error. 'We were upset with you, yes. All right, maybe we'd have beaten you up a little. It's not a nice thing to do to your mates, treason. But we weren't going to kill you. We couldn't have. Physical impossibility, without silver ammunition or the unicorn. I suppose we assumed you'd know that, but—'

'Doesn't matter.' Duncan tried not to look at Veronica, and failed. 'You're right, you're not to blame. You were trying to help. It's just one of those things.'

'Right.'

'And so is this.' He went to the doorway, pushed the door open and whistled.

All his life, he'd been pathetic at whistling. He'd practised for hours when he was young, but all that came out was a rather moist blowing noise. Wrong-shaped face, or something. This time, though, the result was perfect, if a trifle loud. If they failed to hear him in Birmingham, it was because they had earplugs in.

'What the hell are you playing at?' Luke demanded.

'I'm calling for help,' Duncan explained. Odd that Luke, normally so smart, hadn't figured it out for himself. He moved slightly, so as to block the doorway completely.

'Damn it, Duncan, I told you. You can fetch in all the vampires in London and they won't be able to do anything.'

Smile. 'I'm not calling vampires,' he said.

Duncan waited for a few seconds, then sniffed. Sure enough, the smell he needed was there, and a moment later he could hear the soft thump of hooves on carpet. 'Help is on its way,' he said.

'What?' Luke paused, and sniffed too. 'Are you out of your tiny mind?' he said, and his eyes were wide with fear. '*She*'s not going to be able to save your girlfriend. What the hell made you think—?'

'That wasn't what I wanted help with,' Duncan pointed out.

Correction: Luke was pretty smart after all. At least, he didn't seem to have any trouble working that one out. He lunged for the doorway and nearly managed to barge his way through, but Duncan grabbed first his arm and then his neck, and hauled him back into the room. 'I want you to know I forgive you,' he said, as Luke's flailing hand missed his nose by a quarter of an inch. 'Deep down, anyhow,' he added. 'Unfortunately, it hasn't worked its way to the surface yet.'

She was coming; they could both hear her footsteps. Luke turned frantic, kicking and scrabbling with more strength than Duncan would have thought it possible for a human body to contain, a strength matched only by his own. Matched and exceeded. After fifteen seconds or so of the kind of wrestling the big US networks would've paid billions to air, Duncan lifted Luke clean off his feet and threw him against the wall. More damage to the plasterwork. They'd need a full-sized reproduction of the *Night Watch* to cover up that one.

'You can't let her get me,' Luke panted, as he tried to get up. 'It'd be murder.'

Duncan shrugged. 'So don't chase her if you don't want to.'

'You know bloody well I can't help it.'

'Same here.'

Luke sort of tipped himself onto his feet. Duncan picked up the fridge and threw it at him. Either a good aim or a lucky one. Luke stayed still for nearly ten seconds after that.

'Sooner or later, somebody's going to have to pay for all this damage,' Duncan said. 'But we'll cross that bridge when we come to it.'

Luke went for another charge, but he was clearly tired and maybe a little woozy in the head. Duncan sidestepped, grabbed his arm as he shot by and swung him into the corner of the room. Add a worktop, a corner cupboard and a shelf of mugs to the bill. Oh, and the kettle, which Duncan bounced off Luke's forehead for good measure.

'Having fun, boys?'

She was standing in the doorway. But she wasn't a unicorn. Instead, she was just this gorgeous sophisticated-looking female whose face would slip through the meshes of your mind thirty seconds after you left her. She was holding an old-fashioned wicker shopping basket in her left hand.

'Mr Ferris, isn't it?' she said, smiling pleasantly. 'We have met, though never this close. Oh, in case you think that any second now this room's going to fill up with vampires I can pretty well guarantee it won't. I had Carlo – he's my personal chef – knock up two dozen of his special vegetarian quiches, and I've just been round laying them down like landmines. Extremely talented boy, Carlo, though he does tend to be a bit heavy-handed with the garlic. Comes of having no sense of smell, I suppose. Still, you've got to make allowances for the disabled, and being dead's about as disabled as you can get. What happened to her, by the way?'

'Luke murdered her,' Duncan said evenly. 'But he meant well.'

She took a step forward into the kitchen and peered down at Veronica, who was lying perfectly still, on her side. 'Call me picky if you like,' she said, 'but like I told you a while ago, I used to be a lawyer myself, and it's not actually murder until they die.' She frowned, then looked up. 'Oh,' she said, 'I see. That's why you called for me. You wanted me to—' She clicked her tongue reproachfully. 'That's not very nice, you know. If it was anybody else but you, I might easily have taken offence.'

Duncan shrugged. 'Oh well,' he said.

Luke, he noticed, was trying to hide behind the wreckage of the fridge. Pathetic. Hard to believe, really, that he, Duncan, had once been in awe of such an obvious loser. What made it worse was that Luke was clearly in no danger from Bowden Allshapes.

She wasn't remotely interested in him: why should she be, after all? Just another overgrown puppy, all bark and no bite. In spite of himself, Duncan felt a little warm glow of pride, and the muscles that would've wagged his tail if he'd had one twitched slightly, because she wasn't here for Luke Ferris, she was here for him. Furthermore, she was going to be disappointed. He didn't need her after all – why bother with revenge? Being Luke Ferris was plainly the nastiest thing that could happen to anybody, so why try and gild the lily? And by her own admission there wasn't very much she could do to him. He felt not a trace of an urge to chase after her; all that stuff seemed impossibly remote now – silly, like the sort of thing he used to do at school. The hell with the lot of them, he thought suddenly. There's nothing left for me here. I might as well just walk away.

'I can save her if you like,' she said.

There are moments when life freezes. Everything stops. And you know that when it starts up again, nothing's going to be the same.

'Just a thought,' she added. 'Of course, if you don't want me to—'

'Can you?' The words came out like a sandpaper-coated egg out of a chicken. 'You can't, you're bluffing. That'd be—'

'Magic?' She grinned at him. 'No such thing. No, I can save her, all right. It'd only take me a jiffy.'

Duncan looked at her, as though he could peck through her skull with his eyes and see inside her mind. Apparently he couldn't. Pity. 'You're lying,' he said.

'Try me,' she said. 'No win, no fee. Actually, it's pretty simple.' She sniffed. 'Garlic poisoning, right?'

Duncan nodded.

'There you are, then. She'll wake up with slightly red eyes and a runny nose but otherwise fully functional and bursting with rude health. And yes, I can do that. I can also cure lycanthropy and vampirism and a whole range of other minor antisocial ailments, as I'd have told you long ago if only you'd asked. Of course,' she added, 'there'd have to be something in it for me. A little light clerical work, nothing strenuous. I'd like to say *take your time, think it over*, but I'm afraid that's not possible. I figure she's got, what, twenty-five seconds, and then it's goodbye, bat girl. Sorry to pressure you, but time is really rather of the essence.'

Duncan looked down. Veronica wasn't moving. Choice? It had been so long since he'd really had one.

'You promise you can—?'

'No, of course not. But if I fail, you don't have to come and work for me. Look, I hate to harp on about it, but time's getting on.'

'Deal.'

'Duncan, for crying out loud—' Luke's head popped up from behind the heap of fridge shrapnel. 'I don't know who or what this is; all I know is, she kills the likes of you and me, so if you were thinking—'

'Shut up, Luke,' Duncan said. 'Well, get on with it, won't you?'

She was grinning at him. 'It's done. Look, she's starting to come round already, bless her.'

Veronica was yawning and stretching. *So that's what she'll look like in the mornings*, said the lonely, neglected optimist inside Duncan's head. She mumbled something without consonants in it, and sat up.

'Duncan?' she said. 'Oh. Mrs Allshapes. Sorry, do we have an appointment?'

Then, presumably, Veronica felt the difference. She shuddered all over, as though she was cold, then shuddered again, as though it was murderously hot and she was wearing six layers of jumpers and cardigans.

'That's just the blood starting to circulate again,' Bowden Allshapes said cheerfully. 'Oh, and I wouldn't try moving your feet for a bit—'

'*Ouch!*'

'Because of the pins and needles. But that's all right, it'll pass in a minute or two and then you'll be right as rain. Oh, and before you ask, the heavy palpitations in your chest are just your heartbeat. It probably feels like you've swallowed a traction engine, but you won't even notice it after a while. Well,' she added frostily, 'don't bother to say thank you, will you?'

Veronica turned her head and looked at Duncan. 'What happened?' she said.

'He killed you,' Duncan said. 'Him over there: Luke Ferris. He's a solicitor. We were at school together.'

A hand popped up from behind the fridge and did a little wave.

'He poisoned you with garlic,' Duncan went on. 'You died. I think. Anyway, Bowden Allshapes brought you back to life.'

Veronica's eyes widened like ripples in a pond, and she burst into tears. A tug, like a fish-hook snagged in his soul, made Duncan want to grab her and squeeze her in his arms. He didn't, though.

'Men,' said Bowden Allshapes. 'Sensitive as a horseshoe. Anyway,' she added briskly, 'I hate to mention it, but I've fulfilled my side of the deal, and paperwork waits for no one. Come along, Duncan. My car's outside. You can run along behind it if you'd rather.'

Veronica stopped crying in mid-snuffle. 'Deal?' she said sharply.

'None of your business, dear.' Bowden Allshapes frowned. 'Well? Are you coming, or not? I know there's nothing in writing, but I took you for a man of your word.'

Duncan took a step towards her. Moving his leg was like ripping up a tree stump with a tractor and chain. Veronica looked at him and opened her mouth, but no words came out.

'Look, this is all very touching and human, but I simply don't have the time.' Bowden Allshapes held the door open. 'What with one thing and another, it's been rather too long since my last audit, and that's not good for me. Oh, while I think of it. Mr Ferris.'

Something moved behind the fridge.

'Would you be awfully sweet,' said Bowden Allshapes, 'and

have my file couriered round to my office? You'll find the address on the cover of the file – it's the registered office of Allshapes Holdings. As soon as possible, please, unless you want me to come round and fetch it myself. We could all go for a nice run while I'm there.'

'Thassalright,' Luke mumbled very quickly. 'Seetoitstraight-away.'

She smiled. 'Splendid. Feel free to send in your bill whenever you like. It was a pleasure doing business with you, but on balance I think it'll be much better having the work done in-house from now on. Though house,' she added, 'is something of an understatement. Still, a deal's a deal. Isn't it, Duncan?'

The important thing, he told himself as he walked slowly to the door, is not to look round. For once, he was quite right. He plotted a course across the kitchen floor and out through the door, and stuck to it. There were little pastry things in foil cases lined up on the corridor floor, like the landing lights of an airfield. He followed them, down the corridor to the stairs, down the stairs to the entrance lobby, out into the bitter fresh air. It was still dark, but clouds obscured the moon.

'I'm right here behind you,' said Bowden Allshapes, 'just in case you were thinking of straying off somewhere. Maybe I should get you a collar and lead. There's the car, look. George will be pleased to see you again, I'm sure. Did you know that he used to be a Formula One racing driver when he was still alive? Not actually a terribly wonderful qualification for a chauffeur, but I guess I'm one of nature's *collectors*. No, you get in the front, where I can keep an eye on you. And this time, no sneaky grabbing the wheel and making us crash, that'd just be action adventure. The office, George. *Slowly.*'

George was rather a mess – hardly surprising, considering what had happened the last time he and Duncan had met. His face and neck were latticed with deep cuts – no blood, no clots, just empty gouges, which made it worse, somehow – and his left temple was *flattened*, as if his head was made of putty and someone had trodden on it. He didn't seem to bear Duncan a grudge, though; he nodded affably as Duncan got in beside him, and then ignored him. It was, of course, a different car. No traffic on the roads at a quarter to five in the morning. Everything calm, peaceful and civilised.

'You'll enjoy working for us,' Bowden Allshapes was saying. 'Light caseload, just the one file to look after. Nice quiet colleagues, you won't hear a peep out of them from one day's end to the next. Your office will be on the seventy-third floor, so you'll have wonderful views out of the window; and accomodation en suite, so to speak. In fact, you can have the whole floor to yourself. Just you, the file, and a pencil. No calculators or anything like that, I'm afraid, but it'll be pleasantly soothing, just adding up the same columns of figures over and over and over again. A refreshing change, I'd imagine, after all the dashing about you've been doing lately. The best part, though, has got to be the job security. At Allshapes, we don't just think in terms of a job for life, it's a job for *ever*. Though, as I said earlier, we may need to review the position in about twenty years. Still, for someone with your rather unique profile, I'm sure we'll be able to find you something that'll keep you out of mischief. Ah, here we are.'

Out of the car, in through a glass and steel entrance lobby, into a lift that just kept on going up and up. The three of them: Bowden Allshapes, George and himself. The lift stopped at the thirty-sixth floor and George got out. 'Maintenance,' Bowden Allshapes explained. 'Next time you see him, he'll be good as new again, if you don't look too closely. We're very organised here. The only way to be, if you ask me.'

Duncan glanced up at the level indicator; fifty-first floor and still climbing. This high up, of course, all the windows would be sealed. You don't have to be dead to work here, but by God it helps.

'There's no staff canteen,' she was telling him, 'not as such. Mostly because nobody who works here needs to eat. But that's all right, we'll send out for sandwiches and pizzas and things for you. If you're very good, maybe we can think about letting you out on the roof for a run about at full moon. I like to think of myself as an enlightened employer, you see. As far as I'm concerned, investing in people is much more than just a nifty slogan. I think it was the late Richard Nixon who said that once you have them by the balls, their hearts and minds will follow. Here we are, top floor. I think you're going to like your new office. A bit spartan, but loads and loads of room.'

She was right about that. In an area the size of a football pitch, there was one plastic stackable-type chair and one plain wooden table. On the table was a coffee mug full of pencils. Bare floorboards. Nothing else. One very small window, like an arrow slit. Only one door, apart from the lift entrance; it led into another huge room, in the precise centre of which stood a steel-framed bed, the sort you'd expect to find in an army barracks. A chamber pot lurked under it. No window. Home.

'Everybody else in this building is dead, apart from you and me,' Bowden Allshapes said. 'So efficient. No need to bother with all the tiresome, disruptive stuff that *people* feel the need for.' She smiled. She'd be rather attractive if she wasn't the epitome of evil. 'Now I expect you've been under the impression that my dead people aren't really dead at all; they died, and then somehow they were brought back to life, like you were when you bashed your head on that water pipe. Actually, it's not like that at all. The legal definition of dead, as I'm sure you remember from law school, is no brain activity. Well. If you were to hook one of my boys up to a fancy medical scanning thing, the needle wouldn't so much as twitch. What's that expression: the lights are on but nobody's home? That's the way I like 'em, Duncan Hughes. They don't need a brain to tell their bodies what to do. That's my job. It means I've got thousands and thousands of ideal employees: absolute efficiency and no aggravation. One day,' she added with pride, 'the entire workforce will be like this. I don't know what they'll find for the living people to do. I'm not a politician, it's not my business. Really, I'm just doing what every employer in the world wishes he could do; and one of these days I'll make that dream come true, you mark my words. It's inevitable, if we're going to see off the competition from the emerging economies of the Far East, with their minimal labour costs. It won't be long before they elect a government that'll see it the way I do, and then I won't have to bother with all this silly skulking around any more. Well,' she added briskly, 'it's great fun talking to you and getting to know you, but I haven't got time right now. Go and sit in the chair, and as soon as your friend Luke Ferris sends the file round you can start work. You know what to do: just keep on adding up the figures, and when they don't balance, start all over again. You get twenty minutes for lunch, the lights go out at midnight and come back on again at six a.m. I'll drop by every six months or so to see how you're getting on. Welcome to the firm, Duncan. It's a pleasure having you with us.'

A chair. A table. A pencil.

What she hadn't told Duncan was that there was an automatic door-closing mechanism and a time lock on the bedroom door. It opened when the lights went out in the office, and closed again as soon as he'd walked through it; reverse procedure when the lights came on again in the morning. During the third cycle (you couldn't really call them days and nights; it'd be like saying Swindon was the Cotswolds) he tried staying in the office after lights-out. Nothing bad happened, but he had to sleep in the chair instead of the marginally more comfortable bed. A certain degree of rebellion, he realised, had been allowed for in the specification.

The numbers, he noticed after a while, changed from time to time; at least, they shifted their positions on the page, though the actual figures stayed the same. As an experiment, he copied them all out on the floorboards and checked them the next day. It proved his theory, for what that was worth, but he couldn't think of any use to put his hard-earned discovery to. If he put the pencil down and refused to add, the lights went out and it got very cold very quickly. He held out for two complete cycles once, but the satisfaction he got out of it wasn't enough to justify being frozen to the bone, so he gave in and went back to work.

Twice every cycle the lift doors opened (there were no controls on his side of the door, naturally) and a dead girl came in with a tray. The first time he said 'Thank you' out of sheer force of habit. The second, third, fourth, fifth, sixth and seventh time, he tried talking to her, but she didn't reply. The eighth time, he smashed the chair over her head; it made her drop the tray, and he had to stand up for the rest of the shift. Next lights-on, when he emerged from the bedroom, there was another chair in its place, identical in every respect.

After a bit, Duncan stopped bothering to count the cycles. He was only reminded of the passage of time when he came to work and found that his arrow-slit window had been blocked up – shuttered, it turned out, from the outside. The shutter went away again three cycles later, and he eventually figured out that it had been there to keep moonlight from getting into the office. When the shutter was taken away again he didn't bother looking out of the window. The view only upset him, and as time went on he took to sitting facing the other way, so that his back was to it. No measures were taken to stop him, so apparently it was allowed. Jolly good.

His main regret was that he hadn't paid attention to maths lessons at school. If he had, he might have been able to work out how to adjust his calculations so as to convert the result into Base Ten, compensating for the point-one degree of error. He spent many hours trying to reinvent that particular wheel, until the flip side of every sheet of paper in the file was covered in little scribbled sums and he was forced (in the absence of a rubber) to start using the floor and the walls to write on. He couldn't do it, though. He knew it could be done, but he lacked the necessary flair for figures, simple as that. The Management didn't even erase his jottings from the walls while he was asleep, which suggested that they shared his opinion of his mathematical abilities. After a while he gave that up as well. He was rapidly approaching the point where anything not enforced and compulsory was simply too much effort. The worst thing about it was how little he found he was suffering, once he'd settled in and found his feet. He was getting used to it, more or less the same way he'd got used to working at Craven Ettins; and here, he didn't have regular appointments with Jenny Sidmouth to contend with, so in a way it was better—

The one thing Duncan didn't do, for the same reason that people all over the world don't unscrew light bulbs and jam their fingers in the sockets, was think about the people he'd left behind: Luke Ferris, for instance, or Pete, or Micky, Clive and Kevin. Or what's-her-name, Veronica. Especially not her. He expressly and deliberately didn't think about how he'd chosen to come here and do this so that thingummy wouldn't die, which meant that somewhere out there she was still alive, presumably still waking up each morning and going to work and maybe possibly occasionally allowing her mind to drift, during the day's more boring bits, and wondering, in a vague sort of a way, whatever happened to that Duncan Hughes . . . On that score, he was as self-disciplined as a Hindu mystic, single-minded as an ant. In fact, he'd got such a grip on his own brain that, if challenged to do so, he could quite possibly not have thought about an elephant.

Maybe she missed him, too. In which case, surely it wouldn't bloody well kill her to come looking for him, possibly even rescue him; after all, she and her chums had been quick enough to snatch him away from the Ferris Gang when they thought there was something in it for them, and there was a perfectly good window and they could *fly*, for crying out loud, so they wouldn't have to fool around with scaffolding or helicopters or hang about waiting for him to grow his hair till it was seventy-three floors long. And if they were scared of heights or something, there was always good old brute force and violence – they might look all thin and willowy and left over from the 1970s but he knew from bitter personal experience that they were as strong as werewolves or possibly stronger, so bashing in a glass door and beating up a few dead people in the lobby shouldn't present any problem. But of course, if they weren't interested, if one of their number wasn't constantly banging on and on about how they really ought to go and rescue poor Duncan, who was only trapped in that ghastly place because of a selfless and noble act, until the rest of them couldn't stand it any more and were prepared to do anything just to get her to shut up—

No. Nothing of that kind whatsoever crossed Duncan's mind, not even for a fleeting instant. Which was just as well. A man could get depressed dwelling on stuff like that. It might even get to him to such an extent that he'd have difficulty concentrating on his work, and that would never do.

After Duncan had been there an indefinite number of cycles, a visitor came to see him.

'George,' he said, remembering as the bald man put his tray down on the floor. One cheese sandwich and a glass of water. 'That's your name, isn't it? You're her chauffeur. I drove you into a wall or something.'

George nodded. He was looking better now – not good, but better. The gashes in his face hadn't healed, because only living flesh can do that; but somebody had done something clever with it along the lines of epoxy resin, body putty and wet-and-dry sandpaper. You wouldn't notice it if you didn't know it was there.

'No hard feelings,' George said, as Duncan made an effort to stop staring. 'Actually, no feelings of any sort, but you know what I mean. If I could still bear a grudge, I wouldn't.'

'Ah. Well, that's very mature of you.'

'Oh, I'm very mature,' George said. 'Like blue cheese. Luckily, she's got this chemical that stops me maturing any more, or else I'd leave a trail of me wherever I went. How're you settling in?'

Duncan thought for a moment. 'If I concentrate on my work very hard indeed, sometimes I can forget about it for seconds at a time. Otherwise—' He shrugged.

'Wonderful thing, work,' George agreed. 'I brought you a new pencil, by the way. Old one must be worn down to a stub by now.'

He laid it carefully on the floor, then stepped away from it. Duncan looked at it, but didn't move.

'She thinks of everything,' he said.

'Oh yes.' George nodded a couple of times. It was like watching a puppet being operated by a master puppeteer; you could almost believe he was alive.

'I've been trying to remember,' Duncan went on. 'Trouble is, I never liked horror movies. Always scared me stiff, even the really cheesy old black-and-white ones.'

'Me too,' George said. 'Ironic.'

'But there was one,' Duncan went on, 'about zombies. The hero had to kill a zombie, and I've been trying to remember how he went about it. I think he either cut off its head and buried it a long way away from the body, or else he drove a wooden stake through its heart.' He glanced down quickly at the pencil. 'One or the other, I'm sure. I mean, I'm pretty sure the stake through the heart is what you do with vampires, but maybe it works for zombies as well. I suppose you can't help me out here?'

'Sorry.'

'Ah well,' Duncan replied. 'So, do you enjoy being Undead? Everything you hoped it'd be, career-wise?'

George pursed his lips. 'It's a living,' he said. 'And I've got it better than most. I'm a trusty, you see. Great honour. Means I've got twenty per cent autonomous physical functions. Most of the lads are a hundred per cent controlled, but not me. It's so I can do my job. She never learned to drive, so—'

'I see.' George turned his head sideways for a moment, and Duncan caught sight of a neat row of stitch marks. A seam. 'And you can do other things for yourself besides driving the car? Doors, stuff like that?'

'It saves her the bother. It's not easy, controlling the movements of hundreds of thousands of bodies simultaneously. It's marvellous, really, the way she manages it.'

'Very impressive. Oh, while I think of it,' Duncan added conversationally, 'what's ninety-seven plus forty-two-point-six, take away seventeen?'

'I don't do maths,' George replied, straight-faced. 'Sorry.'

'Not to worry.' A seam; stitching. Implying that his head had been – what, sewn back on at some point? Implying in turn that someone had cut it off. But here he was. 'Your previous existence,' he said. 'Can you remember much about it?'

'Not really,' George replied. 'Bits of it come back to me, when I'm driving, mostly. Slicker ways of changing gear, the exact balance of the clutch and accelerator, that sort of thing.'

'Stuff you need for work?'

George nodded. 'But sometimes – well, I remember something about driving, and there's other bits and pieces stuck to it, if you see what I mean, like things stick to your shoes and then you walk them all over the carpet. I forget them later, though. Mostly. Oh, and I can remember going through the windscreen at Le Mans at two hundred and ten miles an hour one time. Very vivid, that is. I remembered it the rest of my life.' He grinned. According to the annoying little saying, it takes a hundred and something muscles to frown and only three to smile. Bowden Allshapes, presumably, cutting corners. 'Not saying much, actually, since the rest of my life was about seven seconds. After that, I didn't have anything to remember *with*, if you follow me.'

'I remember her telling me,' Duncan said. 'You were a racing driver.'

'Was. Now it's mostly just sitting in traffic. And when I'm not driving, I stand in a corner.'

Duncan turned to look at the window – blocked up again – and nodded. 'A bit of a comedown, then.'

'Less stress, though. Especially since they brought in the congestion charge. I miss some things, though. Fear, for one.'

'Fear?'

'Practically essential. Sharpens you up, fires up the reflexes. You try going round Marble Arch when it's busy, not able to be afraid of anything. It's worse than having your eyes shut.'

So, Duncan thought: if decapitation's been tried and failed, and if that rotten old movie had got its research right – which is unlikely, since the people who made it presumably didn't even believe that such things as zombies exist . . . Even so.

'You know what?' he said, as he stood up and picked up the pencil. 'Our little chat's cheered me up no end.'

'Really?'

'Oh yes. You see, sitting here for hours adding up these stupid numbers over and over again – knowing that they're never ever going to balance, too, that really gets to you after a bit – really, I'd come to the conclusion that this has got to be as bad as it can possibly be. Then I listen to you, and I realise, no matter how awful it is, being alive's still better than – well, the other thing.'

'Quite right,' George said. 'Only, there's absolutely nothing I can do about it.'

'Nothing *you* can do,' Duncan said. 'Changing the subject just for a moment, did you leave the keys in the car?'

'Of course not. I may be dead, but I'm not stupid. They're in my left-hand trouser pocket.'

'Left-hand?'

'Mphm.' George walked over to the lift and touched the door. It slid open. 'Silver Volvo. Parked right outside. Would you believe, I found a meter.'

'Your lucky day,' Duncan said, and jammed the pencil into George's chest as hard as he could.

It was just an average pencil, a touch under six inches long. But you only need to go in three inches to reach the heart, and what's a pencil except a short thin wooden stick?

Mightier than the sword, is what.

George looked at the pencil stub sticking out of his shirt. There wasn't much to see, apart from the little rubber on the end. No blood, of course. Then he smiled, and fell over on his face.

Was it sheer luck that led him to fall in such as way as to block the lift door and stop it closing? Or did he, in his last second of not-life, plot a deliberate trajectory? The result was the same either way. Pausing only to snatch the file off the desk, Duncan jumped over the prone figure, fumbled in his pocket till he found the car keys, shoved him out of the way with his foot, and flattened himself against the back of the lift as the door snapped shut like sharks' teeth.

A lesser man, he told himself, listening to George's wretched tale, would have told him to get a life. The exact opposite—

Duncan watched the floor indicator as the lift went down. Not going to get away with it, he told himself, too easy . . . But the doors opened, and there across the lobby was the glass door. Visible through it was the street, bathed in amber light that glowed on the metallic paintwork of a silver Volvo. A quick dash, through the stupid door (literally through it if it wouldn't open); then jump in the car, fire up the engine and go. He still had a wallet, he remembered, with credit cards in it; enough to buy him a certain amount of distance, though he'd need a passport for New Mexico. The destination didn't really matter, though. Anywhere, so long as it was *away*—

He shoulder-charged the glass door and bounced off it like a tennis ball.

Landing didn't hurt, of course, except in the cupboard under his mental stairs where he kept hope, along with all the other stuff he'd never use again but couldn't bring himself to throw away. He'd rammed the door with the full force of his werewolf-enhanced strength, and it had chucked him back like a nightclub bouncer. Meticulous old Bowden Allshapes.

He looked round. An alarm had gone off, and though he was pretty certain that there wasn't another living soul in the building, that wasn't much comfort. Of course, in the circumstances it took a special kind of malice to specify a glass door. He could see the outside world through it, clear as anything, but he couldn't get there. Nasty old Bowden Allshapes.

A *ting* noise behind him made him swivel round. The lift was on the move. He watched the floor indicator: going up, two, three, four, *ting*. Coming back down again, two, three— There was a reception desk. He dived behind it. No heavy books this time, no weapons of any sort. Sod.

The lift door opened, and out came two men and a woman. You could tell they were Security by the way they walked; as if every step they took was an act of stamping on fingers clinging to a ledge. It occurred to him that, to a certain sort of mentality, a practically immortal, practically invulnerable victim would be a whole lot of fun. Lasts longer.

Oh well, he thought.

Security stumped round the lobby a couple of times, checked that the door wasn't damaged, opened a walk-in cupboard to make sure he wasn't in there hiding. They didn't bother looking behind the desk because who in his right mind would choose to rely on such pathetically inadequate cover? One of them shut the alarm up. They stopped, looked at each other and got back in the lift. Going up, two, three, four, fifty-seven, seventy, seventy-three . . .

Just for the hell of it, Duncan tried the door again. This time he took the longest run-up he could fit into the lobby. When the moment came to jump, he hurled himself into the air like a leaping salmon. He bounced back so hard that he ricocheted off a wall before hitting the floor. The stupid alarm went off again, of course. *Ting*, said the lift, smugly. Going down.

He picked up the desk and hurled it at the door. Fortunately, he had the good sense to duck a split second later.

He sighed, and picked up the file. Mental note: when they'd finished beating him up, he needed to ask them for another pencil. That'd be a good joke.

He wandered over to the door for one last look before the lift came back down again. He could see George's silver Volvo, glowing orange in the lamplight as though it had been heated in a furnace. Between it and him was a barrier he couldn't even see, but strong enough to make all the difference. A bit like life, really.

Well, he wouldn't be needing the car after all, so there was no point holding on to the keys. It'd just make trouble for someone. He picked up the desk and stood it back upright again, then laid the keys on it where they'd be able to find them.

Keys. Plural. *How had George got into the building?*

The big one with the black plastic on it: that was the ignition and door key. A small, flat one: that'd be the petrol cap. The third one – long, silvery, not a car key at all. Surely not.

Oh for crying out loud, Duncan said to himself, and unlocked the glass door.

Ting went the lift behind him as he wrenched the door open. Not that it mattered. With the keys in his right hand and the file in his left, he hopped through, out of the building, into the street.

And promptly dropped both the keys and the file. He hadn't meant to. It just sort of happened automatically. That's the thing about prehensile fingers and opposable thumbs. You only really miss them when you haven't got them any more.

Instead, he had paws. Four of them.

For a tiny part of a second, he balanced on just two paws. It's a trick that most dogs can do, standing on their hind legs, but only the specially trained ones can keep it up for very long. Of course, Duncan reflected as his forepaws hit the pavement, the window in my office, it's been shuttered for the last couple of cycles. He looked up and saw the full moon, and howled.

Security was right behind him, and dead people aren't afraid of werewolves. Well, the car keys weren't going to be much use now. Duncan grabbed the file in his teeth and broke into a run.

CHAPTER SIXTEEN

In Year Ten, the maths teacher had been Mrs Hicks. The letters in front of her name implied that somewhere, at some stage, there had been a Mr Hicks, though nothing was known about him; nevertheless, he'd lodged in Duncan's mind as a paradigm of reckless courage. There must have been a moment (candlelit restaurant, lazy summer afternoon beside the river, bright frosty morning in the park) when he'd turned to her, probably but not necessarily got down on one knee, and asked her to be his wife.

There had been many afternoons (Wednesdays – *double* maths), when the yelp of Mrs Hicks's voice had lost the atom-splitting feather of its edge and the distant whirr of maths going way over Duncan's head had lulled him into a dreamy, meditative stupor, when he'd tried to reconstruct the scene. He had no idea what the real Mr Hicks looked like, of course, because nobody had ever seen him – Luke's hypothesis, that she'd killed and eaten him the day after they got back from their honeymoon, was generally accepted throughout the school, so that no further speculation was necessary – but in his mind's eye he had a clear picture of a small, thin weedy man (because that's the type that huge women so frequently team up with), sometimes with a thin straggly ginger beard and glasses, sometimes bald, with little bleary eyes like a mole, clearing his throat nervously, presumably putting up his hand and waiting to be allowed to speak: *Excuse me, miss, but . . .* Then there'd be a short bit of mumbling, because Duncan really couldn't imagine what form of words could've been used on that occasion. Then pan to Mrs Hicks; she scowls as she considers the request, and the little scrawny man waits for the answer, a single drop of sweat trickling its crooked, leisurely way down the full length of his nose. Then *Yes, I suppose so* or *Well, all right, then*, followed immediately by some grim imperative: *But you've got to promise you'll stop keeping terrapins and for pity's sake shave off that ridiculous beard*; and that'd be it. Subject closed, judges' decision is final, no further communication will be entered into. Fast forward to a church (one side practically deserted, the other stuffed to bursting with her loud, enormous, ferocious relatives) and a great white shape barrelling up the aisle like the *Bismarck* bearing down on an unescorted convoy, her train frothing behind her like the incoming tide on a shallow beach.

Well, it had passed the time until the bell went, and a little pity and terror's good for the soul. And besides, Duncan had told himself, it doesn't matter if I don't pay attention in class. It's not as though I'll ever need to know any of this stuff later on, in the real world.

Indeed. Maths? Complete waste of time. Pythagoras. Quadratic equations. Pointless, meaningless garbage. I mean, when the hell are you ever going to need to calculate the volume of a cone, or use logarithms? Or transfer a bunch of numbers from Base Ten to Base Something Else . . .

If only, Duncan thought as he trotted down a subway, it could've been something else, a different subject. Geography: he'd always been keen as mustard in geography. To this day he still knew all sorts of cool stuff about cumulo-nimbus and magma layers and ox-bow lakes and subsistence agriculture in Bhutan. Or chemistry: he'd learned loads of chemistry (mostly things you added to other things to make them blow up, but never mind). Or drama, even. He'd learned how to play poker, blackjack and pinochle in drama, and still got an A-star in his GCSE. But not maths. His worst subject. Now, of course, he knew why, but that didn't make it any better. The fact remained that if only he'd paid attention the day they'd done Bases, he'd be laughing. A quiet room somewhere with no windows, a calculator and a pencil, and that'd be the end of Bowden Allshapes. A few calculations, some straightforward addition, the two bottom lines would balance and that'd be it. Accountancy as a lethal weapon; death by double entry. And then he'd be free.

Duncan stopped in a doorway. Moonlight blanched the walls on either side of him to a pale dead grey. He sniffed. People about, but not many and not close. No trace that he could register of wolves, vampires, unicorns or formaldehyde. He had no idea what time it was.

His first thought, of course, had been to leg it round to Crosswoods and bark and scratch at the door till they let him in. It hadn't taken him long to see the folly in that. She'd have her people (if you could call them that) out in force, guarding every street corner for a square mile, waiting for him to trot tail-waggingly into the trap. The same went for Ferris and Loop. As for going home: highly unlikely that he still had one, after the unquantifiable but substantial amount of time he'd spent on the seventy-third floor. He relaxed his aching jaw muscles and let the file flop out of his mouth onto the pavement.

Base Ten Point One, for crying out loud.

And then there was the matter of the total lack of rescue attempts. He'd tried not dwelling on it, to the point where his mental rubber had worn a big rescue-attempt-sized hole in the page of his consciousness, but the moment he lowered his guard it came roaring back. They'd *left* him there, the *bastards*. Fine, so the vampires didn't owe him anything (apart from the one whose life he'd saved; what's-her-name, begins with a V), but what about Luke bloody Ferris and his other so-called friends? Even if decades-old loyalty and the brotherhood of the pack didn't count for anything, that bastard Ferris had got him into this mess by poisoning Ver – thingummy, the girl whose name he couldn't call to mind. If he had the faintest shred of decency he should be tearing himself apart with guilt, desperate for a chance to atone, even if it cost him his life. Instead, nothing. Not a bark, not a whimper. Times like these, you find out who your true friends are.

A cloud drifted quickly over the moon and Duncan felt his shape relax its grip for a moment. It felt like that point in a dream where you know you're about to wake up, and that the dream isn't real. But he hadn't woken up, and it was still bloody real, thank you very much. Inside him, the horrible reality growled, and he felt a strong urge to find something to chase and, if at all possible, kill – or at least bite. Times like these, you find out who your true friends are; namely, nobody at all. Being a wolf was, all things considered, a bad thing. Being a lone wolf was no fun at all. But, he considered as he lifted his head and sniffed, we aren't put on this earth just to have fun. Mostly we're here to make things as nasty as possible for those around us.

He listened for the nearest main thoroughfare and followed the sound. No pedestrians: it was just an anonymous urban dual carriageway, amber-lit and concrete-bleak. He tucked himself into a shadow and waited for a little while, until a white Transit van appeared in the distance, coming towards him. He let his tongue loll, his best shot at a grin.

To make it a little bit more interesting, he made himself wait until the van had passed him and gone on a good hundred yards or so. Then he let his mind relax and his legs take over. The rhythm of the run came back to him like a favourite tune. When he was close enough, he could see the vague shape of the driver's head, reflected in his side-view mirror. He accelerated.

There was always a moment when the drivers noticed you; at which point, the key thing was to close in. At first they think *Oh look, a dog.* Then it's *That's a big dog,* then *That's a very big dog,* and then *That very big dog's following me.* And then an instinct as old as the species kicks in and overrides centuries of safe, civilised complacency – the pedal hits the metal and the chase is on. At first, the driver only speeds up a bit because, after all, it's just a dog and what can it do to you when you're safe inside your sealed steel box? Just enough speed to shake the stupid thing off, therefore, except that the stupid thing turns out to be much faster and much more tenacious than any dog has a right to be. So the right foot goes down a little further, the frown in the mirror crinkles round the edges with the beginnings of actual fear, and the huge running dog with the big red eyes is still hardly more than cruising . . .

The trick, Luke always said, was to know where the speed cameras were. On urban freeways heavily infested with the things, you could shred some poor bugger's licence in ten minutes flat and he wouldn't even realise it until days later, when the summons hit his doormat.

Tonight, however, it wasn't going to be just about driving licences. There were other games you could play, or so the lads had said; not the sort of activity the Ferris Gang went in for, because – well, they *were* werewolves but deliberately hurting people wasn't really their style. There were other packs, though – the Esher Boys, or the Wealdstone Crew – and you heard things. Discussing them with your pack-mates you might pretend that you approved, at least of the ingenuity and the panache, but deep down where it mattered you knew that we don't do that sort of thing, because fundamentally, staring red eyes, slavering jaws and inch-long fangs aside, we're basically nice.

But there were those other games; and although nobody had shown Duncan how to play them, he reckoned he'd heard enough about them to figure out the basic rules. There was the one where, instead of maintaining that precise, psychologically perfect distance behind the van, you zoomed up flat out, overtook and hurled yourself at the driver's side door, snapping at the handle with your teeth. The scoring system the Esher pack used, rumour had it, was five points for a swerve into the crash barrier, ten points for sideswiping another car, five bonus points for every vehicle that joined the pile-up, double bonus for each one that flipped over. Subtler, according to received opinion, was the Greenford serial kamikaze dive: when you overtook, instead of attacking you shot out in front of the target to give yourself a lead of, say, ten yards, and then stopped dead. The mess your granite-hard invulnerable body made of the van's front end was just the preliminary selection of poppadums and dips. The fun started when the driver got out and tottered back to inspect your flattened corpse, whereupon you got slowly to your feet, hackles up, and did the extra-special growl. Where the fun ended depended on how fit the driver was, and whether he had a latent predisposition to coronary disease. You actually lost points if you had to bite him to finish him off – hence, presumably, the reputation for subtlety.

The van driver had seen him. Duncan speeded up to cover the slight acceleration. Because he knew the driver would be looking at him, he lifted his head and let his tongue loll stylishly. His nose caught a faint tint of human sweat in the slipstream, heralding the start of the *That's a very big dog* phase. He speeded up just a little bit more. Keeping station is one thing, but gaining on them accelerated the lurch into irrationality. There was another game the bad boys played that all depended on getting mental control of the quarry, so that he started paying too much attention to his mirror and not enough to the road ahead. It was a delicate variant, all to do with nuances of pace, instinct and body language, and you got a triple bonus score if they crossed the central reservation and hit something coming the other way.

It was working. The van was swaying from side to side, setting up a feedback loop of panic and over-correction. Duncan lengthened his stride just a touch—

The file.

Well, it wasn't in his mouth. He must have left it behind when he started the game, or else dropped it at some point. He knew that losing the file was terribly important somehow, but he couldn't be bothered with all that now, not when his control over the prey was tightening with each spurt of acceleration, to the point where his nose could already anticipate the smells of spilled diesel and burning rubber. Bowden Allshapes and Luke and all that nonsense seemed hopelessly remote, in any case. He wasn't doing this because he was the victim of some bizarre and complex conspiracy, or because his friends and the girl he loved had left him up there in that office and not even tried to get him out. He was doing it because he was a werewolf; a good were-wolf, possibly even a great one. Because it was fun.

Smells don't carry upwind, so the first he knew of it was a large, solid body looming up on his left side. The collision winded him; he lost his footing, stumbled, felt the hard asphalt slam into his shoulder and squeeze out all the air. Then he was tumbling, head over paws; the tarmac kept punching him – head, ribs, elbows, head again – until something metal and a bit stretchy caught him like a net, and he stopped. When he opened his eyes and saw what a mess he'd made of the crash barrier, he couldn't help feeling mildly impressed. Eighteen-wheeler artics didn't usually do that much damage.

He smelled Luke Ferris before he saw him. The Ferris sweat had a distinctive tang to it that he'd know anywhere. This, how-ever, was the first time he'd smelled Luke's blood. Also quite distinctive, and there was—

– Rather a lot of it.

Duncan picked himself up, gave himself a good all-over shake, and looked round. Luke was a long, splayed shape on the opposite carriageway: he'd burst clean through the barrier (typ-ical Ferris, had to outdo everyone else) and was lying stretched out, as if frozen in the middle of a flying stride. For some reason, all Duncan's anger evaporated. Something was wrong. A healthy werewolf wouldn't be lying like that, not with that rather distinctive newly ironed look that you only get with fresh road kill.

If he'd still been angry, he'd have jumped the barrier. Instead, he walked slowly through the gap Luke had torn in it – taking his time, he realised, because he was in no hurry to get there and see what he had to see.

It's marginally better to travel hopelessly than to arrive, but Duncan got there in the end. Luke was still breathing, but he was making a noise like someone filing the sharp edges off thin sheet metal. He opened one eye as Duncan sidled up to him and sniffed.

'So there you are,' Luke said, and Duncan realised he could hear him the usual way, rather than in his mind. 'I've been looking everywhere for you.'

A bit like a slap round the face with a handful of nettles. 'You have?'

'We all have.' Luke tried to nod, but apparently it was too difficult. 'I asked the vampires where that dreadful woman might've taken you, but they said they had no idea. I think they were lying.'

'But she gave you the address. For delivering the file.'

'Really?' Luke coughed, and something dark red and thickly wet trickled down the side of his jaw. 'Don't think so. The address they gave us turned out to be a key-cutting place in one of those grotty little streets near Victoria. So we split up and went out looking for you. Every night, after work. Pure chance I happened to catch a whiff of you tonight – extreme range, eight miles away.' He glanced down at his back legs. Human legs were supposed to bend that way, but not a wolf's. 'I suppose I just got lucky, wouldn't you say?'

Duncan opened his mouth to say something, but it evaporated along the way.

'Anyway,' he said, 'you're out now, so that's all right. I'd love to hear all about it, but I get the feeling that I'm a bit pushed for time. You know,' he went on, 'I'd always wondered exactly how much punishment one of these bodies could take, and now I know. It'll survive pretty much anything except a fifty-mile-an-hour collision with another werewolf. Only,' he added, 'you don't seem too bad. Which is great,' he said, 'but curious. A mystery. Oh well.'

'Luke,' Duncan said. 'Why did you do it?'

'Do what?'

That infuriating Ferris don't-know-what-you're-talking-about stare; if Luke hadn't been dying, Duncan would've smashed his face in. 'Ram into me like that. Stop me—'

A slight frown, if wolves can do that sort of thing. 'You know perfectly well why,' Luke replied. 'I haven't got the faintest idea what got into you, but I know precisely what you were trying to do, and no, sorry, we don't do that. The Walthamstow mob yes, but not us. It's what you might call a point of honour. If you happen to be a pompous git, I mean.'

Duncan wasn't sure where the anger came from, but there was plenty of it. 'And you think that's worth getting yourself smashed up for.'

'Me? Not sure. It's you I was thinking of. You're the one who'd have to live with it, if you'd caught that van like you were trying to. Stupid bastard,' he added, with a trace of a grin. 'You could've killed somebody. Sorry, am I boring you?'

Duncan lifted his head. Maybe Luke was too badly smashed up to notice it, but the smell was everywhere. 'She's here,' he said.

'She who? Clare Short?'

'The unicorn.'

Luke laughed, messily. 'Then you'd better give her my regards, but she's wasting her time. I won't be chasing anybody tonight, that's for sure. You'd better clear off, though. Go on, don't mind me.'

Duncan turned round slowly. There she was, the milk-white unicorn. If anything, she looked more beautiful than ever, a soft bright glow that was far more than just light. The moon flared on her hooves and horn, as though she was drawing it in.

'You arsehole,' she said. 'You complete shit.'

'Go away,' Duncan said. 'I'm busy.'

'You dropped this.' The Allshapes probate file materialised in the air just in front of his face and flopped to the ground. 'It's a miracle I just happened to trip over it. Do you realise what it'd have meant if you'd lost it? I'm very angry with you. In fact—' She broke off, and her soft white nostrils twitched. Then, apparently for the first time, she noticed Luke. 'Oh for pity's sake, not another one.'

'Afraid so.'

She came closer, and her nose brushed Duncan's shoulder as she lowered her head to look. 'Don't tell me,' she said. 'Another rescue bid.'

'Yes.'

A long equine sigh. 'I must say,' she said, 'I'm glad I'm your enemy, not your friend. You really are a bit hard on the people you like.'

'Yes.'

'Not to mention,' she went on, 'inconsiderate. If you think I've got nothing better to do than go around snatching your nearest and dearest from the jaws of death—'

It was as though what she'd just said was a windscreen, and he was a little slow, soft-bodied fly. *Impossible*, he thought frantically. *She can't possibly save him now, he's all smashed up. She could cure Veronica because all it took was stopping her dying of garlic, which is just supernatural rubbish. This is different, it's splintered bones and ruptured spleens and punctured lungs. Real stuff. There's no way anybody can—*

'You can do that?' he asked.

'Oh yes.' She was managing to sound as though he'd phoned her at five twenty-nine, just as she was on her way out of the office. 'Any time in the next two minutes. After that, no. At least,' she added, with a twinkle in her voice that made Duncan want to growl, 'not in the sense you mean. Though – no offence – he's not quite the sort of person we're recruiting right now, career opportunities-wise. A bit too boisterous and Tiggerish, to be perfectly honest with you.'

'I see.' Duncan looked her in the eyes. It was like trying to outstare a tunnel. 'Same terms as last time, I take it.'

'Basically,' she said. 'Except this time, we're really going to have to put in some kind of guarantee clause, to stop you wandering off every five minutes. I do understand you wanting to stretch your legs now and again, but I'm afraid it's not on. Not when you've got responsibilities.'

'Guarantee clause,' Duncan repeated.

'Oh, nothing too blood-curdling,' she said briskly. 'All I was thinking of was planting a silver bullet in your chum's chest. You know the sort of thing – like old soldiers who carry on quite cheerfully for years and years with huge great chunks of shrapnel still inside them after they got blown up in the war: so long as it stays put and doesn't move about, no bother at all. Same idea. So long as you stay put and do your job, the bullet doesn't move. It's no trouble,' she added, 'I can pop it in now before I close him up. Well, is it a deal?'

'Duncan, for God's sake.' The words came out of Luke's throat like air from slow puncture. 'Don't listen to her, mate. Don't do it. I'm not worth it, OK?'

'Oh dear.' The unicorn sighed wearily. 'You were at school together and everything, and still you don't know him half as well as I do, you silly man. Now please be quiet and don't move around more than you can help. There's enough wrong with you as it is.'

Duncan frowned. All his life, the trend had been for things to get more and more complicated, each set of aggravations and encumbrances impacting on its predecessors and snagging in those that followed. But that was what he'd grown used to, his natural habitat. Moments of perfect simplicity disconcerted him, and he wasn't quite sure how they worked. Still, he thought, I'll just have to do my best and hope I get the hang of it as I go along.

'No,' he said, 'Luke's right. He's not worth it. No deal.'

The unicorn's shocked *'What* did you just say?' coincided so perfectly with Luke's roar of 'Now just a fucking minute' that Duncan heard it as a kind of barber-shop duet. He shook his head. After three decades of uncertainty, he'd never been more sure of anything in all his life.

'Sorry, mate,' he said, as Luke lifted his head a good three inches and glared murderously at him. 'You're my best friend and I'll miss you a lot, and if there was anything else I could do, I wouldn't think twice about it. But not that.' He shuddered. You can shudder really well if you've got a long bushy tail. 'I've been there, and I'm buggered if I'm ever going back. I'll probably tear myself apart about it for the rest of my life, but I'll just have to deal with that somehow. So long, my old mate. And I'll get her for this somehow, one day, you can bloody well have my word on that.'

'You *shit*,' Luke howled. 'Are you out of your frigging skull? You can't just stand there and let me die—'

Duncan clicked his tongue. 'Sorry to seem so callous about it,' he said, 'but yes, I can. Watch me. But it's all right,' he added. 'Now that I'm free of her, I can figure out some way of making these estate accounts balance and then—' He turned to the unicorn and grinned. 'That'll be that, won't it?' he said. 'Goodbye Bowden Allshapes, this was your grotesquely overextended life. Because that's all it'll take, isn't it? Two identical numbers at the foot of a piece of paper, and you're history. Well,' he amended, 'mythology, anyway. That's why it had to be me, I already knew that. If anybody else adds up those numbers, you're finished.'

'I don't think so,' the unicorn said, and he had to admit that she was superb. Every cell in his body wanted to believe her.

'Well,' Duncan replied, 'we'll soon see. But I think I'm right. I think that's why you had me locked up in that tower on my own, so you could be sure nobody who counts in Base Ten ever came near your precious file ever again. I think that's why you got me the job at Craven Ettins, so I'd be there on tap when the special file came in. Oh, you were pretty smart about that, I expect. Lovely piece of creative fiction, that file. Specially compiled so that anybody looking at it would see straight away that it was one of those jobs that's been screwed up beyond all possibility of salvage by whoever had the running of it last; which means it'll be nothing but aggravation to whoever gets landed with it next. Which meant, inevitably, that it'd end up on *my* desk, and nobody else could ever be persuaded to touch it with a ten-foot pole. Well? Am I right, or am I flattering you?'

'Both,' the unicorn said. 'But—'

'No,' Duncan snapped. 'This time, you shut up and listen. Here's the deal. I'm through with you, for ever. Find someone else to do your stupid sums for you, or just roll over and die, I don't care. But I can promise you this. Unless you fix my friend there, and no pissing around with silver bullets, because I'll be watching, then I'm going to take this file and I'm going to buy a maths textbook and a calculator, and you're going to be a very endangered species indeed. You got that? Or do you want me to draw you a Venn diagram?'

There was a slight disturbance in the light, and she turned into a woman. Not the gorgeous-instantly-forgettable one he'd come to know and not remember, but a small, dumpy, middle-aged female with very bright blue eyes and a sort of office-manager look on her face that told Duncan he hadn't just made a new friend. 'Don't be stupid, Duncan,' she said. 'I'm not some little fat kid in the playground, you can't bully me. I, on the other hand, can make life really tiresome for you. For instance—'

A car appeared out of the darkness and slowed down. Duncan could see the driver peering thoughtfully at him before he speeded up and moved on.

'All he saw was a stupid woman walking her dog on the central reservation of a busy dual carriageway,' she said. 'The next one could see something different. Like a fully grown wolf where no wolf ought to be. Oh, I don't suppose the police marksmen could actually hurt you, but I'm absolutely certain you could hurt quite a few of them, and then your life would be really quite interesting for a while. Then they catch you and before they've had a chance to round up a vet with a humane killer, it's morning and you've turned back into a human being. I imagine there'd be quite a tussle between the police wanting to lock you up for murder and the scientists wanting to take you apart to find out how you work. You might be able to find time to squeeze in a little advanced maths, but I certainly won't let them give you my private legal documents, so it won't do you any good. Oh, and by the way, your friend's just about to die, if you're interested. There's still just about enough time to save him, of course, but I don't suppose that matters to you very much.'

Duncan turned his back on her and knelt down beside his best friend's body. 'I'm sorry,' he said. 'But I've had enough. I can't . . .'

'Piss off.' The words were so faint he could barely hear them. 'You always were a selfish bastard. When I think of everything I've done for you—'

'Yes? Name one.'

Behind him, Duncan heard a tongue brusquely clicked; then a sharp whistle. Immediately, Luke jumped to his feet. His ears were back, and his hackles were up.

'It was worth a try,' said Bowden Allshapes. 'But I haven't got all night. Go on, then, Ferris. Kill.'

Luke sprang at him. Some instinct that had very little to do with being human made Duncan back up a step while there was still time, and push with his hind legs. He reared up to meet the attack, and as Luke's teeth met in his ear, his own jaws closed in the loose skin of Luke's shoulder. The growl in his own throat was an echo of Luke's; he had no idea where it came from, but as he made the noise he realised that this time he really meant it. And, as he jerked his head sideways to try and tear a chunk out of his enemy's skin, he thought: *The vampires knew there was a traitor, but apparently it wasn't me after all.* He felt his own skin and flesh give way, but it meant nothing. It wasn't damage sustained that mattered, only damage inflicted. *You set me up,* he thought, trying to ram the thought through Luke's skull like a wooden stake. *You made me choose to let you die. I can't ever forgive you for that.*

Luke snapped at his throat, missed by a quarter of an inch. The click of his jaws meeting in thin air was as loud as a bone breaking. *So what?* Luke's thought stabbed into his mind like a needle. *You thought I was about to die and you could've saved me, and you fucking didn't. I'm going to kill you for that, Hughes. I mean it.*

There are some things words can solve, and other times when words only make it worse. As Duncan scrabbled vainly for Luke's eyes with his claws, he thought: it's true, sometimes you just can't beat good old-fashioned trial by combat. Because I don't know which of us is more in the wrong, and he doesn't either, the only way we'll know is by who kills who. That's a verdict you can't argue with. Not even two lawyers. Especially two lawyers. No matter how good you are, you can't wriggle out of a ripped-open throat on a procedural technicality.

Duncan felt Luke's claws rake the side of his head, and snapped impulsively, just as Luke's foreleg passed though the patch of air between his jaws. He felt bone crunch under his teeth, just as he felt other teeth clamp shut on his right elbow. For a moment they stood upright – a dog walking on its back legs; quaint, but you'd never in a million years mistake it for a human being – and then they toppled over sideways onto the ground. Luke's back legs kicked Duncan and he kicked back. Every muscle and sinew in his body was working flat out: nothing idle, nothing redundant. Sooner or later it'd come down to a slight superiority in physical strength, not that there was much in it. There didn't have to be. Until then, all he had to do was hold on and not let go, which is what being canine is all about.

It all seemed to go on for a very long time. At some point, Duncan reckoned he heard a human female laughing.

Duncan opened his eyes.

Daylight was pouring in through an open window. Immediately, he looked down at his hands. They were hands, not paws, which was good. They were fastened to the steel frame of a bed by thick leather straps. Not so good.

Worse to follow. His right arm was in plaster; likewise his left leg. Bandages wound tight around his chest. Oh yes, and pain. Plenty of that. Special offer on pain this week.

He remembered a fight. That was odd: he hadn't had a proper fight since he was at school. Oh, and the Asterix-the-Gaul dust-up with Wesley Loop, except that that hadn't hurt or done him any harm. He wasn't counting his run-in with Sally, because after all, she was a *girl* . . . He thought about that.

Wesley Loop had hurled him into walls, and he'd left Tom-and-Jerry man-shaped dents in them. This other fight, by contrast, had left him trussed up like a half-finished Pharaoh. Must've been some fight, then. Shame he'd been too involved in it to watch.

Duncan turned his head as far as the collar (right, fine, collar) allowed. There was another bed in the room. What was it they said? *Ah, but you should see the other guy.* All he could glimpse of him was one leg, plastered and winched up on one of those gantry things. He grinned. You look such a prat with your leg in batter and pointing at the ceiling.

'You awake?'

Ferris. He didn't want to talk to Ferris right now. More memories were beginning to seep through the headache (yes, one of them too): nasty memories of what the fight had been about. Betrayal, deceit, manipulation, stuff like that. 'No,' he replied.

'Oh. Pity. I just thought you might know where we are, that's all.'

Don't talk to the nasty man, it'll only encourage him. Duncan could remember what it had felt like: how simple, how joyfully, delightfully simple his life had been for those few minutes when all he'd cared about was trying to kill Luke Ferris. For the first time ever, he'd known what he really wanted to do, and was doing it.

Of course, he tried to tell himself, that was just the werewolf inside him behaving badly – it wasn't really *him* at all. Luke was, after all, his oldest and closest friend. Admittedly, Luke had done his best to sell him down the river to the unspeakable Allshapes woman, but civilised human beings don't resort to violence and attempted murder over a little thing like that. Instead, they cross a name meaningfully off their Christmas card list, sulk for a bit, in extreme cases possibly draw all over the fly-leaves of any books the offending party may have lent them. Ripping out throats, though, simply wasn't acceptable behaviour. Under no circumstances; not even when the horrible trick the bastard's played on you has led you to do something really nasty and mean, which you'll be ashamed of for the rest of your life—

A sharp twang of pain in his right arm drew his attention to the fact that he was straining wildly against the straps that tied him to the bed. He forced himself to calm down (*bad* dog, leave it) and tried to rearrange the known facts in such a way that everything was really Bowden Allshapes's fault. It'd be so much more convenient if she could be made to take away the sins of the world, like some kind of ethical skip, into which the whole neighbourhood dumps its old rubbish as soon as your back is turned. Unfortunately, he couldn't quite manage to do that. Apparently, he was better at being a wolf than a lawyer.

It occurred to Duncan to wonder if that was a good thing or a bad one. But the jury was still out on that one, with the door locked behind them and a chair wedged under the handle. Wolves bite, lawyers lie. In both cases it's just business, nothing personal. A wolf can rip up your body. A lawyer—

He sniffed. A delicate perfume, its fragrance slightly distorted by ambient formaldehyde. He twitched his head, but it wouldn't go back that far. Somewhere behind him, a doorknob creaked a little as it turned.

'You're awake,' she said.

'No, he's not,' Luke said. 'He told me so himself and I trust him. He's a lawyer, you know.'

'How are you feeling?'

Ah, Duncan thought. The other one, so now I've got the complete set. My best friend, and—

'You left me there,' he heard himself say. 'In that hell-hole of an office. For weeks. You didn't even *try*—'

'Who told you that?'

Veronica moved into his line of sight. He'd forgotten how nice-looking she was. Somehow, when he'd thought about her, when he'd been in that place, it hadn't really mattered. 'Stands to reason,' he snarled. 'Had to get myself out, didn't I? You obviously didn't care.'

Her eyes were pointy-ended stakes, like cricket stumps with

attitude. 'Yes, I bloody did,' she snapped. 'Eight times we tried to break in there, and each time they doubled the strings of garlic on the window ledges. It was like bloody Covent Garden market up there when we finally had to give in. Not my decision, by the way. It was Caroline who decided. I threw a copy of Cross and Jones at her. Luckily, she's got good reactions.'

'Oh.'

'And if we hadn't shown up when you two were trying to pull each others' heads off—'

'Sorry.'

Bowden Allshapes had told Duncan there was no such thing as magic, only the occasional very skilful lawyer cutting a deal with the universe. Like a fool, he'd believed her, though why she should choose to tell the truth about magic when she's deceived him on every other point . . . There had to be such a thing as magic, or how else could you account for the change that took place as soon as he said the word beginning with S? One moment the ferocious piercing stare that made him feel as though everything he'd ever done was culpably wrong; the next, a smile you could've fried an egg on.

'That's all right,' Veronica said. 'And I don't blame you for being suspicious, not after everything you've been through. He told us,' she added quickly, 'we know all about it. And—' Slight hesitation. 'I think I'd probably have done the same, in your shoes.'

Something in the way she said it suggested that she was Being Nice; however, Duncan wasn't going to argue with that. The number of people in the universe who thought he was worth Being Nice to, by his calculations, amounted to precisely one. But it's quality that matters, not quantity. 'Thanks,' he said.

'Thank *you*,' she replied. 'For saving my life. When he poisoned me, with the garlic.'

Curious how the same little group of sounds can be simultaneously music to the ears and bone-grindingly embarrassing. There hasn't been a man since the days of the stone axe and the mammoth cutlet who hasn't at some time daydreamed about hearing the girl he loves shyly mumble 'Thank you for saving my life.' When it actually happens, though, the urge to crawl away and hide under something until you've stopped doing incandescent beetroot impressions is practically irresistible. Though, in Duncan's case, the straps tying him to the bedframe helped.

Talking of which—

He didn't phrase it well: *By the way, why'm I strapped to the bed?* wasn't the best follow-up line in history, but what with one thing and another Duncan wasn't at his best as far as dialogue was concerned. She explained, very rapidly, that it was only to stop him and Ferris trying to kill each other, which they'd both been dead set on doing when they'd been brought in, even though they were barely conscious—

'Really,' Veronica went on, 'it was pretty scary, the way you were tearing into each other, even when we got you indoors out of the moonlight. Eventually I guess you were both too exhausted to carry on, you just sort of keeled over in mid-grapple and fell asleep. But then you kept coming round while we were trying to set the broken bones and do the plaster and everything. Well, when I say 'come round' it was more like sleepwalking, except there wasn't much walking going on. So when you both passed out again we, um, kind of tied you down. If we hadn't, you'd just have gone on breaking each other's bones till there weren't any left, you'd have been flopping around like a couple of pillowcases stuffed with Lego bricks—' She frowned, and Duncan guessed she was playing that last bit back in her head and wishing she hadn't said it. Even so. 'Well, you seem to be all right now, so I'll just—' She fumbled with buckles, and Duncan lifted his left arm feebly.

'I was fighting?' he said. 'In this state?'

Veronica nodded. 'Well, it was full moon,' she said, and if that was making allowances, it was a feat of engineering that would've put Brunel to shame. 'And you'd spent all that time locked up in that horrible place, no wonder you were upset.'

Upset. Well, quite. Upset enough to try and club my best friend's brains out with a crushed fist on the end of a broken arm. But what the heck, she seemed to be saying, that's perfectly normal, everybody's entitled to fly into berserk rage after a trying day at the office. If she really believed that – but she couldn't, surely. Except that she had a coffin in her office, and she slept in it. Sure, she was different from all the others. Probably there was a scruffy old teddy bear with a hand-knitted scarf perched on her coffin lid during the day, or at the very least a nice vase of flowers. Lilies, presumably. *I really have turned into a monster,* he said to himself. *I'm surrounded by monsters: my friends are all monsters, the girl I love's a monster, if I was in my right mind I'd pull the sheets over my head and whimper, instead of lying here trying to look soulful and interesting. My entire life is scary monsters, and the scariest of the lot of them is me—*

Veronica was looking at him: uncertain, worried, afraid she'd said or done something wrong or that something was hurting or bothering him. Extraordinary. Judging by what she'd said, she'd *seen* him while he was completely out of control; in which case, how could she possibly bear to be in the same hemisphere as him, let alone the same room? Who could possibly tolerate a monster? Who could *love* a monster?

Well. She could, for one.

And me.

'Is that the time?' she said suddenly. 'I'd better get moving, I've got clients coming in at ten-fifteen and I haven't even read the file yet. It's a dreadful bad habit of mine.'

'Doing things on the fly, you mean?'

A clock would have ticked once; then she smiled. 'If you're up to making vampire jokes, you're obviously on the mend. Will you be all right like that? I'd bring you something to read, only there's nothing in the building except law books and chick lit . . .'

'Megarry and Wade,' Duncan said. 'Or Kemp and Kemp, doesn't matter which. Or Whitehouse and Stuart-Buttle on revenue law, at a pinch. Something meaty, with a bit of weight to it.'

Veronica frowned. 'You actually read that stuff?'

Duncan flexed his left arm. 'No,' he said.

'Oh.'

He smiled. 'I promise I'll be good,' he said. 'It's just that if *he* starts anything, I'd prefer to have the law on my side.'

She nodded. 'Dispute resolution,' she said. 'It's what we're all about, really, isn't it?'

She went away, and for a while Duncan stared at the ceiling. He was just thinking it was a nice ceiling, white artex, restful, ordinary, when he caught sight of a heavy-duty steel ring hanging from it in the corner of the room. Funny, he thought, what's that for? A winch? But that's the traditional argument in favour of a career in the law: no heavy lifting. It was a big ring, made from chunky metal: five-eighths of an inch thick at the very least. What would you want to hang from the ceiling in a solicitors' office?

And then he thought, *upside down, as a change from the box; a bit like sleeping in a hammock in the garden in summer. Or not.*

Monsters.

'I take it you're awake now.'

Duncan didn't turn his head. 'Maybe,' he said.

'Just one thing I'd ask of you,' Luke went on. 'Next time you two are planning on a cosy tête-à-tête, would it be too much trouble to ask you to give me a massive dose of anaesthetic? Only, throwing up when you're completely immobilised is probably a bad move. At the very least, a pair of industrial-grade earmuffs'd be nice. There are times when having supernaturally enhanced hearing isn't the blessing you'd take it for.'

'Piss off, Ferris.'

Mistake; the bully looks for a reaction. 'Thank you for saving my life, you wonderful big, strong man,' Luke falsettoed. 'For crying out loud,' he added. 'If I could've reached I'd have chewed my leg off just so as to escape. You may have noticed I'm still strapped down, incidentally. Strikes me this bird – no, sorry, this *bat* of yours has got a bit of thing about—'

'She's not my bat. Bird. Girlfriend.' Stop it, Duncan ordered himself; but it wasn't any good. Luke had figured out long ago that the needle is mightier than the sword. 'Just shut your face and leave me alone, will you?'

'Wish I could. Unfortunately—' He didn't need to look; he could picture the smug expression on Luke's face even with his eyes shut. 'Bondage girl's seen to it that I'm stuck here, with you. What shall we talk about? Oh yes. See that ring over there in the ceiling?'

'No.'

'Well, I was thinking. If that's how vampires sleep . . . Actually, I'd rather not turn my imagination loose on that one, not stuck here like this, I might find myself plagued with mental images I could well do without. I mean, rope burns, sprained ankles, dizziness—'

'Shut *up*, Luke.' Megarry and Wade and a clear field of fire . . . 'Considering you nearly murdered her, I'd keep a low profile if I were you.'

'You think that'd do any good? Use your brains, Duncan, they're *vampires*. Our natural enemies. *She* might be all over you like a pair of pyjamas. I'm prepared to bet the rest of them have something entirely different in mind.'

'Really.'

'Yes, Duncan, really. Get a fucking grip, for God's sake. Yes, I know we've had our differences lately—'

'*Differences*—'

'But,' Luke said firmly, 'the fact remains, they're them and we're us. In the end, it's always about sides: whose side you're on, whose gang you belong to. You may be lying there dreaming of hanging cheek to cheek from the rafters with the bat of your dreams, but I know about these things. Them and Us. Sides. That's all there is.'

'Shut up, Luke.'

'All you've got to do—' It was the other Luke Ferris voice: the calm, authoritative, Luke-knows-best voice, rather than the loud, overbearing one; he'd never been able to withstand it. 'All you've got to do is get up, come over here, undo these straps and leave the rest to me. I'll get us out of here, we'll go back to the office and we'll be *safe*. The others are there. We can just carry on as normal, and everything'll be fine. Look,' he went on, modulating the voice like a precision instrument, 'I know I was out of order last night, it was wrong of me and I feel pretty bad about it. I expect you do, too; neither of us was exactly at our best, really. But there's no point either of us bearing a grudge. Never solved anything. The truth is, deep down where it matters we're on the same side. Always have been. You and me, and the others. Occasionally we make mistakes, it happens. But we're big enough to put all that stuff behind us—'

Well, he had to ask, and now seemed as good a time as any. 'Why did you do it, Luke?'

'Do what? Oh, that.' Pause. 'Simple, really. Fear.'

'Oh.' Actually, it was a good answer.

'I was scared shitless, if you must know,' Luke went on; and it wasn't either of the voices this time, it was just *a voice*, the sound Luke made when he talked. 'She said she'd run me to death if I didn't cooperate. Well, not straight away. First she'd pick the others off one by one – Pete, Micky, Kevin, Clive, and finally me – and by then she'd have figured out another way of getting to you, so it wouldn't actually matter: all of us dying wouldn't actually have achieved anything, it'd all have been a stupid waste.' He hesitated, as though dwelling for a moment on something he'd rather not put into words. 'And she gave me her word that nothing really bad would happen to you. Like, she wouldn't kill you, it's in her interests to keep you alive as long as possible—'

Dead or alive, Duncan thought. But possibly Luke hadn't thought that one through.

'Well, anyhow,' he added lamely. 'Like I said, I was scared. That's it, basically.'

'I see,' Duncan replied.

'That and the money.'

For a moment, Duncan struggled to remember what the M word meant. '*Money?*'

'That's right, yes. Well, not cash in hand, thirty pieces of silver, that'd have been in dubious taste, obviously. But she said she'd give us all her commercial leasehold work . . . you know, I never realised, their investment property portfolio alone is bloody *awesome*, and then there's the development side—'

For a whole second, Duncan searched his vocabulary for an expletive: the nastiest, filthiest, most appalling word he could possibly think of. He found it.

'Luke,' he said.

'Well, it wasn't the deciding factor, obviously,' Luke said quickly. 'I mean, it was the threats that did it, no question about that. But after all, if you've got to betray your friend and pickle your immortal soul in shit for the rest of eternity, you might as well have something to show for it as not, it's only common sense. Apparently, she's got two hundred acres slap bang in the middle of Leeds, vacant possession, planning consent, venture capital all lined up—'

'You bastard, Luke,' Duncan said. (And he thought, two hundred acres. *With* planning. Actually, that's a lot of leases, we could really—)

'Look, it was you or the rest of us,' Luke said. 'Basically, your bog standard *Star Trek* ethical dilemma: the needs of the many outweigh the needs of the few. It's the sort of decision a leader's got to make, and I made it. If you want to hate me about it, go ahead. You have my permission. And I can hate you back for making exactly the same decision – except you were prepared to let me die just so that you wouldn't have to do a boring, rotten job; it wasn't like you were thinking about Pete and Clive and all the others, the way I was. Bloody hell, Duncan,' Luke went on, his voice rising, 'how the hell could you do something like that? It's not as though it's even the shittiest job in the universe: you sit in an office all day adding up meaningless numbers – so fucking what? Millions of people do that every day of their lives, all over the world. You'd have been no worse off than if you'd stayed at Craven Ettins. Oh, you were happy enough to sacrifice yourself for the bat girl, who you'd only known five minutes; but not for me, your oldest friend, who took you in hand when you were just a sad, pathetic kid whose mummy sent him to school with a *vegetarian packed lunch*. You still owe me for that, Duncan.

Whatever else may have happened since, you still owe me for that, and you always will.'

Uncomfortable silence; because it was true, even though Luke had said it. Even a lawyer can tell the truth sometimes; and the fact that it's a lawyer saying it doesn't change anything. 'I always wondered why you did that,' Duncan said quietly. 'I mean, like you just said, I was the freaky little loser and you were – well, the Ferris Gang. What did you want me for?'

'I don't know, really,' Luke replied. 'Maybe I felt sorry for you, maybe I had a sort of instinct. It's so long ago I can't remember now. It doesn't matter, anyway. You're not the freaky kid any more, because of us. You're what we made you. We're all what we made each other. That's the point.'

And Duncan shook his head (ouch) and said, 'No, it's not. The thing is, Luke, you may still be the Ferris Gang, but – well, I didn't stop growing when I turned seventeen.'

'Yes, you did. You were six foot two then, and you're still six foot two. You can see it on the school photos, where you're standing next to Clive—'

'Let's call it quits, shall we?' Duncan said, and if it wasn't the Ferris voice, it owed a lot to it. But there's a difference between what we learn and what we are. 'For years I tried blaming everything that's wrong with me on you, but that doesn't add up. No pun intended. I used to think, it's not that I'm some kind of bizarre freak of nature or anything. I just got this way because of hanging around with those meat-heads for so long. But now it turns out I really *am* a bizarre freak of nature: point one of a decimal place out of synch, whatever the hell that means. And I got this way because Bowden Allshapes has been frigging around with my destiny, and I've been programmed as a sort of human computer, or a secret weapon, or something. Well, screw that, I've had enough. This worm's going to turn so fast you could use me to drill holes. As soon as I'm fit enough to get out of here—'

'You and the bat girl?'

Like a trail of tin-tacks strewn in the path of a speeding car. 'Well, possibly. I hope. If she'll have me.'

Luke made an exasperated noise. 'Same old story, nothing special at all. He meets some girl, and straight away all his old friends go out the window. Well, in this case it's the other way around, she's the one who can bloody *fly*, but that's beside the point. Don't try and dress it up in melodrama, Duncan. It didn't work the last time, did it? With that miserable cow, that Sally. Stitched you up like a hemline, didn't she?'

'Yes, but—'

'They're all the same,' Luke said wearily. 'Vampires. Women. You make the mistake of confusing Them with Us, and next thing you know you're back living in a bedsit paying school fees for a bunch of brats you never even wanted. Bowden Allshapes really hasn't got anything to do with it. She may have set you up for the last time, but this one's all you. Your own free, unfettered, bloody stupid choice. Oh, the hell with it. I wash my claws of you.'

Duncan thought about that for a moment. 'Promise?' he said.

'You know what, Duncan Hughes? You're a disgrace to the legal profession.'

As Jenny Sidmouth used to say. It's awkward, lying perfectly still in the same room with someone you know really well, for hours on end, not talking. To fill up the time and keep his mind from straying where he didn't want it to go, Duncan tried to figure out a solution: a Clever Plan that'd solve everything and leave him free to go away and have a life. But he couldn't. This was sad but hardly surprising. Duncan knew perfectly well that finding solutions just by thinking about problems is like trying to catch your own shadow. He tried to be logical about it. (What would Mr Spock do?) He tried to be creative, lateral, outside the box. He tried creeping up on the problem, outflanking it, wandering off in the opposite direction and suddenly turning round and pouncing . . . It reminded him a bit of chasing the unicorn, which killed you by letting you chase it. The more he chased, the more he had a problem.

Disgrace to the legal profession indeed. Look who's—

He tried breaking the problem down into its component

parts. He tried nibbling little chunks off the edges, to make the problem smaller. He tried thinking of a number and doubling it. What would Napoleon have done? Gandhi? Philip Marlowe? Indiana Jones?

What exactly had Luke meant by that, disgrace to the legal profession? All right, so Duncan wasn't the greatest lawyer that ever was. He'd been known to make mistakes: documents not filed at HM Land Registry, draft wills sent out with typos in them, advice to clients that was sometimes not as clear as it might have been, or even just plain wrong. Big deal. Everybody made mistakes, even partners; especially partners. What made a good lawyer wasn't avoiding cock-ups: it was knowing how to dance on top of them, like a crane-fly on water, until they no longer mattered or they'd been put right.

A disgrace, though? Well, he undercharged. That is, he tried not to overcharge, which was pretty much the same thing. He wasn't passionate about the job, which was Jenny Sidmouth's way of saying he didn't spend every waking moment creeping round everybody he met trying to sell them expensive legal services that they didn't need and couldn't afford. Fine. He'd never be a *great* lawyer, but that was a long way from being a disgrace to the profession. For two pins, he'd have broken the silence and asked Luke what he'd meant by it, but nobody wandered by and gave him two pins, so he didn't. Instead, he thought: it's not incompetence, it's not lack of greed and ambition, so what am I doing wrong? I do lawyers' work, I act like a lawyer, therefore I am one. I think.

I think, therefore—

I think like a lawyer, therefore—

But of course. I don't think like a lawyer. Because if I'd been doing that, I'd have seen it a mile off. It'd have stood out like a lighthouse in the dark. Instead, I've been lying here bothering my head with clever plans and outsides of boxes and Gandhi.

A lawyer would've known what to do straight away. A real lawyer. Someone like, say, Bowden Allshapes. Or Luke Ferris.

Duncan wriggled round so that he could see his watch, which

was lying on the chair next to his bed. Four o'clock in the afternoon. If he was quick, he could—

In a proper hospital, there's a bell or a buzzer to call a nurse. Duncan had to do the best he could with shouting and banging the bed frame with his good hand.

'Are you all right?' He was pleased to see concern in Veronica's face, rather than annoyance at the row he was making. It took him a certain amount of effort to sideline that train of thought.

'Do me a favour,' he said.

'Sure,' Veronica replied. 'What?'

He grinned. Pity there wasn't a mirror handy (but of course, no mirrors in the Crosswoods building), because he'd have liked to have seen the expression on his face. Just for once, he reckoned, he'd have looked like a lawyer.

'Could you fax the probate registry for me?' Duncan said pleasantly. 'I need a copy of a will.'

CHAPTER SEVENTEEN

There is an office high up in a government building in Kingsway. It's the kind of office people end up in rather than aspire to. The work that gets done there is largely unimportant, though generally inoffensive, and although many of the people there are lawyers, they hardly ever sue anybody or make nuisances of themselves. They don't buttonhole slow-moving people at parties or hand out business cards at accident scenes; they don't pad their bills or charge their clients for sending them a card at Christmas. Work trickles in; it gets done, sooner or later, and everybody goes home at five o'clock.

'Your ten o'clock's here, Mr Eddison,' squeaked Reception. 'I'll put them in the interview room.'

Mr Eddison sighed, straightened his tie and put on his jacket. He didn't get many people coming to see him, and that suited him just fine. His preferred method of working was to bleat letters into a dictating machine, wherever possible using the standard forms set up on the computer: number thirty-four or number seventy-two, like ordering takeaway. If he'd wanted to be creative, he liked to say to himself, he'd have been a novelist. Still: the callers were from two well-known firms of solicitors (at least, he'd heard of them before). It wasn't as though he was going to have to face the General Public, or anything frightful like that.

There were three of them. There was a big tall man with long grey hair and a beard; another, rather similar; and a nice-looking young woman dressed in black, with rather alarming eye make-up. None of them looked like lawyers – that is, none of them looked like Mr Eddison – but he made an effort and rose above the incongruity. He read them their names from the note Reception had given him, and asked them to sit down.

They told him a story. It was, they assured him, quite true. He believed them because they were lawyers, and if you can't trust a lawyer, who can you trust?

Even so: 'Are you sure about that?' he said eventually, when he could hear himself speak over the pounding of the blood in his ears.

The slightly less hairy man smiled at him. 'Here's a copy of the will,' he said, 'and certified-copy death certificates – I've numbered them all, look, they cross-reference to the will, and I've highlighted the names. The schedule of assets is mostly just what I was able to get from Companies House, so it doesn't include bank and building society accounts, land and property, minority shareholdings, anything like that. Probably just the tip of the iceberg, in fact. But I know for a certainty there's a complete schedule in the file, when you get hold of it.'

He pushed the papers across the table. Mr Eddison picked them up as though he'd just been handed a magic sword he didn't particularly want. 'You're *sure* about this?' he said. 'Only—'

'Quite sure,' the other man said. 'Take a look at the documents if you don't believe me.'

Mr Eddison winced. 'Oh, I believe you,' he said. 'Only . . . Are you *quite* sure? It seems so—'

'You've got everything you need to get the court order,' the nice-looking woman said briskly. 'I wouldn't hang about if I were you. The sooner you make a start, the better. After all, there's a great deal of money at stake here.'

'Of course, yes,' Mr Eddison said. 'Um – could you possibly give me a very general—?'

The less hairy man said a number.

Mr Eddison opened and closed his mouth four times. Then he said, 'Are you *sure*?'

'Yes.'

'Ah.'

'Quite a feather in your cap, I expect,' the hairier man said. 'A bit of a coup for your department, and I don't suppose it'll do you any harm, either. Pity you're not on a percentage.'

The same thought had slipped quietly into Mr Eddison's mind, where for about five seconds it had much the same effect as a lighted match in a firework depot, before Security turned up and threw it out. 'The sums involved are immaterial,' Mr Eddison heard himself say. 'We just do our job, that's all.'

'Of course.' But the very hairy man was grinning. 'I can see you aren't in it for the thrill of the chase. Still, it'll be a bit of fun, won't it? I mean, one of the biggest corporations in the UK—'

'Yes,' Mr Eddison said faintly. And because he was neither a werewolf nor a vampire, because he wasn't (he knew perfectly well, deep in his heart where he kept the poor, wilted thing that comprised his self-esteem) really a proper lawyer at all, he wasn't thinking about the money, or the conflict, or the intellectual challenge, or the irresistible scent of the prey. He was thinking, wretchedly, about all the extra work. 'Yes, well. Leave it with me, and I'll—' He'd what? He had no idea. It was all too—

But there was one thing he had to ask. It was none of his business, he didn't need to know it, and quite probably it was something he ought not to know, in case it made things even more tiresome than they were inevitably going to become over the next year or so. But he was still at least nominally human, and so he asked, 'Why are you doing this?'

The three of them pursed their lips almost simultaneously. Thinking about it later, Mr Eddison came to the conclusion that they were trying not to laugh.

'It's our duty,' said the less hairy man, and the nice-looking woman made a soft noise that could well have been a suppressed giggle. 'As citizens.'

'And officers of the court,' the other man put in. 'Duty of utmost good faith, and all that.'

'Snrg,' said the woman, and she made a fuss of blowing her nose on a bit of tissue.

'Yes,' Mr Eddison said firmly; because when someone looks you straight in the eye and lies to you, there's not a lot you can do about it if you're a civilised person. 'Well then. Jolly good. Thank you,' he added. 'Um, have a nice day.'

When they'd gone, Mr Eddison sat alone in the interview room for a good ten minutes, staring at the papers on the table in front of him. Not reading them; on the contrary, he was doing his best not to look at them, as though they were people he knew and didn't want to talk to. Most of his mind was simply numb with shock, but a small part of it was trying to remember: is a billion a million million or just a thousand million, or is that only in America?

She came in like any other client and sat, peaceful and well-behaved, in the waiting room until Veronica came down to fetch her.

'Sorry to keep you waiting,' Veronica said. 'Would you like to come on through?'

Bowden Allshapes smiled. 'Is that necessary?' she said. 'You can just send him out. Unless you'd like a receipt or something.'

'Oh, there's just a few things. Nothing important.'

Bowden Allshapes shrugged. 'Fine,' she said. 'Nice to see you looking so well, by the way,' she added. 'Last time we met you were—'

'At death's door, yes.' Veronica held the fire door open for her. 'And I never had a chance to thank you properly.'

'It was nothing,' Bowden Allshapes replied. 'I just happened to be in the right place at the right time. Aren't we going to the interview room? It's down this way, isn't it?'

'I thought we'd have our little chat in my office,' Veronica replied. 'Less formal. Cosier. We can have a nice cup of tea.'

'Please don't go to any trouble,' said Bowden Allshapes. 'I'm sure you're very busy.'

'It's no trouble,' Veronica said.

Duncan was there, looking subdued but calm, leaning against the coffin. Behind him, rather unexpectedly – 'Mr Ferris,' Bowden Allshapes said. 'This is a pleasant surprise. I suppose you've come to say goodbye to your friend.'

Luke Ferris shrugged. 'Let's say I always like to be in at the kill,' he said, as he flipped open a big brass Zippo lighter and lit a stub of candlewick in the middle of a little dish floating in a bowl of water. 'Essential oils,' he explained. 'It's meant to be feng shui or something, but I don't understand that stuff. I like it because it's *smelly*.'

Bowden Allshapes smiled politely. 'I don't blame you for taking precautions,' she said. 'But I do hope that, after today, we can all be friends.'

'Absolutely,' Ferris said. 'Here's to no more running about.'

Bowden Allshapes nodded, making a mental vow as she did so that Luke Ferris would die gasping on some moonlit patch of urban waste somewhere. As for the girl – well, why single out individuals? They'd all have to go sooner or later, the bloodsuckers and the ambulance chasers. Duncan Hughes would give her control over the werewolves, thanks to his ability to defy the pack leaders; he'd also be a paw in the door of the vampire community, and that was all it'd take . . . *Three* birds with one stone. Hurrah for efficiency. It was simply a matter of time, a commodity of which she'd very soon have a more than adequate supply. 'Well now, Duncan, ready when you are. Bags all packed?'

Duncan Hughes looked at her. 'No,' he said.

'Not to worry,' she replied. 'Everything you need will, of course, be provided. I'm pleased to say that you can have your old room. We've made a few changes, upgraded the security just in case you should ever get itchy feet again. Oh, and George is waiting for us in the car. I expect he's looking forward to seeing you again.'

'I bet he is.'

She nodded pleasantly. 'His kind don't bear grudges,' she said. 'Nothing to bear them with, you see. A zombie, I'm so sorry, a *revenant* needs a grudge like a fish needs – well, anyway. I'm so pleased, by the way, that you decided to – well, to come quietly, if that's not too melodramatic. So sensible of you; and of course, absolute peace of mind for your friends here. It's a far, far better thing, and all that. After all, I can't always be there to snatch them from the jaws of death. And your nearest and dearest do seem to have a knack of needing to be snatched. But that'll all change now, of course.'

The three of them exchanged glances, which was odd. Exchanged glances weren't on the agenda.

'Before you go,' Veronica said, 'perhaps you'd care to have a look at this.'

She was holding out a piece of paper, bless her, as though she was doing something clever. Bowden Allshapes smiled nicely at her, and took it—

'That's right,' Duncan said. 'It's a court order. Well, a copy of one. You're not actually entitled to see it, strictly speaking, because it's addressed to the board of your company, not you personally. But you'd know that,' he added sweetly, 'being a lawyer yourself.'

Bowden Allshapes was reading. Duncan was astonished to see that her lips were moving slightly. 'This is *silly*,' she said at last. 'It says I'm dead.'

'Well, you are, you know,' the woman said cheerfully. 'We got a copy of your death certificate. At least, we got a copy of Bowden Allshapes's death certificate. Are you really sixty-seven? You don't look it.'

'Thank you,' Bowden Allshapes said gravely. 'Actually, I'm not. I'm well over seven hundred. And, of course, I've never died.' She lowered her voice. 'Between you, me and Man's Best Friends over there, the certificate wasn't come by honestly. When I told them I was dead, I was fibbing.'

'Doesn't matter,' Veronica said. 'It's what's on the register that counts. Besides, if you aren't dead, how can Duncan have been winding up your estate all this time?'

'But that's not the clever bit,' Luke said, and Duncan was – well, *touched* to notice that he was using his best leader-of-the-pack voice. 'You're a lawyer. Tell us what happens when somebody dies without leaving a will.'

'Mr Ferris—'

'Oh, go on. It'll be more fun if you tell us.'

She scowled at him, but said, 'His property—'

'Or her property,' Luke put in. 'If it's a woman, I mean.'

'Indeed. His *or her* property goes to the next of kin, according to the intestacy rules. I'd have thought you'd have known that, Mr Ferris. After all, you're a lawyer too.'

'Oh, I am. All lawyers together. And what happens if all the dear departed's relatives died before she did?'

Just the faintest flicker in Bowden Allshapes's bright, clear eyes. They were brown, Duncan realised. Never noticed that before. Or maybe, before, they hadn't been any colour.

'Maybe you don't know, so I'll tell you,' Luke went on. 'If there's no will and no next of kin, everything goes to the government. The whole lot, right down to the shoes you're standing up in. Though, of course,' he added with a nice smile, 'you can't be standing up, because you're dead.'

'That would be the position,' Bowden Allshapes said, her voice as brittle as glass, 'if I hadn't left a will. But I did, and a very good will it is, too. I drafted it myself.'

'Quite right,' Duncan said, pulling a thick document out of the desk drawer. 'Beautiful piece of work. Interest in possession trusts, protective trusts, nil-rate-band discretionary trusts: you're clearly a very trusting person—'

'Well, of course,' Luke muttered. 'She's a lawyer. And if you can't—'

'And plenty of named beneficiaries,' Duncan went on. 'I can remember their names quite well without even having to look. God knows I should do, after the hours I spent doing all those sums. But the thing is,' he continued, 'they're all dead. Every single one of them. And their children and grandchildren and great-grandchildren, everybody who'd be entitled to inherit in their place. All gone to their everlasting reward, and quite some time ago, too. Centuries. Oh, I expect you could make a few phone calls and in they'd all come, happy, smiling, healthy people. I mean, you can't get healthier than a walking corpse, can you? They never get ill, not even colds. But not alive,' he added with obvious pleasure, 'in the eyes of the law. Not when we've got office copies of their death certificates. More to the point, not when the public trustee's got office copies of their death certificates. You know who the public trustee is, don't you? Nice man, with an office in Kingsway. It's his job to wind up estates that pass to the government for want of an heir.'

'Heir today, gone—'

'Quiet, Luke.' Duncan realised some time later that he'd said it in a Luke Ferris voice. 'We took the whole lot round to him a few days ago. He didn't really know what to make of it all, but the court order seems to imply he got the hang of it after we'd left. Of course, I feel bad about giving him so much work to do. I expect he's understaffed and underpaid, like all these government lawyers. But he'll get there in the end, I'm sure of it. And when he does—' Duncan paused, allowing himself to savour the moment: the unicorn, finally brought to bay. 'He may not be the sharpest knife in the drawer, but he can add up. In Base Ten. And when he does, what do *you* think'll happen?'

Bowden Allshapes was staring at him. Duncan was rather ashamed to say he knew that look. He'd seen it in the eyes of a few small, insignificant animals – squirrels, rats, urban foxes – when the pack had run them to a standstill. If he'd been quite human, maybe it would have bothered him rather more than it did; because humans can't help feeling sorry for the hunted animal, the small and furry, the sleek, slender and beautiful, the underdog. But he wasn't human, not any more. And besides, he was an underdog, too: leader of the underpack, maybe, but that didn't really change anything. Besides, every dog must have its day.

'I'll die,' Bowden Allshapes said. 'Is that what you want? To kill me?'

Duncan looked at the other two, who nodded. 'Yes,' he said.

'Oh. That seems so—'

'Quite.' 'Pretty bloody brutal, is the way I see it. Of course,' he went on, 'it had to be a lawyer's way of doing it. Stakes through the heart and silver bullets and garlic poisoning and even being hunted down and torn limb from limb by savage wild animals are all very well, but they're so – what's the word I'm looking for? Unofficial, I suppose you could call it. Taking the law into your own hands. Not on the register – and in the end, that's what really counts. Just killing the body's no good at all, when there's someone like you out there who really can deliver on a fate worse than death. But you can't argue with a court order, can you? I mean, it's got its little printed crown on it and everything.'

'Red in tooth and law,' Luke said, and this time Duncan didn't shush him. He had the feeling Luke had been saving it for a special occasion, and the moment certainly qualified as one.

There was a brief, icy silence, and then Bowden Allshapes seemed to pull herself together. 'How very naive you are, Mr Hughes,' she said. 'For a lawyer, I mean. You know perfectly well that I can fight this. We'll appeal, naturally. We'll take it to the House of Lords, Strasbourg, the whole tedious, interminable grand tour. It'll take years.'

'Oh, absolutely,' Duncan said. 'I'd hate to think I hadn't given you time to set your affairs in order. It'll be a good, long hunt, I'm sure of it, before they finally run you down. But that's the joy of getting the government involved. I mean, they aren't like *people*. They've got infinite time and infinite money; sooner or later they'll have you, and until then it's the thrill of the chase, isn't it? I have it on good authority that that's what a *real* lawyer lives for. Of course, I'm not a real lawyer, not inside where it matters, I just got bitten by one at an early age. I think you're going to have the time of your life over the next few years, now that there's actually something at stake at last. Nothing like

putting your life on the line for helping you get into the spirit of
the thing. And when it's all over and you've lost – well, you
know what they say. Death and taxes.' He grinned, showing all
his teeth. 'An extra big helping of both, in your case. And you'll
have the added satisfaction of knowing that everything you've
worked so hard for, all your very long life, will eventually go to
build a bypass somewhere, or finance a war for a whole week.
You won't be around to see it, of course, but I expect you'll feel
so much better knowing it'll be there when you've gone.'

Bowden Allshapes looked Duncan in the eye for a very long
time. Then she smiled. It hit him like a slap across the face, but
he knew there wasn't really anything behind it, not any more.

'See you in court,' she said, and left the room.

'I'd better go after her,' Veronica said quickly. 'Just to make
sure she doesn't set fire to the building or anything.'

Duncan nodded. 'I have an idea she may be a bit of a sore
loser,' he said. 'Just a feeling, you know. If she offers you something to eat, don't forget your rubber gloves.'

She went away, leaving Duncan and Luke together.

No reason why there should be any awkwardness. Not
between such old friends.

'Well,' Luke said. 'I suppose this is it, then.'

'Yes.'

'Final parting of the ways.'

'I suppose so.'

Luke jumped up – always so full of energy – then sat down
again. 'This is a bit bloody silly, isn't it?' he said. 'I mean, after
all these years. The big goodbye scene. Melodrama. I thought
you didn't like melodrama.'

'I don't.'

'Well, then.'

'As a rule.'

They looked at each other: eye to eye, man to man, werewolf
to werewolf. Then Duncan said, 'You take care, all right? Look
both ways before crossing the road. Don't go chasing horses
with pointy bits sticking out of their faces. That sort of thing.'

Luke frowned. 'The others—'

'Give them my . . . Say hello to them from me,' Duncan said. 'Especially Pete.' He paused, then added, 'I always liked Pete.'

It took a moment for that to sink in. 'Ah,' Luke said. 'And the rest of us—'

'Bit like family, really. Whether you like them or not doesn't enter into it. They're always there, like the sun or the sky, so when they aren't around any more the world changes. It's like a whole slice of your past life has suddenly vanished into thin air. Liking them's a bonus, if it happens. But I always liked Pete. Couldn't tell you why.'

'We'll miss you.'

Duncan nodded. 'Yes,' he said. 'I expect you will.'

'And her?' Luke's eyebrows suggested where a scowl might be. 'You think it'll all be different and right this time. With her. Because of her. I mean, you hardly know the woman.'

'That's perfectly true,' Duncan said. 'But what the hell. If not her, someone else.'

'Anybody so long as it's not us.'

'Yes.'

Luke nodded. 'Ah, well,' he said. 'A solo werewolf. Can't see it myself. You'll forever be an unpaired sock in the laundry basket of eternity. And to be honest, I don't see it working out – you and Little Miss Eyeshadow there. After all, there's Them and there's Us. Brave, upbeat words don't change anything. The jury's heard it all before.' He stood up; wearily, no spring in his step this time. 'I think I'd better go now, before I say something nasty. Take care of yourself, Duncan. You know where to find us.'

'Yes.'

The door closed. Duncan shut his eyes and counted to fifty, listening to the sound of Luke's footsteps, tracing his scent through the corridors. His oldest, best friend. His past. Oh well, he thought. And the others . . . But they'd never really been *friends*, had they? Too close for friendship.

He opened his eyes, made an effort to unclench his clenched muscles, sighed, sat down. It was only when he was leaning back in the chair with his feet on the desk that he realised he'd turned round three times first. Can't be a lone wolf, he thought, they just don't happen. Not a human being any more. Not anything, really. It'd be nice to be something, though.

The phone on the desk rang. He frowned, then picked it up. 'Me again.'

He caught his breath. Bowden Allshapes. Now he really *hadn't* been expecting to hear from her. 'Hello,' he said.

'I forgot to mention,' she said. 'You do know I've got the power to turn you back into an ordinary human being again, don't you? Easy as pie. For me, not for anybody else.'

Duncan tried to breathe out, but something had got itself stuck. 'Really?'

'Oh yes. I was going to mention it earlier, but then you ambushed me with your nasty, spiteful trick, and that drove it clean out of my mind. So sorry.'

'You mean—' Pulling himself together took an effort that was nearly beyond his strength. 'You could really do that? Put me back the way I was.'

'Absolutely. No more superpowers, of course, but so what? Everybody else makes do without them. And everybody else – practically everybody else – is happier than you. Now if I was a small-minded, petty, vengeful person who bore grudges, I'd say no, the hell with him, he'll just have to get on with it. Why should he have his nice old life back again, after what he's done to me? Especially since there's nothing you can do about it, now that that dreadful Mr Eddison's taken charge of the case. A lot of people in my position might think that way, wouldn't they?'

'Well, yes,' Duncan said quietly. 'I suppose so.'

A theatrical sigh. 'I suppose it means I'm a small-minded, petty, vengeful person,' she said, 'because as far as I'm concerned you can stay a werewolf till you die of mange. Just thought you ought to know what your precious revenge has cost you, that's all. Straight back to the office, George, and don't take any notice of those silly red-and-green lights. Life's too short for traffic signals.'

The line went dead. Slowly and carefully, Duncan put the receiver back. Shit, fuck and bugger, he thought, but on the other hand, never mind. It'd only be really bad for a few days each month. (And if women could cope with that sort of aggravation, so could he, probably.) Apart from that; well. There may be troubles ahead, but while there's moonlight and howling and love and romance, let's face the music and chase lorries.

'Where's Luke?' Veronica was back in the room. Her office, after all. He looked up and caught sight of the coffin. A vampire: he was in love (probably) with a vampire. Marvellous. Then he noticed that there were picture postcards Blu-Tacked on the side of it: white hotels standing out against royal-blue skies. Did the secretaries remember, when they sent holiday postcards to everybody at the office, that *having a great time on the beach soaking up the sun* wasn't the most tactful message, in context? Apparently not. It was, after all, just an office. If you like your boss, it's only polite to send her a postcard . . .

If they can forget, Duncan thought, maybe I can, too.

'You just missed him,' he said. 'She's gone, then.'

'Yes, I'm delighted to say. Horrible woman, and I don't care if we have lost all that business. I never thought I'd hear myself say this, but there're some people you'd really rather not work for, even if they do pay on time and don't argue about the bill. Oh, while I think of it, what do you reckon to us getting married?'

Duncan frowned. 'I don't know,' he said gravely. 'I think, on balance, probably yes.' He nodded toward the coffin. 'Do you think there'll be room for both of us in that thing? Only I'm blowed if I'm going to hang upside down from the ceiling all night, so—'

'You can get double ones,' Veronica replied. 'Special order, and you get ever such funny looks in the showroom. Also they do lids that fold up the middle, like pianos. I prefer to sleep with the lid down, you see, but—' She shrugged. 'You do realise that that'll be the least of our problems?'

'Yes.'

She nodded. 'That's all right, then. I'll have to check my diary, but I think I'm free all day on the twenty-third, if that suits you.'

'I expect so. After all,' he added, 'the rest of my life's my own.'

Then she smiled at him; a big, sunny smile. He hadn't actually seen the teeth before. He decided they weren't too bad. Suited her, if anything.

'Don't you believe it,' she said.

George was waiting in the car.

It was a nice car. The seats were real leather, the dashboard was real burr walnut, the floor carpet was real wool. It was quite probably the realest car in the world, or at least outside California. But humans, even dead humans, can only stand so much reality, and George spent a lot of time waiting in the car. Because he was brain-dead, his muscles, nerves and tendons operated by an external power source and guided by an external intelligence, it shouldn't have mattered terribly much. The George (it wasn't his real name) who'd once been a racing driver no longer existed in the eyes of the law, which held that once the brain stopped working, life was extinct, and the parcel of meat wrapped in skin that was left over was neither here nor there. Quite so. You couldn't argue with that.

George's hands, folded in his lap, twitched. Very slowly, his thumbs began to move, circling each other like wary boxers.

The thing about the law is, though, that from time to time it contradicts itself. There was no George, because he was dead. But the driver of the car existed; and, because the traffic police have this tiresome habit of pulling people over from time to time and asking to see their papers, George had been issued with a driving licence. It gave his full name (George Non Cogito Ergo Non Sum Watson), an address, a date of birth, stuff like that. It told the world that George was qualified to drive cars, motorbikes, passenger-service vehicles, articulated lorries, combine harvesters and tanks. There was also an endorsement for speeding.

George's thumbs slowed down and stopped turning. Then, as the wind stirred and the moon broke through the heavy layer of black cloud, they started turning the other way.

Someone with a lively imagination, reading George's driving licence, could make up a life based on those sparse facts. He'd been born – well, you could picture the scene. Father standing out of the way looking petrified, mother pulling faces and yelling for more pethedine, nurse calm and brisk, various relatives sitting glumly on the vinyl-covered benches in the corridor. At some point he'd learned to drive; an examiner had shown him a page of colourful symbols and he'd said, 'I think that one's beware of migratory toads crossing a dual carriageway.' And so many different classes of vehicle, everything from milk floats to self-propelled artillery. You couldn't help being intrigued by that.

George's hands clenched. The knuckles showed white.

And the point was, the law believed in the man in the licence. The traffic policeman wouldn't hand it back with a sad smile on his face and say, *pull the other one, it's got bells on it.* The law had faith. It trusted itself; because if you can't trust the creation of lawyers, what could you trust?

George glanced at the clock on the dashboard. She'd said, Wait here, I'll only be a minute, and that had been five hours ago. A little voice that shouldn't have been there clicked its insubstantial tongue and muttered, *women.*

Impatience: a human trait. George felt in the inside pocket of his jacket and took out the driving licence. He looked at it for a moment, then put it back, reached forward and turned the key in the ignition.

There was no voice in his head telling him where to go, but he drove anyway. The name he'd read on the licence was a joke at his expense, he knew that: George I-Don't-Think-Therefore-I-Am-Not. She liked to make little jokes like that. Lively sense of humour. Well.

I drive, therefore I am. You can't not be and still manage a gearbox. He headed down a slip road onto the dual carriageway and let his foot snuggle a little more firmly on the accelerator. Because the moon was full and the moonlight was as bright as day, he turned off the headlights. His eyes, expertly maintained by the finest technicians, didn't need great vulgar jets of artificial brightness. He wound the window down and felt the slipstream on his cheek.

And he thought, I'm thinking.

The same technicians had done a bang-up job on his brain, too. He thought: if I'm thinking, it implies that her power is waning, something to do with the trick the werewolf played on her, the one we're not supposed to know about. But his dead ears had taken in every word she said into her mobile phone as she sat in the back, oblivious to his presence; he knew that she was – dying? Not the right word, but the effect would be the same. Her power was slipping back like the tide (influenced, he vaguely remembered, by the phases of the moon; now there was a coincidence) on the ebb – he was suddenly thinking once again.

He thought: I hate my job.

Which goes to show just how good those skilled technicians were; because very few of the millions of people who hate their jobs ever get around to admitting it in so many unambiguous words, and of that small minority, only a fraction ever take it into their heads to do something about it. Which was what George did.

I'm driving without lights, he thought, and I'm doing, what, (his left foot pressed a little harder) eighty miles an hour in a forty limit. I could get busted. They'd have my licence. And no licence, no job—

He checked his mirror and frowned. There's never a copper around when you need one.

No police car – but there was *something* in the mirror. He looked again, and made out five dark shapes, following him. Too small for cars, but moving fast. He slowed a little, and saw that he was being followed by what looked like five long black dogs. Big dogs. Enormous dogs with red eyes and lolling tongues, chasing behind him at seventy miles an hour and closing—

He remembered being stabbed with the pencil. There had been a moment when her power had let go, and the man whose name wasn't George had woken up inside the perfectly maintained dead body, realised where he was, and screamed.

He checked the petrol gauge. Nearly empty. She'd said something about filling up on the way home, now he came to think of it. Running out of fuel while being pursued by wolves: the stuff of nightmares.

The car had central locking, naturally. He leaned across and lifted the little peg thing. Down to lock, up to open. Five locks clicked simultaneously, like the heels of Prussian officers.

He grinned. 'Catch me if you can, boys,' he said, and stood on the gas.

In the white heat of the New Mexico desert, a long way from anywhere, there's a small town. Nothing much: a diner, a gas station, a general store, a feed and seed merchant, some grim-looking frame houses and a small building right out on the edge of town where people only go if they absolutely have to.

On the door of that building there's a brass plate: *Hughes & Hughes, attorneys-at-law*.

There's nothing much to do in that sort of small town except spread malicious gossip about your neighbours, especially if they happen to be incomers, so it's hardly surprising that there were strange rumours about the young couple who ran the law office. Odd things happened, they said, particularly at night, particularly at certain times of the month. Long-distance truckers had seen things they didn't want to talk about. A few head of cattle had gone missing. Folks took care to get the chickens in at night, and not because of the coyotes.

Some people figured it was because the young couple liked to go for picnics out on the old military ranges, where they'd done the secret tests back in the 1950s. Mostly, though, people reckoned it was because they were British. Enough said.

It didn't stop the townsfolk going to them when they needed their services. They had a reputation for being bright, cheerful and efficient, their charges were quite reasonable and their clients *always* paid on time, just in case. Maybe there was something a bit odd about them, but the same goes for everybody, to a greater or lesser extent. In small communities you get used to people after a while. You make allowances, even for late-night howling, fluttering black shapes in the twilight, calling cookies biscuits and drinking tea. But you keep your distance, all the same. (The way they see it in small desert towns is that everybody's weird, deep down under the skin where it doesn't necessarily show. Maybe it's radiation, or something that bit you, or the intrusive surgery the aliens performed on you when they snatched you out of your car one moonlit night, or the side effects of a damp climate and tannin addiction; maybe it's human nature. Inside every normal person there's a strange person, a wacko; probably in no hurry to escape, because wackos don't get out much, preferring to stay inside and brood on their particular obsession. Slice open anybody's head, they reckon, and you're more likely than not to find the walls of the skull papered with hundreds of photographs of the president or Jodie Foster, while 'Mister Tambourine Man' plays softly in the background on a continuous loop. But that's no big deal, they say; because inside every wacko inside every normal person, there's an even smaller normal person waiting to get out, and so on for ever, like Russian dolls. Of course, they would think that, living miles from anywhere in the desert, hopelessly inbred for ten generations, their poor brains fried by the fallout from the secret weapons tests. People like that are capable of believing in any damn thing. Werewolves, even.)

And, when the full moon shines on Chiswick, five wolves stand motionless on the moonlight-bleached grass beside the dual carriageway. They sniff the air, and the biggest wolf lifts his head and howls. They wait, listening for an answer, which never comes.